CAPTIVA

"Inventive"
Playboy

"Enticing"
Entertainment Weekly

"Superb"
The Denver Post

"Dramatic"
The Miami Herald

"Compelling"
San Francisco Chronicle

B

NEW YORK TIMES BESTSELLING AUTHOR

RANDY WAYNE WHITE

BERKLEY

ISBN 978-0-425-15854-8

5 0 7 9 9

S ▷ EAN

continued on next page

CAPTIVA

RANDY WAYNE WHITE

BERKLEY BOOKS, NEW YORK

THE BERKLEY PUBLISHING GROUP
Published by the Penguin Group
Penguin Group (USA) Inc.
375 Hudson Street, New York, New York 10014, USA
Penguin Group (Canada), 90 Eglinton Avenue East, Suite 700, Toronto, Ontario M4P 2Y3, Canada
(a division of Pearson Penguin Canada Inc.)
Penguin Books Ltd., 80 Strand, London WC2R 0RL, England
Penguin Group Ireland, 25 St. Stephen's Green, Dublin 2, Ireland (a division of Penguin Books Ltd.)
Penguin Group (Australia), 250 Camberwell Road, Camberwell, Victoria 3124, Australia
(a division of Pearson Australia Group Pty. Ltd.)
Penguin Books India Pvt. Ltd., 11 Community Centre, Panchsheel Park, New Delhi—110 017, India
Penguin Group (NZ), Cnr. Airborne and Rosedale Roads, Albany, Auckland 1310, New Zealand
(a division of Pearson New Zealand Ltd.)
Penguin Books (South Africa) (Pty.) Ltd., 24 Sturdee Avenue, Rosebank, Johannesburg 2196,
South Africa

Penguin Books Ltd., Registered Offices: 80 Strand, London WC2R 0RL, England

This is a work of fiction. Names, characters, places, and incidents either are the product of the author's imagination or are used fictitiously, and any resemblance to actual persons, living or dead, business establishments, events, or locales is entirely coincidental.

CAPTIVA

A Berkley Book / published by arrangement with the author

PRINTING HISTORY
G. P. Putnam's Sons hardcover edition / 1996
Berkley Prime Crime mass-market edition / May 1997
Berkley mass-market edition / August 2005

Copyright © 1996 by Randy Wayne White.

ISBN: 978-0-425-15854-8

BERKLEY®
Berkley Books are published by The Berkley Publishing Group,
a division of Penguin Group (USA) Inc.,
375 Hudson Street, New York, New York 10014.
BERKLEY is a registered trademark of Penguin Group (USA) Inc.
The "B" design is a trademark belonging to Penguin Group (USA) Inc.

PRINTED IN THE UNITED STATES OF AMERICA

25   24   23

THE AUTHOR WOULD LIKE TO THANK KAREN BELL, Captain Kim Gerz, Dr. Roy Crabtree, and Lieutenant Gary Beeson for kindly sharing their time and knowledge. I would also like to thank the many Floridians on both sides of the net ban controversy who, out of concern for the fishery, generously provided information and opinions on this complex issue. Any factual errors or misrepresentations of fact are entirely the fault of the author. Finally, I would like to thank my friends Glenn Miller and Susan Beckman for dutifully reading the early drafts.

FOR WOMEN WHO BURN BRIGHTLY AND CAST A POWerful wake: Debra Jane, Mother Marie, Jayma Gillaspie, Sherry Lavender, Katy Hummel, Renee Wayne Golden, Rilla Kay White, Lorian Hemingway, Phyllis Wells, Gigi Cannella, Debbie Flynn, Jennifer Clements, Deb Votaw, Cheryl Moore, Gloria Osburn, Chris Allman, Jacquie Meister, Janet Henneberry, Sandra McNalley, the Wilson sisters—Georgia, Jewel, Della Sue, JoAnn, Johnsie, and Judy—and for Kimberly Gerz, who left a comet's trail.

Captivity is Consciousness—
So's Liberty.

—EMILY DICKINSON

What thou lov'st well is thy true heritage. . . .

—EZRA POUND

CAPTIVA

ONE

THE REASON I WAS AWAKE AT FOUR A.M. WHEN THE bomb that killed Jimmy Darroux exploded was that my friend Tomlinson and I were on the dock taking turns squinting through a telescope, inviting—or so said Tomlinson—"ocular confirmation" that telepathic messages he believed he had received were, indeed, being transmitted by space creatures.

"It's *loaded* with them out there," he told me. "Sentient beings? For sure. Real living souls who generate very heavy vibes. They're aware a few of us earthlings are tuned in. Seriously; I shit you not. Couple of weeks ago, I just flashed on it. The whole scene. Trust me. They're definitely out there."

I thought: So are you, Tomlinson. So are you.

But I didn't swing out of bed on a cold January morning in the hope of contacting Tomlinson's deep-space kindred. He's a believer; I'm not. However, one of my journals promised there was an interesting planetary oddity to be seen in the pre-dawn sky. Venus was in apogee and, over the period of a few days, would seem to pass in front of Jupiter. I'm not an astronomer. It's a sometimes hobby. Over the years, I've acquired a working knowledge of the night sky because my poor sense of direction has gotten me lost often enough to know that stars are handy navigational aids—that, plus it makes me uneasy to see something over and over again that can't be identified. Which is why I've learned enough waypost constellations to keep me comfortable. So, as long as Tomlinson was badgering me to break out the telescope, I decided the best time to do it was when there was something interesting to see. Tomlinson could look all he wanted for signals from space. I'd look at Jupiter and Venus.

I awoke a few minutes until three, just before my alarm clock clattered. First thing I did was look across the bay to make sure Tomlinson was awake. Lights were on aboard the thirty-five-foot Morgan sloop that is his home, the portholes creating lemon-pale conduits in the darkness. The guy was up, probably meditating, burning incense, drinking green tea, no telling what else. I lit the propane ship's stove, listening to *Radio Habana* on the portable shortwave—my thought patterns switching comfortably into Spanish—as I dressed in chino pants and a soft sailcloth shirt. When the coffee was ready, I poured a mug and took it outside. The sky was clear: glittering stars suspended from a purple macrodome. Checked the weather station on the outside wall and found the barometer steady, temperature 49 degrees—cold for the southwest coast of Florida, even in January. Got a bomber jacket from one of the storage lockers and checked my watch: 3:13 a.m.

Later, I would relay some of those details to the police detective who investigated Jimmy Darroux's death.

There is a weight to the early-morning hours; a palpable density that's a little like being underwater. You can feel the press of it on your shoulders, the pressure of it in your inner ear. The resonance of one's own heartbeat is the test of silence—a fragile, fragile sound. I went through the list of my morning chores: Check the fish tank, clean the filters, check the complicated pulley system I use to moor my boats . . . confirm that some late-night visitor hadn't swiped an engine or the onboard electronics. Lately, a lot of that had been going on up and down the Florida coast. Everything was in order, but I moved more methodically than usual, slowed by the weight of the hour. Then poured another mug of coffee, hunkered down on the porch and listened to the night noises, waiting for Tomlinson.

I live in a remodeled fish storage shack in Dinkin's Bay, Sanibel Island. The shack is built over the water on pilings, so I could hear the draw of tidal current, a mountain stream sound . . . the knuckle pop of pistol shrimp . . . the *bee-wah* croak of catfish. The lower level of the house is dockage, the upper level is wooden platform. Two single-room cottages sit at the center of the platform, both under the same tin roof. One of the cottages is home, the other I've converted into a lab. The lab is necessary because I run a small company, Sanibel Biological Supply, selling marine specimens, alive or preserved, to schools and research firms around the country. It's a good place for a biologist to live and work, particularly when the biologist is a bachelor who likes living alone but who occasionally wants company. Dinkin's Bay Marina, located down the mangrove shore, provides that when I want it, just as the marina store provides staples such as chips and conch salad and cold beer in quart bottles.

From across the bay, I heard the ratchet cough of an

outboard too cold to start on the first pull. After a couple of more tries, I heard Tomlinson's muted voice: "Japanese scum!" Then the engine caught, and a few minutes later, he was tying his Zodiac up at my dock, saying: "Um-m-m, coffee. I smell coffee . . . or yeah, maybe a beer would be good. Something light, a breakfast beer. Maybe loosen up the receptors, make it easier to communicate." He climbed barefooted up to the main platform, combing fingers through scraggly blond hair, tugging at his beard, intense, focused, ready to communicate with the universe. As always, he smelled of Patchouli, the old hippie perfume.

I said, "Interesting choice of clothing, Tomlinson."

"Got to look sharp—that's what I always say. Look sharp, feel sharp."

"The serape makes sense. Nice Clint Eastwood touch. But a sarong? Isn't it a little cold to be wearing a sarong?" With his long bony legs showing, the man resembled a stork.

"*Sah*-rong," he said, correcting my pronunciation. "Night like this, my body wants to breathe. Teach Mr. Happy the world's not always a warm and cheery place. Living in Florida has spoiled the both of us."

"Ah."

"Self-deprivation is a forgotten path to spiritual awakening. The Buddha didn't live naked in the desert just for laughs."

"Nothing funny about that," I said.

"Pain purifies."

"Yeah, well . . ."

He was trying to hold down his billowing skirt. "Shit! That wind comes blowing right up the prune whistle, huh?"

"If you're cold, I've got some sweatpants you can wear."

"Goddamn right I'm cold. Take a whiz, I'd have to goose myself and grab Mr. Happy when he jumped out." He was pulling open the screen door, headed into the house. "You want a beer too?"

"I'll stick with coffee."

"Just in case, I'll bring a couple." Meaning he would drink them both.

AS I TOLD THE DETECTIVE (HIS NAME WAS JACKSON), we heard a boat enter the bay sometime between three-thirty and quarter to four. There was no moon, just a haze of stars, but I could tell it was a commercial netter's boat by the sound. Net boats are usually open boats, twenty to twenty-four feet long, and their engines are mounted near the bow through a forward well. Because of the well, a net boat can run forty miles an hour in nine inches of water and turn as if on a spindle, but the prop augers a lot of air. The cavitation noise is distinctive.

Tomlinson and I noticed it at the same time, a bumblebee whine at the mouth of the bay two miles away. "This time of year," Tomlinson said, "those people don't sleep at all. The netters." He had his eye pressed to the telescope, looking and talking at the same time. "They got what? Five months left? Six?"

"The net ban goes into effect in July. After that, they're out of business."

"Yeah," he said. "Permanently. People wonder why they're desperate? Fish all day, all night, trying to bale all the mullet they can before the clock runs out. Babies to feed, mortgage payments to make. Shit. Out there alone in a boat, all that on their shoulders.''

I said, ''You voted for the net ban. The guilt starting to get to you?''

He looked up from the telescope as if mildly surprised. ''I did? Jesus, I guess I *did*. Oh man. . . . That's exactly why I hate politics. Always having to make decisions. But they were wiping out all the fish, and fish can't vote. You're the one told me that.''

It was true, but had I told him that? I couldn't remember—although lately, it seemed, I'd been saying and doing more small dumb things than usual. ''What I meant was, it's the migrant netters who come down and strip the place bare. The ones from North Florida, Georgia, Texas; all over. They come down for December and January, take the fish, dump their garbage, and leave.''

''The mullet roe season,'' he said. ''That's right, I remember now. They sell the fish eggs to the . . . Taiwanese.''

''Taiwanese. Filipinos. The Japanese. They dry it, consider it a delicacy. Or can the milt.''

''Take the seed stock and the fish can't reproduce. Exactly.''

Which was also true. But he was missing the point—rare for Tomlinson because the man has a first-rate intellect. Granted, he's eccentric, often bizarre. As a late-sixties drug prophet, his mind sometimes takes odd and quirky turns, though it's impossible to say whether it's through enlightenment, as he claims, or because he has done serious chemical damage to the neural pathways and delicate synapse junctions of his brain. Tomlinson's genius is nonlinear, empathic, able to make intuitive leaps from illogical cause to logical effect. There are times that I don't take Tomlinson too seriously, but neither do I discount anything he says. That's not true of the general cast of New Age mystics, crystal worshipers, alien advocates, astrology goofs, macrobiotic back-to-the-earthers, and their politically correct brethren. If one of them told me they had been communicating with extraterrestrials, I would nod, smile pleasantly, then angle for the door. But when Tomlinson says it, you think: Well . . . probably not, but . . . *maybe*. He possesses a kind of stray dog purity that is without ego or malice. I have never met anyone anywhere who didn't like and trust Tomlinson.

"He must have struck fish," I said. The sound of the boat had traced the western bank of Dinkin's Bay . . . kicked up mud at the shallow Auger Hole entrance—I could hear it—and grown louder as it neared the marina, then stopped abruptly. The mullet fisherman had dumped his net, probably, and was now hauling it in.

"Yeah," Tomlinson said. "Or maybe *she* did. I see women working right along, out there no matter what the weather. White rubber boots and plastic rain jackets, picking fish all by themselves. Couple of 'em." Tomlinson had begun to tinker with the telescope again, scanning through the viewfinder. We'd already taken a good long look at Venus. It appeared as a tiny moon in crescent phase, gold-tinged by the reflected light of its own yellow clouds. Jupiter was an ice-bright globe, its four visible moons suspended around it. I was satisfied. Felt it was worth getting up at three a.m. because looking through a telescope creates, in time, a pleasant converse perspective. You naturally imagine what it is like to be seen from space: a milk-blue planet, the peninsula of Florida dangling into the sea, the Gulf Coast, a sleeping island, the clustered lights of Sanibel and Captiva, clustered stars and infinity beyond.

I stood shifting from one leg to the other, trying to stay warm now that Tomlinson was free-ranging the Celestron. To the west, the marina was still. Occasionally, a refrigerator generator would kick in or the sump of a bilge pump. I could hear the desert-wind baritone of surf on the Gulf side. The only other noises were the squawk of night herons and, once, the cat scream of raccoons. In another couple of hours, the fishing guides would be stirring, getting their skiffs ready for work. But now the docks were deserted. In the harbor's deep-water slippage, the trawlers and cruisers and doughty houseboats were as dark and motionless as a charcoal sketch. People aboard were buttoned in tight against the January cold. At the shore docks, near the gas pumps and bait tanks, smaller boats—the Makos, Aquasports, Hydrasports, Lake & Bays, Boston Whalers, and Mavericks—were tied incrementally and in a line, like horses.

My eyes swept past . . . stopped . . . and swept back again. I had seen something on the docks. What . . . ? For an instant, just an instant, an image lingered—the suggestion of a human figure hunched down, moving past the bait tanks.

"Far . . . out," whispered Tomlinson. "Hey—I think I've got it!" He was folded over the telescope, holding his hair back in a ponytail. "Yes . . . a signal of some sort . . . definitely a signal. Flashing light . . . getting . . . getting . . . brighter." He stood, motioning with his bony hands. "Take a look, Doc. I think my space buddies are sending us their regards."

I looked once more at the docks . . . saw nothing.

"They're *waiting*."

I removed my glasses, stepped to the telescope, and leaned to see a pulsing dot move across the optic disc and gradually disappear. I adjusted the focus, disengaged the clock drive, moved the scope's tube on its axis, and found the dot again. As I followed the light, I listened to Tomlinson's running commentary. One night, in the cockpit of his boat, he had been in deep meditation, just him and the stars. A meteorite—a comet, he called it— had swept down out of the sky and the shock of its appearance, its brilliance, had vaulted him through into another dimension of awareness.

"An awakening is often catalyzed by a shock or a surprise," he explained. "In the fifth century, a simple monk gained enlightenment and became Buddha after he stepped on the tail of a very vicious dog."

The comet, Tomlinson said, had drawn his consciousness outward, beyond the confines of earth. All that night he sat in meditation, allowing his brain waves to probe the stars. It was cold out there, he said. He sensed the infinite chill of nothingness, the black abyss of space.

"It was a serious downer, man; a very heavy mojo. I mean, *scary*. That emptiness, it was like pulling me apart, molecule by molecule. Diluting me. You know how the beam of a flashlight diffuses over distance? Like that. But I kept going, fighting the panic."

Finally, he said, his mind had sensed a flicker of warmth. "It was sentient consciousness, man. You hear what I'm saying? Life, energy—whatever you want to call it. It was out there, very frail at first. Still a long way away, but I was homing in on the signal. It got stronger. Then—truly *amazing*—I began to sense other signals, but from different directions. Spread out all over the place. Thought . . . power. In far corners of the universe, these little islands of . . . divinity. I was making contact! This was . . . two weeks ago. Every night, I do deep meditation, man. Bypass all that deep-space bullshit so it's gotten to be like dialing from a cellular. If I had a cellular.''

He chattered on and on while I used the telescope to chase the flashing dot. Universal energy fields. Chakras, auras. Life registered a specific measure of electrical current—that, at least, was true. All matter in the universe was structural repetition. An atom with electrons, a planet with moons . . . adapted fins which were a bird's wing, the fingers of a child's hand. And had I looked down to notice that a stream of urine spirals like a DNA helix? Communication was nothing more than conduction; the dipoles could be at opposite points in the universe and it would make no difference. Tomlinson had simply accessed that current . . . and made a few new friends.

"God's out there!" Tomlinson said. "God is out there, and He's *not* us. What a relief!''

I stood from the telescope, cleaned my glasses and put them on. "Tomlinson?"

He had been curling his fingers in his hair—a nervous habit. He moved toward the telescope. "The Big Guy wants to talk to me now?"

I didn't want to have to tell him. "Not exactly."

"Then what?"

"It's . . . an airplane. That's what you were seeing. An airplane.''

"*What?* Naw. . . .''

"It took me a while to figure because the running lights weren't quite right. And it was moving so fast.''

"An airplane? They were going to give me some kind

of signal. It popped right into my mind: ocular confirmation. Just the other night, making very heavy contact. Those very words. Right there on my boat, they were telling me to look."

I shrugged. "Yeah, well . . . but this is some kind of fighter jet, probably out of MacDill or could be Homestead. Maybe a Tomcat with its war lights on, an F-14. Pretty strange. They do strafing and bombing runs in a restricted area off Marco. Remember that time we were anchored off the Ten Thousand Islands and heard explosions?"

Tomlinson said, "*Shit.* Wouldn't you know."

"They like to scramble early, avoid the civilian traffic. They've got Air Combat Maneuvering Instrumentation towers out there, built way off shore."

He said glumly, "The military industrial complex is going to fuck with me one too many times. Seriously. Mark my words."

Disappointing Tomlinson is like disappointing a child. I nodded toward the Celestron, checking my watch as I did: 4:00 a.m. We had a good hour of darkness left, and I was about to suggest that he scan another part of the sky. I was facing the marina . . . had, once again, confirmed that there was no movement on the docks; realized I had probably imagined the human form . . . and I had begun to say, "Check the northern sky—" when the dock exploded. An orange corona bubbled up over the water, I heard a suctioning *ka-WOOF*, and then the entire marina was illuminated . . . illuminated just for an instant, as if a flashbulb had gone off. All this in a space of microseconds.

I yelled without thinking: *"Incoming!"*—a response programmed long ago. Yelled it even before I realized what had happened; yelled it as I collapsed, dragging Tomlinson to the deck.

A fireball ballooned above the dock, back where they kept the sportfishing boats. Not a big explosion, but it generated enough energy to arch debris, rubble, burning slats high into the air, toward my stilt house. And I thought stupidly: Grenade? Light mortar?

Tomlinson poked his head up. "Holy shit! The sons-abitches opened fire on us!" Which didn't make any sense either . . . nothing was making sense . . . then, out of the confusion, his meaning took form: He was referring to the jet. He thought the jetfighter was attacking us.

Ludicrous; it should have been funny . . . but the dock was blazing, looked like a couple of the boats had caught fire too. By then I was thinking: gas fumes in the bilge, ignited by a spark. It was a reasonable explanation, even probable, but I didn't pursue it because out of the flames stumbled a human figure . . . no, a human torch, clothes ablaze, arms clawing, sputtering, whooshing, making a guttural *caw-w-w-w*-ing sound. I was already on my feet and running toward the marina when the torch seemed to kneel, a gesture of submission, then tumbled, hissing, into the bay.

IT WAS A MAN. NOT THAT I COULD TELL AT FIRST. I went sprinting down the dock past the bait tank and gas pumps . . . then tried to stop so quickly that my feet went out from under me and I bounced along on my butt. I had realized something: If the fire got to the gas pump, the fuel tank beneath the marina's deck would blow. Instead of one burn victim, there would be dozens— myself included.

I found the storage tank's emergency shutoff switch
in a gray box beside the pumps. Hit the switch, took two
strides and leaped off the dock into the water. The tide
was up, but that area of the harbor is so shallow that I
had to half swim, half slog to what, in the copper light
of the fire, resembled an inflated garment bag. Grabbed
it without knowing what or where I was grabbing . . .
pulled it to me, felt weight, felt life . . . and the thing
rolled over in my arms to reveal a mask of black from
which two bright, dazed eyes blinked.

A hole formed in the mask and a croaking sound came
from it: "I can see . . . Jesus. I can see *Jesus*."

The image of a human who has been maimed goes
straight to the motor reflex region of the brain. It touches
all the genetic coding for flight and survival, leaching a
primitive, chemical excitement from the adrenal gland—
which is probably why the trash newsmagazines and
some of the trashier media have come to rely on human
suffering as stock-in-trade. If they can't create excitement one way, they'll serve it up in another. Their
favorite shield—"We're journalists, trained professionals"—is as clouded as a pornographer's videotape,
which at least makes their cry "It's what the viewers
want!" analogically accurate.

What I knew was that I wanted to pull this guy onto
the dock and get him covered up before the gawkers
arrived. Tragedy is a personal thing; a human property
to be shared—if by choice—but not stolen away in film
bites.

I moved to touch the man's head; realized I shouldn't.
Instead, I said, "I'll get you out of here. You'll be
okay." Wondered if he had even heard the lie.

There were people shouting now . . . the heavy thump

of bare feet on wood . . . the whine of a boat engine. Tomlinson came racing around the corner in his Zodiac as someone called in a panic: "Is he hurt? Who is it?"

I looked toward the flames, saw silhouettes, and I answered, "Don't know. I can't tell who it is"—pleased, on some perverse level, that my voice remained calm, controlled. "He needs help. Call nine-one-one, tell them we want a medevac. A chopper."

I was slogging around with the man cradled in my arms, trying to find enough footing to swing him up onto the dock, but Tomlinson interceded. There would be less stress, he said, if we rolled him into his rubber boat. "Plus, we can flood it with cold water. That's what he needs now. Until the paramedics arrive."

The two of us lifted the man into the inflatable; then Tomlinson took charge, calling for the water hose, calling for buckets of ice while he got the man's legs elevated, already treating him for shock.

I had a dim memory of Tomlinson telling me that, at some time in his life, he had taken an emergency medical technician course. Tomlinson, an unlikely person, often did unlikely things. Already, there were a couple of marina regulars sloshing around with us . . . people who seemed to know more about first aid than I. Once they had a blanket over the guy, I left them to their work and hoisted myself onto the dock to help fight the fire.

It wasn't as bad as it could have been, but it was pretty bad: Four small sportfishing boats—known locally as flats boats—were ablaze. Mack, who owns the marina, was doing what he could, getting people organized. While some cut the lines of nearby boats and drifted them to safety, others used fire extinguishers and water to control the fire. Just as a precaution, I took another look at the fuel tank's emergency shutoff switch—and was very glad I did. Some well-intended person had come along after me and switched it off again, thereby switching it on.

The marina is connected to the main road by a sand road. The Sanibel Fire Department is located just a few hundred yards from that intersection. The trucks arrived in minutes, lights flaring, and they had the fire under control not long afterward. But they couldn't save the four boats, and two others were badly damaged. Nor could the emergency room doctors save the man I had pulled from the bay.

He died later that morning, with Tomlinson at his side.

TWO

I HELPED AROUND THE MARINA UNTIL MY HELP wasn't needed, then shuffled back to the cottage to hang bomber jacket and clothes out to dry. I'd been slogging around in boat basin muck; the stink of it was still on me. I took a cold-water shower. Kept lathering and rinsing, lathering and rinsing. Decided there are some things—the memory of an odor, for instance—that cannot be washed away with soap.

By then, it was nearly ten a.m. I felt as if I had been awake for days, but didn't feel like sleeping.

Because of the petroleum and spent chemicals that had gone into the bay, I was worried about the fish tank aquarium where I keep live specimens—some to sell, most just for my own research and pleasure. I had built the fish tank on a reinforced section of my lower deck, using half of an old wooden cistern. From a distance, the thing looked like a whiskey barrel. Raw water is constantly drawn into the tank by a Briggs pump housed on shore. Then the water is aerated and clarified by a hundred-gallon upper reservoir and subsand filter, then sprayed as a mist into the main tank.

But even the multiple filter systems couldn't protect

the aquarium from big doses of chemical contaminates. That's why I was concerned. Because of the cold weather, I had a Styrofoam cap on the tank. But the sun was out now—the norther had blown through, and the temperature had already climbed to 65—so I removed the cap and let the sun in. The water in the tank was clear, three feet deep. I released a long slow breath, relieved: everything was still alive. Snappers, with their black masks, were doing slow figure eights, flushing shrimp before them. There were whelks and banded tulip shells, and one great big horse conch, its orange foot out, suctioned to a clam. There were also sea squirts and tunicates—the bay's natural water filters. The most delicate animals in the tank are my reef squid. It took me a while to find them. They can change colors and blend in, their chromatophores changing with the background. But they were alive too . . . and so were six immature tarpon that I had recently rescued from a drainage ditch near the island's Pirate Playhouse.

I stood watching the tarpon, debating whether to switch off the raw-water intake. The fish held nose-first into the current; thin bars of silver that seemed to generate their own light. Over at the marina, the cleanup continued. The tide was still carrying out charred fragments and white pellets of synthetic goo. I decided that cutting the raw-water intake was the safest course. For a day or so, the recirculation system and aerator could keep my animals isolated and alive.

"Dr. Ford? It's doctor, right?" I looked up to see a sheriff's detective: sports coat, loose tie. He had introduced himself earlier, asked a few questions, then dismissed me. Ron Jackson. He was on the boardwalk that connects my stilt house to shore, coming toward me.

I waited until he was closer before I said, "Just Ford. I'm not a physician."

He smiled a cop smile, illustrative of genial mistrust. "Out on the islands, I keep forgetting. Everything's informal. Probably why the tourists like it." He had his notebook out; found a piling on the lower deck and leaned against it, making himself at home. "Let's see . . . I've already got your number, your name. So . . . just a coupl'a other things. You got a spare minute?"

I'd already told him everything there was to tell. "Not really. I was getting ready to . . ." I cast around for an excuse. Sleep was out of the question and I didn't feel like working. "I was just getting ready to go for a run."

The smile again. "There you go; best way to get rid of stress. I'm a runner myself. You don't mind, I'll follow you around while you change. It'll save us both some time."

Jackson didn't look like a runner—short, bull-necked, hair sprayed smooth—but then I don't look like a runner either.

He followed me through the companionway into the cottage and took a seat at the dinette table, allowing me to change in private while he made small talk. Stress fractures were on his mind—he'd recently recovered from one. The Gasparilla Run, he'd done that, was thinking about the Seven Mile Bridge run, and wasn't it hot as hell, running in the summer? Then he got to the point, saying, "I have two or three more questions."

"Ask away."

"Let's see. . . . You didn't know the deceased, right? That's what you told me."

I hesitated. "The guy died?"

"Yeah . . . you couldn't have known. One of our guys

just talked to them, the hospital. Tentatively, we've got his name as Jimmy Darroux, a commercial fisherman from Sulphur Wells. That's an island near here, huh?''

I said, ''That's right. Darroux . . . the name's not familiar. It took us about an hour to count heads, me and the others from the marina. Make sure it wasn't one of us. But the way he was, I wouldn't have recognized him if it had been my best friend.''

Jackson had the soft, rounded speech pattern of the southern regions of the Middle Atlantic. All *o-u* combinations rhymed with ''boot.'' He said, ''Yeah. Burns are the worst.''

He told me about finding a boat with a commercial sticker hidden in the mangroves; they had traced the numbers. As I listened, I guessed he was from Virginia, maybe Maryland. Hadn't been here long; wasn't familiar with the agricultural and fishing island of Sulphur Wells.

Jackson was reviewing his notes. ''You described the explosion . . . the fire . . . what you did. You and your buddy out with the telescope. . . . Is he around? I need to speak with him, too.''

''Tomlinson rode in on the medevac, him and a paramedic. He didn't know the guy either. But I've got your card, I'll have him call you.''

''He didn't know Darroux, then why did he—''

''Tomlinson is . . . a very religious person. He went to the hospital because he felt he could help.''

''I see. Um-huh . . . what I was wondering about—'' Jackson looked up when I came around the locker that separates my bed from the kitchen. I had changed into shorts, sweatshirt, and Nikes, and began to stretch, hands against the wall. ''What I was wondering about,'' he said, "were some of the things you told me earlier. Some of the phrases you used."

"Oh?"

" 'Point of detonation.' You said that. 'Accelerant flare.' What you said was"—he was reading from the notebook—" 'I saw the accelerant flare before the noise reached me.' You said 'magnitude of compression.' "

"So? I was telling you about the explosion, what happened. It was a small explosion with a lot of fire. I don't understand your—"

"The way you told me, that's what made me curious. The phraseology."

"Phraseology? What was I supposed to say?"

Jackson's laugh dismissed it as unimportant. "Before my wife and I moved here, I was in D.C., the capital. Jesus, it was like living in Ghetto National Park. Nothing but brothers and half-assed political flakes, and all these squirrelly little bombers. You ask somebody what they saw, they say, 'It just went boom!' Or, 'Blowed up, man.' Or, *'Ka-POW.'* See where I'm headed? In D.C., I heard a lot of people describe a lot of explosions. But you say, 'I saw the accelerant flare before the noise reached me.' You say 'point of detonation.' "

"I was trying to give a precise account of what occurred."

The notebook again. "A guy at the marina told me. His name is Graeme. . . ."

"Yeah, Graeme MacKinley, the owner. Mack."

"Mr. MacKinley told me that you're a biologist. I wouldn't expect a biologist to be familiar with those terms." Jackson looked at me blandly. "So how do you know so much about bombs, Dr. Ford?"

"Bomb? I never said anything about a bomb—"

"Well . . . explosions then. Were you in the military or something?"

I paused a beat before I said, "I worked for the government for a while. We had a few courses, I probably picked up the language there."

"The government. What did you do for the government?"

"I was with the foreign service."

Jackson chuckled. "Up in D.C., saying you work for the foreign service is like a hooker saying she works with people—no offense. But it's pretty broad—"

"I did clerical stuff," I said. "A paper shuffler." I was getting tired of Jackson. Law enforcement people are the standard—and the victims—of the unappreciated imperative. Day in, day out, they deal with misfits, liars, drunks, and head bangers. Their only reward is low pay, bad hours, and a firestorm of criticism if they make a mistake. If you're a bureaucrat and screw up, you get a private memo from the department head. If you're a cop and screw up, you get headlines. As a result, law enforcement people are usually a hell of a lot more efficient and professional at their jobs than professionals in other fields. But they also develop a myopic under-siege view of the world. They trust no one—why should they? I didn't blame Jackson for being suspicious. But now he was prying into unrelated affairs—things that were none of his business.

"Where did you work? Countries, I mean."

"Quite a few. Lots."

"Don't get shy on me, Dr. Ford."

"Then let's get something straight: You're not suggesting I had anything to do with the explosion?"

"You mean you *didn't* do it?" He was looking at me,

smiling like we were buddies and it was a joke. But it wasn't a joke. He wanted to see how I reacted.

I didn't react. I didn't smile. I said, "I've got a lot of work to do today, Detective Jackson. Anything else?"

He was nodding his head, confirming something. "The people I talked to, that's exactly what they said. You're kind of bookish and straitlaced, everything's work work work. No, I can't see the motive. Everybody over there likes you, so why blow up their boats? See, what I'm doing . . . I'm trying to neaten things up, get them straight in my mind. It was bugging me. But the way you told about it—it makes sense now."

"Fine."

He tried to parry my sudden coolness by being conversational. "You ever get to Central America?"

"Once or twice."

"Yeah? I almost went there with my wife on vacation. Costa Rica, Panama, Colombia—one of those cruise ship deals? But all the stuff you read, the violence and stuff. I asked this guy I knew, if we went, should I maybe pack a side arm. He worked for one of the federal agencies. Least, I'm pretty sure he did. Know what he said? He said, 'You take a gun down there, make sure you file off the front sight before you leave. That way, it won't hurt so bad when the guerrillas stick it up your ass!' "

I had gone to the screen door, was holding it open. "I think of anything else, Detective Jackson, I'll call you."

"And your buddy—"

"He'll call you too."

•   •   •

"THOSE WERE HIS LAST WORDS; THE LAST THING HE said to me. Practically the only thing he said."

I asked, "What? His name?"

"His name? He never said his name. Man, he could hardly speak. The ER doctor said the vacuum—from the explosion?—it forced this intense heat down him. His pharynx, his lungs, everything. I know there's perfect symmetry to every event, every little thing that happens, but that is one shitty way to go, man. No, the last thing he said was, 'Take care of Hannah for me.' He told me that. 'Take care of Hannah.' Said it about three times, the name. Hannah. I was holding his hand. By then, the ER doctor said that contact, the risk of infection . . . well . . . it just didn't matter."

Tomlinson was flopped down in the reading chair by the north window. I was on my bed, head propped up with pillows. Crunch & Des, the black marina cat, was down by my feet, projecting enough lazy indifference to create his own space. I had been trying to read my new *BioScience Journal* but kept dozing off until Tomlinson rapped at the screen door. It was a little before six p.m. The chemical stink of melted fiberglass, charred wood was still in the air.

"Who's Hannah?"

Tomlinson shrugged. "Jimmy Darroux's daughter? His wife? I don't know. Maybe his one true love. He didn't say." Tomlinson looked exhausted, shrunken, all the joy sucked out of his eyes. He was wearing green physician's scrubs. Apparently the sarong had seemed out of place in an emergency room, even to him.

"That's what I was asking you. How did you find out his name?"

"One of the cops gave me a lift to the marina. Mack told me. A detective told him."

I got up on an elbow and looked out the window to see if Detective Jackson was still around. There were a few gawkers milling near the site of the fire, but they couldn't stray into the area because of the yellow crimescene tape. There were a couple of policemen in uniform and a couple of men wearing blue windbreakers, *ATF* in white letters on the back. The feds. But no one wearing a green, checked sports coat like Jackson's.

"Did Mack also tell you the guy probably blew himself up with his own bomb? That's what the police are working on. He was a commercial fisherman, probably mad about the net ban. That mullet boat you and I heard—they found it tied over in the mangroves. He'd apparently waded in, had the flats boats targeted. They got his name through the registration."

Tomlinson put his face in his hands and made a wincing noise, like pain.

"That poor, poor fool."

"Jimmy Darroux isn't getting much sympathy around here. Two of the guides are out of business because of him. Nelson and Felix both. They'd just gotten those boats, a new Parker and a Hewes. The one just like mine."

"He was carrying the bomb?"

"I don't know. Carrying it, trying to put it someplace. That's what they're working on."

"But they're not sure."

"They didn't confide in me, but it's not that hard to figure out, Tomlinson. Renegade commercial guys have been vandalizing marinas up and down the coast, stealing engines, electronics. Setting boats on fire, trying to even the score. They blame the sportfishermen for pushing the vote.''

"Revolution, man, right on. That's how it starts. I thought they'd been stealing stuff just for the cash.''

They'd been doing that, too.

Tomlinson paused. "So now I've got to find Hannah.''

It took a moment for it to register—Darroux's last words. "If he and Hannah were close, I'm surprised she didn't show up at the ER.''

"I told you, no one knew who he was. By the time I left, they still didn't know. If they did, they didn't tell me.''

"So, you find her, what are you going to do?''

"I don't know—ride the Karmic Highway. Nothing happens by accident, man. There's no such thing as coincidence. I ended up with Jimmy Darroux for a reason. At first, I thought it was to heal him. Use my hands to fill him full of universal energy, take away the pain—''

"It didn't work?'' I wondered if Tomlinson would admit it.

"Well . . . his dying sort of put the nix on the whole approach. So now I've got to find Hannah.''

"Look, that guy . . . his bomb, he could have killed one of the guides. Hell, if the fire had gotten to the fuel storage tank, he could have killed us all.''

"He was a human being, man. I'm not here to judge him. And I'm not saying the vibes weren't bad. There was a darkness in him, I sensed that, but let's face it: He'd just gotten blown up. A thing like that will definitely darken the mood ring. The man died holding my hand, Doc. It's what we call a karmic obligation.''

I stood up, stretched, returned the magazine to the

bookshelf. "Terrorism is what I call it. I don't share your sympathy."

"I'm talking about the girl. The woman, whatever. You need to help me find her."

"His last words to me were about Jesus—"

"See? At least he was a religious man—"

"That he could see Jesus. Nothing about a woman. I don't understand how that obligates me."

Tomlinson was out of the chair, some of his energy returned. He still looked tired, but he was as serious as I have ever seen him. "Come on, Doc. You were the first one to him. No coincidences, remember? You're good at this stuff, finding people. Me, I'm a concept person. In all the years we've known each other, have I ever asked you for a favor before?"

I almost answered truthfully—seldom a day went by that Tomlinson didn't ask me for something. Instead, I said, "They know his name, where he lived—Sulphur Wells. You don't need me for that. Check the phone book, under D for Darroux. Someone at his house will know."

"See? You're already getting things figured out. What would it hurt to hop in your boat and run over there? A ride, that's all I'm asking for. Then I'll buy you dinner. Find a place at Sulphur Wells or stop at Cabbage Key. You name it."

"The guy dies and we just pop in, start asking questions."

Tomlinson made an open-palmed gesture—he was going. "I'd ask to borrow your truck, but you have to drive halfway up the mainland, then way south again to get there. Two hours minimum by road but only about an hour in a fast boat. Or I'll take my dinghy . . . ?"

I pictured Tomlinson pulling into the commercial fish docks at Sulphur Wells, all those rednecks staring at him, probably wearing some beer by this time of day. And already pissed off about losing one of their own. "It'll be dark in an hour."

"Then I'll need a light. Can I borrow your spotlight?"

I swung open the door and stepped out to see if my bomber jacket was dry—the norther had slipped through, but it would still be cold out there on the water. "I'll go, I'll *go*. We'll take my boat."

I MADE A STOP BEFORE WE GOT UNDER WAY. AFTER MY talk with Ron Jackson, I'd found Janet Mueller out by the front gate loosening up to run, so we'd jogged a couple of miles together before I broke away and headed to the beach to finish my workout. As I left her, I'd suggested that we get together later for a beer and something to eat.

Now I had to cancel the date.

Marina communities are gypsy communities—boats are, after all, built for travel. If you're sailing the Intercoastal north to Texas or Mexico, or south to the Keys or Yucatan, Dinkin's Bay is just off the main channel, Marker 5 on the chart. The cruising guides list it as a "quaint" back bay marina hidden in the mangroves, electrical hookups, showers, laundry, and ground transportation available . . . but not recommended for vessels over forty feet or that draw more than six feet. So we get a steady turnover of small cruisers and gunkholers. Usually couples, often retirees—"When the kids were young, we always dreamed of buying a boat,"—but almost never women traveling alone.

Janet Mueller was an exception.

She'd come chugging into the marina a couple of weeks earlier in a little Holiday Mansion houseboat that was so beaten up that the bright blue paint job couldn't disguise the misuse . . . unless you were an absolute novice—which Janet was. She'd banged the docks, fouled her lines, then banged the docks some more. By the time we got her tied up, her hands were shaking, she seemed near tears. She kept saying, "I just bought this. I don't know anything about it!" She continued to apologize, even as we said our goodbyes.

Because marinas are gypsy communities, the cruisers and the marina regulars usually mix easily. Not Janet. She stayed to herself; spent a lot of time above deck in the heat of the day, scrubbing, polishing, studying manuals. Sometimes she would throw off the lines and chug around the bay. My impression was that she did it so that she could practice docking. I liked that—she seemed determined, independent; a stubborn lady.

But Janet Mueller also had the shell-shocked look of a person who is trying to recover from some debilitating event. You see it often in Florida: the introspective stare, the weighted shoulders, the slow declination of chin. They don't say much, they sigh a lot. They seem to have trouble concentrating, as if some private chord echoes in their ears. They are traveling, they say, or on sabbatical. It's not true. They are in flight; trying to escape the divorce or the death or the bankruptcy that has dismantled their lives. They come down hoping the beaches, the sunsets will provide a curative—just like the brochures suggest. Yet, all too often, the abruptness of the change, the neon glitz and ocean space of Florida only add to the shock of being untethered. You can escape everything by leaving home . . . except yourself.

The only thing I knew about her was that she was from a place called Montpelier, Ohio—she told me that—and she liked oldies rock and roll. I could hear it coming from her boat when I walked past on the dock. Also, she knew a great deal about computers—Tomlinson told me that. She was a plain-looking woman. Not unattractive, just plain. She was probably in her early thirties, had short brown hair, a round face, a body prone to plumpness, legs, hips, and torso not constructed for the cargo shorts and pullovers she usually wore. I could picture her sitting at the back of the classroom, not saying much but getting good grades. I could picture her in business clothes, neat, punctual, indispensable at her work. She had that aura of steadiness. But, in the very few times we spoke, I also got the impression that had I clapped my hands unexpectedly, she would have dived for cover or burst into tears. Post-traumatic stress syndrome is not the exclusive province of war veterans. Women, particularly the quiet ones, the plain ones, can suffer it as well.

In a small community, romance segregates, so I've made it a rule not to date women who live at the marina. But that morning, Janet had been among those in the water with Tomlinson trying to help Jimmy Darroux. She hadn't been shy or timid then. We had the explosion in common now. And suggesting that we get something to eat had seemed to provide polite closure to our run. It was an offhand invitation, innocent, but I didn't want her to think that I'd simply forgotten it.

As I idled over to the marina, Tomlinson jogged over by land to see if anyone knew where, exactly, Jimmy Darroux had lived. It wasn't his idea, it was mine. Sulphur Wells is a big island. There are several waterfront

settlements; five or six commercial fish houses, and unlike Tomlinson, I didn't trust karma to steer us to the
right one. I nudged my skiff around the oyster bar off
the T-dock, then along B-dock where Janet's houseboat
was moored. She had it bumpered nicely, stern to, cur-
tained pilothouse windows clean, lines coiled. I glided
in and caught the safety rail, calling, "Hello the boat!"

I felt the little houseboat's trim shift slightly; then she
poked her head out of the pilothouse door, grinning. She
was wearing a terrycloth robe, scrubbing at her hair with
a towel. She had just gotten out of the shower. For absolutely no logical reason, I had the terrible feeling that
she had washed her hair and was about to get dressed
up just for me. She said a little shyly, "I didn't know
you wanted to go so early. You want to come in for a
drink? Or I can . . . geez, just give me ten minutes and
I'll be all ready. I promise. I'll put on some music."

I said, "Well, that's not exactly why, uh . . . Something's come up, you see and . . . I know I said earlier
that we would, uh . . ." the whole time wondering how
a grown man could sound so stupid.

Her smile began to fade. "We're not going?"

"Sorry, can't. I have to do a favor for a friend."

The smile disappeared. "Oh. Well . . . I know you're
awfully busy."

"It's not that. It's just that this thing came up."

"Honest, don't worry about it." She said that in a
soothing way, as if more concerned with my feelings
than her own. The smile was back in place, but she had
withdrawn, eyes avoiding me, casting around as we continued to talk; those green eyes reminding me of some
shy small creature that had retreated to the safety of its
cave, peering out.

"We'll do it another time."

"Sure we will, Doc, sure. Or maybe just go for a run."

When her door closed, I punched the throttle, wheeling my skiff around on its own length. Looked up to see several of the fishing guides—Jeth Nicholes, Nelson Esterline, Felix Blane—staring at me, probably wondering why I was kicking up a wake. Jeth used his hand to signal me, and when I'd swung into the dock, he said, "You muh-muh-mad about something?"

"Yeah, I guess I am. Have you seen Tomlinson?"

Nels said, "What'a you got to be mad about? They didn't burn *your* boat. I'm the one's got a right to be mad. Me and Felix both. Jesus Christ, I've got charters booked and my wife, she just bought a new washer-dryer!"

I'd meant to talk to them about losing their boats. "How long before you get your checks from the insurance company?"

"They said two, but it'll be more like four. Weeks, I mean. A whole damn month at least, which will ruin a big chunk of the prime season for us."

I said, "I don't have any orders right now. Well . . . I've got one for sea horses, but I can catch them with my drag boat. What I'm saying is, any way you two want to split it up, you can use my skiff for a while."

Jeth looked at Nels. Said, "See? People don't loan their boats, buh-buh-but here's Doc doing it."

Which seemed an odd thing to say, until I took a look at the faces of Nels and Felix and several other men who had gathered around them in a tight little pack. A kind of physical hostility emanated from them, directed at me. I couldn't understand it. We were all friends, Jeth a close friend. Just two months ago, Nels and I had placed our boat orders together to get a better price: each buying a twenty-foot Hewes Light Tackle flats skiff, a kind of maximum-length fishing sled, beautifully designed and built, huge live wells and plenty of storage, rigged with jack plate, power trim, and a big Mariner outboard. Mine was gray. Before the explosion, his had been teal green.

I looked at Felix, then back to Nels. "You guys want to tell me what's going on?"

Felix shifted from one foot to the other, stared at my skiff for a moment before he said, "That's up to you, Doc. We got something we want to ask."

"Yeah?"

Nels said, "What we're wondering is where you stand on all this."

"All this . . . what?"

"Those goddamn netters, that's what. They think they can come over here and screw with our livelihood, they bit off more than they can chew. The voters kicked them out of their jobs, that sure as shit don't mean we're gonna stand around with our thumbs up our ass while they take it out on us. They want a war, they got it."

"As of tonight," Felix said, "we're doing shifts. Guarding the place. It's the same with the other marinas on both islands, Sanibel and Captiva. I didn't get into the guide business to carry a gun, but that's what we'll be doing, by God."

What the hell were they talking about? "I'm going to ask you one more time: What's this have to do with me?"

"We know you spoke at some of those meetings," Jeth said softly. "That's what it's about. Some of the guys think you were on the nuh-nuh-netters' side. And

Tomlinson was just over here asking about the guy who buh-burned up, where he lived, saying you two were goin' up there to help his family, some woman."

"We're asking how you voted," Nels said. "That's what we're asking. Whether you're on our side or theirs. That's what we're talking about."

I was in my skiff; they were on the dock. I looked up at them: big men in fishing shorts, ball caps, pliers on their belts, their faces scorched black from three hundred days a year out there on the flats, burning up their lives to make a living. You don't try to manipulate this kind of men and you can't finesse them. Not that I would have tried. So I did exactly what they expected me to do—I told them the truth. It wasn't a question, I said, of me being for the netters or for the sport fishermen. Yes, netting was an indiscriminate and destructive method of fishing. And yes, the netters were their own worst enemy. They had used spotter planes to exterminate the king mackerel. Once snook and then redfish had been protected, the netters—pushed into a corner—had competed to exterminate the mullet. Each winter, migrant netters came down and trashed the beaches, trashed the islands, and trashed the canals, outraging equally hardworking home owners. I knew all that too.

But had the state legislature done anything to stop it? No. As usual, legislators shied from making the tough decisions. They could have implemented a lottery system to control the fishery and drastically reduced the number of netters. Or they could have legislated riparian rights, allowing netters to fish only where they lived.

There was an incontestable fact that pro-net ban advocates conveniently ignored: Every netter who fished Florida waters was issued a commercial saltwater-products license by the state. The state did not hesitate to sell those licenses to any wandering, itinerant fisherman who could plunk down the money. They sold the licenses to out-of-state netters as eagerly as they sold them to native Floridians whose families had fished the same waters for a hundred years. While the state stamped out licenses, state bureaucrats sat back, brows furrowed, expressions aloof, and made dire, but accurate, predictions about the imminent collapse of the fishery.

The irony was lost on legislators, who chose an uncharacteristic haven—silence—then watched safely from the background as special interest groups battled it out and finally brought the net ban to the ballot.

Would the ban revitalize Florida's shallow water fishery? Absolutely. But there would be a long-term price. When disturbed, water oscillates far beyond the point of contact. The same dynamics apply to the environment—and to society. With netting banned, many of the back-bay fish houses would be forced to close. Most of them were located on the water in delicate mangrove littoral zones. They were already zoned for commercial use, they already had docks and dredged canals. Who would buy them out? Big condo developers and marina investors, that's who. No permits required, no environmental hoops to jump through. And where would Florida's banished netters go? They would join the growing numbers of migrant fishermen and thereby contribute to the decimation of fisheries in states—such as the Carolinas—that still allowed netting.

The world market demands sea products. Nothing is going to change that. When there are innate conflicts between man and the environment, I believe it is wiser to dilute the problem by sharing and wisely regulating the burden. Saltwater and sea creatures do not acknowledge the boundaries of states or nations.

I told the guides that. I could have added that because the amendment had been couched as an ultimatum, a reasonable person had no choice but to vote *for* the ban—unless that person wanted to register a protest vote against the spineless behavior of the legislature. But I didn't tell them that. Didn't want it to sound as if I were trying to contrive an excuse. Instead, I said, "Truth is, I voted against the ban."

Nels looked at Felix and nodded: *See? I told you.*

The men shuffled around on the dock, no longer hostile, but neither were they conciliatory. Nels said, "I'm sorry to hear that. I truly am. I always figured you for a friend of ours."

Jeth was upset, becoming impatient. "He told you why he did it. Jesus damn! He had reasons. What's the big deal? A lousy vote."

"The big deal," Nels said, "is, you looked at my boat lately? I'll shoot the next one. You tell your netter buddies that, Doc. I swear to God I will. When you're up there on Sulphur Wells, trying to make 'em feel better 'cause that sonuvabitch burned up, you tell 'em."

I was getting a little impatient myself. "You think I approve of them blowing up boats because of the way I voted? That's stupid. You can take that any way you want to take it, Nels. Like you said—I thought we were friends."

"Well . . . it's something we're gonna have to think about. Yes it is. This is serious shit and we need to know who stands where."

I started the engine and pushed away from the dock.

Tomlinson was over by the canoe ramp talking with
Mack. When he saw me, he strolled out. I pressed bow-
up to the pier so he could step aboard, then backed into
deeper water.

"Just like you wanted," he said, "I got the information. Gumbo Limbo, that's where Jimmy Darroux
lived." He held up a six-pack of Coors Light. "Brought
the entertainment, too."

I didn't say anything; wanted to get away from the
marina first. When we were out of the harbor, I let it
go: "You damn dumb old hippie! Why'd you tell the
guides we're going to Sulphur Wells?"

"Hey," he said. "I'm not that old. What's this 'old'
business?"

"It didn't cross your mind they might be just a little
upset about their boats?"

"For sure. Exactly what I intended, too. Those fellas—I love 'em, don't get me wrong—but those fellas,
they're way too hung up on material possessions, man.
Man gets killed, all they can think about is their boats."

"Yeah, and making their mortgage payments and
feeding their kids. Jesus, Tomlinson!"

He was making a calming motion with his hands.
"Don't freak out on me here, Doc. You'll ruin the whole
ambience of the trip. Although . . . although . . . at least
you're showing some emotion. A growing experience—
that's good. *Any* kind of emotion—for you, that's real
good."

"A growing experience, my ass! Like you're doing
me a favor? Let me tell you something, Tomlinson—I
may have lost a couple of friends tonight. And I disappointed a lady who doesn't appear to need any more
disappointment. All because of you."

He was suddenly interested. "A lady, huh? No shit. Pretty? Who's the lady?"

I told him. Watched him fold his hands and nod sagely. "Yes, Janet has had some trouble. Heavy domestic stuff . . . but I can't go into it. We've had some long talks."

I found that irritating—was there anyone who didn't pour out their soul to the guy? But I didn't want to hear any more of his Ping-Pong talk. I stood at the wheel and pressed the throttle forward. Felt the wind-roar torque, felt the trim of the skiff settle low and fast over the water as I steered us out past Woodring Point, then west toward the Mail Boat Channel, running backcountry as far off the Intercoastal as I could get. The sun was low, diffused by clouds. The clouds resembled desert mountains . . . bronze-streaked, like an Arizona landscape. To my right, far across the water, was St. James City. To the left, Sanibel was an expanding mangrove hedge above which a crown of milky light bloomed: They were playing softball at the school field; already had the lights on even though there was an hour of daylight left.

Tomlinson went forward and began to rummage through the cold-storage locker. "Want a beer?" he yelled.

He'd forgotten that I no longer drank beer during the week. Popping three or four Coors prior to bedtime had gotten to be a habit, and habits have a way of ultimately dominating the host. So I now drank only on Fridays and Saturdays. Today was Thursday.

"Nope," I said.

Ten minutes later, when Captiva Pass was a small breach of silver in the charcoal void, he was pawing through the ice again. Looked up at me to say, "You ready for another one?"

THREE

SULPHUR WELLS WAS A BACK BAY ISLAND NAMED for the artesian springs that Spanish fishermen found when they settled there in the 1700s. The island was isolated by shallow water and a haze of mosquitoes that bred in the mangrove fringe. Because Sulphur Wells had no beaches, it had yet to be divvied up, reconstituted, and sodded by resort conglomerates and international investment groups. But the island's day would come. Florida developers were running out of beachfront property, so the back bay islands were the next logical target of the concrete stalwart. Now, though, the economy of Sulphur Wells—what there was of it—was still based on agriculture, commercial fishing, and blue-collar winter residents who didn't have the money for big-ticket properties over on Gasparilla Island or Manasota Key.

In this way, Sulphur Wells was a Florida anachronism. The people grew peppers and pineapples and mangoes; they wholesaled mullet and blue crabs caught from boats that they had built up from wooden stringers and glassed themselves. There were a couple of stores, but no mall, no 7-Elevens, no car lots. The Florida of Disney World and Holiday Inn, the slick destination of interstates and jetports, was far away, over on the mainland, across the steel swing bridge that joined Sulphur Wells with the current decade; a decade which, inevitably, presaged the island's own future.

I ran up the eastern rim of Pine Island Sound toward Charlotte Harbor, hugging the mangrove banks. I had visited the island a few times by truck on recent buying trips. Still had a few friends who lived there; guys I'd known back in high school. But it had been years since I had boated to the small settlement where Darroux was said to have lived, Gumbo Limbo.

Which meant that I wasn't familiar with the submerged creeks and gutters that constitute channels on the flats. The water was seldom more than a couple of feet deep and, worse, the weak light made the bottom tough to read. The tide was up but falling, so I held to the wind-roiled water; avoided the slick streaks that can be created by the surface tension of protruding sea grass or oysters. Had the engine jacked high, Tomlinson on the bow, running sheer.

Sulphur Wells lay to the east, a long ridge of mangroves and casuarinas. Occasionally, the mangroves would thin to reveal the docks of a fish camp or a cluster of mobile homes. The trailers were set up on blocks, like derelict cars, their aluminum shells faded a chalky white or pink. As we flew past, a man looked up from a fish-cleaning table and stared. A woman gathering wash gave us a friendly wave. Both were quickly absorbed by the marl shore and crowding mangroves. Just east of a mangrove thicket called Part Island, we raised Gumbo Limbo: a curvature of land that extended into the water, its perimeter fringed by a strand of coconut palms. Now, at afterglow, the trunks of the palms were yellow, the canopies black, their heavy fronds interlaced like macaw feathers. A dozen or so wooden houses were elevated on shell mounds beyond. I could see the glow of their windows through the bare limbs of gumbo-limbo trees. Some of the windows were still trimmed with Christmas lights. Houses and palms appeared buoyant on the small raft of land, supported by the mass of water, but adrift, as if the freshening wind could blow the village out to sea.

"I don't suppose you know which house was Darroux's?"

Tomlinson was standing beside me at the console, staring. Probably tuning in the vibrations, expecting karma to point to the place. "Don't know," he said. "One of them." He shrugged. "There aren't many."

"Then we'll have to use the commercial docks. I don't want to beach it. The tide's going, we're losing our water."

"Those hills, the shell mounds. Reminds me of Mango." He was talking about a place where an uncle of mine, Tucker Gatrell, lived. "Old Florida, man, with those Indian mounds. They still do farming—smell the cow manure?"

"I smell it. Open that bow hatch and get the lines ready."

The channel into Gumbo Limbo was lined by a bank of limestone—that much I remembered. Miss the cut and you could kill your boat—maybe even kill yourself—on the rocks. So I used the good water to run in close to shore, then dropped down off plain when I picked up the first wooden stakes that served as markers. The markers led us into a dredged canal, at the mouth of which was a warehouse on pilings. The docks were lined with simple plywood boats that were brush-painted blue or white.

Men in jeans and white rubber boots moved around beneath the lights. Someone's radio was blaring. The whine of twangy, achy-breaky music was louder than my outboard. There were commercial scales and a cable hoist mounted on the loading platform. A sign above the warehouse read: *Sulphur Wells Fish Company.*

As we idled down the channel, men on the dock stopped what they were doing. Put down the crates they were carrying and watched us.

Tomlinson smiled, waved—got blank stares in return. Still looking at the workers, he spoke to me out of the corner of his mouth: "These fellas don't seem too friendly. Kind of standoffish."

"That's one way to put it. Standoffish."

"The way they're staring at me."

"I noticed."

"Hey . . . I'm not still wearing that damn sarong, am I?" He had his chin on his chest, inspecting himself.

"Nope."

"That woulda explained it. A sarong would get some funny looks around here. Not as sophisticated like Sanibel."

"What you look like is a soap opera doctor in those scrubs."

"There's a possibility. Maybe they think I'm on TV."

Was he serious? "No, what they're thinking is, we're crazy. Come here in a flats boat at night, enemy territory. And they're right. The smart thing to do would be turn around and head back to Dinkin's Bay. You want to talk to Hannah? Track her down over the phone."

"Let's at least ask somebody first, okay? They probably don't get many visitors. Like country people, not used to dealing with strangers.''

We had come to the end of the canal, and I swung into an open area of the dock. ''Yeah,'' I said, ''probably just shy,'' as a couple of men who had been trailing us along the dock caught up.

AS THE MEN APPROACHED, I CALLED, ''YOU MIND IF WE tie up here for a while?''

They waited until they were above us: both of them tall, one maybe six three, bony-looking. Probably in their mid-twenties, jeans and T-shirts with long arms hanging out, showing their biceps. The taller one was the talker. Had a couple of generations of Georgia piney woods in his voice, and proud of it. He answered, ''Tie up? Sure, you boys can tie up. Tie up just long as you like.'' Which came out: ''Show-er, yew boys kin tah up,''; the dialect exaggerated, and with a mock friendliness that Tomlinson took at face value.

''Thanks, man.'' Tomlinson had the bow line in his hand, already reaching for the galvanized cleat. Then, as he reached up over the dock and took a wrap, the talker—he was wearing a bandanna on his head knotted pirate style—moved with an amused, catlike laziness and used his rubber boot to pin Tomlinson's wrist between the deck and the cleat.

''Uh-h-h—whoops-a-daisy—you're stepping on my hand, man.''

''Huh?''

''My hand. You've got your foot on my hand.''

The talker turned and looked at his partner blankly. ''What the hell this boy talkin' about? He got an imagination in his brain, don't he?''

The partner was laughing—big joke. "That's what he got. 'Bout the only thing, Julie."

I thought: *Julie?*

Tomlinson gave a yank, trying to get free. "Seriously, man . . . really! You're like cutting off the circulation."

"Naw-w-w. Me?"

"See—there's your boot. That thing under it? My hand. Look for yourself."

Julie lifted his right boot, putting the full weight of his left on Tomlinson's wrist. He peered at the space beneath his right boot, said, "You must be invisible 'cause I don't see a damn thing."

If Tomlinson hadn't already taken a solid wrap around the cleat, I would have backed away. Let Julie decide if he wanted to be pulled into the canal, then pop my skiff up on plane and wash all those net boats into the pilings to thank Sulphur Wells Fish Company for its hospitality. But I couldn't go anywhere because we were already secured to the dock.

When I switched the engine off, the blaring radio became the dominant noise: *Redfish ain't ro-o-o-ses to my baby*—lyrics that were strangely familiar, but I didn't take the time to try and remember why. I stood there a moment, not saying anything, letting my inactivity draw their attention. When they were both looking at me, I said, "The smart thing to do would be get your foot off him."

"Hoo-wee, a tough boy! You don't mind, I'll stand where I damn well please."

"Just a suggestion."

"You take your suggestions and leave. That's my advice."

"Move your foot, we will."

"You have a mind to do somethin' about it?"

I was shaking my head. "Walk clear up his arm for all I care, I'm not going to help him. Take a look at those clothes he's wearing. Those are hospital clothes. You know why? Because he's sick. The guy's a leper."

Julie made a face, saying, "Huh?" then lifted his foot just as Tomlinson gave a tremendous pull . . . and back-pedaled across the bow . . . teetered for a moment, almost caught himself, then sprawled into the water.

I leaned away from the splash, aware that other men were now coming along the dock toward us, hurrying.

"He ain't sick. You serious?" Julie was thinking maybe he'd been duped, but didn't want to show it. I ignored him, waiting for Tomlinson to scull to the surface. Held out a hand to help him vault back aboard as the partner said, "He ain't no leopard, what a bunch'a shit. It ain't a disease anyway. I seen pictures'a leopards."

Heard Julie say, "Mr. smartmouth fuckin' with us. Got his girlfriend all wet!" Laughing, as if that had been his plan all along.

To Tomlinson, I said, "You okay?"

He was wringing out his hair. "Water's kind of refreshing. Cold but nice."

"One of these days, you'll learn to listen to me. See that mob coming?"

He didn't; he was looking at Julie. Wiped water from his eyes and yelled, "Violence covereth the mouth of the wicked, and the name of the wicked shall rot! You hurt my hand on purpose!" As an aside to me, Tomlinson said, "That's from Proverbs, man. When you're pissed off, the Pali just doesn't have the juice."

I was shaking my head. "Just close your mouth and

do what I tell you to do. You start the engine while I try to get the bow line. When I tell you, gun it. Run us straight into the bay.'' I stopped to place my glasses on the console . . . and the world became a blurry place of bright coronas and moving shapes. Then I stepped up onto the casting deck to confront Julie.

I am not an eager let's-prove-something-here fighter. I'd much prefer to talk it out. Or leave. Or even run. Which is probably why I have been in so few street fights. But when there are no options, when it is fight back or else, I do not double the fists and start swinging—except, long ago, when they placed us in a training ring with leather gloves and substantial chunks of Everlast headgear strapped around our ears. But no bare-knuckled boxing. Ever. By the time I was nineteen, I'd seen enough fistfights to know that no one ever wins; one man just loses more painfully than the other. I also knew that the clean, bare-knuckled choreography that constitutes fighting in books and movies has no more basis in reality than film's absurd lionization of the martial arts. A fistfight—or any fight—is ugly, bloody, and brutal; a quick descent to the primate roots. It is proof that, in the deepest wells of our own brains, Neanderthal man still lives. There is always a lot of grunting and growling. A lot of scrambling and panicked scratching amid the sweat and adrenal stink. And a fight always, *always* ends up on the ground. Which is why an average college wrestler could humiliate any one of Hollywood's kung fu movie stars—or a good professional boxer— were he so inclined.

As our instructor told us in that long-gone boxing ring, ''We're teaching you this because, someday, you might have to fight a man that you're not authorized to kill.''

Which, if nothing else, demonstrated that some of our instructors had a flair for exaggeration.

I didn't want to fight Julie, and I certainly wasn't going to climb up on the dock and try to slug it out. All I wanted was to get my bow line and the opportunity to run back to Dinkin's Bay . . . tail between my legs, if need be.

Behind Julie and friend, I could hear men asking, ''What's going on? These guys giving you trouble?'' Heard Julie say, ''Couple smartass sportfishermen. One just went for a swim.''

He had an audience now, plus backup, so I didn't have much doubt about what he'd try to do. As I reached for the cleat, he lifted his left boot to stomp me—which I anticipated. I jumped to reach him, grabbed his right heel and pulled. Julie seemed to hang suspended in midair for a moment, then crashed spine-first onto the dock, both legs hanging over. I locked his knees under my arms and let my body weight—about 220 pounds— snatch him crotch-first into the cleat. A cleat is a mooring device with pronounced metal horns at each end, and both of those horns disappeared into Julie. He made a falsetto cry of shock, tried to sit up when I applied more pressure, then settled back, hollering for help.

To Julie's partner, I yelled, ''Know what a wishbone is? Take one step toward this boat, your buddy better make a wish.'' I turned to Tomlinson. ''Start the engine.''

''You boys just hold 'er right there! You ain't goin' noplace!'' A small man had pushed his way through the ring of fishermen, something in his hand. Without my glasses, I couldn't tell what. "Let go'a that man's legs or you'll wish you had. Don't be reaching for that line, neither!"

Tomlinson said very softly, "He's got a gun."

I released Julie and told Tomlinson, "Kill the engine."

I HAD MY GLASSES ON, TRYING MY BEST TO BE CONCILiatory. The man's name was Futch, Arlis Futch—he told us that—and he was the founder, sole owner, operator, and the only one who much mattered around the docks of Sulphur Wells Fish Company. He told us that, too.

Judging from the way the fishermen deferred to him, I didn't doubt it.

"You boys get back to work. This ain't no dance. I need any help, you'll hear shots. By then I won't need no more help." He didn't laugh when he said it.

Futch had a body type that I had come to associate with the male descendants of Gulf Coast settlers: narrow shoulders, blunt fingers, bandy legs, but with hands and forearms large and out of proportion, and trapezius muscles so pronounced that his head seemed to sit atop a pyramid. Also, he had the characteristic myopia. His eyes, magnified by the thick glasses, were owl-sized.

"You hurt bad or just making noise?"

Julie had his arm over his partner's shoulder, sucking in air. "The sonuvabitch 'bout crippled me."

"He draw blood?"

"I'd rather bleed than have my nuts squished out my nose. That cleat liked to ruin me."

"Well, don't be feelin' your thingumabob around me, goddamn it! You want to inspect your personals, find a bush. Now somebody tell me what happened."

Julie still had enough wind to talk. "What happened was, these here two come in high and mighty thinkin' they could tie up. When I told 'em it was private they got smartmouthy, kind'a pushy. He tripped me, the big one, and I fell wrong or they wouldn't be here botherin' you now."

"That's how it happened, huh?"

"Ask J. D. Ain't that how it happened?"

J. D.: Julie's partner had a name.

Arlis Futch looked down at me, asked, "That the whole story?"

I said, "Not much that I recognize," but didn't offer any more.

"You gonna believe him? *Shit*." Julie was up pacing around now, kept glancing over, eager to take another shot at me, I could tell. "I was just tryin' to help, Mr. Futch. They come in here acting like big shots, what you want me to do?"

Futch had the shotgun tucked in the crook of his arm. Now he levered it open, looked as if to make sure it was loaded. "What I want you to do is mind your own affairs. Someone wants a slip, they ask me, not you. That's just about exactly the way she goes 'round here."

"I didn't know you wanted flats boat business."

"Don't use that tone to me. What I want ain't none of your concern. You ain't from around here and you ain't no kin—"

"We been sellin' you fish for the last month, that's all—"

"And I paid you cash for 'em. Don't owe you diddly-squat. Don't even know your damn names and I don't want to know 'em. What I do know is, you and some of the others camped up the shore drink way too much whiskey, smoke your damn dope, and you're tryin' to get my local boys mixed up in matters they're damn near desperate enough to try. Somethin' else I know is, you're trouble. Just plain dog-mean trouble." Futch snapped the shotgun closed, but kept it pointed at the dock. I noticed just the wryest hint of a smile as he added, "So what you boys gonna do is jump in your skiff and disappear. Want to take a minute, hunt around the dock for any small things you lost, your thinguma-bob, whatever, that's fine. But don't come back."

"You sayin' you ain't buyin' no more fish from us?"

"You find someone else to haul it in, that's your business. Just don't let me catch the two of you on my property."

J. D., it turned out, was a talker, too. He took turns with Julie hollering at Arlis Futch. They made obscene and impossible suggestions; they offered vague threats. Each was prefaced by "old man." Futch ignored them until he'd heard enough; then he looked at his watch before saying softly, "You boys want me to tell you when your time's up? Or should I jes' surprise you?"

Which sent the two of them walking toward their boat. When they were under way and out of the canal, Futch turned his attention to us. Because of the way he'd treated J. D. and Julie, I expected him to assume that we were the wronged parties and behave cordially. He didn't. He popped open the shotgun and shoved the shells into his pocket, saying, "What you waiting on? Get out. I don't want you around here neither."

Tomlinson said, "We need a spot to tie up," and told him who we were looking for and why.

Futch worked at appearing indifferent—he yawned a couple of times—but I could tell the story touched a chord. When Tomlinson had finished, he asked, "You was there when Jimmy Darroux burnt up? Maybe you're just sayin' that 'cause you're a cop or somethin.' "

Tomlinson said, "Do I look like a cop to you?"

"You look like just one more damn Yankee tourist to me."

"I was with him at the hospital. When he died. That's why we're looking for Hannah."

"Hannah, huh? Tell me somethin'—did he suffer real bad. At the end, I mean. Jimmy?"

"It didn't last long. If you were a friend of his, you can take comfort from that."

"I don't need no comfort, not from you I don't. Common sense gives me all the comfort I need." Judging from Futch's tone, his expression, I got the impression that he hoped Darroux had suffered, and was irritated that Tomlinson didn't offer more details.

"Jimmy Darroux made a request of me on his deathbed," Tomlinson said. "I'm determined to honor it."

Futch thought for a moment, stared along the dock where the commercial fishermen had returned to work but were still keeping an eye on us.

"You looking for Hannah," he said finally, "that would be Jimmy's wife, Hannah Smith." In reply to my sharp look, Futch added, "I won't call her by her married name. She was always Hannah Smith to me, still is to this day."

"Do you know where we can find her? If she doesn't want to talk, considering what she's been through—"

"Hannah ain't no prissy, mopey kind'a woman. She doesn't want to talk, she'll tell you plain enough. I ain't the one to make her decisions for her. She lives down the road a couple hundred yards, the yellow cabin up on the Indian mound.'' Futch pointed vaguely. ''The cops've already talked to her, so if you're here to ask more questions she'll figure that out quick enough, too.''

''So it's okay to tie up?''

''Didn't say that.''

''We . . . can pay you.''

''Don't want your money. You boys just ain't clear about the way things stand, are you? You own this here boat?'' He was talking to me. I nodded. ''Let me explain the way it is. You paid more for this fancy boat than some'a these men make in a year. Boat with a fancy platform over the motor so you can stand up there, dressed real nice, and look for fish when you got the time. Well, mister-man, those used to be our fish. Used to be our bay until the rich sports got their lawyers together and found a way to push us out.

''Time was I'd see only one or two of these here boats in a month. Helped 'em out many a time, too, tellin' where I saw the tar-pawn schoolin' or when the tripletail was around the traps. Tarpon and tripletail weren't nothin' to me, and it was the neighborly thing to do, I figured. Now'days, though, there're hundreds, hell, thousands'a these boats ever'where you look. Can't hardly strike a mess'a mullet without one'a these here flats boaters blastin' through givin' us their dirty looks.'' Futch hacked, spat, hacked, and spat again. ''What you think it does to our boys, see a boat like yours? They got the whole world comin' down on their heads, sick kids, payments to make, banks yammering for their money and not a cent comin' in after the nets is banned in July. A lot of 'em didn't even finish high school, figuring they could always make a livin' fishin'. Now what they gonna do? You sports in the fancy boats got it all. You sports in the fancy boats took it all. Now you come in here lah-de-dah-de-dah askin' to tie up?'' Futch had his face squinched into a thoughtful frown. ''I reckon I jes' couldn't be responsible, you tie your boat here. One of the boys might mistake her for a two-holer and poot his mess on the deck. Or maybe worse. Lines might break and it'd drift off and catch fire, nobody's fault. My advice to you fellas is get the hell out an' don't come back. Hannah wants to talk to you, that's her business. But my docks ain't got no room for a boat like yours.''

FOUR

TOMLINSON SEEMED SURPRISED WHEN I BEACHED MY skiff in the mangroves south of the fish house so that we could look for Hannah Smith Darroux on foot. He'd been scolding me for skewering Julie on the cleat—"Violence is like a boomerang. It always comes back at you"—but he paused when I swung toward shore, favoring me with his you're-growing-as-a-human-being expression—a look, happily, that I seldom receive. But I didn't beach my boat out of sympathy or to please Tomlinson. The way Arlis Futch had behaved interested me . . . interested and angered me both. I admired the fact that he empathized with the younger men, and he had summed up the inequities of the net ban accurately. Yet he also seemed to take perverse pleasure in being defiant and intractable. That kind of belligerence enjoys a mythos to which every region lays claim: the flinty Yankee, the bow-necked mid-westerner, the resolute cowboy. It is a character standard from folklore in which "good old common sense" is an essential bedrock ingredient. But too often, "common sense" is the safe harbor of ignorance and an excuse for intellectual laziness. They don't need the facts because they already

know the truth—their common sense has spared them
the effort of investigation or thought. It was precisely
that attitude which too many cottage industry netters
brought to the fishery, and, in doing so, they helped destroy their own way of life. Arlis Futch was an intelli-
gent man. Stupid people don't build successful
businesses or earn the respect of their peers. So why
would he cloak himself in stupid indifference?

But that's not the only reason I swung into shore. The
way Futch had reacted to Tomlinson's story piqued my
interest. He had asked about Jimmy Darroux hoping to
hear that the man had suffered. I was sure of that. It was
in Futch's tone, his eyes. He hadn't approved of Darroux
as a husband for Hannah Smith—a woman he spoke of
with a degree of respect he certainly didn't show the
men who worked around the docks. Tomlinson says my
best quality and my worst quality are the same: an orderly mind. I think he's half right. Tomlinson is mysti-
cal, I am methodical. He believes in the Great Enigma,
I do not. The behavior of any organism should be understandable once external influences are deciphered.
When an otherwise predictable animal behaves oddly on
the tidal flats—or on the docks—a little alarm goes off
in my head. The inexplicable attracts me because there
is nothing that cannot be explained. When the explanation is not readily apparent, I become compulsive about
isolating the external influences. It attracts me in the
same way that jigsaw puzzles and chess draw in similar
types of people. Assemble enough pieces, make the right
moves, and the reward is clarity.

The alarm had gone off when Arlis Futch asked about
Jimmy Darroux, and when he spoke of the wife. Not a
loud alarm, just a gentle chime of suspicion. But that,

connected to the experience of holding a charred body in my arms, was enough. I wanted to meet Hannah Smith Darroux. I wanted to see for myself why Futch held her in such high regard.

I idled in close to shore, looking up at the lights of houses built on Indian shell mounds. When I judged we had gone a couple hundred yards, I tilted the engine and poled us toward a patch of mangroves. I didn't want to leave my skiff unattended in the open. There was no moon, but the night sky was star-bright, and Julie and J. D. were out there cruising. I stern-anchored so that we could haul the boat off when we got back; then we waded through muck and oysters to the road that ribboned between the houses and the bay.

Tomlinson stood in the middle of the road, fingering a braid of his hair. There was no traffic. It was quiet but for crickets and the whine of mosquitoes. "I have a feeling it's that one. I don't know why, man, I just do." He was pointing to an old cottage with an open board porch. The porch light showed peeling, colorless paint. "I'll walk up and ask."

"No," I said, "we stay together. We'll start with the first house. If they don't know where Hannah Darroux lives, someone at the next house will."

But the elderly man in the first house knew. Turned out that Tomlinson had guessed correctly.

HANNAH SMITH DARROUX WAS NOT THE SUN-WIZENED fishwife that I imagined she would be. She was like nothing I could have imagined—my imagination is not that fanciful. When Tomlinson knocked at the screen door, the floor of the porch on which we were standing began to vibrate with the weight of approaching footsteps; a steady, authoritative thud. I expected a man to answer. Instead, the door swung open and a woman confronted us, asking, ''Help you?''

Tomlinson didn't speak for a moment, and then he said, ''Huh?'' as if he'd been dozing.

The woman said, ''Huh what? Do I know you men?''

''We're . . . looking for Hannah Darroux.''

''Pretty close, but what you found is Hannah Smith. What's your business?''

Tomlinson cleared his throat; he seemed to be having trouble speaking, but he was probably reacting to a kind of sensory overload. He had been as unprepared as I for the woman who stood in the doorway. Hannah Smith Darroux was well over six feet tall—probably six two, six three. Balanced on long crane legs, she had a busty, countrified body: big hands, shoulders, and bony bare feet. I guessed she would weigh 155, maybe 160. She wore jeans and a blue denim work shirt with the tail knotted and bloused loosely above skinny adolescent hips. I guessed her to be in her mid-twenties, maybe a shade older. Her hair was Navajo-black, the whole heavy gloss of it combed over onto her right shoulder as if she didn't want to be bothered with it. She wore no makeup, no jewelry of any kind—not even a wedding ring. The result was a kind of unconscious stylishness. She had wide, full lips, deep sun lines at the corners of her brows, good cheekbones, a squarish quarterback's jaw, and dark perceptive eyes that looked from Tomlinson to me, then back to Tomlinson, taking us in, assessing us, then dismissing us as unimportant. I saw no telltale redness in those eyes. The widow Darroux hadn't done much crying.

''I know this hasn't been the best of days, Mrs. Smith,

but I'd like to speak with you. For just a few minutes.''

"If I had a few minutes, I'd throw you in my dryer and close the door. You're drippin' all over my porch.''

"Oh . . . well, see, I had a little . . . encounter down at the fish house—'' Tomlinson was backing down the steps, trying to wring more water from his shirt.

"Arlis Futch throw you in, or just have one of his boys do it?''

"Actually, I sort of fell—''

"Men that fall off docks ought to live in the mountains. If you're sellin' something, I suggest you try Denver. Wet the porches there.''

"Seriously, I'm not selling anything, Mrs. Smith—''

"I should say you're not. Question is, why are you bothering me?''

Tomlinson opened his mouth as if to speak, then stopped to collect himself. By continually anticipating what he was going to say, then interrupting to reply to it, the woman was not only keeping Tomlinson off balance, she also was establishing a weird dominance that had even me wishing he would finally say something that would interest her.

After a second or two, he chose the direct approach. "I'm here because your late husband asked me to come. My friend pulled him out of the water this morning; I was at the hospital with him when he died. My name's Tomlinson, his name's Ford.''

Which threw her off her rhythm. Caused her to narrow her focus, partly out of suspicion, I sensed. "Jimmy told you to come here?''

"Sit down, I'll tell you everything.''

"Before he died, right? Not something crazy, like talking from the hereafter? You seem that kind to me.''

"I am! You've got a good eye for people, Mrs. Smith.
You want to give transsphere communications a try, we
can discuss the possibilities later. For now, though, the
only thing he ever said to me was while he was still
alive. His last words."

"But the cops told me, this Lieutenant somebody, that
Jimmy never regained consciousness. Now you're saying he spoke to you?"

"The police haven't interviewed me yet. I'll tell them,
but I'd rather tell you first."

"I see." She pressed a long index finger to her lower
lip, a reflective pose. "You could be cops just tryin' to
trick me into something. The county cops or the
A.T.F.—they already took up half my day. And me with
mortuary arrangements, a million things to do. You try
to trick me, I reckon my attorney would have to nail you
to the wall. Or you could be reporters, same thing. They
were nosing around here earlier."

I found it impressive that she differentiated between
the sheriff's department and the federal Alcohol, Tobacco, and Firearms officers.

Tomlinson said, "We're not cops and we're not reporters. Civilians, that's us. Just concerned human beings. I'm telling you the truth."

"Jimmy told you something before he died."

"He spoke to me. Yes."

"What about your friend?" She turned and gave me
her full attention for the first time. For a moment, just a
moment, I thought I saw her react: a mild flash of rec-
ognition, as if she had seen me before, so was scanning
the memory files, searching for confirmation.

I said, "A few words. Not much."

She was still staring at me, pondering, when from inside the house came a man's voice: "Anything wrong, Hannah?" Looking through the doorway, I could see a man walking toward us through what appeared to be a sparsely furnished living room. He wore a desert-gray safari-style shirt and matching shorts; a big man in his mid-thirties who took his appearance seriously; the contemporary backpacker and kayaker look—which seemed out of place on Sulphur Wells. He wasn't quite as tall as Hannah, but he had the tight muscularity that I associate with collegiate sports—soccer, lacrosse, tennis, that sort of thing. He had to poke his head over the woman's shoulder to speak to us. "Can we help you fellows?"

"They're here to talk to me, Raymond, not you. You stop by tomorrow, we'll finish our business. 'Bout four or five, before I go to work."

"Do you know these men?"

She gave him a warning look. "Tomorrow, Raymond."

Raymond reached around and placed his hand on the woman's arm, a territorial gesture. "Hannah's had a terrible shock today, fellas, so I think it would be best if—"

That quick, the woman had Raymond by the elbow and was hustling him past us down the steps, off the porch, and into the shell driveway where some kind of utility vehicle sat in the shadows, a Ford Explorer maybe. Heard her say, "Damn it, Raymond, if I want a guardian I'll have you fill out an application. Not that you'd be high on the list. You want to talk business, come tomorrow. You don't, that's fine, too."

Raymond mumbled something, mumbled something else, then started his car.

Striding back to the porch, Hannah said to Tomlinson, "You get those clothes off. Yeah—right where you stand. Nobody comes down that road much, but I'll turn off the porch light if you're modest. You"—she was speaking to me—"take your muddy shoes off and get inside out of the mosquitoes while I find your friend a towel and some of Jimmy's dry things. . . ." She was still staring at me. "What did you say your name was?"

I told her . . . and watched her expression soften slightly. "I know who you are; I've seen you. At the Conservation Board meeting at Tallahassee. You were 'bout the only one that had anything good to say about us commercial people."

Which wasn't true, but Hannah Smith had the politician's knack of making people eager to please.

I said, "I told them what I believed, that's all."

"But you had a good way about you. You talked soft. All those facts and numbers—but not too many. People listened. When you got done, I thought maybe, just maybe, we had a chance."

"I'm surprised I didn't notice you."

"Oh, I was in an' out of the room, carryin' papers, makin' sure our men were where they were supposed to be. Tryin' to organize fishermen is like trying to organize a bunch of snakes. I had my hands full. I was there—one of the green hats. I just blended in."

"No, I think I would have remembered."

Which earned me a quick smile . . . and then she was done with me, her attention back on Tomlinson. "Hurry up now! I don't care a thing about seeing your skinny little butt. Hand me your wet stuff." She grabbed the ball of clothes out of Tomlinson's hands. Tomlinson, naked, gave me a wan look, shrugged, then followed her into the house. Heard her say, "Well, you got hair like a woman, but that's 'bout as far as she goes. Towel off in the bathroom. Jimmy's stuff may be a little big around the shoulders, but it'll do. Might as well just keep it. Lord knows, Jimmy, he won't need it no more."

"RAYMOND TULLOCK IS LIKE MOST MEN. HIS BALLS tell him he should be in charge, but his brain's just not big enough to steer the load. You want ice tea? I had some Co-Colas but I handed them out to the cops."

I was sitting in the small living room on a rattan couch waiting for Tomlinson to come out of the bathroom. He was showering. The water had just started. Hannah was puttering around in the kitchen. She had the clothes dryer thumping on the back porch; something was simmering on the stove: smelled like black beans, a cumin and bay leaf smell.

"Raymond used to work for the marine extension agency, a government job. Worked with the oystermen, the netters, tellin' us how we could do our business better. A liaison—you know what I mean?"

I said, "Sure."

"Now we've got a woman. She was down here . . . Tuesday? No, Monday. Brought another woman with her to tell us how to make low-cost meals, where to go for food stamps. Getting us ready for welfare handouts because of the net ban. Had a meeting at the Community Center, all these island women sitting around in their print dresses. What they did was treat us like a bunch of snot-nosed kids who'd starve if they weren't there to show us how things're done. Know what the government woman said? Wendy something. Wendy graduated Duke, knows everything there is to know. Wendy says,

'I strongly recommend you try to limit fats in your families' diets. Too expensive and bad for the heart.' She says, 'Seafood is a good low-cost substitute, the cheaper grades of fish.' ''

Hannah poked her head out from the kitchen to see how I'd reacted to the punch line. "Get it? This bossy college woman, teeth like ice, tellin' us to eat fish now that we can't net them. Jesus! She says, 'I recommend broiled fish as opposed to frying. Peanut oil is so expensive.' That's exactly what she said. I grew up cookin' for my daddy and brothers up in the Panhandle, Cedar Key, down here. *Knowin'* how to cook. But there's Wendy, an easy government job and all the gall in the world, telling us about fish."

I said, "I can see why you find that offensive."

"Damn right we were offended. After the meeting, this little old lady, Miz Hamilton—she's some relation of mine, way, way back; little bitty thing—Miz Hamilton totters up to Wendy, and she says, 'Missy, if the gov'ment paid you a dollah to come heah' ''—Hannah had thickened her own accent, making it sound real— '' 'the gov'ment paid you a dollah too much. I think them micra-waves done boiled your brain!' ''

I sat there listening, smiling. The woman seemed to be on a talking jag, and I wondered if it was because she was trying to avoid the subject of her husband's death. Denial is the first stage of mourning. So far, the talking jag was the only slim sign of bereavement that Hannah Smith had displayed.

"That's what he did up till about three years ago. Then he went into the private sector." She was back on the subject of Raymond Tullock. "I guess he got tired of the bad pay, carryin' a clipboard around. Driving those white state cars everywhere he went. You know they got to keep track of every single mile? With all the connections he had, Raymond got himself appointed to the state Fisheries Conservation Board—'bout the only one on it who talked against the net ban. And he set himself up as a kind of wholesale seafood agent. A restaurant needs softshell crab up on the Chesapeake? They call Raymond and he works it out, top price. He's the one that found our Japanese buyers for mullet roe. Some other place, too—Indianesia? He goes to those places, scouts around. So instead of Arlis Futch sellin' to the big fish wholesalers, we sell direct to the buyers from over there. A better deal for them, a lot better price for us, and Raymond takes his piece off the top. Does it all over the phone and fax, doesn't even own a boat. Pretty smart, huh? For a man like Raymond.''

She appeared long enough to hand me a mason jar of iced tea, wedge of lime, then carried a second glass into the bathroom. Heard her say, ''Don't be leaving hair in the tub, neither!'' Heard Tomlinson make some enthusiastic reply; couldn't understand the words.

The tea was made with local water. Had a heavy, sulfuric musk to it that she had tried to cover by making it very sweet and strong. Tasted as if she had mixed in some New Age herb for spice. Boil any dried leaf, they call it tea.

It was different, but good. So I sat there with tea, feeling the house shake beneath me. Whenever Hannah walked—whenever anyone walked—the whole house vibrated. It was one of those old Florida cottages built of heart pine on foot-high shell-mortar blocks, raw shell beneath. The living room had a varnished oak floor and a brick fireplace. On the mantel were arrangements of dried flowers in wicker baskets, a feminine touch. There were also four or five small glass spheres, dark green in color. The spheres were smaller than a tennis ball; reminded me of old glass net floats. Hanging from the ceiling were mobiles made of seashells, and on the walls, a couple of strange paintings: dark backgrounds with fluorescent loops and whirls. The furnishings were inexpensive, simple. Wood frames and bright cushions, beanbag chairs, a rocker, a Lay-Z-Boy, and a Sony television mounted on an orange crate in the corner. A small foyer with jalousie windows faced the bay. There was a breakfast table there covered with baskets of food, cakes, a roast chicken. The kind of gifts that country people bring when there has been a death in the family.

I tried to picture the charred creature I had held in my arms sitting at that table, eating a meal, sipping coffee after a hard night on the water. Tried to picture him walking to the refrigerator for a beer, plopping down on the couch to watch a ball game . . . pictured him taking Hannah into the bedroom.

But the imagery didn't work because the props wouldn't fall into place. There was no man-spore around the house. No heavy boots on the stoop, no tangle of clothes in the corner, no sports page folded beside the Lay-Z-Boy, no tools scattered around the porch. It had been only, what? sixteen hours since Jimmy Darroux had come tumbling out of the flames. My eyes drifted up to the mantel: no wedding picture. Married couples who are childless (I saw no sign of children in the house) usually keep a wedding picture prominently displayed— a gesture I have always found touching. It is as if they are reminding themselves that they are, indeed, a family.

''Sounds like your friend's enjoying his shower. But

he surefire can't sing worth a flip. What's his name again?'' She was still in the kitchen, but didn't have to talk loud to be heard, the place was so small.

"Tomlinson," I said.

"He always so happy?"

"Always." Why tell her that Tomlinson also had a dark side? Twice since I had known him, he'd descended into a depression so emphatic that he did not eat; would barely speak.

She said, "He's kind'a different. No offense."

"None taken."

"I didn't mean it bad, because I like people who are different. I really do. The poet types, people who paint. That sort. See, because I'm kind of like that myself. Different. Since I was a little girl, always sort of, you know—weird. Even my daddy said so. I think I scared him."

Because I could think of no other reply, I said, "You seem normal enough to me."

She poked her head out of the kitchen just long enough to smile and say, "That's because you don't know me very well yet," then vanished again, still talking. "Part of it's I'm a Gemini born on the cusp. But with Leo rising. Like two people in one body, both of us bossy." Her chuckle was a series of soft bell tones. "Women aren't supposed to speak their minds, do whatever they please. Know why? Because it reminds men how much spunk they lack. Scares 'em, makes them feel sheepish. What about you, your sign?"

I wasn't even sure I knew. When I took a guess, she said, "Gad! We're complete opposites. You're the real logical type, everything real orderly. I bet you think astrology's a bunch of crap. Well . . . how about this? You know what a birth veil is? Mama said I was born with a veil over my face. This flap of skin or something, the placenta, I guess, connected when I came out. Like I didn't have eyes or a mouth or nothing. The midwife about fainted—that's what Mama said—because a baby born with a veil is supposed to have the power of second sight. That's what the midwife believed. She was my mama's closest friend, Miz Budd. A colored woman.''

All nonsense. But I liked the sound of her voice, the vitality of it. I said, "Tomlinson's the one you should be telling. He's interested in folklore."

"There. I knew he was different. What's he do?"

"Tomlinson? He lives on a sailboat and . . . well, that's what he does. He pulls up anchor occasionally, cruises around, then comes back."

"To make a living, I mean. For money."

I'd wondered about that myself. "I think he has a small income from his family. He does research projects for organizations. Scholarly things. He's written some books—"

"Books!" She was suddenly very interested. She stood in the doorway for a moment, a wooden spoon in her hand. "What kind of books? You mean that he wrote himself?"

"Well . . . yeah. I haven't read them . . . not clear through, anyway." I'd given Tomlinson's most recent volume, *Variations of the Yavapai Apache Sweat Lodge Ceremony*, a determined effort, but failed.

She paused for a moment, thoughtful. "I'm writing a book myself, but don't know nothing about how to get it published. Hell, truth is, I don't know nothing about how to write it. It's about the fishermen. We're the last of about ten generations—if the bastards get their way.

And about my great-grandmother and my great-aunt, too, Sarah and Hannah Smith. You ever hear of them?''

I told Hannah that I hadn't, then listened as she told me that, back in 1911, Sarah Smith had driven a two-wheeled oxcart across the Everglades—the only person to ever do it, man or woman.

"Just her alone, doin' what she wanted to do," Hannah said. "Some of the history books, they've got a picture of her. All the Crackers called her the Ox Woman. Because of what she did, and because she was so big. Made her money chopping firewood. Swing an ax like that, you've got to be stro-o-o-ng. Sarah had a sister named Hannah—my great-aunt—and she was big too. Like six two, six three. My size, so the old-timers called Hannah Big Six. Because she was more than six feet tall? Sometimes I think I'm Hannah come back. You know . . . like another life?''

I told Hannah, "When Tomlinson gets out of the shower, you two will have a lot to talk about."

I COULD HEAR A BLOW-DRYER IN THE BATHROOM. TOM-linson was getting himself spruced up—a measure of Hannah Smith's effect on him.

"I almost telephoned you after that meeting." She was still making noises in the kitchen: the clank of a steel lid, the clatter of dishes being washed. I wondered if she expected us to stay for dinner—and why she would want us to. She said, "The meeting in Tallahassee? You impressed me, that's the truth. No fancy talking. Just the facts. The sportfishing guys, they didn't like it, neither. Didn't want to hear nothin' but their own lies."

Which wasn't true. Most sportfishermen wanted what

was best for the fishery. They were willing to listen. I opened my mouth to correct her, but hesitated, allowing the opportunity to pass—and realized that I, too, was oddly eager to please her. A powerful woman.

She came into the living room, wiping her hands on a towel, adding, ''You didn't have an ax to grind, just told it out straight,'' then dropped down into a beanbag chair near the fireplace, one stork leg folded over another. ''Truth is . . . that wasn't the first time I seen you.'' The expression on her face intermingled amusement and challenge. She waited for a reply; proof that she had my full attention.

I said, ''Is that so?''

''Yep. It was maybe a year ago. I was down fishing in Dinkin's Bay, just me. 'Bout sunset, just after. Still some light but not a lot. I was pushing along the bushes looking for a mess of mullet to strike, when I see this big blond hairy man come waltzing out on the porch. Stripped his clothes off and started washing himself from the water cistern. Brushing his teeth, scrubbing all the shady spots. I banged my paddle a couple times, figuring it was the polite thing to do. Let you know you had an audience. But you never heard. Like you was a million miles away. I found out your name after that. Some people on the island knew. Then I saw you at that meeting.''

I remained indifferent—but it took some effort. ''I must have had a lot on my mind.''

''I'm not complaining. Quite a show you gave me.'' Her frankness seemed an innocent conceit; a friendly affection. She added, ''The Punta Gorda Fish Company built that shack where you live. My daddy, when he was a boy, he and his daddy used to stay there sometimes. Fished for the company. That was before they moved to Cedar Key.'' Then she lifted her knees above the vinyl bag, pirouetted on her buttocks, and tossed the towel she had been holding into the kitchen. It landed— still folded—on the counter.

She was graceful for a big woman; had a lazy fluidity of movement that you only see in good athletes or very young children. I found myself looking at her, staring, and when I tried to look away, my eyes drifted back to her again. Hannah Smith was one of those rare women who, the longer you're around them, the more attractive they become. At first glance, she was just a tall, gawky girl with big hands and a blank, unremarkable face. Then gradually, very gradually, the unnoticed details revealed themselves and soon dominated. It wasn't that she was beautiful. It had nothing to do with beauty. It was in the cat flex of thighs when she moved, the taut, countersync jounce of breasts when she walked. Beneath the blousey shirt and jeans had to be an extraordinary body. Her skin, which initially appeared sun-blotched and salt-dried, was also a peculiar, lustrous shade of gold. I had seen beaches in California with that same sun-burnished coloring. Her hair, her nails, her muscle tone, all exuded the body gloss of a healthy young female, a prime example of her species, who was in the ripest years of her fertile life. It took a while, but Hannah projected that kind of sexuality. A ruddy, musky, robust sexuality. Projected it, at first, on a noncognizant sensory level that was very slow in alerting the conscious. Which was probably why Tomlinson was in the bathroom blow-drying his hair.

''You still listening? Or just thinking with your eyes?'' Hannah was sitting there grinning at me, her stare burrowing into me, as if she knew where my mind had been, letting me know it, enjoying my discomfort.

I fought the perverse urge to say something about the man I had held in my arms that morning. . . . Then I didn't fight it anymore. "Sorry, Hannah. I guess I was thinking about the way your husband died."

The grin faded, but her eyes still held me. "Like hell you were. You weren't thinking of Jimmy no more than I was." She let that settle before adding, "And I *know* what I was thinking about." Then she stretched, fists together, hands over head, breasts arched high, before favoring me with a softer look, the vaguest trace of a smile. "You bite back, don't you, Ford? Go right for that soft vein in the throat."

She waited; I remained silent.

"Mind if I call you Ford? It's a simple, no-bullshit name. Seems to fit."

I stared back; wasn't surprised when she refused to look away. Said, after a long silence, "You can call me anything you want." Then the stubborn set of her jaw, the cattish expression on her face somehow struck me as funny, and I began to laugh . . . then we were both laughing. Hers was a heavy, guileless guffaw, not at all like the bell note sounds she made when amused.

Wiping at her eyes, she said, "Truce? I'll put the knife away if you will."

"Only because I'm so outclassed."

"A gentleman about it. Damn!" She sat up straighter in the beanbag chair, getting serious. "See, the thing you don't know about that bastard Jimmy is—"

"Sorry I took so long." The bathroom door swung open, emitting a steamy effluvium. Tomlinson came out wearing a red T-shirt and green denim pants that were bunched tight at his waist with a leather belt, everything very baggy but a couple of sizes too short. His blond hair was fluffed and combed smooth, like a shampoo commercial. I'd never seen his hair so carefully arranged. Even had it parted in the middle. He said, "You live on a boat, man . . . shower out of a rubber bag, you come to appreciate the finer things in life."

Hannah was using her hand as a fan. "Whew, you smell like the perfume counter at Eckerd's."

"You've got a nice selection in there. Hope you don't mind."

"See? That's Jimmy's stuff I never got around to throwing out." To Tomlinson, she said, "Set yourself down. I was about to tell Ford about Jimmy Darroux."

Tomlinson's expression described compassion. "A terrible thing. Awful. He was a good spirit."

Hannah said, "Jimmy was an asshole."

Tomlinson shrugged. "The man had his problems. That much even I could tell."

FIVE

HANNAH HAD MOVED TO THE ROCKER. THE TOPIC seemed to require the added dignity of elevation. First off, she wanted to know what Jimmy had said to us, why we'd run clear up the bay after sunset on a falling tide. Tomlinson talked, then I talked. Then Tomlinson talked some more. She had a good way of listening, the natural-born-executive's talent for nodding at the appropriate time, asking just the right question to lever more detail, letting you feel the full force of her attention as she followed along. She didn't want to be spared anything. She wanted it all.

When we had finished, she sat quietly for a while. In the big rocker, she was the portrait of an anachronism, the pioneer woman at peace. She looked solid. Maternal. But through the open bedroom door, I could see the emblems of a woman who had yet to abandon all adolescent interests: big poster of a country music star tacked to her wall; a banner from Disney World; lazy, whirling ceiling fan with some kind of corsage dangling from the middle. After a time, she said, ''Jimmy said he could see Jesus?''

"That's right. He was in shock, I guess."

"Jimmy finally met up with Jesus—you'd have to know him to understand just how funny that is. *Jimmy?* If the medical examiner hadn't told me himself on the phone, I'd think somebody else burnt up. But they called me and I told 'em how to get the dental records. He'd gone for some fillings just last month. Dr. Gear."

One of Tomlinson's great gifts is his ability to empathize. "If you're feeling bitterness, it's understandable," he said. "Your husband left violently, without explanation. So it's natural. Don't feel guilty, just let it out."

"Guilty? I don't feel guilty one bit. Bitter, sure. But not guilty. You never knew the guy—"

"His last words were about you, Hannah. Looking out for your welfare. I was *there*, holding his hand. I mean— seriously—the guy obviously cared deeply."

She sat up a little straighter, spread her fingers wide to brush the hair out of her face. "That's another thing that doesn't make sense. Why would Jimmy say that? What'd he say? 'Take care of Hannah for me'? Is that what he said?"

"His exact words."

"See, that wasn't like him. Know what I think, Tomlinson? I think—this may sound crazy—but I think you and Ford were sent to me for a reason."

"Of course we were. Except for Doc, a person would have to be a dope to doubt it."

"No, that's not what I mean. Not just to comfort me, but something else. Bigger, you know? It's this feeling I've got."

"Could be, Hannah. Wouldn't be the first time in my life."

"You really believe it's possible. What I'm saying?"

"I'm just a tool. You wouldn't believe some of the stuff God's gotten me into."

Hannah leaned forward slightly, ready to share. "Then you'll understand this. What I think is, that was Jimmy's body there on the table, and it was Jimmy's voice you heard . . . but those weren't Jimmy's words. Couldn't have been."

"Yeah? You think so?"

"I really do. It's just an idea. No way to prove it—"

"He . . . was a bad person?"

"Yes, he was." Her voice dropped a note or two—a confessional tone—making her point. "Jimmy was self-ish as a three-year-old. And lazy. Trust me, if it wasn't for his pecker, he'd've never even learned to drive. Mean, too. Just plain, downright mean. Jimmy didn't give a damn about me."

"There was a darkness in him. I even told Doc that."

"There you go. But do you see what I'm getting at?"

Tomlinson held his hands out, palms up. "No, but I love the concept."

Hannah said, "What it could be—I'm just thinking out loud—but it could be that something, some force, spoke *through* him. Wanted us three to meet. 'Take care of Hannah for me.' Jimmy wouldn't say that. The words just came through his mouth, see? When I first saw you on the doorstep, I gave you a hard time, but what I was feeling was—"

"You don't even have to say it." Tomlinson was nod-ding his head, way ahead of her. "Like I already knew you. That's the way I felt. Saw you standing in the door—"

"Exactly."

"That's just the way it happens. I *knew* this was your house."

"You took your clothes off, no questions asked!"

He was chuckling along with her, his hair showing a lot of sheen and bounce. "Yeah . . . well . . . I've done that for strangers many a time. But, with you, I couldn't even talk. I mean, *wham*. Like, there you *were*."

"This doesn't sound weird to you?"

Tomlinson made a fluttering noise with his lips. "Let me give you some words to live by: Weirdness only seems weird if you fight it. Believe me, I know about these things."

I sat there listening, trying to make sense of it . . . then abandoned any hope of trying to reassemble their exchange into rational conversation. What puzzled me most of all, though, was this troubling reality: No matter what Hannah Smith said, no matter what ridiculous opinion she fronted, I still found myself inexorably attracted to her.

Tomlinson was saying, "As a phenomenon, it's not that uncommon. Some person, dead or alive, serves as the medium for a larger voice. The power speaks through them. Some spirit who has left this world and gone to another. Or some sentient consciousness that has no other means to verbalize . . . Hey . . . wait . . . a . . . minute! I'm getting something here—"

Hannah said, "A larger voice," pondering it.

"This morning, when Doc and I were using his telescope, I was expecting a sign. This deep meditation I've been into, I've made daily contact with a very powerful consciousness—"

She interrupted him. "That's just what I want to learn. Meditation. Can you teach me?"

"It would be an honor. But listen to what I'm saying. I've been locking onto these signals, these little islands of . . . divinity. I mean, I really *knew* I was going to receive some sign from them." He looked at me. "What did I tell you this morning, Doc? What did I say?"

It startled me for a moment, being included in the conversation. "You said something about ocular confirmation," I said. "That's what you told me."

"My very words. Ocular confirmation. You understand, Hannah? I was looking for a light, some kind of signal, way out in space. So what do they give me instead? A fucking explosion that knocks me right off my pins. I'm so damn dumb! Typical unenlightened earthling. I keep forgetting that time and distance mean absolutely nothing."

"Then Jimmy spoke—"

Tomlinson's head was swinging up and down; already knew the direction she was headed. "He spoke, but it could have been this power, this consciousness speaking through him. Jimmy was going to be at our marina anyway. He was going to be carrying the gas or bomb, whatever the hell it was. Free will—never underestimate it. He had his own plans. Blow up boats, burn the marina. Whatever. Destructive behavior, a very negative gig. Not that it mattered, because it was his time to pass on, so they just *selected* him."

Hannah stood, touched her fingers to my shoulder—a brief conduit of heat—then placed her hand on Tomlinson's shoulder. "Right or wrong, I feel like something brought you here. Things like this don't happen by accident."

"Exactly."

"Ford said you write books."

"Several. I have a small but enlightened following. Some truly twisted souls, as well, but that goes with the territory. They send me letters . . . strange clippings . . . interesting herbs . . . once, a dried bat. They're devoted people, my readers."

"I want to write a book. Maybe you could help me."

Tomlinson smiled at her. Said, "I'm here for a reason."

IT WAS MORE THAN AN HOUR LATER. HANNAH HAD walked us down and introduced us to Arlis Futch. When she told him I could dock my boat there "any damn time he wants," I was surprised that Futch simply smiled meekly, as if arguing was futile. "Whatever you want, Hannah. If they're friends'a yours."

We had eaten, and now were sitting on the porch, in darkness, looking at the bay through a framework of palm fronds. The January sea breeze was chilly, blustery; blew the mosquitoes away. I was worried about my boat. The tide was still falling. If I wanted to run back to Dinkin's Bay across the flats, we'd have to leave soon.

Yet I didn't want to leave. Hannah sat between us, kicked back in her chair, bare feet on the railing. Every now and then she'd reach over and squeeze my wrist to amplify what she was saying, or give me a rough shove after the punch line of some joke. Most people are reluctant to violate the perimeter of space that defines the boundary of another person's body. But she was a toucher, a patter, a nudger. Her effective way of bonding, of breaching the chasm.

"I expect you wonder why I married him. A creep like Jimmy. If he was so bad."

"It doesn't make a lot of sense, I have to admit."

"Everybody makes mistakes, man. Kids are young, they think getting married's a way to change their lives."

"Nope, Ford's right. It didn't make sense, doesn't make sense, never made sense." She sat quietly, thinking it over, then began to tell us how it was. "I first met Jimmy . . . yeah, just a little less then seven years ago. Some girlfriends and I loaded up a car, this big green Bonneville convertible that had a dented-in front fender. So old we had to play eight-track tapes—The Doors, Steppenwolf, Cream, that stuff, and it sounded great. Just loaded it up and headed for New Orleans. Had the top down, wine coolers in an Igloo, smoking cigarettes, acting wild. I was . . . eighteen?" She touched a long finger to her lips, thoughtful. "Yeah, eighteen. All of us. Lissa Kilmer and Mary Lou Weeks. We'd just graduated high school from Cedar Key, fishermen's daughters, and we thought, what the hell, let's get out and see the world. Lissa had a brother who crewed the shrimp boats outta Morgan City, right there near New Orleans, and that's how I met Jimmy. Jimmy was . . . different. I told you I liked people who were different?"

"Know what? I could tell that about you. The moment I walked in here, the whole aura of this place."

For just a moment, she rewarded Tomlinson with her full attention, a kindred acknowledgment—they were still on the same cerebral frequency. "Jimmy was twenty-some years older than me, more than forty. I liked that. Liked the way he looked, the way he smelled. Kind'a spicy with some sour mixed in. He was a Creole, what they call a mulatto. Not real black but butterscotch-colored. He had these long arms, real strong, and, truth is, he was 'bout the first man I ever met that wasn't scared of me. Jimmy didn't yap at my heels trying to please me, didn't slobber from the tongue because he wanted in my pants so bad. I'm not bragging—no reason to, it's such a pain in the butt—but nearly every man I've dated ends up hounding me till I can't stand it. It's like a sickness.''

I thought: Understandable.

"But Jimmy wasn't that way," Hannah said. "Nope, with him everything was smooth and easy. If I wanted it, fine; if I didn't there were plenty of other women. First time, we were on the bow of a shrimp boat, the *Baffin Bay Bleu* out of Corpus Christi—can you believe I remember the name of it? It was night, and he stripped my clothes off so quick we just did it right there on that wet deck. Bruised myself, I pounded those boards so hard, humping away like dogs in the diesel fumes. Spray coming over the bow, both of us bareass-naked, headed out Pontchartrain Cut, with the whole crew watching from the pilothouse for all I knew. I didn't care. Didn't care about anything but what we were doin' and what we kept doing. Every spare minute, grabbing each other anytime we wanted, squeezing into every little cubbyhole on the boat, for three days, Pontchartrain to Morgan City, out in the Gulf. It was like I was drunk and feverish both. That's the way it was with Jimmy at first.''

I thought: Why is she telling us this?

Hannah said, "He told me later he'd put a spell on me. Like he was joking. When I got to know about him, I wasn't so sure.'' She exchanged a glance with Tomlinson, confirming that he understood. Then looked at me to see how I was reacting to the story . . . before explaining patiently, "I say things the way they are. The

truth doesn't embarrass me because I've told no lies to
be ashamed of. You knew Jimmy, you wouldn't think
the business about spells was so silly. I said he was a
Creole? He spoke the language better than he spoke English. His people were all swamp people. Coon Asses,
he called them, but that's because he liked to think he
was better. He grew up in a place called Calcasieu
Marsh, this village of shacks up on stilts. He took me
there, showing me around, and these people had Catholic
stuff on the walls—plaster crucifixes, Virgin Marys—
but they had another religion, too. The families from
way, way back did. And the Darrouxs had been there
forever.''

"Obeah?'' Tomlinson offered. "The slaves, they in-
tegrated it into Christian ceremonies. Blood sacrifices,
occult rituals. Scares people shitless, plus plenty of social outings—a first-rate theology, you ask me.''

Hannah shook her head. "Jimmy never called it that.
He just outright called it voodoo. His mama was like
the main witch lady. He showed me all her stuff, which
really pissed her off. Not that she didn't take to me. But
she didn't like Jimmy, and Jimmy hated his family. So,
what did he care?''

Tomlinson was warming to the topic, enjoying the
opportunity to be talking about something that interested
her. "The woman, Darroux's mother, did she have an
altar in her home? Some kind of a carved head with a
cigar, or maybe a cigarette, sticking out its mouth?''

"Yeah . . . a cigar, and some beads on this blue velvet
tablecloth. Feathers . . . and a shot glass full of liquor.
The liquor, it was always there. I remember, because
Jimmy, he'd walk past and drink it, then laugh like
crazy. Rum. I could smell it.''

Tomlinson winced. "Oh man, no wonder he and his mother didn't get along." He turned to me to clarify— "That's like a Baptist stealing from the collection plate"—before asking Hannah, "You happen to notice any small brown bottles around? About this tall?" He held his thumb and forefinger a few inches apart. "Rows of them, probably hidden out of sight, but not anywhere close to the altar. And a Bible nearby?"

Hannah stared at him a moment, impressed—or maybe uneasy—but a little impatient, too. "I don't remember. What I meant was—" She stood up suddenly, went into the house and returned with the pitcher of tea. "What I meant was, it was *like* being under a spell. Not that I really was. By the time Lissa and Mary Lou and me got back to Cedar Key, I didn't much feel one way or the other about him. Just sort of burnt itself out. It was fun, but that's about it. He'd telephone sometimes, always late at night and pretty drunk, which really pissed off my daddy. Next day he'd be roaring, 'She's got Negroes callin' her! *Negroes!*'" She was laughing as she finished filling my glass. "I'd heard through Lissa that he got into trouble down in Mexico. Campeche, I think. For buying cocaine or selling cocaine. Some of the shrimpers, they were into that.

"Then, about two years ago, he shows up here. He'd been mullet fishing in Texas, but the nets got banned there, so he and about a jillion others naturally come to Florida to steal our fish. I was working my own boat by then, rentin' this place, but I wanted to buy. My daddy'd just died, and, in his will, he left me a little more than ten thousand dollars. But there was a . . . what'a you call it? . . . a stipulation. I had to be married and settled down for at least two years before I could touch the money.

That's what the lawyer told me: married and settled down." She chuckled softly. "Even from the grave, Daddy was still scared of me. Of what I'd do." She shrugged, a display of indifference.

Tomlinson said, "So you decided to marry Jimmy."

"That's right—two years ago come May. I coulda married about any man on the island, but guess it was the devil in me that made me choose him. Just meanness. What did I care who my husband was? I wasn't ever going to get married, and I'll never get married again. Maybe I was tryin' to show how independent I am, marrying somebody Jimmy's color—but island people are a lot more accepting than you'd think. If Jimmy'd been worth a damn, they'd have taken him right in. But he kept a dirty boat. He'd cut in on somebody else about to strike fish. When he wasn't drunk, he was high on crack. That man purely loved the rock."

I said, "You stayed married to a man you didn't like or trust just to get your inheritance."

The fingernails of her right hand found the back of my neck, flexed briefly into the skin, then began to make a soft, affectionate circular motion in my hair. "That's right, Ford. I'm greedy. I'm going to buy this house. The net ban's not gonna run me off. My Great-Aunt Hannah, Big Six herself, lived right here on Sulphur Wells. I need that money. I'm starting some kind of business, Arlis Futch and me. Maybe Raymond Tullock, too."

When I asked, "What business?" her fingers found my ear; touched it delicately, explored around inside, then began to stroke the lobe. Normally, such an intimate gesture would have made me uncomfortable. But now it seemed weirdly natural; homely and friendly and simple-hearted. I leaned closer to her, so that our shoulders touched.

Heard her say, "I'm not sure, but it's gonna take money. These little fishing shacks like mine used to sell for next to nothing. A pine house and a chunk of shell on the bay islands. Who'd want it? Like old Mr. what's-his-name at El Jobean, he gave away most of the beach-front over on Gasparilla just for back taxes. But it's getting to be worth something now. Arlis has developers snooping 'round his place all the time, askin' how much he wants. They're chomping at the bit, can't wait till us netters are gone. That's why everybody on the island's so pissed off at Jimmy for getting himself blowed up. I told you we're still fighting the net ban? What we're doing, we found a lawyer in Gainesville who's going to file a lawsuit. Ask a state judge to grant an injunction against the ban, and also seek economic relief."

"Make the state buy back your boats and nets," I said.

"Yeah, or let us keep fishing. Which is why the stupidest thing a netter could do is cause trouble. Give the state a reason to refuse. But there goes Jimmy and some of those other idiots, stealing motors, starting fires. Mostly, they're white trash outsiders, but there're a few local boys, like Kemper Waits and his crew. Like they're getting even, but really just hurting us all."

She had become increasingly animated, this gangly twenty-five-year old woman waving her arms around. Now she leaned back in her chair. "Well . . . I say good riddance. I'll see that he's shipped home. I'll see that his family knows what happened. But I won't miss him, and I won't shed a tear. Does that sound mean?"

Tomlinson said very softly, "He hit you. That was it."

Hannah was nodding slowly—amused that Tomlinson already knew. "Yeah, that was it. Part of it. After we got married, he'd only lived here about two weeks when he got drunk and started slapping me around. I tried to fight back, but ended up with two black eyes. The cops took him off to jail, but that didn't last. So I went to a lawyer, got a judge to sign some papers, and we tossed his stuff in the yard the next day.

"About a week later, after midnight, I heard him outside. Kicking down the door. I'd been expecting it; knew just exactly what I was going to do. Had it all planned out because I swore to myself that no man would hit me again. Ever. One of us would die first. But instead of fighting him, I talked real sweet, real nice, getting him calmed down. Then I brought out the rum bottle. For about two hours, I just kept talkin' and feeding him rum. It took the whole bottle. Then, when he passed out, I dragged him down to my boat and ran him into Boca Grande Pass. By then, it was daylight." She paused for a moment, remembering it.

"This was a year ago last June. You've been in Boca Grande Pass in June? I found a spot off the beach, away from the fleet that's always there. Tarpon were rolling all over the place, these big hundred-pound fish kicking water into the boat. First thing Jimmy sees when he wakes up is these tarpon flashing all around. He kind of shook his head—he didn't know what to make of that. Then he realizes that his hands and feet are tied, and he's not wearing any pants. He didn't know how that happened, and he's getting worried. Then he notices that there's a loop of fishing line knotted tight around his

pecker, and he looks up to see that I've got the other
end of the line in my hands—I'm just sitting there smi-
lin' at him—and there's a hook on the line baited with
a live mullet.

"He looks at his pecker, looks at that baited hook,
thinks about all those hungry tarpon. Then he begins to
sort of sob. His face screws up like a baby's face, and
he starts beggin' me not to throw that bait in the water.
I just sat there real calm . . . and tossed that live mullet
into a pod of tarpon. Then I said to him, 'Jimmy? That
little bit extra you got just ain't worth the bullshit. So
you want to come to an agreement? Or do you want to
fish?' "

Tomlinson said, "*Far out,*" his voice a constricted
whisper.

"I know, I know—but for a long time after that, I
didn't have any more trouble with Jimmy." Hannah
laughed, sighed; a weary sound . . . and I watched her
lean her head on Tomlinson's shoulder; turned to notice
for the first time that the long, lean fingers of her left
hand were resting on Tomlinson's thigh. Heard her say,
"So that's why I'm glad Jimmy's gone."

MY BOAT WAS NEARLY HIGH AND DRY. THE NEW MOON
had sucked so much water out of the bay that I spent a
soggy half hour slogging around in the muck, pushing,
pulling, and rocking to get the thing out into the foot of
water it took to float it. I had to brace my back against
the transom and lift until my muscles creaked and my
shoulders popped, just to budge the damn thing.

That was bad enough, but I had begun to feel mildly
sick . . . a little woozy and dazed, probably from lack of
sleep. I'd been up since, what? before three? Not that I

was sleepy. After four or five glasses of Hannah's strong tea, sleep was out of the question. All that caffeine had my heart pounding; created an unpleasant roaring in my ears.

Every time I stopped to rest, I could hear the murmur of voices. Tomlinson and Hannah were still up on the porch, chattering away.

For some reason, that infuriated me.

Both of them way too involved to lift a finger to help me get my boat ready to run back to Dinkin's Bay. Probably talking about mystic revelations. Karmic spirits. Voices from the grave. Space creatures who inhabited the walking dead and blew up boats. Who the hell knew? Or cared?

Well . . . the two of them were a perfect match. A drug-addled, draft-dodging hippie peacenik and a superstitious, manipulative, domineering twenty-five-year-old sex commando who netted mullet for a living when she wasn't busy marrying any sadistic Hottentot who happened to show up on her porch step, just to qualify for her inheritance.

That's what I was thinking. Mean thoughts to go with the roaring in my ears.

When I had the stern of the boat out deep enough, I plunked the anchor into the water, took two steps toward shore . . . and nearly knocked my toe off on something beneath the surface. I reached down and yanked out what proved to be about a five-pound horse conch shell. Looked at it, shook it at the sky, then threw it savagely out into the bay. *Son of a bitch!*

Which is when I caught myself. Made myself take a deep breath and review just exactly how I was behaving. Reminded myself that, woozy or not, irrational anger—

like jealousy—was the province of the forever adolescent. Stood there in knee-deep water, actually feeling a little drunk because of all that tea.

Thought: That's just the way I'm acting. Like a drunk.

I checked to make sure the anchor was holding, then splish-splashed my way back to the mangroves, toward the road. Saw a silhouette ahead. Realized it was Tomlinson, so I waited for him to come down the path. When he was close enough, I said, "Did you bring my shoes?"

"Got 'em, man."

I took the shoes and began to put them on. "I nearly severed my toe, getting that boat out. Spend an hour listening to Hannah, you feel obligated to walk around barefooted. I should have known better."

"Isn't she something?"

"She's something. I'm just not sure what."

Tomlinson can communicate through the tone of his laughter. The sound he made now was one of understanding . . . but also condescension, which I found irritating as hell. He said, "You don't like her."

"It's not that I dislike her. It's just that I think I see her a bit more objectively than you."

That laugh again. "You know what it is? Hannah and I talked about it. What it is, you and she have the same linear qualities, the same drive to be independent. You and Hannah are both . . . *extreme people*. See what I mean? In that way, she's like you in a woman's body. Just as smart, too. Which may get into a whole male ego thing . . . but the point is, you are also emotional opposites, man. She's a Gemini, but she's got Leo rising—"

"No more astrology lessons," I said. "Astrology lessons I can do without."

"You're sounding a tad grumpy. Come on . . . let's see a smile. Who's your buddy—?"

"Damn it, Tomlinson, I'm not grumpy. Judging from the blood and the swelling, my toe may be broken, but I'm not grumpy."

He remained silent while I finished tying my shoes. Then: "You felt it, didn't you? That's what's troubling you. The lady has some very serious juice, and you felt it. When she'd touch me, it was like. . . . *zap.*"

"Nope. No zaps."

"Like electric. I could feel it in her hands, man, her fingertips. A higher level of consciousness. And her lips—my God."

I stood abruptly. "Her lips? What the hell were you two doing up on that porch—?" I stopped myself. I didn't want to hear it. Used my hands to wave him along, and said, "Get in the boat. The tide's so low we'll have to run the channel all the way back to Dinkin's Bay. Which will take two hours, unless I stop at Cabbage Key for a beer. Which I plan to do."

"On a Thursday night? You're the one keeps reminding me you don't drink—"

"They're my rules. I can break them when I want." I turned toward the bay, took a few steps before I realized that he wasn't following along. "You forget something?"

"Well . . . see, Doc, it's like this—"

"Nope, I'm not waiting. You want to talk to her, call her on the phone. Or drive over. You've fulfilled your karmic obligation . . . or the directive from Mars—whatever it was. I'm leaving."

"Yeah, well, I think I'm going to stay."

"You mean . . . stay here. Gumbo Limbo."

"She asked me. I said yes." He was stroking his goatee, pleased with himself.

"Sleep in her house."

"We've got so much to discuss, man. All these avenues to explore. Meeting Hannah has been . . . just the *impact* of it. Jesus. She wants to learn sitting meditation. Do a sort of *zazenkai,* just her and me . . . only as an ordained monk, her *Roshi,* I have to give serious thought to the moral limitations that would put on our relationship. Then there's this book she wants to write. It could be an important historical document."

I started walking toward my boat.

"Doc—before you go."

I turned.

"Can I ask you something?" Tomlinson stepped close to me, very close. For an uncomfortable moment, I thought he was going to give me a brotherly hug. Instead, he said, "Can I borrow maybe ten bucks? Or a fin? If we go out for breakfast, I'd like to at least offer to pay—"

I took out my wallet, handed him a twenty. As I did, I heard familiar bell notes of amusement; then a woman's voice called, "I'll stick him in my boat and bring him home. Don't you worry, Ford." Looked up to see Hannah standing in an orb of streetlight, the long, lean shape of her, hands on her hips, pelvis canted to the left like a bus stop floozie, loose blouse and black hair catching the sea breeze.

I got in my boat and headed out of the channel.

SIX

NORMALLY, I ENJOY RUNNING A BOAT AT NIGHT. I like being out there alone in the darkness, suspended above the water, going fast. Like gauging my progress by the shapes of islands, by the positions of distant lights. Like the way the wind washes past, a force so steady that, at times, it seems as if my boat is being held motionless by a jet stream of black air.

It's nice and private: dark water, bright stars. But I didn't enjoy the long run back to Sanibel. I was preoccupied. My mind kept wandering. It had plenty of opportunity to wander. Running the Intercoastal Waterway is like running a well-marked ditch. You leapfrog from flashing light to flashing light, from a red to a white, from a flashing white to a red or green. The lights become hypnotic and soon reduce the brain to little more than a dependable autopilot.

So it wasn't as if navigation required a lot of thought.

What I was thinking about, and what I couldn't seem to stop thinking about, was Hannah Smith. I'd lied to Tomlinson—of course I'd been affected by her. Not on some fanciful telepathic level, but on a marrow-deep physical level. Powerful people are attractive people.

The whole process of natural selection is based on the allure of strength. For a species to remain successful, the best genes must be passed on. The gauge is always emblematic: the largest horns, the loudest mating cry, the brightest display of plumage, the lushest body, the biggest bank account. But there are other indicators of power: self-confidence, intellect, humor, independence. Combine these characteristics with long legs, lean hips, and heavy country-girl breasts, and you are dealing with a powerful woman indeed.

Standing at the wheel, peering beyond the feeble glow of my own running lights, I pictured Hannah. Felt an electric rush of longing in abdomen and thighs, and winced, as if in pain. Tried to will the image away . . . but the picture wouldn't disappear. Could still see her standing in the disc of yellow light, taunting me . . . enjoying it.

The problem was, I was jealous. That's what it came down to. Before I could even admit it to myself, I was well past the shoals off Patricio Island, almost to Cabbage Key. I didn't want to be alone, at night, on my boat. I wanted to be in Gumbo Limbo, alone, with her, in that creaky little tinroof house. Wanted to sit there feeling her eyes burrowing into mine, giving me her total attention. Wanted to hear more about her outlaw behavior. Wanted to pull her face to mine, then peel her out of those tight jeans . . .

But she had chosen Tomlinson. She preferred him over me—that was pretty obvious. Skinny, frazzled Tomlinson, with his Jesus eyes and Joe Cocker face. Over me.

Why? Well . . . that was pretty obvious, too: He could help her with the book she wanted to write; help her find a publisher. That was his power. Pure opportunism on her part.

Which is what I told myself . . . then wondered if it was true.

I was thinking irrationally, and knew it. The realization was so strong that I throttled the boat back to idle, then switched off the engine. Drifted along in the darkness, the silent flare-burst of channel-marker lights flashing all around.

Nothing I had felt in the last several hours meshed with my own image of self. It was a red flag. When your emotions or your behavior are contrary to your own self-image, it's time to stand back and reassess. Yes, I had met two, maybe three women in my life for whom I had felt an instant, marrow-deep sexual attraction so strong that it had almost knocked the wind out of me.

Hannah undoubtedly could now be counted among them.

But I had never reacted so emotionally before. Yeah, I had been irritated at Tomlinson all day—the man wore at the nerves. But to be jealous? And obsessive? It wasn't me; it was nothing at all like the man I perceived myself to be. Realizing it seemed to help.

I started the boat and got under way again.

It is impossible to force a topic of thought from your own head. But it is possible to substitute one topic of thought for another. So what I did was spend the next few miles making a cold unemotional assessment of Hannah Smith.

It produced a less attractive picture. By her own admission, she was greedy. She was also self-obsessed. "I do what I damn well please!" How many times had she said that? She used people, she bullied people. The hangdog deference of Arlis Futch—a powerful man himself—was proof. Perhaps most troubling, though, was that Hannah was capable of extreme behavior, the extreme gesture. I believed every detail of her story about taking Jimmy Darroux into Boca Grande Pass. Not that I blamed her. The term ''spousal abuse'' is much too meek to represent the kind of humiliation and fear that those two words actually define. Any man who hits a woman is mentally unstable and should be forced to get help. Immediately. Just as any man who rapes a woman should be treated as if he has forfeited all considerations of help.

But this is the modern world. People don't take the law into their own hands. The fable of justice has become just one more Walter Mitty dream. Oh, they like to talk about revenge. They like to watch movies about it. But to actually do it . . . to actually cross the border into the netherland, to actually make the extreme gesture, is far too frightening for most.

Not for Hannah Smith. She didn't hesitate. Knew just exactly what she was going to do and how to do it— she'd told me that herself in her rowdy, piney woods voice. I admired her for it. Also, she scared me a little because of it.

For a while, I felt better. Reason and logic were familiar territory. They were the tools out of which I have created my own refuge. Emotion, any emotion, was a symptom of perceived reality, not reality itself. Become the slave of it, and you paid a heavy price: wives, lovers, divorces, children, mortgages, corporate infighting, charge cards, early retirement, two cars in the driveway and a dog in the garage.

I preferred my solitary island world. A house and lab

under one roof. My boats, my specimens. The clarity of a microscope, the precision of a trip-balance scale. Just me, living my work, doing what I wanted to do.

Which is when, for no good reason, Tomlinson's words tumbled me back into the cycle of obsession: *You are both extreme people.*

A thought that was all the more unsettling because it had the ring of truth.

IT WAS NEARLY ELEVEN P.M. WHEN I APPROACHED THE channel markers off Cabbage Key. Cabbage Key is a hundred-and-some-acre-island, mostly mangrove, but with enough Indian shell mounds to keep its dozen or so houses high and dry. There are no bridges or landing strips. Boat access only. The biggest house on the highest mound is a sprawling one-story: white board-and-batten with green shutters; a long open porch that, this time of year, was buttoned tight with canvas, the only way to keep out the chill. The house was built in 1938— which made it ancient by the standards of transitory Florida. In the fifties, it was converted into a public inn. A bar was built in what was once the library, and a restaurant was added. Over the years, Florida changed; the old house on the hill did not.

I considered running right on past. If I pushed it, I could make Dinkin's Bay in a little less than half an hour. But I was feeling restless. Dissatisfied with myself, and oddly dissatisfied with other things—what, I didn't know. Still felt as irritable as some moonstruck adolescent. So what could it hurt to pull in for a beer?

I tied up near the boathouse. There were a couple of mansion-sized yachts moored in the deep-water slippage. One looked like a Hatteras, the other a beautiful old

Trumpy. On the Trumpy, people were milling around above deck, drinks in hand. A couple of corporate types in blazers along with what looked to be a cluster of sorority-age girls. The music being piped out of the main salon was vintage World War II, Glenn Miller. The gal from Kalamazoo had just become the girl who was drinking rum and Coca-a-a-a-Cola, as I trudged up the path to the inn. I wondered if the corporate types really believed the antique music would put their MTV generation guests in the mood.

Rob, the owner, wasn't around, but Captain Doug and a couple of other guys I knew were at the bar. I had a Heineken, then another. The guys had heard about the explosion; wanted me to give them all the details. We kept buying rounds and Bob, the bartender, kept serving them. Pretty soon, the party from the Trumpy came spilling in. I found out that the men in the blazers were, indeed, corporate types, but they were neither ego-brittle nor stuffy—the good ones seldom are. Also, the women, though attractive and pert enough, were neither sorority-age nor were they college girls.

"What we do is market cellular phones," one of them told me—a chunky little blonde with pale, Germanic eyes. "This is sort of like a convention, only it's really not, 'cause we had to market more units than anybody else to win this trip. Our regions, I'm talking about. All seven of us, we were picked the top marketers. All women!"

It took me a moment to translate: "marketers" meant "sales staff." Like "educator" and "refuse attendant," it was another one of those inane euphemisms that, instead of clarifying, only murk their own definitions.

She said, "So we won two days at Orlando, then three

days at this place on Captiva Island. I just loved Epcot, but Captiva . . . well, that's been sort of boring. It's so . . . *quiet*. But then we met Charlie, and his corporation leases this great big boat, complete with captain, two weeks every year. You see it down there? *Huge*. And Charlie, he's such a nice man, Charlie said, what the hell, he'd take us on an overnight cruise so we could see the islands. But no strings attached. He made that real clear.'' She poked my arm with an index finger to emphasize the importance of that. Said, ''What we found out is, Charlie's corporation does a lot of business with the group that owns us, so we're like business associates. Just down here networking, doing our jobs!'' She giggled and beamed at me.

I could see Charlie across the room. He was engaged in the delicate task of cutting one of the seven women out of the group. He had selected an aloof brunette—by far the most attractive woman in the room. The two of them were hunched over a table, insulated from the rest of the bar by the intensity of their conversation. The brunette had the look of country clubs and tasteful dinner parties and expensive boutiques. I wondered what circumstance had motivated her to get into the very tough world of sales. Also wondered if Charlie had noticed the sizable diamond on the ring finger of her left hand.

Watched the brunette scoot away from the table; then, very deliberately, very privately, place her hand on Charlie's thigh—a brief, intimate gesture—before rising to go to the rest room.

The ring, apparently, wasn't a problem.

''You want another beer? But you have to let me buy this time. I always pay my own way.''

The little blonde was drinking margaritas. She loved the salt. I stuck with beer because that's what I drink. Her name was Farrah. I didn't ask, but I assumed her mother had watched a lot of television back in the seventies. Farrah was from Granite City, Illinois, right there on the Mississippi River, so close to St. Louis that it was like just one great big city now. She'd graduated from high school six years ago, was accepted into the University of Missouri's nursing program, but just hated it. What she really wanted was a nice car and a nice apartment—both of which she now had. "All because I went into cellular marketing. You wouldn't believe the benefits our company gives. Just for the team members— that's what they call us, the people who work for them. They've even produced an exercise video just for us. 'Cause we're all a team, understand?"

I understood. She kept ordering margaritas, and I continued to pour down beer. Normally, I limit myself to three. But I wasn't in the mood for rules or limits. If I allowed myself to pause, to examine what I was doing, the image of Hannah and Tomlinson popped into mind . . . that small house, just the two of them . . . cricket noises outside and the ceiling fan whirring overhead.

Farrah was telling me, "I like you, Doc. No, I mean it. I first saw you, I thought, whew, he's got cold, cold eyes. But I was wrong. You're just a big ol' sweetie. Hey—your turn to buy or mine?"

Through the gradual process of increasingly familiar body contact, Farrah let me know—and those around us know—that she had made her selection. Now she sat on a barstool, just high enough to throw her arm casually around my shoulder. Just close enough so that I could feel the heat of her left breast as it traced designs on my ribs.

Jerry came into the bar, saw the crowd, and began to play Jimmy Buffett on the keyboard. Farrah wanted to get out on the dance floor with the rest of the group. I told her that there were few things more ridiculous than a full-grown man trying to mimic jungle ceremony. She said, "Huh?" then, "You better not go anywhere," before giving me a moist kiss on the cheek and shimmying out among the dancers. I watched her nudge one of her girlfriends, heard her say, "You meet the guy I'm with? He doesn't even *own* a cellular unit." As if it was proof they were on a tropical island, a million miles from the regional office.

I stood there watching, a cold green bottle in my hand. Farrah was wearing beige pumps, a black T-length sweater dress—looked like cashmere—that fit snugly enough, and was cut low enough, to show the weighty bounce of breasts, the slow roll of buttocks as her body absorbed the music and reissued it. Every so often, she'd look over and give me an owlish wink . . . which caused me to consider just what in the hell I was getting myself into. I was no meat market predator; I'd never gone to a bar and tried to pick up a woman in my life. "You want to come home and see my specimens?" would have been a lackluster line. So I had just about decided to quietly disappear, when I felt a tap on my shoulder. Turned to see a face that was familiar. Finally realized it was Garrett Riley, a deepwater guide out of Naples.

"What are you doing this far north, Garrett?"

He said, "You got your skiff handy?"

"Yeah."

"There's something you need to see."

I looked at the empty bottle I was holding, looked at Farrah on the dance floor.

Garrett said, "Hell, don't worry about that. She ain't gonna catch a cab, and I'm a little drunk myself. I don't need you to make *sense*. What I need is somebody to give me a hand." When I hesitated, he added, "Hurryin' wouldn't hurt none."

I put the bottle on the bar and followed him outside.

SEVEN

GARRETT HAD BEEN HIRED TO RUN THE HATTERAS that was moored down by the boathouse. The charter was a three-week island hopper, he said, Key West to Tampa and back, that he wouldn't have taken, this being the prime day-tripper season, except his own forty-two-foot Johnny Morgan had spun a prop, which scored the drive shaft and stripped the bearings just inside the stuffing box.

"I figured three weeks at half pay was better than waiting on parts, sittin' home whackin' off to the Weather Channel," he told me.

He made a stop at the Hatteras. Signaled me to wait, then scrambled gibbon quick up the ladder to the fly bridge. He returned carrying an industrial-sized bolt cutter.

"You mind telling me where we're going, Garrett?"

He held a finger to his lips—his clients were asleep. Said, "Not far. Where's your skiff?"

Once I got my boat away from the seawall, I let him take the wheel. He hurried us out the channel, no lights at all, then gunned us onto plane. Directly to the east lay Useppa Island. At the turn of the century, back when

West Florida was still considered wilderness, Useppa had been a sportsmen's enclave, host to people like Teddy Roosevelt and Joe Kennedy. The Kennedy connection proved useful in the sixties when Useppa was leased by the C.I.A. to train Cuban exiles for the Bay of Pigs invasion. Now the island was a graceful private community: palm trees and white houses built on rolling hills. Garrett ran toward the island, obviously in a hurry; didn't throttle back until we had snaked our way past the oyster bar near the private channel. Obviously, whatever he wanted to show me was on Useppa.

"That's where it is," he said, motioning.

"Where what is?"

"Where they strung the cable."

"What cable? What the hell are you talking about, Garrett?"

We were idling along now, through the island's harbor. "Little more than an hour ago," he said, "I was over here in the dinghy, plug-casting the docks for snook. Noticed a boat up there in the shallows, somebody poling it along. Didn't look to me like they was up to any good. You know how men'll act when they're tryin' to be real quiet? It was like that.

"Watched'em dump something. Something heavy, too." He pointed to the shoreline. "Right there. They had to do some gruntin'. Then they fired up their boat and purely tore ass out of here. Still no lights. Shit, they about run me down. It was a mullet boat, two guys in it. But the weird thing was, they run clear out around the island, *then* north toward Charlotte Harbor. Why not just pop through the Pineland cut? I couldn't figure it out." He pulled the throttle back to neutral and switched off the engine. "But I found out. That's what I'm going to show you."

The momentum of the boat carried us forward along an old mortar seawall into a narrow cut. The cut was only a few boat lengths wide, but it was deep enough to navigate on any tide. That made it a popular passage for small-boat traffic. The markers to the pretty little village of Pineland, and Pine Island, began on the other side.

"It's right in here someplace." Garrett was standing on the casting deck, his hands out, searching around in the darkness. "Watch yourself. . . ." Then: "Got it."

I felt the boat jolt abruptly.

"What is it?"

"You got a spotlight? Or just come up here and feel."

I reached under the console, brought out a flashlight. What Garrett had found was a length of what appeared to be quarter-inch steel cable. It was stretched tight across the cut, connected to something above the seawall on one side, then to a channel marker on the other.

Garrett said, "After they pulled out, I came blasting over here to see what they'd dumped. If I hadn't been in the dinghy, it'da cut my head off. As it was, it just knocked my hat back and scared the shit out of me. Didn't even see it. Hell, even in daylight, you probably wouldn't notice it—until it was too late."

He was pulling us along, hand over hand, toward the seawall. Had I been sitting at the wheel of my flats boat, the cable would have been about neck-high. Now that I was standing, it was belly-high. I projected what would have happened had a boat come wheeling through that cut doing twenty or thirty knots. A couple of fishermen, maybe, headed out at morning dusk . . . or a family with two or three children perched on the bow of their Bay-liner. Whatever the scenario, it was a bloody scene to imagine.

It sobered me. It leached the alcohol out of my brain. Stringing a cable across a busy waterway was not van-dalism, nor was it a statement of political dissent. It was attempted murder, nothing less.

Garrett said, "Hand me those bolt cutters. I'll snip this side, then we'll pull our way back and get the other side, too."

I said, "No. Not yet."

"Huh? Why the hell not?"

"Did you contact the Coast Guard?"

He said, *"What?"*

"The Coast Guard."

"I hope you're not serious. There's plenty of time for that later."

"I *am* serious. Did you call them?"

Garrett demonstrated his impatience by being metic-ulously patient. "No, Doc, I didn't call the Coast Guard. I don't keep a VHF in a rubber dinghy. An idiot might, but I don't. What I did was go bust-assin' back to Cab-bage to get the bolt cutters, then decided I could use some help. Which is where I felt kind'a lucky spotting you. Because I figured you'd be a good man to help me cut this bastard down before some poor sonuvabitch comes flying around that corner and cuts his head off. Which could happen any minute now!"

I told him to calm down, take it easy. Used my hand-held VHF to raise the Coast Guard on channel 16. I asked for the duty officer. The Coast Guard had me switch to 22-Alpha for extended traffic. While I waited, I opened the forward locker and broke out the big spotlight and plugged it in. Also got out the disposable gas air-horn. Handed them both to Garrett and told him that unless deaf and blind people were racing around Pine Island Sound, he should be able to stop any boat for miles.

It took quite a while to give the Coast Guard all the information they wanted, and the duty officer finished by suggesting we stand by.

"Christ awmighty, are you happy?" Garrett sputtered when I was finished. "This'll take all night."

I didn't need all night. All I wanted was a few minutes alone with the cable. Anyone sick enough to rig such a thing was also sick enough to include a booby trap. Jimmy Darroux was a failed bomber. But there might be other, more skilled bombers waiting in the wings.

I handed Garrett the VHF. "If a judge ever starts questioning you about mishandled evidence, you'll thank me."

"*Right*. . . . Where the hell do you think you're going?"

I had grabbed the flashlight, Leatherman pliers, a chunk of heavy monofilament line, and had slipped overboard into waist-deep water. "I want to take a closer look at the cable before we cut it."

I WATCHED WHILE GARRETT AND MY SKIFF DRIFTED away on the incoming tide . . . then used the flashlight to follow the cable up over the seawall.

The cable appeared to be belted around the base of a palm tree. Before approaching the palm, I tied my Leatherman pliers to the monofilament, thereby making an effective plumb line. Then I walked slowly, very slowly, holding the plumb line out just as far from my body as

I could get it. If there was a trip wire in my path, the monofilament would catch harmlessly on it.

There was no trip wire.

Even so, I remained cautious. Garrett had told me the men had lifted something heavy out of their boat. Something that made them grunt. The typical marine battery weighs thirty-seven pounds. A five-gallon can of gas weighs more than forty. Add a blasting cap and you have the ingredients for a powerful bomb.

I had good reason to be cautious.

I used the fishing line to probe around the cable. No strings or wires running from it. Used the flashlight to check overhead. No strings or wires to be mistaken for harmless vines. The cable was secured with a common screw-down bridle. I slid the fishing line delicately, very delicately, into the chock, alert for the first slim resistance of wire.

Nothing.

I took a couple of deep breaths . . . relaxed . . . used the screwdriver head on my Leatherman to free the cable. Then I half swam, half waded across to the channel marker, where, after a less exacting inspection, I disconnected that end, too. Had there been a mad bomber, he almost certainly would have placed the device on the Useppa side of the cut, where it could do the most damage.

Garrett came puttering up as I was coiling the cable. Shut off the engine and, after a properly dramatic pause, said, "You get a few beers in you, you act like a damn lunatic. I'm serious."

"Nothing but screws and chocks holding it. So I figured, what the hell, why wait for the Coast Guard?"

Garrett said, "No shit, Sherlock," as I climbed into the boat.

As we idled back toward Useppa's harbor, I asked Garrett what he thought the men might have dumped. He said, "You didn't see? What the hell were you doing up there?" Before I could invent an answer, he said, "Here—take the spotlight. I'll show you." Then turned the wheel. When the bow nudged the beach, he took the light and began to sweep it back and forth. "Probably wake up everybody on the whole damn island. There—see that? There's another one . . . and another."

What he was showing me appeared to be lengths of bar stock, chunks of two to three feet, scattered along the northwestern fringe of the island. I removed my glasses, polished the salt spots off, and looked again.

What I was seeing were fish. Dozens of them. I stepped out of the boat, carrying the flashlight.

They were big snook, ten-to-twenty-pounders. The snook is a prized saltwater game fish; an extraordinary animal, both in terms of behavior and physical beauty. It has an efficient, cartilaginous jaw that flares cutlasslike around black peregrine eyes that are ringed with gold. Its body is pewter-bright, amplified by yellow, with an armorwork of scales covering a dense and broadening musculature. It is a heavy, functional, predator's body, as if all the thousands of years of the species' evolution were the refinement of one moonless night in murky, prehistoric water. The black lateral line, running from gill to caudal fin, is a sports car touch, something that might have been dreamed up in Detroit. On any other animal, the stripe would appear frivolous. You see a snook for the first time and, along with the lingering impression of beauty, you think: Survivor.

But these animals had failed the genetic mandate. They had not survived. I went from one to another, touching, lifting, inspecting. They had been dead for more than a day and not kept on ice. The scales were loose. The eyes milky. Their skin had the withered look of roadkill. On several, I found telltale geometrics as if etched in blue, then baked hard: net scars.

I retrieved one of the smaller fish and carried it back to where Garrett waited.

"The marine patrol stops you, Doc, they'll take your boat. Snook are out of season."

"I've got a collector's permit. I'm taking it back to the lab to see if I can find out how it died."

Garrett made a grunt of contempt. "How? Shit, that's not obvious? The two guys in the mullet boat strung their catch wire, then carried up a couple of boxes of illegal fish and dumped them. Let people know who did it; show just how pissed off they are. A lot of sportfishermen live on Useppa. The mullet guys were just saying thanks for the net ban."

I panned the spotlight once more over the rows of carcasses, switched it off, and backed out. Most of the way back to Cabbage Key, we both kept a glum, funereal silence. Then Garrett cleared his throat, said in a soft, musing way, "You know, I voted *against* the net ban. You believe that?"

I knew a little bit about his background. "You come from a family of commercial fishermen, so it's understandable—"

"Yeah . . . but that's not why. You know what it was? It was those fishing magazines, the way they preached for the ban, but still ran their ads for big engines and lorans and sonar. You know as well as I do, *that's* what destroyed the offshore fishery. Damn hypocrites. Least they coulda had the balls to *admit* it. Hell, I do. Anyone who runs a boat is a hypocrite, right?''

He said, ''You know what else? Those stupid commercials about the mullet fishermen netting dolphins and turtles and manatees—what bullshit. Nothing but lies. Hell, it was almost funny to people who really knew something about it. But you know what really did the trick?'' Garrett paused, thinking about it. I got the impression he was trying to explain it to himself. ''What really did it was this guy named Tullock, used to come down to the docks, this state guy, a marine extension agent. He's the one—''

I interrupted. ''Raymond Tullock?'' It had to be—there weren't that many marine extension agents named Tullock around.

''Yeah. Why, you know him?''

It wasn't so unusual to hear Tullock's name mentioned twice in the same day. Florida's fishing community is large, but intricately connected. Still, I found the coincidence striking. I asked, ''Tullock's the one who talked you out of voting for the ban?''

''That officious little prick couldn't talk me into anything. He's the guy that lifted my commercial sticker because I told him I didn't have time to fill out his damn forms. What fish we caught, where we caught them, how much they weighed. He'd come around the end of the month if you didn't mail them. Hell, I about had my boat repossessed because of him. No, Tullock wasn't against the ban. He was *for* the net ban. He'd say, 'I shouldn't be tellin' you this, but—' Or, 'Don't tell anyone you heard this from me.' I figured whatever Tullock was for, I was against. But now . . . after seeing what we

just saw . . . well, sometimes you have to throw out the
good to get rid of the bad. Know what I mean? I kind'a
regret not voting for the damn thing.''

I was beginning to feel the same way.

When we got to Cabbage Key, I asked Garrett to write
his name and number in my notebook. I wanted to talk
to him when we weren't beer-bleary and sullen, and
when it wasn't one o'clock in the morning. I watched
him swing cat-footed aboard the Hatteras and disappear
into the cabin.

Then, just as I was pulling away, I heard a whoop
and a holler, and turned to see chunky, blond Farrah
waving at me. She was calling, ''Is that your boat? I
love that boat,'' as she hurried along the dock in her
tight black dress, moving with the exaggerated self-
control of someone who is very drunk. When she was
close enough, she slowed to a dignified pace, flashed me
a sloppy grin, and reached to steady herself on a piling
. . . but missed. Then I watched her grin broaden into a
wild leer of surprise as she cartwheeled off the dock into
the water.

THE GALLANT THING TO DO WOULD HAVE BEEN TO LEAP
into the water, scoop her up, and carry her to safety. But
I am not gallant. I swung the boat to her, and as she
came clawing her way up on the casting deck, I held her
motionless until she answered some questions. Did her
neck hurt? Any tingling sensation in hands or feet?
Drunks have been known to hobble around sprightly
while internal bleeding or the leakage of spinal fluid
drains the life out of them.

''Damn right I'm tingling, ya big horse. 'Cause I'm
freezing. Lemme up!''

She sat groggily. Used her fingers to strip the water from her hair as I tied the boat. I took my bomber jacket off, wrapped it around her, and helped her to her feet. She was weaving badly. I wondered how many more margaritas she'd had after I left.

"You bazzard, you went off and lef' me. Tol' you not to go, but did you listen? Nope, nope, nope, nope." She was wagging her finger under my nose. "Don' lie to me. Do-o-o-on' you lie to Farrah."

I looked around, hoping to see her girlfriends, hoping to see Charlie. But the big Trumpy was quiet at its mooring. I looked up the mound toward the bar: no movement, no music, no noise. The party was over.

"Hey! You know what I wanna do? Less go for a ride in your boat. How 'bout it." She banged her hips against mine. "Scooch over. I'll drive. Don' you worry. You ever hear of the Miss-pippi River? I drove boats all over the Miss-pippi."

It took maybe ten minutes to talk her out of the boat ride. You can't reason with a drunk, you have to barter with them. Yes, I would take her for a boat ride. Yes, I had heard of the Miss-pippi, and yes, she could drive. But first she would have to go back to her cabin and get into some dry clothes.

"We ga' lots of boats in Illinois," she said solemnly, just before I hefted her up onto the dock.

The Trumpy was about a sixty-footer. We entered through the main salon. It smelled of marine varnish and synthetic fiber. There were courtesy lights glowing from behind the mahogany bar. I tried to turn Farrah loose, but she stumbled as she was going down the companionway steps, and insisted that I help her.

Her stateroom was forward, just behind the master

stateroom. I looked at the door of the master stateroom, all the brass fittings, and wondered if Charlie was in there with the aloof brunette. If so, I wondered if the aloof brunette had bothered to take off her wedding ring.

"See! Just me, all by myself." Farrah had the door open, a light on. It was a tiny cabin with bunks. There was a collapsible table, a stainless steel washbasin, and a combination shower and head. The layout reminded me of an Amtrak sleeper. I guessed it was designed to be the children's quarters, handy to the master stateroom.

"No, don't you leave! I'm keeping you with me till I get that boat ride." She had me by the hand, trying to pull me into the cabin. Then she stopped suddenly, touched fingers to her forehead, and said in a softer, more articulate voice, "Whew, I feel a little dizzy. Don't go. Please? Not till I feel better."

I sighed, shrugged; stepped into the room. Turned around to pull the door closed, and when I turned back, Farrah was stripping the wet dress over her head . . . found a hanger . . . had to arch her back to reach the simple white pearl necklace she wore . . . placed it on the vanity.

"You mind waiting while I jump in the shower? I'm freezing," she said.

"So I see."

"You do?"

I did. Very clearly. Farrah wore only a transparent nylon bra and blue bikini panties. The wet material clung to her, showing the mounds and pink circles and curling pubic folds of her body. She was not nearly so bulky as the tight dress had made her appear. She held the pose for a moment, grinned, then hip-wagged her way into the tiny head, and closed the door. I took a seat on her bunk; sat there breathing in steamy, fragrant odors, telling myself I should leave . . . wondering why I didn't.

A friend of mine once made me stand back and look at a wall map of the United States. "Do you see it?" she kept asking. "Do you see the subliminal message? Students grow up staring at a map just like this." Her theory being that the testicular and penile shape of Florida caused those students, as adults, to suffer a feverish subconscious libido on their Florida vacations. Over the years, I had observed enough tourist behavior to believe that her weird theory had merit. Maybe Farrah was another example. Or maybe hers was a drive more complicated.

Whatever Farrah's reasons, they weren't good enough—that's what I told myself. I had no interest in one-night stands—right? Why intentionally diminish myself—right? Nor did Farrah strike me as the type to engage in that kind of destructive behavior. She had been drinking, I told myself. Her reasoning was fogged—right?

Well . . . *right*.

Even so, I sat there debating it, wanting to stay, trying to ferret out an acceptable excuse. . . . Then I didn't have to debate or rationalize anymore because Farrah came stumbling, naked, out of the head, a towel clutched in her hands, her face as pale as her milkmaid breasts, saying, "I . . . feel . . . sort'a *sick*."

Then she *was* sick. Not just once, either. I helped her as much as I could. Helped her get cleaned up and into bed; then I sat there patting her back, making comforting noises, feeling old and far more chivalrous than I actually am. I also felt relief . . . and a curious sadness, too.

Farrah was one of the winners. Her employer had ac-
knowledged that. She had a nice car and nice apartment.
She had the dental and medical and retirement plans. She
had a fitness program and vacation getaways. She had
joined the team, so the corporation was providing for
her every need. Lately, I had been meeting more and
more team members—but fewer and fewer individuals.
It was beginning to worry me.

When her breathing became a steady series of soft
poofing sounds, when I could feel the involuntary mus-
cle-twitch of legs and hands, I stood and found a blanket.
Covered her from toe to head, tucked her in tight.
Leaned to kiss her forehead and, as I turned out the light,
said, "Have a good life, lady."

Then, as I snuck out of her stateroom, I nearly collided with what turned out to be Charlie. He was in the
process of sneaking out of *his* stateroom, headed for the
main salon to get a snack. I followed him up the companionway, prepared for the chummy locker room winks
and nudges that he would offer. *Hey, we got laid, buddy!*
The aloof brunette was none of my business, but I felt
an unreasonable animus toward him because of her. Instead, Charlie said, "These corporate junkets, they can
wear you out, you let 'em. Lot of craziness down here
in Florida."

I said, "Yeah, Charlie, it's just a crazy mixed-up
world."

He seemed a little surprised by my tone, but pressed
on. "So what I did this time, I had the wife fly down.
Just . . . *missed* her, I guess. So I called her up, had her
book first-class."

Wife?

Charlie was beginning to think me dense. "You didn't

meet her? The brunette I was sitting with. My *wife*.''

I left berating myself for being presumptuous and judgmental and cynical, but heartened that, for some, maybe the world wasn't such a crazy place after all.

EIGHT

T HE NEXT MORNING, LATE FRIDAY MORNING, THE phone woke me. I was talking into the handset before I was even conscious of being out of bed: "Sanibel Biological Supply."

Silence.

I said, "Hello?"

No reply—but there was someone on the other end, listening to me. I could hear a distant strain of music, an old song: "Everyone's Gone to the Moon."

Was just about to hang up when a gravelly, muffled voice said, "You asshole, you tell the hippie to get the hell off'a our island. He snoops around, we'll cut 'is nose off."

Click.

I stood looking at the phone dumbly, then replaced the handset. Like everyone, I get my share of crank calls. Usually from kids having fun while Mom and Dad are away, dialing randomly, acting tough. But this call had a specific message, and the voice—though obviously disguised—had an edge of crazed intensity that cut to the animal core. I crossed the room, heart beating faster than normal, and checked the clock: 10:17. Very late in the day for an early riser like myself. Even so, I felt as if my body needed a few more hours of sleep. My eyes burned and my head throbbed. I had a hangover that seemed out of proportion to the seven or eight beers I'd had. Felt more like a minor bout of the flu. My stomach was making gaseous rumbling noises. Each rumble produced the residual taste of Hannah's sulfuric tea.

Not a nice way to start the day.

I turned on the stereo and spun the scanner until I heard the last, fading refrain of "Everyone's Gone to the Moon." It was a local FM station. I turned it up a little before lighting the propane stove and putting coffee on. As I did, I made a mental list of people who knew that Tomlinson was on Sulphur Wells. I came up with only two who had an obvious reason to make threatening calls: the mullet fishermen, Julie and J. D. But why call me? And how could they have gotten my name?

As the coffee perked, I got the phone book and found the listing for Sulphur Wells Fish Company. Dialed the number and, when an unfamiliar voice answered, listened carefully for music playing in the background: Garth Brooks. My station was now playing John Lennon.

No match.

I asked, "Is Julie or J. D. around?" The unfamiliar voice said, "Nope, and they ain't gonna be around, neither," and hung up.

I found Raymond Tullock's number, dialed it, and got an answering machine. I found Tullock Seafood Exports in the business pages, dialed the number, and got his answering service. I didn't leave a message.

The only other people I could think of who might have a motive were the marina's two guides, Nels Esterline and Felix Blane—but they couldn't know that Tomlinson had remained on Sulphur Wells. Also, I'd known both men for several years. Angry or not, they weren't the type to make anonymous calls. Even so, I tried their home numbers, listening for music in the background as I told their respective wives, "Sorry, wrong number."

No match.

Finally, I tried to find a listing for Jimmy Darroux. There was none. Had to leaf my way through a couple of pages of Smiths before I finally found H. S. Smith, Gumbo Limbo. Dialed it, let it ring and ring before Tomlinson finally answered. He told me he was just on his way out—Hannah was in her truck waiting for him. "Can't talk, man! When she wants to go, she goes. Innocence without patience—can you imagine that combination?"

"She's going to have to wait," I said, and I told him about the call I'd gotten.

"Cut my nose off?" Tomlinson said. "Why would anyone want to cut my nose off? I'm not one to brag, but I think I've got a pretty nice nose."

"He was talking metaphorically, for God's sake. It was a threat. Maybe it was a crank, maybe it wasn't. But you need to be careful. Have you been out this morning, met anyone new?"

"Yeah, bunches of people. Hannah's had me all over the island already. I stayed up till three reading her notebooks; then she had me on the road at six, visiting the fish houses. Completely screwed up my meditation schedule. But she said I needed to get to know the place before I start work on her book. I agree. The ambience—

you know? Tone? This island has a whole different *feel*.''

"Did you mention my name to anyone you met?''

"She's honking out there, man. I don't get out the door quick, she'll leave me. She'd do it, too.''

"Did you mention—''

"Maybe. I don't know. Hannah, she could have mentioned you. Seriously. You're like one of her favorite topics.''

I felt an unreasonable surge of pleasure at hearing that. "What I'm saying is, you need to be careful, Tomlinson. That's all I'm telling you.'' I hesitated. What I wanted to ask, I couldn't ask. So instead, I said, "She's bringing you back to Sanibel tonight, right?''

He said, "I don't think so. Whatever she wants . . . hey . . . Jesus, she's—'' His voice suddenly contained the flavor of panic. Maybe Hannah was pulling out of the drive. Heard him yell, "HOLD IT! I'M COMING!'' before he said into the phone, "Gotta go, man! I'll call you. Okay?''

I said, "One more thing—''

Tomlinson said, "Can't. The magic bus is rolling. *Mañana!*'' Then he hung up.

THE COFFEE DIDN'T HELP MY HEAD OR MY GURGLING stomach. Decided what I needed to do was sweat my system clean.

So I put on the Nikes and ran down Tarpon Bay Road to the beach and did five killer miles on the soft-packed sand. Ran east along Algiers Beach almost to the golf course and back, forcing the pace, ignoring my swollen toe, checking the watch, making myself sprint two minutes, then stride three minutes, never allowing a peaceful anaerobic moment.

The last lingering chill of the cold front was gone. Clear, sun-bright January morning. Heat radiating off the sand. A mild tropical breeze huffing from the south, out of Cuba. Vacationers already out with their beach towels and tanning goo, eager to bake in the first summer-hot day Sanibel had presented them in more than a week. Around the hotel pools, the uniformed staff members were busy shuttling towels and drinks, renting sailboards and paddle pontoons and jet skis. Scattered all along the beach were little strongholds of oil-coated flesh; some, truly spectacular women in their thong bikinis or sleek one-piece suits. I didn't linger. Didn't let myself pause, or even slow. Kept right on hammering away at the sand, through the lotion stink of coconut oil and Coppertone, lungs burning, sweat pouring, until I was back to my starting place just off Tarpon Bay Road.

After that, I did an ocean swim. Twenty minutes up the beach, twenty minutes back—more than a mile. Swimming is so deadly boring that the brain, in defense, compensates with an alluring cerebral clarity. That's what I like about it. While swimming, I could think intensely and without distraction. Thought about the anonymous phone call: *He snoops around, we'll cut his nose off.* Idle threat or not, it took a lot of anger to generate a call like that. If the call came from Sulphur Wells— which seemed likely—Tomlinson had already added two or more enemies to a life list that contained no enemies anywhere. It was precisely because Tomlinson had so little experience in dealing with personal menace that he was so vulnerable. The question was: How could I make him believe it?

Also thought about Hannah. Still felt the familiar abdominal squeeze when I pictured her eyes, that long body, but the symptoms of obsession had faded. I was relieved, because there were things about Hannah Smith which I found unsettling. Her judgment, for one thing. She apparently believed that Raymond Tullock, her prospective business partner, had worked hard to prevent the net ban. But Garrett Riley's story was more convincing: Tullock had actually lobbied hard to get the net ban passed. He was lying to Hannah and the other commercial fishermen to protect his own interests.

But that was *her* problem. Maybe Tomlinson's, too. Which would probably delight Tomlinson. The man was never truly happy unless he was involved with a woman who was struggling with interesting and complex personal difficulties. The more personality quirks, the better. Life was never too strange or complicated for him. As he had told me more than once, "I am, above all else, a divine healer."

Actually, I believed him to be, above all else, a divine flake. Yet I also knew that no one would work harder for a friend. If Hannah wanted him to help her write and publish a book, that book would be written and published—or Tomlinson would collapse trying.

After I had showered and changed, I telephoned the Coast Guard just to make sure they had found the cable where I left it. The duty officer said that they had, then told me the investigation had been turned over to the sheriff's department and the marine patrol. I told the duty officer that I hoped both agencies dropped everything until they found the people who were responsible. The duty officer reminded me that both agencies were trying to patrol several thousand square miles of water and shoreline with just two or three boats and limited budgets—the equivalent of a couple of beat cops trying to patrol all of Rhode Island, alone and on foot.

Then I called a friend on Useppa, Kate Schaefer, to make sure that the community had been alerted. Kate had heard, and so had everyone else on the island. As one of the community leaders, she'd made certain of that. "It made me so mad I was shaking," she told me. "I'm *still* shaking. All those poor fish, that was bad enough. But to come here and rig a trap like that—Doc, are they *insane*?"

Nope, I told her. Probably not. In all likelihood, they were ruthless, indifferent, and more than a little stupid. But mostly, they were mean. Just dumb-dog mean. I told her to stay on her toes and to call me if she needed any help. Kate said, "The only thing I want from you is the dinner you owe me. Some restaurant that isn't too loud or too smoky, and has a superb menu. Sarasota is nice." She had a very bawdy chuckle for someone with her business accomplishments and political clout. "Or I could fly us to Omaha. I know how much you love a good steak."

I took a rain check. Then, after we'd said our good-byes, wondered why in the hell I hadn't taken her up on the offer. Kate was a great lady. She was smart and tough, but she was also elegant, tender, and she had an outrageous sense of humor.

So why not? Or why not telephone Dewey Nye? See how her campaign on the pro golf tour was going. Offer to fly up to New York . . . or wherever she happened to be, and spend a few days buddying around. Nothing physical—not with Dewey. Her psychological makeup wouldn't allow it. Still, it would be nice to spend some time with a woman I cared about. Get away from my damn fish for a while. Have my Hewes put in dry storage and go. From what I'd seen lately, dry storage was the only safe place for a flats boat—until after July, at least, when the net ban went into effect.

A five-mile run, a one-mile swim, and a hundred pull-ups, I decided, were not sufficient to dissipate a blooming case of male restlessness.

So I futzed around with my damn fish for a while. Got the raw-water intake pump going again. Paid special attention to the six immature tarpon I had in the tank. The fish looked healthy. No apparent ill effects from spending twenty-four hours in water that did not circulate. I wasn't surprised. The tarpon is a euryhaline species, which means that it can live in a wide variety of saline and nonsaline environments: from open ocean to the muckiest landlocked sulfur pit. In Central America, I had seen tarpon in the leaf-choked jungle ponds of Guatemala and Honduras, and as far inland as Lake Nicaragua, 127 miles from the sea. One reason for their hardiness is that tarpon can supplement their oxygen supply by rising to the surface and gulping in air. The mysterious thing is, tarpon surface—or "roll," as it is called—whether the water they inhabit is rich with oxygen or not.

That was my current interest. And why I paid special attention to the six metallic-bodied animals in my tank.

In the early 1940s, biologists Charles M. Breder and Arthur Shlaifer had published articles in *Zoologica* which suggested that the behavior of tarpon was not just respiratory, it was social. I had obtained copies of those papers from the New York Zoological Society. It was my plan to duplicate their experiments and, perhaps, expand on them.

Also, I wanted to necropsy the snook I had brought back from Useppa.

But that was spare-time work. Sanibel Biological Supply, my small company, presently had an order on the books for two dozen sea horses. Eighteen were to be shipped alive, six were to be dissected, their circulatory and reproductive systems injected with contrasting dye. It would take me a whole day, maybe two, to collect that many sea horses. The dissection work would be precise, tricky, and demanding.

I was looking forward to it.

IT WAS AFTER MIDNIGHT BEFORE I FINISHED IN THE LAB, showered beneath the cold-water rain barrel, then switched off the lights. I padded barefooted across the plank flooring. Found my portable shortwave, a Grundig Satellit, on the table beside the reading chair, then flopped into bed, holding the radio on my stomach. Used the autoscan button to surf the bands, and discovered Radio Vietnam at 7.250 MHz, all programming in English. Drifted off to sleep listening to a woman's silken, accented voice, live from Hanoi, telling me about the noble Communist party's legalization of capitalism, a celebrated event called Doi Moi.

Then I was awake again. . . . Groggy. Confused. The radio was no longer on my stomach. Apparently, I had set it aside when I covered myself with the soft wool navy-issue blanket. Looked at the phosphorus numerals of the alarm clock beside my bed: just after three a.m. Why was I awake?

I had heard something. What? I lifted my head, listening. Lay there motionless for what seemed a long time, all senses straining. Could hear the wind blustering against the windows; once heard the primeval squawk of a night heron. Nothing more. Had just about decided that I'd been dreaming, when I felt the slightest of tremors vibrate through the wooden scaffolding of my house. Then felt another . . . and another. It took me a moment to identify the rhythm . . . then I knew: Someone was coming up the steps.

I turned my head just enough to see the gray scrim of window by the door. Saw the sillhouette of a human head materialize, then grow larger, distorted, as a face pressed against the window. I remained motionless, the face peering in, me staring at the face. The face was unrecognizable; a black smear that was magnified by the glass, its hot breath illustrated by a vaporous fog on the windowpane.

I wondered what those unseen eyes could decipher from my darkened room. Not much, I decided. Wondered if the face was that of a friend . . . or a foe . . . or some late-night wanderer who, perhaps, thought my stilt house was part of the national wildlife preserve. A taxpayer had the authority to inspect government property any time of the day or night, right?

I waited. Watched the black shape drift across the expanse of window and disappear. Expected to hear a knock at the door; expected to hear the voice of some troubled friend saying, ''Sorry to bother you so late, Doc, but I need your help.'' Boats break down. Boats get stranded. It had happened before.

But there was no knock. Instead, I felt the rhythmic tremor of careful feet on wooden steps. My visitor was returning down the stairs.

I swung out of bed, found my glasses, and went to the window. Saw that my visitor was a man: big, heavy-set man in a dark shirt. It was too dark to make out facial features. Watched him stop on the lower platform, glance back at my cottage, then study the sleeping marina—the behavior of someone who doesn't want to be seen. Watched him move along the dock toward the mooring area where I keep my boats. Thought about trying to spook him off by hitting the deck lights . . . decided that would be too kind. He seemed to have burglary on his mind, and I don't share the sympathies of some for the economic quandary of thieves. Yet I didn't want to confront him. Maybe he had a knife. Or a gun. Or a knife and a gun, plus a head full of drugs. It is the unwise citizen who challenges a late-night prowler. That's what cops are for.

Still watching the man, I picked up the phone, planning to dial 911. As I began to dial, I saw him go to my fish tank and lift the lid. Saw him reach down into the tank, as if attempting to find the water pump. My visitor, I decided, wasn't a thief, he was a vandal. In a minute or less, he could destroy the whole circulatory apparatus of a very delicate system that had taken me a lot of very frustrating hours to build.

So much for playing the roll of respectable citizen. I didn't have time to wait for the cops. Furthermore, I no longer wanted to wait for them. Stealing was bad enough, but attempting to damage my aquarium was, in my mind, a hell of a lot worse. This bastard had crossed the line; deserved my personal attention.

I reached for the door, then remembered the squeaky hinges that would telegraph my approach. Instead, I moved the reading chair, then quietly opened the big trapdoor through which the fish merchants had once hoisted crates of fish and blocks of ice. I lowered myself through the floor, grabbed a crossbeam, then hung there suspended above the water, wearing nothing but my glasses and old khaki swim shorts.

My visitor was still hunched over the fish tank.

I grabbed the next crossbeam, and the next, moving hand to hand beneath my house, away from the tank. My house is built of old Florida heart pine. The beams creaked, but not much. It was a noiseless way to move. When I was close enough, I reached out with my legs, got my feet onto the platform, and stood. Turned to make sure the visitor was still on the front deck—he was—then I went belly-down on the dock and slid into the January water. Staying beneath the dock, I sculled my way around the house, then under the main platform. I could hear my visitor above me: the gentle shifting of weight a few inches from my head. I continued onward until I was out from under the platform; then I laced my left arm around a plank in the boardwalk that leads to shore. The water was shallow—only about four feet deep—and I had firm footing on the muck bottom.

I tapped the dock with my knuckles, then snapped my fingers a few times, hoping to get my visitor's attention.

Heard the lid to the fish tank creak closed . . . then silence.

Snapped my fingers twice more. Heard the scuff of shoes on damp wood: My visitor had heard the noise and was coming to investigate.

I stood beneath the dock, knees bent, head back, only my face out of the water, looking up, waiting. Heard a whispered voice say, ''Is that you?''

Thought: Who the hell is he talking to?

Snapped my fingers once more, then heard a dull thud above me—my visitor was getting down on his knees—and then watched the dark shape of a head extend out over the dock, looking for the source of the noise, my visitor's face only a foot from mine. There wasn't enough light to see his expression. . . . I knew it would take a moment for his brain to interpret what his eyes were seeing . . . lunged up out of the water before he had time to react, grabbed him by the throat and swung him into the water with me.

My visitor's first terrified instinct was to flee—maybe a gator had grabbed him. He came up spitting water, throwing elbows, struggling to get to shore. But I got my legs threaded through his legs so he couldn't move, still had a good grip on his throat, tilted his head back and said into his ear, "Hey . . . *hey!* Talk to me, you won't get hurt. Fight me, you'll drown."

He decided to fight. Tried to find my eyes with his fingers; elbowed me hard in the ribs . . . so I took him under. Took him down to the bottom and waited until his movements became panicked, frenzied before allowing him up to take in air.

"Quit fighting!"

More elbows. Then he lunged backward, ramming me into the dock. So I took him under one more time; waited on the bottom with him until the thudding of my eardrums told me my own lungs were empty, then hoisted him back to the surface . . . only to be clubbed hard above the ear by someone behind me. Stupidly, I turned to look . . . and just had time to get my arms up as a man standing on the dock swung at me with a long plank. Took a glancing blow off forearm and head . . . disentangled my legs from those of my visitor and lunged underwater, swimming hard. I wanted to put some distance between myself and the guy with the board.

Came up twenty yards or so away to hear: ". . . dumb ass, I told you to wait for me. Let 'im go!"

"The sonuvabitch almost killed me!"

"You want to tell it to the cops? Get your ass outta there!"

From neck-deep water, I watched my visitor walrus up onto the dock, and then he and his buddy went jogging along the boardwalk toward shore. A minute or so later, as I was climbing onto the platform, I heard their vehicle start—it sounded like a truck; a manual transmission. Took a quick look at my fish tank. He had ripped out the PVC spray rail, but the pump was still working. Even so, the idea of him trying to futz my aquarium infuriated me. I hustled up the steps, took the keys to my own truck from the hook beside the door, and then drove down the shell drive, hoping to catch them.

At the end of the drive was a four-way stop. Turn left, you'd soon be on Periwinkle, Sanibel's main road and the only route to the mainland causeway. Go straight, along Tarpon Bay Road, and you'd end up at the beach. Turn right, the road led to Blind Pass, across which is the bridge to Captiva Island. The Sanibel Causeway was the only mainland umbilical; there was no highway egress from Captiva, so it seemed unlikely that they would have turned right. Yet a lingering haze of dust told me that they had gone toward Captiva.

I turned, powering through the gears, driving fast. There was no traffic: black two-lane road; black hedge of trees on both sides. There were a couple of fishermen on the Blind Pass Bridge—no matter what time of the night, there were always fishermen—so I stopped long enough to ask one of them if a pickup truck had recently passed. Got a shrug for a response. "Little bit ago. Maybe."

I crossed the bridge, onto Captiva. Pale rind of beach and night sea to my left, winter estates to my right: vacation homes set way back in, cloaked by tree shadow, their driveways marked by driftwood signs. Over on Sulphur Wells, winter residents hung plastic placards from their mailboxes, naming their mobile homes as cleverly as they named their cheap boats: Lay-Z-Daze, Snow Bird, Sea-Ducer. Here on Captiva, though, the names— carved into the driftwood—communicated the power of old money and lofty society: Sea Grape Lodge, Casuarina, Tortuga, White Heron House. Why would two vandals flee to Captiva?

At a resort and marina called 'Tween Waters, I turned into the parking lot. Plenty of rental cars, but no pickup trucks. Headed back onto the beach road, still determined to catch them—at the very least, get their license number. Drove clear to the security gates of a massive resort, South Seas Plantation—as far as you can drive on Captiva Island. Nothing but private tennis courts, condominiums, and a golf course beyond. No sign of a truck anywhere. Didn't pass a single car. So maybe I'd guessed wrong. Maybe they'd turned toward the causeway bridge, not Captiva. Or maybe they had detoured down one of the side roads. Whatever they'd done, I'd lost them.

I turned around and headed back toward Sanibel, driving my normal speed—slow—arm out the window, feeling the sea wind, feeling the anger recede, but still wondering why anyone would want to destroy my fish tank.

It was nearly four a.m. by the time I got to Dinkin's Bay.

NINE

ACH SATURDAY AT SUNSET, THE FISHING GUIDES and the live-aboards throw money in a pot to finance Dinkin's Bay's weekly Pig Roast and Beer Cotillion. The name is misleading because pigs and cotillions don't play a role. Beer, however, does. Ice is shoveled into Igloos, and the beer is buried deep. Kelly, from the take-out, loads the picnic table over by the sea grape tree with platters of shrimp and fried conch and anything else that happens to be lying around the kitchen. The live-aboards begin socializing on the docks, freshly showered and drinks in hand, at sunset. Which is usually about the time the guides finish washing down their skiffs.

For the first hour or so, it's marina community only. No wandering tourists allowed, no locals looking for a free meal. There is a chain-link gate on the shell road that leads to the marina, and Mack keeps the gate closed. But after all the food has been eaten, and if there's still enough beer, Mack strolls out and opens the gate. After that, the length of the party is commensurate with the endurance of marina residents and outsiders alike.

Saturday morning, I forced myself to get up at a re-

spectable time—seven—and spent the whole day working. First, I replaced the PVC sprayer bar on my fish
tank. Then I went to work in my lab. I'd gotten the sea
horses I needed, and the dissections and mounting process went pretty well. I also took a look at the snook
that I had retrieved from Useppa. Aside from the netburn
scars, I could find nothing unusual. No trauma that might
have occurred from an explosion, no metallic discolor-
ation of key internal organs that might indicate death by
poisoning. My guess was, someone had netted the fish
and allowed it to die slowly on the deck of a boat.

Most of my work was done. So, just before sunset, I
showered, changed into jeans and a gray flannel shirt,
and ambled through the mangroves to the marina. Found
that the mood around Dinkin's Bay did not have its
usual screw-it-all-this-is-Saturday-night ebullience. The
marina had officially closed for the day, but Mack was
still busy serving as line chief to the cleanup operations.

They had floated in a crane mounted on a barge. The
crane was fitted with a dinosaur-sized bucket that would
swing down onto the charred dock, bite off a chunk, then
pivot shoreward to regurgitate the mess into a dump
truck. When the dump truck was full, it would rumble
away, only to be replaced by another.

A yellow Detroit diesel engine dominated the stern of
the barge. The diesel made a deafening roar, exhausted
a lot of blue fumes. The live-aboards were locked tight
into their boats, probably trying to screen the noise with
loud stereos. Or earplugs. Who knew? They certainly
weren't out socializing on the dock, so there was no one
to ask.

But Kelly was already laying out the platters of fried
conch and shrimp on the picnic table. I could see a cou-

ple of industrial-sized Igloos that appeared to be straining at the seams. So the Dinkin's Bay Pig Roast and
Beer Cotillion—"Perbcot," as it is known locally—
would go on as usual.

At the good marinas around Florida, the old and important traditions die hard.

I strolled over close enough to one of the dump trucks
so that Mack would see that I was there. He is a com-
pact, muscular man—a native New Zealander—whose
laid-back Kiwi qualities have made him a big success
on the island. But he wasn't laid-back now. He was
having some kind of loud conversation with a man who
was wearing a sports coat and carrying a clipboard. Not
an argument, just loud, so as to be heard above the din
of the diesel. The man with the clipboard was an insurance adjuster, I guessed.

Mack saw me, waved, then held up five fingers after
pointing to his watch. Pantomimed a drinking motion
and grinned.

Which meant we wouldn't be bothered by the noise
much longer.

Beyond what was once a dock, I could see Nelson
Esterline. Nels was hammering at the wreckage of his
skiff. Trying to remove the jack plate, it appeared. His
teal-green Hewes had once been a pretty thing indeed.
Teal green, polished bright, with functional lines—the
prettiest quality of any boat. Now it looked like a Clorox
bottle that had been accidentally left on a hot stove.

I considered walking over to offer him a hand. Sound
him out about my two early-morning visitors; see if he
knew anything about it; see if he was still mad at me.
Decided against it. Men like Nels make up their minds
in their own fashion, their own good time. Instead, I put

a coin in the slot and read the local newspaper.

The day before, the death of Jimmy Darroux had made front-page headlines. I had read the story carefully. Darroux had been described as Hannah described him: a native of Louisiana. A commercial fisherman who had migrated to Sulphur Wells only a few years before. The story related that he had had several minor run-ins with local law authorities. He'd been arrested in a bar brawl, charged with public intoxication, but the charges had been dropped. On his record was also a charge for misdemeanor battery related to spousal abuse. He had pled no contest, was fined five hundred dollars and given a year's probation. Within the last two months, he had been arrested for possession of less than three grams of cocaine. The case had been scheduled to go to court in early February. He had also been arrested and fined for fishing outside proscribed times, and for having illegal fish in his possession.

Judging from the newspaper article, Jimmy Darroux had been just one more habitual loser. Not so hard to imagine him getting a belly full of booze, or a head full of crack, and setting out with a jerry can of gasoline to punish the people he perceived to be responsible for the net ban and his own troubled life. The article said the Bureau of Alcohol, Tobacco, and Firearms was assisting local authorities in the investigation. An A.T.F. officer said it was too early to tell if an explosive device had played a role in starting the fire, or in the death of Darroux. I knew that the A.T.F. officer wouldn't have admitted it even if he had known.

I glanced over to where the crane was still gobbling up wreckage. The yellow crime-scene tape was gone. The A.T.F. people, apparently, had found all they needed to find. If not, they wouldn't have released control of the area.

In today's paper, though, Jimmy Darroux rated only a token mention. His name was included in a story about the increase in thefts and vandalism up and down the coast. The story implied a connection between the crimes and the recent vote to ban the nets. In the last two months, the story read, fifty-four boats had been stolen, stripped, and destroyed—most of them small sportfishing boats. Sixty-seven outboard engines had also been stolen. A sheriff's department spokesperson speculated that a well-organized theft-and-chop-shop ring was involved. Two other skiffs had been set afire at their dock. In Naples, an unknown and unsuccessful arsonist had attempted to raze a marine storage barn. A night watchman had smelled the smoke and put out the fire before it had a chance to spread. In other places, arsonists had been more successful—they had burned several of the few remaining old stilt houses to the water. Also, sheriff's department records showed a report of someone stringing a cable across a waterway near Useppa Island.

I was relieved to see it reported. The more people who knew, the better.

The story also named several local sportfishermen who claimed that net fishermen were harassing them on the flats. Intentionally spooking the fish, yelling threats, throwing bottles. Finally, the story quoted an anonymous net fisherman: "They're taking our jobs away. They're taking our houses, boats, everything. They expect us to smile and be nice about it? You tell them paybacks are hell."

I folded the paper and dropped it in the trash can

beside the bench outside the marina store. I had grown
so accustomed to the roar of the diesel engine that when
the noise abruptly died, the fresh silence made my ears
ring.

"HEY, FORD, GET YOUR BUTT OVER HERE!" I LOOKED
to see Rhonda Lister waving to me from the stern of her
water-bloated Chris-Craft cabin cruiser. There were Japanese lanterns hanging from the cabin framework, and
painted in red script on the stern was the name: *Tiger
Lilly*. Rhonda was wearing an elaborate green gown and
a lot of complicated jewelry. Her caramel-bright hair
was coiled into a towering bun, and there was a pale
yellow hibiscus blossom behind her ear. Rhonda is a big,
busty, hippy woman. Dressed the way she was, she
looked like the proprietor of an 1850s whorehouse.

I walked over, accepted the bottle of Steinlager she
held out to me, and said, "You are unusually lovely
tonight, Miz Lister."

She curtsied daintily. "Thank you, kind sir." Then
did a quick double take. "Hey—how'd you get those
scratches on your face? You get in a fight? You look
like hell."

I felt lucky that a few scratches and a knot above my
ear were the only injuries I'd suffered.

"I spent the day wrestling sea horses."

"Which means you don't want to talk about it?"

"Which means I'd rather talk about that gorgeous
dress. Why the costume?"

Rhonda made a flittering motion with her hands; a
regal effect. "The ladies who inhabit this fish palace
have discussed it among ourselves, and we've decided
that tonight should be a special night. A real celebration.

Our little family of gunkholers and misfits endured a great trial by fire on Thursday, and we ... and we ... we ..."

"Triumphed?" I offered.

"Damn right we did. Triumphed. So what we ladies have decided is, we are all going to wear our best gowns this evening. Show you men just how tasteful we are. Show we own something besides boat shorts and aren't always up to our elbows in engine grease. But mostly to prove that those sonsabitches can't scare us!" She smiled demurely and fanned herself with an imaginary fan. "Because we are, after all, ladies, sir."

I laughed as she whirled around, billowing her skirts. "What do you think, Doc? Pretty fancy, huh?"

"Stunning. The tennis shoes make just the right statement."

"It was JoAnn's idea. She said we'd get stuck in the dock. If we wore high heels? She said it wouldn't be ladylike because we'd fall and spill our drinks. Plus, it would make us easy prey for you vultures."

JoAnn was JoAnn Smallwood. She and Rhonda were roommates, and co-owners of *Tiger Lilly*. Several years ago, they pooled a couple of hundred dollars and started an advertising sheet they called *The Heat Islands Fishing Report*. The advertising sheet was well accepted. Sanibel and Captiva certainly qualified as heat islands, and advertisers knew there was money in any publication that had to do with fishing. JoAnn and Rhonda worked eighteen hours a day, and pumped every dollar they made back into the business. Now their advertising sheet is a magazine-sized weekly. They've started a sister publication that deals with real estate. They are in the process of buying their office complex over near Periwinkle Place Shopping Center. They've made way too much money to be living on a rot-pocked cabin cruiser in Dinkin's Bay. JoAnn says they stay on the boat because their business eats all their liquid assets. But I know, from a good source, that each of the women owns at least one island home—which they lease—plus a couple of choice building lots. I suspect they continue to live on their roomy cabin cruiser because that is how they started life on Sanibel, and they still enjoy being a part of the marina community.

Rhonda said, "Look, do me a favor. If Tomlinson shows up wearing that Dorothy Lamour thing of his, the sarong, send him back to the boat and make him change. I don't mind, but I've got a couple of important clients coming later. No matter how many times I remind him, he still spreads his legs whenever he sits down. God knows, he's not the only one around here doesn't wear underwear, but it upsets some people."

I was in the process of telling her that Tomlinson was still on Sulphur Wells. But Rhonda interrupted me, saying, "My God, it's . . . it's . . . it's Princess Di!"

I followed her gaze down the dock to see Janet Mueller approaching. Janet had a shy, crooked grin on her face and was making a hushing motion with her hand. Her gown was some kind of peach-colored gauze over a silver skirt and peach bodice. Apparently she, too, had visited one of the Dinkin's Bay hibiscus bushes. A bright red flower bloomed from her mouse-brown hair. She wore a light dust of makeup—pale lip gloss, some cheek highlighter, a darkening mascara—that reduced the roundness of her face. It was strange to see Janet wearing makeup. But she looked . . . nice . . . sweet. There was something touching about her appearance, as if she were a plump, wistful little girl who had used her older, prettier sister's clothes to play dress-up.

I said, "Can this be the same sweaty woman I ran with? No. It's impossible."

Janet seemed pleased and chagrined all at once. "This was all their idea, Doc. I mean it. I don't even own a gown . . . I don't have one with me, I mean. So Rhonda, she insisted on loaning me one of hers. Then we had to spend half the night altering it, trying to get the hem even—"

"And drinking wine!" Rhonda hooted.

"I didn't drink nearly as much as JoAnn did. You either."

"Janet honey, no one ever drinks as much wine as JoAnn does. Doc, you should have seen the three of us. None of us knows a thing about sewing, but there we were, trying to measure this, trim that, poking ourselves with needles. Then JoAnn started telling those raunchy jokes of hers!"

"I didn't even try the dress on until about midnight," Janet said. Then she looked at Rhonda; a friendly expression of mock threat. "If I look as stupid as I feel—"

I took Janet by the elbow, then held her away as if inspecting. After a critical pause, I said, "You look great. I mean it." I did, too. Janet had lived isolated and alone on her dumpy Holiday Mansion houseboat long enough. Didn't mix, didn't fraternize. Now, finally, she was allowing herself to be accepted into the marina community. She looked happy, and I felt happy for her.

"Ladies," I said, "if you look toward the picnic table, you will notice that Mack is already serving himself. That wouldn't be so bad, but Jeth is next in line. Jeth will eat anything, but he prefers shrimp. We'd better hurry, or the only thing left will be little bits of shell and Styrofoam.''

I extended my arm to Janet. She wagged her eyebrows at Rhonda, then allowed herself to be escorted.

MACK OPENED THE MARINA GATES AT AROUND EIGHT, thereby allowing a steady flow of locals and lost tourists to join the party. The locals wanted to inspect the damage caused by the explosion. Most of them had done that on Friday, but now they wanted to do it on a social basis. The tourists just wanted to have fun. They did— except for a dour young French couple who showed up asking to see ''ze attrac-she-uns.'' Someone had apparently told them about the party and, due to a miscommunication, they had expected Perbcot to be the island's version of Epcot.

As Jeth Nicholes watched them stalk away, he said, ''Jesus Christ, them French people are so dense you couldn't climb 'em with an ice ax. Know what I heard? They'll piss right in the sink, you give them a chance. French people, I mean.''

At about nine, I was sitting with Janet—she was telling me about a conservation project for which she had volunteered; the St. Joe River cleanup. In northwest Ohio?—when Nels approached me, saying, ''Doc, you got a minute?'' Felix Blane, all six feet six inches and 250-some pounds of him, stood directly behind Nels, shadowing us both from the dock lights.

It wasn't ideal timing. Janet was finally starting to open up a little, starting to talk about herself instead of relying on me to carry the conversation. It wasn't that she sat there mutely. But she knew how to deflect attention from herself by asking leading questions; timing them so that I, or someone else, was always in the process of answering. As a result, I hadn't learned much about her. She was from Ohio—which I knew. She was in her mid-thirties—which I had guessed from her taste in music. She'd never spent any time around boats—no surprise. She had taught biology and chemistry at a high school near her home—I hadn't known that—and she was just telling me about the conservation project on the St. Joseph River when Nels interrupted.

I said, "I want to talk to you guys, but—"

"Doc, please go ahead. Really. I need to . . . check on something anyway." That quick, Janet was up and gone, as if glad for the opportunity to escape.

Nels watched her walk away, shrugged, and said, "Sorry, Doc. I didn't mean to chase her off. She seems like a nice girl."

I said, "She is."

Felix said, "I told you we should'a waited." Then to me, he explained, "This big dumb ass forgets that he scares most men and just about all women. The way he looks; just the sight of him."

Among men, hyperbole and character assassination mark the parameters of friendship. I found it heartening that I was still included.

Nels said, "You want to go after her, we'll wait. Whenever you got the time."

"Nope. She's just a friend."

Felix said, "Well, go ahead then, Nels. Spit it out."

Nels was suddenly uneasy; having a hard time getting started. Finally, he said, "It's like this, Doc. I was wrong to say to you what I said the other day. I was pissed off about my skiff, and you were a handy target. Shit, I felt like unloading on somebody, and there you were."

I said, "Don't worry about it. It was a tough day for all of us." I started to stick out my hand, but Felix interceded.

"Tell 'im the rest of it, Nels, before you go to shaking hands."

Nels fixed him with a sour look. We had been sitting beneath the porch that shelters the bait tanks. Now Nels stood and motioned with his head, telling me he wanted to get away from the people who were milling around. As we walked toward the end of the T-dock, he said abruptly, "I did something stupid the other night. Thursday night."

I said, "Oh?"

"Yeah, and I want to be right up-front about it. There's this thing that happened."

What had happened was that Nels, distraught about his boat and his money problems, had gotten falling-down drunk.

"I don't know how much I drank," he said. "A lot. Way too much. I hit about every bar on the island. One thing about being a drunk, you never lack for company. I talked to people I knew, and I talked to a lot of people I didn't know and hope to hell I never see again."

Felix said, "That's what Nels needs to tell you. That night? I was standing guard duty. We told you we were going to start patrolling the marina? So I'm sitting on the dock, my thumb up my butt, feeling like an idiot. I'm carrying a shotgun around. Shit, a *weapon*. It was like Highway One, back in Danang. That's how long it's been since I've carried anything. Except I'm doing it at Dinkin's Bay, where the only dangerous thing around is Jeth, who might walk out on his balcony to say hello, then fall on me, he's so clumsy. I mean, it's *stupid*."

Nels said, "Damn it, don't start. We've still got to keep a guard. I don't even have a boat left, and I think so."

Felix said, "Yeah, well, the point is, Nels is like an hour overdue for his shift, when this big-wheel truck comes barreling down the road—"

I said, "A pickup truck?"

"A pickup, yeah. It's like one in the morning. I'm dozing, I'm cold, I've got to take an all-time hellish dump, and I wake up with this vehicle charging me. Jesus Christ, Doc, first thing that pops in my mind is it's Sir Charles. Mr. Sapper about to come down hard, and the only general order I can remember is: If it flies, it dies. You know? It *startled* me. I'm thinking it's a bunch of dinks until I'm full awake, which is the only reason Captain Nelson Esterline here didn't get himself waxed."

Felix was having fun with the story—he had an incongruously high laugh for a man his size—but Nels wasn't enjoying it. He seemed increasingly sheepish. I wanted to hear more about the pickup truck, and tried to hurry him along. "Whose truck?"

Nels said, "I don't know. I'm in a bar, then I'm in their truck, and they're bringing me to the marina because I'm late to relieve Felix. That's what I remember. There were three of them, I guess. I don't remember any names." He looked at Felix. "Is that right? Three?"

Felix said, "Three kind of rough-looking dudes. Fancy truck. I'd never seen them before, but they're like Nels's best friends 'cause they're all so drunk. The four of them come staggering up, and who they want to see? You, Doc. They're pissed off, in a mood to fight, and they want to see you. They're asking, 'Where's the goggle-eyed bastard?' '' Felix had begun to laugh; was relishing Nels's discomfort. "What Nels had done was, he'd convinced them you're like a spy for the commercial netters, living over here in flats boat territory. A traitor. He was out there flapping his gums, yammy-yammy-yammy, and they all wanted a piece of you—''

"Would you shut up a minute so I can explain it?" Nels was tired of Felix provoking him. "Truth is, I said a lot of things to a lot of people that night. I hate a person who sneaks around and says stuff about someone else, so that's why I'm telling you. I didn't mean what I said. Hell, I can't *remember* most of the stuff I said. But that night, right or wrong, you just seemed a big part of what happened to my boat."

I said, "You can't remember anything about the guys in the truck?"

"Nope. They were staying on Captiva, so they must have money. All-pro sportfishermen to hear them tell it. I don't think I'd ever seen them before."

"You're sure this was Thursday night, not last night?"

Nels said, "Last night, I was still in bed with a hangover."

"So who patrolled the marina?"

Felix said, "Jeth, supposedly. But probably from his bed."

Nels interrupted. "The point is, I'm not the type to go around back-stabbing friends. You know that." He wiped a leather-dark hand across his wide face. "After Felix got me sobered up a little, we had a long talk about this whole business. Over the years, you've helped us, Doc, and we've helped you. Dinkin's Bay may be a weird-ass family, but it's still a family. The way I see it, we stick together. I don't agree with the way you voted—''

"It was a dumb-shit way to vote," Felix put in cheerfully.

"Yeah, it was. That's what I think. I'll say it to your face, but I'll never say it behind your back again. It's your business how you voted, not mine. And . . .'' Nels shrugged. "That's what I wanted to tell you.''

I asked, "When you came looking for me Thursday night, did you stop at my place before you pulled into the marina?''

"Yep. That much I remember. But you weren't home. I know you don't lock it, and you showed me where the key is if you do. I just knocked and left.''

"The three men were with you?''

Nels thought for a moment. "One or two of them, yeah. But we didn't touch anything.''

"You think they live on Captiva, or just visiting?''

"I think they live on the Keys. Marathon? Maybe Marathon.'' Nels was getting suspicious. "What's that have to do with anything?''

I was tempted to tell Nels that in all probability, his drinking buddies had returned to vandalize my house last night. Gave it some thought before deciding not to. Why add to his guilt? It hadn't been easy for Nels to come to me with his story. Most wouldn't have had the courage. It's easier to allow a friendship to fade away than to suffer the occasional awkwardness it takes to maintain it. And he was right about the importance of allegiances in a tiny community.

Felix said, "What I bet he does remember is getting sick off the dock, barking like a damn dog. I told 'im, 'Nels, just keep puking till something hairy and round comes up—that'll be your asshole.' Told 'im, 'You'll be needing that, so try to catch it before it hits that water.' "

Nels said, "Don't remind me." Tired of talking about it.

So, to seal and bury the subject, I changed the subject. Then, as we were returning to the party, I once again offered Nels and Felix the use of my flats boat. Why miss all those charters?

But Nels said very quickly, "Nope. I couldn't do that. Not now."

Which sealed that subject, too.

TEN

I DIDN'T HEAR FROM TOMLINSON ON SUNDAY, OR ON Monday, either. Tried to call him a couple of times. No answer. I didn't receive any more anonymous threats—*Tell the hippie to get off'a our island*—but that didn't mean that someone on Sulphur Wells wasn't targeting him, just as the sportfishermen from Captiva had targeted me. In any emotional debate, the first casualty is reason. Not that Tomlinson is a reasonable person— I had already warned him once, and there was no cause to believe that a second warning would convince him to return to his sailboat. He would stay on Sulphur Wells as long as he wanted; at least until his karmic mandate was fullfilled.

So, because he might be gone for a while, I hauled his Zodiac up on the deck, and tied it fast near the storage locker where, days earlier, I had already stored his little Yamaha outboard.

On Tuesday morning, I put off my run and swim until later, and I got to work trying to re-create Dr. Breder's and Dr. Shlaifer's tarpon procedure. What the two biologists had done was establish a control group of five immature fish in a small area, and observe how often the fish rolled. Then they charted the behavior in elapsed time, real time, and kept careful notes on how frequently a solitary rolling fish appeared to catalyze the same behavior in the other fish.

I already had my control group of immature tarpon, and I had a contained area—my big fish tank. It wasn't as large as the tiny pond Breder and Shlaifer had created—ironically, they had dug it on what was then Palmetto Key, now Cabbage Key—but the water in my tank was clear. Their pond was not. The clear water would give me the added advantage of being able to identify individual fish. To make it easier, I had already tagged my six fish with tiny color-coded tags.

It was not exciting work, sitting there in the January sun, watching tarpon drift to the surface, breach, then bank off in descent. But the marine sciences are seldom exciting—unless you happen to be fascinated by the quirks and oddities of animal behavior. Few are; I am.

During a break, I saw Janet Mueller on the docks, and told her what I was doing. She insisted on stopping by to have a look. Within an hour, she had read the Breder-Shlaifer papers, and had a clear grasp of what I was trying to accomplish. Not long after that, she had taken my place in the cane-backed chair beside the tank, and was using the stopwatch, making fastidious notes in a tiny, spidery hand on a log sheet attached to a clipboard.

It is said that the human eye cannot show emotion. That is true in a specific sense, but false in general application. When a person becomes consumed by a project or a thought sequence, it shows in their eyes. The eyes seem to glaze and radiate light at the same time. Janet was consumed by what she was doing, sitting there lost in the world of precise time and the strange behavior of those silver-bright fish. For the first time since I'd met her, she seemed free of her introspective burden, free of whatever it was that had created her expression of chronic shell shock.

The lady was happy in her work, so I went off and let her work. Did my run—four cheerful, bikini-studded miles in which my damaged toe didn't hurt at all, and only bled a little bit. Did a lazy mile swim, and I was only half finished with my daily assault on the pull-up bar, when the phone rang. It was Tomlinson.

I picked the phone up to hear, "Doc? Sorry, brother; sorry I didn't call you back, but I am having one of the most un-damn-believable experiences of my life. I mean, it's like I've been invited to explore the inner sanctum; the workings of a whole, tight traditional society. Seriously."

I said. "You sound serious."

"Oh man, if you only knew."

"You're talking about the commercial fishermen."

"Of course! You got the ol' thinking cap on backward, or what? *Yeah*, the commercial fishermen. Men, women, their children. The island, man—Sulphur Wells. The whole scene is like a living laboratory. Can you imagine what that means to an eminent sociologist such as myself? Thing is, it was here staring me right in the face the whole time. The whole time! I'm skipping off to Appalachia, the Yavapai reservations of Arizona, Brazil—hell, *Fumbuck Egypt*—to write papers about traditional people, and here I've got them living and working just up the bay, but I don't even realize till now. Go figure!"

I could remember Tomlinson skipping off to Key West quite often. Arizona occasionally. Maybe Appalachia; I wasn't sure. Brazil—that had to have been before I met him. But Fumbuck Egypt? The man lived with a memory fractured by dealing with the real and the imaginary; factors I didn't even care to guess at. I changed the subject. "Anybody giving you a hard time? I told you about the phone call—"

"No problem, man. People here love me. It's like a gift I've got. People just naturally love me."

"How could I have forgotten?"

"Search me. But what I'm calling about is my boat."

When I told him I'd already hauled out his Zodiac, he said, "No, my sailboat. What you could do is let the engine run for a while, charge up the batteries some. And in the icebox. By the sink? I've got a couple fish fillets. A guy in a little boat came by and gave them to me, and I meant to give them to you for your cat."

Crunch & Des, the marina's black cat, was lying on the desk beside the phone. I reached out and scratched his ears as Tomlinson said, "They're probably pretty stinky by now. Who's got time to buy ice? So I'd hate to come back to that. Just one of the many, many reasons I don't eat meat. And hit the bilge switch. I've got it on automatic, but you never know."

"Bilge switch," I repeated.

"And my dinghy outboard—"

I told him I'd already taken care of it. He seemed relieved. "Thing is, I got so wrapped up in Sulphur Wells, I forgot about everything else, man. See, what I didn't realize was, traditional people don't have to be isolated from the outside world. They can be isolated by the imperatives of their own *lifestyle.*"

"Fascinating," I said.

"Fucken-ay! These people, these fishermen, their

lives revolve around their work. The migration patterns of fish, season to season. That's the link. Those patterns haven't changed in two hundred years. Hell, forever! It determines how they fish, when they fish, how often they go out. It defines interaction between family members. It solidifies the bonds of families within the fishing community. You see where I'm headed?''

''No, but—''

''I'm saying it's *tribal,* man. You ever hear a kid from Kansas say, 'When I grow up, I want to be a mullet fisherman'? Of course not. It can't be learned in school, man, and it can't be learned from a book. You've got to be *born* into it. These traditions, they're handed down, father to son, mother to daughter. You know the way farming families used to stay on the farms, inheriting the fields? It's like that here, man. Only it's water.''

When Tomlinson gets on a roll, all you can do is sit back and listen. I moved away from the desk just enough to see through the window. Janet was still down on the deck, hunched forward in her chair, pencil in hand, clipboard in her lap.

Heard Tomlinson say, ''Are you still there?''

''Yeah, I'm here.'' Apparently I had missed something.

He said, ''What I mean is, that's another thing that insulates them. The economics. The best ones make a pretty good living. But no one gets rich. It's strictly lower-middle-class, and that's another thing that binds them but also sets them apart. See? Outsiders have no reason to want to join the tribe. Not enough money in it, understand? It's not like some company that pays hospitalization.''

I said, ''I'm with you so far.''

"So the society is a caste within a caste; sets up a whole hierarchy. They've got their outlaws, they've got their tangent groups. People wrapped a little too tight for the general population. You know? They have all the tools to upset the whole applecart. Which brings up an interesting question: Should the scientific observer ever intercede? Like the Rockefeller expedition into New Guinea. Do you try to help settle obvious conflicts between natives, or do you just sit back and let the natives find their own solutions?"

I didn't like the sound of that. "Getting caught in the middle," I said. "That's what I'm talking about."

"Hey, man, no one's going to hurt me. I'm strictly the passive resistance type. Even if they did try to hurt me, I wouldn't fight back."

"That's why you need to watch your step. Already, you're talking about conflicts."

"In a hypothetical sense. That's what I'm saying. The main problem here is alcohol and drugs, man. Just like my brothers on the reservations—they've taken their toll. But mostly, it's close-knit. I'm talking about Sulphur Wells now. Sure, there's some infighting. Name a group that doesn't have that. But there's also an infrastructure that sets the boundaries of what's acceptable, what isn't. Remember Arlis Futch? He's like one of the tribal elders. People don't screw with Mr. Futch. And Hannah, man—she is like the young chief. The way the men react to her. Seeking her approval, but not wanting to show how much. 'Cause they're men, right? And she's a woman. But she's stronger than them. She's stronger than them, and they *know* it."

Hearing her name for the first time keyed the abdominal twitterings. I wondered if she was there, in the room with Tomlinson. Her bare feet thumping along the wooden floor; reaching out to touch her fingers to him as she passed. Maybe listening in, knowing I was on the other end of the line, but not acknowledging it, not even calling out a greeting.

The sensation of her fingernail tracing the shape of my ear flashed and lingered. I said, "By the way, if she's around—Hannah—tell her I said hello."

"I will, man, I will. She's down at the fish house with Mr. Futch now. Those two—that's a whole other intense story. But I will."

"Things are going okay?"

"With Hannah, you mean?"

"Well . . . sure."

"I can't even tell you, Doc. Seriously. The whole karma thing is just too heavy. It's like mixing LSD-25 with IBM—the most radical fucking business trip since Rasputin met the czar. I mean, my head is *spinning*. Mostly, I eat a lot of collard greens, drink a lot of well water, and work on her book. Doesn't even have a typewriter. We had to borrow one."

As I tried to interpret that, he added, "She starts out with all this beautiful fishing folklore. Never carry money on a working boat. It's bad luck. Same if someone says the word "alligator." The blade end of an oar *has* to be facing the stern. If a pregnant woman goes into labor after dark, panthers will gather outside the house to watch. Or to stand guard. You get the shits, you make tea from this tree called white stopper. You get snake bit, you make a poultice from Spanish moss. Very heavy into the medicinal stuff. She knows about herbs I've never even heard of."

He hadn't answered the question that I could not bring

myself to ask outright. "So you and Hannah are . . . you two are . . ."

"Yeah, we're up to our *Haras* in work, man. People keep stopping around. What happened to Jimmy, the cops are still interested in that one. Plus, there's a lot of weird jockeying going on here. Because of the net ban? You know: who's going to sell what. There are about three hundred commercial fishermen on this island; most of them own property. So what happens in July if they all try to sell their homes at once? The property values, I'm talking about. Gumbo Limbo is a busy little place these days. People are trying to get themselves into position for when the big ax falls."

I found that interesting, so pressed Tomlinson to expand on it. "Arlis Futch," he said, "is one of the main players. If he gets some cash from Tallahassee, maybe he can convert his fish house into a little marina. If not, he'll go out of business. Mr. Futch is like: Screw it, pay me, don't pay me. What's he care? He's no kid and he owns it free and clear—that's what Hannah told me. That, plus some acreage across the road where he keeps cattle. Another one's this guy, remember the guy we met? Raymond Tullock? He's part of the picture, too, trying to pick his shots. Comes on very smooth, you know—'Hey, I'm just here to help out'—but he puts off very bad vibes. Hannah, she doesn't care. Nothing bothers her. Far as she's concerned, Tullock's just another guy who's got a terrible set of the hots for her. And let's face it, man—who doesn't?"

From outside, I heard Janet's voice call, "Doc? There's a man here to see you." She sounded preoccupied—all her concentration still on the tarpon.

Looked out to see Detective Ron Jackson standing on

the deck, as Tomlinson rattled on about Hannah shipping Jimmy's remains off to New Orleans—she wouldn't even let him say a few words over the coffin—and how he, mostly, was just keeping the ol' nose to the grindstone. Death of a traditional society. That was the theme.

He was talking about the book again.

I said, "Anything else you want me to do with your boat?"

"What I wanted," he said, "was to sail it up here. But there's not enough water to get a boat that size into Gumbo Limbo. So what I guess I'll do, Hannah's fishing tonight. She won't let me go because I won't help her pick mullet out of the net—no way will I kill a fish. So I told her, she gets down to Dinkin's Bay, you'd have my clothes in a bag, and you'd help her rig a towline for my dinghy. That way, at least, I'll have some transportation."

I resisted the urge to offer to deliver his gear to Gumbo Limbo.

Tomlinson said, "One more thing. About Hannah?"

Detective Jackson was standing on the deck, trying to make conversation with Janet. Janet was being polite about it, but she was also trying to concentrate on the tarpon. "Make it quick," I said.

"Hannah is, like . . . her own woman, man. She thinks of something? She *does* it."

What the hell did that mean? "So?"

"No restraints, man," he said. "Hear what I'm saying? She won't play the role. It's Hannah's way or the highway. Hell, I *hinted* at it, and she sat me right down. Made me see I was behaving like a typical male goof. She was right, too."

I said, "Huh?" Was he talking about sex . . . the book
. . . what?

"She's *free*. That's what I'm saying. She'd be pissed
if I let you think anything else . . . which is a scene I
genuinely choose to avoid. Like, no strings attached."

I said, "Tomlinson, if I'm supposed to understand
anything you've said—"

"Can't make it any plainer, man. And, Doc? Don't
forget about those fish fillets, okay?"

JACKSON WAS WEARING THE STANDARD UNIFORM OF
the five-day-a-week county-salaried detective: inexpensive brown sports coat, dark stay-pressed slacks, and
comfortable wing tips. He was so thick and bulky that
everything he wore appeared to be a size too small . . .
and he was still trying to talk to Janet when I appeared
outside. He looked up and fixed me with a thin, formal
smile. Said, "Seems like I'm always interrupting your
workouts." Meaning my running shorts, Nikes, and
sweaty T-shirt. "Are you all done? Or just getting
started?"

I said, "Just finishing up."

He seemed disappointed. "Too bad. I brought my
running clothes just in case. I was hoping we could
maybe go for a jog and have a little chat. You know—
mix business with pleasure."

I wondered if he was bluffing. Also wondered why he
wanted to waste my time and his with more questioning.
I had already told him everything I knew. Looked at him
standing there—two hundred or so pounds loaded onto
short, stubby legs—and thought about him hanging
around my fish house while I tried to shower. Pictured
him trying to pass the time with Janet while she was

attempting to work. The woman was just sitting there watching fish, couldn't possibly be doing anything important, so why not talk to her?

I shrugged before saying with measured indifference, "I guess a couple more miles wouldn't hurt. If you're serious."

"You feel like it?"

"Go ahead and change your clothes. Use my house."

Jackson went loping off to his car and returned with a gym bag. As he disappeared into the house, Janet said, "Thanks. He was starting to irritate me." As she spoke, she never took her eyes off the fish tank.

I said, "They're interesting animals, aren't they?"

"They're . . . gorgeous. Those big silver scales, the way they seem to change color."

"They're mirrors," I said. "A tarpon's scales? So they reflect the color of their environment. Brown sand, brown tarpon. Gray bottom, gray tarpon. See? It's an uncomplicated but effective method of disguise."

"*Right.* I hadn't even thought of that." One of the tarpon—a red pellet was attached to its tail—drifted to the surface, gracefully breached the water's film of surface tension, then flashed a brilliant silver as it rolled toward the bottom. It was followed by two more fish: yellow and blue.

Janet took up the clipboard and made careful notes.

I said, "Janet, I appreciate you helping out. But I'm starting to feel a little guilty about taking up so much of your time—"

"Don't you dare try to run me off now. I'm just getting to know these fish. That's the—" She lifted the clipboard as if to look, then decided against it. The fish might roll again. "I can't tell you right now, but that's at least the fourth time that Red has been the first to roll. Always followed by one or more of the others. You think that could mean something?''

I said, ''I think it's way too early to tell.''

''Oh, I know that. But I was just thinking—''

''Never theorize in advance of your data. It can cause you to manipulate your own observations.''

She had a pleasant, gusty laugh. ''I know, I know— that's exactly what I used to tell my students. My kids, wouldn't they love it if they could see me making the same mistake? I used to take them on all these crazy field trips, all these mini-research projects I'd set up. That was the first rule: Record first, interpret later.''

I decided the kids at her small high school had been very lucky students indeed.

Jackson was coming down the steps. He wore black running shorts, no shirt. The man was as hairy as a Kodiak bear. More muscular than I'd suspected too.

I touched Janet's shoulder. ''We won't be gone long.''

She nodded, her attention already back on the tarpon.

''Nice life,'' Jackson said to me. ''You've got an assistant to do all your work.''

I found the familiarity of that grating. I replied, ''Actually, Dr. Mueller is my associate, not my assistant.'' Which caused Janet to roll her eyes and smile. Then, without waiting for Jackson to follow, I walked down the fifty yards of wobbly dock, then charged off.

My plan was childish. If Jackson could catch up with me, fine. And if he did catch up, I'd run his stubby little legs off before he could find breath enough to ask a single question. It was his idea to run and talk at the same time. Mix a little business with pleasure, he had

said. I wondered just how much pleasure he'd get out
of collapsing like a winded bull.

So I was pushing it. Running at a pace slightly faster
than I normally run on my very best day. Trying to put
some distance between myself and the pushy detective.
When I lost him, when he was so far behind that he had
to strain to see me, I would then stop and patiently wait.
Let him know that next time—if there had to be a next
time—he would be wise to simply question me over the
phone.

Less than a minute had passed when, behind me, I
heard a heavy crunch of shell, *ka-thump-ka-thump-ka-
thump,* getting closer, growing louder . . . heard the
flesh-slap of swinging arms. Heard the comfortable
rhythm of controlled breathing. Then saw the bear shape
of Jackson out of the corner of my eye. Heard him say,
"Mind if we pick up the pace a little?" as he strode
past me.

I accelerated until I was even with him, then fell into
step.

"Nice day for a little jog," he said.

"Not too hot, not too cold," I replied, fighting to
restrain my breathing; keeping my voice nonchalant.

"No humidity," Jackson said. "Humidity, that's what
kills you."

"Yeah, humidity's the worst."

"But now—like *Arizona*. Great place to run, Sanibel."

"A day like this," I said, "it's perfect."

"Good surface, too." He was talking about the bi-
cycle path. We were headed northwest toward Captiva.
Coconut palms and oaks; egrets spooking—everything

moving past in a blur. He said, "Makes me want to stretch it out a little bit."

"Stretch it out all you want," I told him, hoping like hell he wouldn't—but he did.

That's the way it went for the next three miles or so. Ran way too far, way too fast, each of us pushing the other. We didn't talk. I didn't have air enough to speak, and my throat was too dry had I tried. I had the strong impression that it was equally painful for Jackson, but the stubborn little bastard wouldn't quit. And just when I was beginning to wonder which would fail first, my lungs or my courage, Jackson said in a raspy wheezing voice, "So it's kind'a like the tree-falling-in-a-forest deal. If we both keep this up, will anyone be around to hear our hearts explode?"

I broke stride, laughing. Began to walk in a slow circle, hands clasped and overhead, sucking in air. Jackson was doing the same. After a minute or two, when I was able, I said, "Uncle. You win."

He grinned. "Bullshit. I can't even remember the last quarter-mile or so. I died way back there."

"Nope. That was a stupid kid's stunt I pulled. You gave me exactly what I deserved."

"You?" He seemed honestly perplexed. "It was me. I was trying to run *you* into the ground. Soften you up a little so we could talk. I mean, no offense, but you don't exactly look like a runner. I figured you for a nine-minute-mile guy. The way you're built. One of those 'Oooh, look at the birds' or 'Oooh, aren't those flowers pretty?' types."

I said wryly, "And you're such a wispy little bit of a thing. Lucky for me I'm not the kind to judge people by their body types."

Jackson was nonplussed, wearing an expression that read, *Damn*. He said, "Three years playing defensive back at Maryland, four years in the Marines, and very few people ever stuck me like you just stuck me, Ford." He placed hands on hips, bent deeply at the waist, sucked in a little more air before extending his right hand. "So call me Ron from now on."

"Okay . . . Ron." I took his hand. "But tell me one thing: Why soften me up before talking? What's the point? I've told you everything I know."

"I don't doubt it. But I've got a problem." He had begun to walk along the bike path, back toward Dinkin's Bay. "The problem is, I drove up to Sulphur Wells yesterday. About my sixth time just for this case, trying to talk to people, make a few contacts. What do I find? I find your buddy Tomlinson. The guy never called me for an interview, by the way. So I spent half an hour or so talking to him there. He's kind of an . . . unusual person."

"Unusual" wasn't strong enough—Tomlinson, the dope fiend, had just spent ten minutes with me on the phone, pondering everything but the air quality on Sulphur Wells, but he couldn't take the time to tell me he had been questioned by the police?

"I have to admit," Jackson said, "the connection kind of surprised me. Jimmy Darroux's widow, your buddy. Knock on the door and there they are. Less than a week after the husband gets fried at your marina. Mrs. Darroux is a real looker, your buddy's there smiling at me. But kind of nervous. Both of them living there under the same roof."

I stopped. "All cops make Tomlinson nervous. I think he took one too many shots to the head back in the sixties. He was the draft card-burning, protester type. So if you're still thinking that I or Tomlinson had anything to do with the explosion last Thursday—''

He made an impatient hushing motion with his hand. ''Relax. Don't be so damn touchy. If I thought either one of you had anything to do with it, you wouldn't see me until I had the cuffs ready. No—it's kind'a strange, you can't argue that. That's all I'm saying. Your buddy and the widow. If I hadn't already checked both of you out pretty closely, I might come to a different conclusion. But I did, so that's not the problem. It's something else. I figure, maybe you can help me with it, maybe you can't.''

I began to walk with him again. Said, ''So tell me about your problem, Ron.''

RON JACKSON'S PROBLEM WAS THAT RESIDENTS ON SUL-phur Wells wouldn't talk to him. Weren't being very helpful at all. Not just the people of Gumbo Limbo, either. Same was true of the island's other small settle-ments: Barrancas, Key Lime, Rancho, and Curlew.

The Bureau of Alcohol, Tobacco, and Firearms was assisting in the investigation, Jackson told me. Which meant the A.T.F. would do the lab work, all the intricate, complicated tracing of evidence, while he and one other detective did the local legwork. But after half a dozen trips to the island, Jackson had yet to assemble much more than was already in Jimmy Darroux's police file.

''It's getting embarrassing,'' he said. Judging from the rueful tone of his voice, he meant it.

One of the reasons the job was so tough, he said, was that his department didn't have a single cop who had roots on the island. There were a couple who lived on

Sulphur Wells, yes. One had grown up there. But none were from the commercial fishing community. Because of that, he said, the normal sources for gathering information weren't there to cultivate.

We were still walking along the bike path. I did most of the listening; he was doing most of the talking, explaining how it was. "I told you I once worked in D.C.? You go into one of the projects there, one of the housing slums, it was like that. Code of silence. Never tell the cops anything. In a way, I didn't blame them. They're practically living under siege. Nothing much good had ever come from the outside, so why help? I'm starting to think it's the same sort of thing on Sulphur Wells."

I was thinking: Is he telling me this for a reason? But I said, "Could be some similarities. The fishermen have spent the last couple of years under attack. The attacks have come from some sophisticated sources; sources they were never equipped to deal with. The state government, newspapers, regional publications. Probably people who live on their own island. Not everyone's a commercial fisherman up there. They've got a few retirees, a few businesspeople. People who probably see themselves as sportfishermen. They got it from all sides. That would make anyone defensive."

"See?" Jackson said. "Already you're helping me get things clearer in my own mind."

I thought: Quid pro quo; you'd better give me an explanation in trade. But I said, "There's an additional element you wouldn't find in the projects. A reason they probably don't want to talk to you. The commercial fishing community can't afford any more bad publicity. One of their outlaws torched some boats and was killed in the process. There's a good reason they want it to stop right there.'' I explained to him about the injunction the commercial fishermen had filed, and about the economic relief they were soliciting from the state. Then I said, ''The point of your investigation is to find out who helped Jimmy Darroux build a bomb, right? So you can add some more commercial fishermen to the list. More bad publicity. Or else you wouldn't be talking to me.''

Jackson became noncommittal. Evasion is always couched as innocence. ''I'm just trying to collect what I can, see where it takes me. Hell, I don't know much more than you do, Ford.''

I was tempted to start running again, make him suffer just for lying to me. If my legs hadn't been so noodle-weak, I might have. Instead, I said, ''So maybe we ought to drop the subject. Usually—what I do when I run?— I take time out to enjoy the birds.''

He said, ''What?''

''Birds. When I run, I like to look at the birds.''

He made a groaning noise. ''Jesus.''

''Have you noticed all the pretty flowers we have on Sanibel? Too much talking ruins the scenery.''

He said, ''Okay, okay. Enough.''

I said, ''It can't be all give and no take.''

''I see that. So I tried, okay?''

''I doubt I can help you anyway.''

''What'll it take for you to give it a try?''

''Simple. Tell me what I'm getting into. And why. That's all. You tell me that, we'll talk. You can't tell me . . .'' I shrugged, letting the sentence trail off.

We walked along while he mulled it over. Finally, he said, ''Where I grew up, up on the Chesapeake, my grandfather and his grandfather were oystermen. My dad, he got seasick, so he went into the state troopers.

So it was my job to help Grandpa. I'm telling you why I'm interested. Understand?"

I said, "The Chesapeake. Nice area."

"We did a little striped bass fishing, but mostly oysters. I saw what happened to our fishery—hell, they nearly netted it clean—but I still had mixed feelings about the regulations, and then the bans, because I was one of them. One of the fishermen, see? It was like, who the hell are these outsiders coming in telling us what we can and can't do? So I can understand that a little bit. It was pretty nasty. Seeing it happen, you know? What happened to the people."

I said, "Oysterman, huh?"

He held out his arms and smiled. "I didn't get these forearms in a weight room. Tonging oysters; a forty-five-pound rake. My grandfather'd drop a galvanized chain off the stern of the boat. He could tell when we were on oysters by holding the chain, feeling the vibrations. Made a pretty fair living, too. I bought myself my first car with tonging money. But it wasn't the environmentalists who finally put us out of business. It was the way the water quality went to hell when all the new people started flooding in."

I said, "So you do know a little bit about it."

He was nodding. "About the kind of people involved. I imagine they're about the same. Most of them are pretty good people. Solid. Don't ask for anything, stay out of trouble. In D.C., the kids couldn't wait until they were old enough to qualify for welfare. First of the month, some of the lines were four blocks long. On the Chesapeake, a lot of those men and women, the government couldn't force them to take it. Welfare? Not them—they had too much self-respect. Personally, Ford,

I admire that. I don't know much about the situation here. Maybe it was smart to ban the nets, maybe it's all a bunch of crap. I do know it's a shitty situation. And I know . . . well, there was this thing that happened when I was a kid.'' He made an effort to continue, then: ''Ah, hell—''

I tried to goad him along. ''You mean with the commercial fishermen.''

Jackson thought for a moment, not sure he wanted to go into it. Finally, he said, ''Let's just say I saw what can happen when people are pushed into a corner. I was like, seventeen, and this kid I knew got burned really bad. For what? Some idiotic demonstration. Trying to get even because his dad had to sell out, look for new work. It's not a nice thing to see.''

''No, I imagine not,'' I said.

''Five thousand people get laid off by General Motors, it's no big deal, right? But somehow, it's different when it happens to people who . . . just do what they do, on their own. No unions to back them up, just them, just people. Know what I mean? So what I'm saying is, I'd like to get in there, if I can, and stop some of it before it starts. Yeah, I'd love to nail the whole Jimmy Darroux business shut. But I'd also like to get the right people under my thumb before anyone else gets hurt.'' He looked at me. ''To do that, to stop anything, I need information.''

Which I had already guessed. I said, ''You think because Tomlinson is involved with Hannah Darroux, I can pry information out of him, then feed it to you.''

''Maybe. She's an important woman on that island. People wouldn't tell me much, but I learned that. She's an insider, and I'd be willing to bet she knows a hell of a lot more than she told me or the A.T.F. guys. But no—'' He was making his gesture of impatience again. Apparently, we were getting off track. ''Where you could help is, the people I talked to on Sulphur Wells, the people I've talked to around here. Your name kept popping up.''

''Oh?''

''Yeah. That surprise you?'' Jackson had a crafty, troublemaker's smile. ''Maybe you were with the National Security Agency so long you're not used to that. Where you were a . . . a paper shuffler, right?''

Who the hell had he been talking to? ''What I am,'' I said, ''is a biologist.''

His expression said: *Sure, buddy, sure.* He shrugged. ''Okay. We leave it at that. What I'm saying is, you're the only guy who seems to be accepted by both communities. The sportfishing guys are your buddies, right?''

''I know quite a few of them, yeah.''

''This guy on Sulphur Wells—Tootsie Cribbs?—he told me you were about the only so-called sportfishing guy who came down on the side of the netters. He said you spoke for them a couple times at meetings.''

I'd known Tootsie since high school. He ran a little fish wholesale place in Curlew. ''I did that. Yeah.''

''People on both sides of the line know you, they respect you. That's the way I read it. Couple of people on Sulphur Wells mentioned you. Said you come over there sometimes and buy fish and stuff for your lab. Know what they said?'' He looked very smug—I was the guy he'd lured into a schoolyard footrace. ''What they said was, they think you're fair.''

I said, ''Spare me the flattery.''

"No, I'm serious. Fair. That's the word."

"They think that? Good. But what you're saying is, you think I can act as an intermediary. My question is: What's left to mediate?"

"For one thing, I know some of the sportfishing guys are going around with guns. That's bullshit. They catch someone stealing their outboard, what they gonna do, blow them away? Kill somebody over a motor? You can start there. Talk it around among your friends. Reason with them. They ever shoot anybody before? They have any idea what it's like?"

I got the impression that Ron Jackson had . . . and did.

"And on Sulphur Wells . . . some of the other commercial places, too. I've heard—not from a very good source—but I've heard they have some real nasty stuff planned. Most of it's probably talk. People, you get them loaded up on whiskey . . . hell, you know the type. They like to talk big, but very few are actually stupid enough to do the big deed. That report about somebody stretching a cable across some markers—" He gave me a nudge: *See? Your name again!* "That report tells me we've got a couple of legitimate bandits. Sure, if you can get some information out of Hannah Darroux . . . love to have it. Through your buddy Tomlinson, I don't care how. Go over there and buy some more fish, ask around. Don't get the wrong idea. I'm not deputizing you or anything. If I thought you were the type to go out and strut around, bang your chest, we wouldn't be having this conversation. This isn't official. I'm asking a favor. Keep it low-key, nothing obvious." The crafty, troublemaker smile again. "But there I go telling you your business."

"That's your proposition? I find out what I can, help you keep a lid on things?"

He was nodding. "How many times do cops have a chance to stop trouble before it starts? Yeah, you could help me do that. Little things. You hear something, you give me a call. We get back, I'll give you my cellular number, my beeper. Anytime, day or night." Ron was pleased with how this was going. I could tell. "Up on the Chesapeake," he said, "maybe if some cop had jumped into the middle of things, Terry . . . that friend of mine . . . would have lived beyond the ripe old age of nineteen."

"There's one thing you've left out."

"There is?"

"Yeah. The bomb. Tell me about Darroux's bomb. Why it's got you on the move. Why you don't believe he built it by himself."

"I never said that."

"Let's not play games. Darroux was the impulsive type, right? He gets mad, he starts a brawl. His wife tries to lock him out, he smacks her. A guy like him wants revenge, he might steal some engines, or he might dump some gas and light it. My guess is, you read him the same way. But your people found something at the marina, something at the bomb site, that tells you whoever made the bomb had to do a little tinkering first. They had to sit down and think it out. That wasn't Darroux's style." In reply to his quizzical glance, I said, "You know a little bit about fishing. I know a little bit about bombs. Accelerant flare, remember? Point of detonation?"

"Okay. So, if you were a pissed-off netter and wanted to torch some boats, how would you have done it?"

"You trying to steer me off the subject?"

"No. I'm trying to decide if it would make any difference me telling you something I'm not authorized to tell you."

I thought for a moment before saying, "Do you want casualties, or just structural damage?"

"That's the scary thing. I don't think the people who built this bomb cared."

"That simplifies it. Then all you need is an initiator, a power source, and the accelerant. The accelerant is easy—go to a gas station or any hardware store." I touched the cheap Ironman model watch on my wrist. "I've got enough voltage right here to detonate a standard commercial blasting cap. So power source is no problem. But even that's a lot more complicated than it needs to be."

I described a couple of basic explosive devices—booby traps, they were once called.

When I was done, Jackson gave a soft whistle. "The first two, I've heard about. Lids from a tin can, a clothespin. Sure. Very effective, very easy. But that last one. A Ping-Pong ball and a hypodermic needle? Jesus, that one's spooky. That one really would work?"

I almost said, "I've seen it work." Instead, I said, "That's what I read. Since the late sixties, the revolutionary types have published black market booklets on the subject." I listed some of the names.

Jackson knew them. We talked about that. We talked about the lunatic fringe. We talked about the political far right and the political far left being different sides of the same frightening coin. We talked about dangerous times, and maybe Australia would be nice, or New Zealand. Go down there to Auckland, watch the America's

Cup races. Finally, as we turned at the shell road into Dinkin's Bay, Jackson began to tell me about the bomb. "What the A.T.F. people found," he said, "was enough to tell us that it was probably too sophisticated for Jimmy Darroux. Like you said, he was the impulsive type. This bomb would have taken some sober thinking and some reading."

"The A.T.F. is sure about that?"

"Yeah. What they found were the leg wires from a blasting cap, some bits of wire from the internal workings of an outboard motor, and a chunk of timing switch off a battery charger."

I said, "So, when they trace the components back, you'll have your bad guys."

Jackson was shaking his head. "The wire was from a two-hundred-horse Mercury built two years ago in Fond du Lac, Wisconsin, sold out of a Bonita Springs marina to a guy we've already interviewed. He reported the motor stolen three months ago. The battery charger was the type fishermen use to keep their trolling motors charged up. Same thing. It was on a boat stolen last month. Listed on the insurance claim sheet along with the other stuff the owner had on the boat. Everything the A.T.F. found was stolen material."

"The blasting cap?"

"The leg wires were off a Combie Model 305 L-P, made within the last two years and used commonly by contractors. Build roads, blast rock quarries. That sort of thing. The A.T.F. people haven't been able to trace it that fine yet. They're not sure they'll be able to. A blasting cap always maintains a paper trail—least, it's supposed to—but there are a bunch of them out there."

That was certainly true. I'd used blasting caps to do

fish-census work on small bodies of water.

Jackson said, ''So that's what we're faced with. We'll have your standard pissed-off, drunk commercial fishermen out there setting fires, stealing engines—maybe stretching cables. We'll have your standard pissed-off, drunk sportfishermen out there trying to get even. But a guy who will sit down with a book, figure out how to make a bomb, then actually do it—that's a whole different animal.''

I said, ''Yeah, but they're novices. There's no doubt about that.''

In reply to Jackson's upraised eyebrows, I added, ''Jimmy Darroux? The guy who carries the bomb isn't supposed to get blown up, right?''

ELEVEN

THAT AFTERNOON, I MOTORED OVER TO TOMLIN-
son's sailboat to get the gear he said he needed. I
had no idea what time Hannah would come by to
get his stuff. Presumably, she would be out mullet fishing, so it might be dusk or it might be midnight. Some
perverse side of me hoped it would be late; the later, the
better. I was, perhaps, suffering what the writer Jack
London, in his letters, referred to as the urges of "ani-
mal-man." It is described less succinctly now: horny . . .
pocket-proud . . . three-legged and dumb. All of which
were accurate enough, but realizing it made me feel no
less insipid.

Even so, motoring toward Tomlinson's *No Más*, I
tested out potential scenarios: Invite Hannah in, show
her around. Put on some music—see if she liked Crosby,
Stills, Nash, and Young as much as The Doors. Offer
her a drink—that was the sociable thing to do. Someone
had left a bottle of wine in my refrigerator, but it had
been opened . . . three weeks ago? Maybe longer. Well
. . . she might enjoy it anyway. It couldn't be any
stronger than that sulfur-water tea of hers. Let her walk
around my place, wineglass in hand . . . feel the vibra-

tion of her weight through the wooden floor—just like at Gumbo Limbo, where she'd traced the shape of my ear with her fingernail, and told me about watching me take my rain barrel shower.

Then I caught myself. Was it happening again?

As I stood at the controls of my boat, I made a conscious effort to shift the subject to other matters. . . .

No problem. Not at all like the previous Thursday night when, for a short time, I had so clearly demonstrated symptoms of obsession that I still found it surprising . . . a little troubling, too.

I smiled; spoke aloud: "You dumb ass." And thought: If I invite Hannah in, it will only be to gather information for Jackson.

But, at the same time, my perverse side whispered: A glass of wine . . . music. Remember? *No strings attached . . .*

ONCE ON TOMLINSON'S BOAT, I DIDN'T EVEN HAVE TO step down into the cabin to realize that no, there was not sufficient ice in the man's ice locker, and yes, the fish fillets had been unhappily decomposing in this happy vegetarian home.

So, using a plastic bag in lieu of gloves, I dropped the mess overboard. Was tempted to drop the plastic bag and plate overboard too, but enough people were already using the coast as a garbage dump. Finally decided what the ice locker needed was a bucket of Clorox water, a lot of scrubbing, then a good airing out. If it wasn't done now, the stink would seep into the cushions.

Each time I lifted out some remnant of macrobiotic, vegetarian goo, each time I had to lunge up out of the Clorox fumes to suck a fresh breath of air, I reminded myself that Tomlinson would not have hesitated to perform the same nasty task for me.

If he wasn't too preoccupied to think about it . . .

When I got back to my fish house, Janet was just finishing up. By my reckoning, she had notes on four separate hours of tarpon observation, those hours spaced between ten a.m. and five p.m. She looked pretty proud of herself, standing there in baggy jeans and brown sweatshirt. Stood by my side as I went over her field notes on the clipboard; had a nervous habit of licking her lips whenever I paused over an entry or seemed even mildly confused.

"At this point—" She was pointing to one of the field sheets I had composed. "That's when the man showed up to see you. Uh—"

"Ron Jackson," I provided.

"Yeah, but what happened was, I lost my concentration, so I was unsure if I'd seen Green Flag roll first or the Red Threat, so I just—"

"The Red Threat?" I asked, smiling at her.

She whacked me on the sleeve and said, "You spend four or five hours watching a bunch of fish, I'd like to hear the names *you'd* give them! You know, from history class? The *red threat*?" As if I were being dumb. "I'm a teacher, for God's sake. You think they only let us teach one subject at a school with only four hundred kids? But what I was telling you about was that entry—"

"The other fish is Green Flag? Is that like Greenpeace or—"

"As in the Green Flag Moslems? In Egypt, but after the decline? Geez, Ford, you must read nothing but journals."

Now I really was beginning to feel dumb.

"Okay, okay, they are very . . . well thought-out names."

Janet lowered the clipboard. Had a nice little energy in her laugh. "You think it's silly, don't you? Naming the fish. Honest now, all the time you spend with them, you never gave them names?"

I had never even named my boats. "Let me think here—"

"Because to me, they seem to have individual . . . It's like they behave differently, one not like the other. The Red Threat, he's the mobile type. He doesn't wait for the others to act, he just does it. Swoops around in there when he's in the mood, and the others follow." She paused, looking at me. She was serious. "You never have favorites?"

"Well . . ."

"But don't think it influenced any of my observations," she added quickly; she'd realized what I might have been thinking and wanted to put my mind at ease. "Everything's there on the field sheets, just how I saw it."

I took the clipboard from her, leafed through the sheets. "You know what you've done here? When Breder and Shlaifer did their work back in the forties, they observed their tarpon for one hour a day over a period of twenty-two consecutive days. Today alone, you've broadened the standards."

On the field sheets were entry columns for: "Time; Water Temperature; Rises per Fish Hour; Greatest Time Between Rises; Percent of Minutes with No Rises." Each column was neatly filled with her penciled entries. Four pages—one for every hour of observation. I said,

"I don't expect you to spend every day sitting with those fish. . . . What I'm saying is, you've already done four days of work here." I glanced at the clipboard again. "Looks like very good work, too."

She was pleased. Made self-deprecating remarks about how she had been a little sloppy here, could have done a little better there. I put my hand on her shoulder; felt her pull away instinctively, then relax enough to lean briefly against me. "It's all fine. Hell . . . it's great."

"I can keep working on the project?"

I told her, "Lady, it is now *our* project. If I get around to publishing something on it, instead of saying Breder-Shlaifer it'll say Mueller-Ford."

"Nope—you've got to at least take top billing."

"If I ever get to know the fish on a first-name basis, then we'll discuss it."

We stood there talking about the project. We shouldn't be surprised, I told her, if our results differed from Breder-Shlaifer, because we were doing the procedure in January. They had done it in June, when the water was much warmer. Then we talked about the possibility that at least some tarpon behavior was social behavior . . . and of course, mature fish might behave differently than immature fish . . . and Janet said it might be interesting to see what happened if a glass plate was suspended at the water's surface so that the fish could not roll.

"That procedure's been done," I told her. "Even in water that was heavily oxygenated, the fish died. Might be interesting to duplicate that one, too, try to find out why—"

"Oh, no way," she said with feeling. She glanced toward the tank: the Red Threat, Green Flag, and the others were in there. "I couldn't be a part of that."

I dropped the subject. Mostly what I did was wrestle with my own conscience. It was getting late. The sky had taken on the slate-gray and raspberry hues peculiar to the Gulf Coast in January. High, high up in corridors traveled only by tourist jets and the combat jockeys, wispy cirrus clouds showed the pathway of global winds. But down in Dinkin's Bay it was balmy, warm. . . . It was also dinnertime. I owed Janet a dinner . . . owed her a lot more than that for all her work. But I also knew that if I left, I risked missing Hannah. Why hadn't Tomlinson offered a time? Why hadn't I asked? Or he could have had Hannah call me on the VHF . . .

Caught myself and thought: You're a dumb ass, Ford. A familiar charge from a familiar source.

I looked at Janet standing there: solid, pudgy, plain face, short mousy hair, good eyes. Saw that a little light had come back into them after her day with the tarpon.

"You want to go get something to eat?" I was saying it before I had even decided to speak.

"Are you sure you have the time? There's not something else you'd rather—"

I took her by the elbow and steered her toward the boardwalk. "Mueller, just give me time to grab a shower and change. Twenty minutes?"

Nice smile; a touch of irony in it. "Make it twenty-five, Ford. I'm the one who's been working. Remember?"

WE CHOSE THE LAZY FLAMINGO, NEAR BLIND PASS. ONE of the few restaurants on Sanibel or Captiva that had a kicked-back, shorts-and-thongs, out-island quality to it. Since they'd closed Timmy's Nook, anyway. Heavy raw

wood furniture, ceiling fans whirling, some palm thatching for effect. Go to the bar and place your own order,
then sit in your booth while the waitress brings beer that
is served from buckets of ice.

I chose the raw conch salad, lots of onion and lime
juice. Also ordered the grilled grouper sandwich, plus a
large Caesar salad—heavy on the anchovies—an order
of fries . . . and garlic bread.

Janet said, "Is that for both of us, or just you?"—
her tone pleasantly sarcastic.

I told her that a day spent on a chair watching fish
was slothful compared to the day I had had. She ordered
the grilled grouper . . . canceled it, just asked for the
Caesar—the extra weight she carried was probably on
her mind—then we found an open booth by the window.
She sat there looking around; I guessed she was wondering what to talk about—there's a limit to how much
can be said about fish. So, when I felt the silence become
strained, I told her about the Ford-Jackson hell run.
Which got her laughing. She said she could just picture
us out there, two huge kids lumbering along, both of us
too stubborn to quit. I told her about Tomlinson's icebox. She made the appropriate grimace of disgust, but
had to add: "Have you ever looked into his eyes? Tomlinson has the most wonderful eyes. I know he's . . . unusual. Where I'm from? He'd be considered some kind
of eccentric up home."

I said, "I've yet to find a place that wouldn't consider
him eccentric. That's on his quiet days."

"I know, but . . . he has the most . . . gentle way about
him. Don't you think? You meet him, you feel as if
you've always known him. He . . . empathizes with people. No, that's not the word." She puzzled over it for a

moment before saying, "He *feels* for people, that's what
he does. Not just empathizes, but gives you the impression he actually feels what you are feeling. I don't know
how he does it. Telepathy? I'm not sure I believe in that.
But somehow he does it, and he seems like . . . such a
nice and gentle man."

I took a sip of my beer; should have considered it
longer before speaking, but I asked the question anyway:
"Is that why he's the only one you told why you left
Ohio?" Saw the reaction in her face—a nervous,
stricken look—and instantly regretted my words.
Reached out, patted her hand. Said, "I'm sorry. It's none
of my business. I had no right to ask."

She sat there for a moment—at least she hadn't pulled
her hand away—head down, staring at the table. Finally,
she lifted her face to me—the cloudy expression of shell
shock had returned—then asked in a small, small voice,
"Tomlinson *told* you?" as if she had been betrayed.

There have been times in my life—too many times,
I'm sad to admit—I have spoken or acted so unthink-
ingly that I do not doubt that civilized people would be
better off if I simply returned to the jungles where I
spent so many of my years. Build myself a bamboo hut.
Hang a sign over the door: *Beware the Big Dumb Shit.*
Use a stick to bang a hollowed-out log if I absolutely
have to communicate.

I took her hand in both of mine, and squeezed. "No,
Tomlinson wouldn't do that. All he told me . . . the *only*
thing he told me was that you and he had had some long
conversations. Because I know Tomlinson, I assumed
the rest. It's one of my eccentricities—prying into other
people's business just to remind myself how rude I really am. Which is a nicer way of saying that I'm way

too nosy. I'm sorry. Please believe me, Janet.''

It was a while before she spoke. I sat there feeling helplessly big and clumsy. Finally . . . finally, she patted my hand . . . looked at me with cool, remote eyes and said, ''Of course I believe you. I'd . . . like to tell you about it. But it's not easy for me. It's taken a long time to—''

''Forget it,'' I interrupted. ''When you're in the mood, I'm ready to listen. A couple of weeks from now . . . or after we finish the tarpon procedure. Or not—you decide.'' I glanced around at the busy waitresses. ''Jesus, where *is* that food?''

A gusty sound of laughter burst from her lips—an emotional release. She said, ''No one would ever say that you have kind eyes. But you're kind. I used to watch you around the marina, and you seemed . . . so remote. Like you're there, but you're really someplace else. When I first saw you? That's what I'm talking about. You actually seemed kind of scary.''

''I scare myself,'' I put in helpfully. Didn't add: *Beware the big dumb shit.*

''But then I saw the way you treated that poor man. From the explosion? And the way you are with the others around the marina. Mostly, though, I know you're kind because you let me do all the observations today, and I know—don't tell me otherwise, either—I know you really wanted to do it.''

''Baloney,'' I said. ''I took advantage of you. I lazed around on the beach and did other childish things while you worked. Which is why I'm paying the tab.'' The food was coming. I was more grateful for the opportunity to change the subject than the chance to eat.

We ate in silence for a time. Good raw conch salad,

good sandwich. When we did talk, I was careful to keep the topic within safe borders. Fish, biology, running. She spoke of trying to lose weight—I could hear the frustration in her voice. These are modern times. All men and women are required to fight hard to maintain the preferred Prime-Time American uniform: thin. But it's harder on the women because they must not only be thin, they must be fashion model-gaunt. Television commercials, like certain poisons, have to have a cumulative effect. So Janet was one of the ones who battled daily in an attempt to match the images they saw in the mirror with the images pressed upon them by the television screen.

As she picked at her Caesar salad, she said things like, "If I just had more willpower . . . exercise till I drop, and things still don't seem to change much . . . have you heard of that new powder diet?"

I said things such as "Genetic coding . . . the effective storage system of wandering Nordic tribes . . . think in terms of fitness, not fat."

WHEN WE WERE FINISHED, I WALKED HER OUTSIDE TO-ward my old chevy pickup truck. I'd had the engine overhauled recently, the brake pads and brake lines replaced, then had the truck painted a very handsome—I believed—shade of navy gray. I liked the pearlike shape of the cab, and the fact that its six-cylinder engine was so simple that even I could work on it. The color seemed to match the functionality of the truck.

That was what I was explaining to her—why I maintained an old truck rather than buy a new one—when, as I reached for the passenger's-side door handle, Janet suddenly took me by the elbow and said, "Let's walk."

She used her chin to motion toward the beach across the road.

So we walked. It was a good night for it: blustery January sea wind pushing surf onto the beach, making a surging, waterfall roar. Black night with a new moon drifting down the western sky; winter stars gauging the velocity of scudding clouds. Tropical Mexico and the jungles of Yucatan were somewhere out there, beyond the far range of horizon. But here, on Sanibel, a Canadian wind culled sand from the beach and stung us.

We were walking south, away from Blind Pass. Probably walked five minutes or so before she pulled my arm tight to her—an attempt to conceal herself, I sensed, rather than a gesture of affection—and she said in a steady, controlled voice, "I want to tell you about what happened. It would be good for me to talk about it, they . . . That's what I've been told. But it's not easy, and I want you to understand that I'm getting better. I don't want you to think I'm the kind who goes around whining about poor me me me. But there are things—I know this now—there are things that you can't keep bottled up inside."

I said, "Then you probably need to talk about it."

She sighed. I could feel her body shudder involuntarily. "Okay, what happened was, the reason I left Ohio was . . . I had what you would call a nervous breakdown. Those words—nervous breakdown—you hear them all the time, so they don't seem like much. You know, so-and-so had a nervous breakdown? But when you go through it . . . it's not so simple. I was convinced that I really had gone . . . gone completely insane. Only I hadn't. The doctors, it took them a long time to convince me. I spent nearly a year under their care, and it was several months before I finally began to believe that I wasn't really crazy, I was just reacting to . . . what I'd been through. I was suffering severe depression and what they called anxiety attacks. These things, the attacks, would seem to just descend on me—in the classroom, at the store, anyplace. Like poison gas almost, and it was the most terrifying experience. . . .''

She paused, trying to wrestle her emotions into control. I said, ''You don't have to go on with this. You became ill. Human beings are susceptible to illness—there are emotional viruses just as there are physical viruses. So now you're in Florida recuperating, and things are going better—''

She tapped my arm, hushing me. ''That's not it,'' she said. ''I'm avoiding it again. I started to tell you what happened, and that's what I'm going to do.'' She cleared her throat . . . made a brave attempt to continue, then completely broke down. I patted her, I made little clucking noises. She told me what she could in little spurts. Over the next hour and several miles of beach, the whole story came out. She kept saying, ''I know *worse* things have happened to people.''

Sadly, it was true. But not much worse.

As early as grade school, Janet had known that she was not, and would never be, drop-dead attractive. But she grew up with enough good people, and enough self-esteem, that it didn't matter much. At one point she said, ''You've seen those women—women who are smart and talented but, because of the way they look, they end up with men no one else would have? I wasn't going to let that happen to me.''

She didn't. She dated occasionally, but not much. What she did was wait . . . and wait . . . and wait until just the right man came along. Four years ago, he finally did. His name was Roger Mueller. Roger worked for some state agency, and he was assigned to the northwest section of Ohio. Roger was good at his work. He also played bluegrass music—even made his own instruments—and had personal interests that were far-ranging. He liked to read. He liked to laugh. True, he was no screen idol. What he was was an average-looking but very kind and decent man. Janet fell madly in love with Roger; he fell madly in love with her.

"From the moment we met, it was like we were meant to be together," she told me. "Roger felt the same way. All those years, he'd been waiting for just the right person to come along, too. Then, to finally find each other . . ."

They married. They bought a small farmhouse north of town, which they completely remodeled. Did all the work themselves after dinner, on weekends. Because they both wanted to start a family, part of the remodeling included a nursery just off the master bedroom. The first year it didn't happen, but the second year it did. Janet was pregnant. "Up to that point, I'd had a good life," she said. "Pretty well-adjusted and happy. Then to find Roger and get pregnant, too . . . I'd never imagined that kind of happiness."

And that's when the big hammer fell.

Roger was driving home late after work one snowy night. On the same road, coming from the opposite direction, was a woman who had no license because of her long history of alcohol abuse.

All that Janet could remember from that night, and the week that followed, was a highway patrolman coming to the door . . . then a nurse crying with her, at her bedside, because of the miscarriage.

Janet tried to resume her teaching duties, but couldn't function in the classroom. She took sick leave, but couldn't function at home. Finally, she ended up in a hospital, then a mental health facility.

"Learning how to deal with the panic attacks," she said, "was the thing that finally convinced me I wasn't completely crazy. When I'd feel one coming I'd keep reminding myself what the doctors told me: The attacks were unpleasant as hell, but they were harmless. All that fear was being manufactured by my own brain. I didn't have to control it. All I had to do was learn to wait it out, and it would leave. That's when the attacks began to go away, and I began to get better."

We were walking north now, quartering into wind. Janet had cried herself dry. Her voice was weary, but solid; it had an even timbre that I liked. The woman was a survivor. She would be okay.

"I came to Florida because they suggested I have a complete change of scenery," she said. "They said I was well enough for it. I'd had enough solid weeks in a row. Buying the houseboat . . . I don't know—living on a boat was something I'd wanted to do since I was a girl. I had the money from the insurance, so . . ." She shrugged. "It still isn't easy. I feel myself getting scared sometimes, all the old fears coming back. But I've learned to ignore it, and it doesn't last. I'm glad I ended up in Dinkin's Bay. The people there are . . . such a funny little group." She chuckled. "I think the other night—at Perbcot?—was the first time I'd really laughed in a long, long time. But the best thing . . . the best I've felt since it all happened, was taking notes on your tarpon today. It was all so . . . focused, watching those tarpon . . . so analytical that I didn't have time to feel any emotion. You know? Those tarpon, the way they behave. Every movement is so strong and sure. Perfectly alive, no regrets, no fears. Right there in the tank, living and so damn . . . pure.

We had been walking side by side. Now she laced her arm through mine. "What happened to Roger and our . . . our family . . . was a terrible, senseless, tragic thing. I know that, yet there's nothing in the world I can do to change it. But Roger was no quitter, and neither am I."

I said, "I think you're going to be fine, Janet."

"Maybe. No, I *will* be okay. I don't let myself think about the future. I take it one day at a time. I wake up in the morning and try to think good thoughts. Do the same when I go to bed at night. I miss him. I miss them both. It will be a long, long time before I'll be able to get involved with anyone else emotionally or physically." She looked up at me and added quickly, "That's not bitterness, Doc. It's what I know is best for me. I'm going to live a constructive life. As soon as I can, I'll go back to work. I *miss* my kids. For now, though"— she put a fist to her mouth and stifled a yawn—"what I need now is a lot of time. And probably the same thing you need after listening to all my blubbering—some sleep."

We walked on in silence. For some reason, I started thinking of this looney old uncle of mine, Tucker Gatrell, who lives down in the Everglades. Tuck had an old gator-poaching and drinking partner by the name of Joseph Egret. It was Joseph who once told me that life was scary enough to make a sled dog shiver. How an Everglades Indian knew anything about sled dogs is im-

possible to say. But Joseph was right. I couldn't relate
to Janet's account of psychological problems—Tomlinson often claims that emotion is the only quality I lack
as a human being. However, I could relate to her sense
of loss, and I was impressed by her determination. The
good ones do not always die young; neither do they ever,
ever quit. They keep finding ways to create and con-
struct, struggling all the while to endure, because we are,
above all else, a species of builders—though it seems
that more and more aberrant destroyers live among us.

Janet was one of the good ones. The good ones always
find a way.

When we got to the truck, I leaned down and kissed
her on the top of the head. Told her, ''Just don't be late
for work in the morning.''

TWELVE

IT WAS A LITTLE AFTER EIGHT P.M. WHEN HANNAH Smith arrived to get Tomlinson's gear. I was in the lab, futzing around with a box of old slide plates that I had collected over the years. Some people keep scrapbooks; I acquire slides. One of my favorites is of a newly hatched tarpon that is still in the eellike leptocephalus stage. Beneath the lowest power of my Wolfe stereomicroscope, the tarpon resembled a thread of translucent ribbon that was attached to a set of dragon jaws spiked with needlelike teeth.

If tarpon continued to grow in that form, if they did not metamorphose into an entirely different animal, no human being would have the courage to go near the water.

I had the goose-necked lamp on, clamped to the stainless steel lab table. In the next room, I had a new selection of Gregorian chants on the stereo. As I tinkered with the slides, I also deliberated over my decision to provide Ron Jackson with whatever information I could gather. I had agreed to help him, of course. I am not the Rotarian type; one who attends meetings, then volunteers for good causes. Nor am I a political animal. My previous work left me cold on politics. But I do believe that if you live in a community, you are obligated to contribute what you can. Jackson's offer was an opportunity to play a small part. Maybe I could help, maybe I couldn't, but I would try.

I had already spoken with Felix and Jeth about their armed patrols. They were tired of doing it anyway, they said, and agreed that it was a bad idea. They said they would try to talk some sense into Nels, and the other guides around the island.

Other than that, I had provided Jackson with the first names of the two troublemakers I knew about: Julie and J. D., whereabouts unknown. Gave him the name of a Sulphur Wells man that I remembered Hannah mentioning in association with boat thefts: Kemper Waits. Also told him about the sportfishermen in the big-wheeled truck who, presumably, had tried to vandalize my aquarium.

It wasn't much; I told him I would try to do more. In return, Jackson had promised to ask the Sanibel police to keep a close eye on my place.

So I was sitting there mulling over different methods I could use to gather information. Legal methods, I had to keep reminding myself. I was so involved with the novelty of that, plus my slides, that I had almost . . . *almost* . . . forgotten that Hannah was coming. Which is when I heard the outboard whine of an approaching boat. Heard the boat slow to idle, then felt my house jolt slightly as the boat swung up against the pilings of the dock. Heard a twangy, alto woman's voice call: "You coming out, Ford? Or you want me to come in and get you?"

I turned on the big deck spotlight, pushed my way out

the screen door . . . and there was Hannah. She was
wearing yellow Farmer John-style rain pants and a damp
green T-shirt. The pants bib was cinched up with sus-
penders. Her black hair was frazzled by the wind, and
she had used a red ribbon to tie it back into a ponytail.
She stood toward the bow of her little boat, one arm
thrown lazily over the PVC tube she used to steer it, and
was grinning up at me: wind-burnished skin, dark eyes,
white teeth, creases of dimples running from cheek to
chin.

"Tell you the truth," she called up, "I liked the way
you were dressed better last time." Referring to my out-
door shower.

"Are you always so dirty-minded, Hannah? Or just
with me?"

"Not always," she answered wryly. "And not just
with you." She was tying her skiff to the pilings; using
a very simple quick-release knot that very few boaters
seemed to know anymore. Stood there for a moment,
hands on hips, before saying, "I've already had a pretty
good night. You want to see?"

I clumped down the steps and swung onto her boat.
She kept things neat. There was a wooden push-pole
stowed along the plywood-thin gunwale, a bailing can,
and a couple of bottles of outboard motor oil wedged
into the stringers so they wouldn't bounce around while
she was running. An orange gas can was placed out of
the way, just behind the tunnel of engine well. Pretty
new engine: ninety-horsepower Yamaha. Toward the
stern was a big fiberglassed icebox. Astern of the box
was a bundle of nylon gill net. The net's brown foam
plastic floats were buried among the folds of translucent
nylon, like Christmas ornaments.

"I caught a pretty good mess," she told me as she hefted up the lid off the icebox. "About eighty head of blacks, and maybe a dozen silvers."

I looked into the box to see a slag heap of cobalt-silver fish, most of them close to a foot and a half long. The black mullet—known around the world as the striped mullet—is a strange-looking creature. It has a blunt, bullet-shaped head and big saucer eyes. It is as aesthetically pleasing as an old Nash Rambler automobile. Because a mullet feeds mostly on detritus and other vegetable matter, it has a gizzardlike stomach that pre-grinds food before passing it into a freakishly long digestive tract.

Earlier in the century, a Florida court once ruled that the mullet, because it had a "gizzard," was actually a bird—thus freeing a commercial fisherman who was charged with fishing out of season. The incident is but one measure of what a strange fish the mullet is.

As I peered into the box, Hannah said, "I did a strike off Cape Haze and did okay. You know that point just before you go into Turtle Bay?"

That was a little north of my normal cruising area, but I was familiar with it.

"I took most of them there. Then I struck this little sandbank I know near White Rock and got the rest. I'd have more, but I know Tommy needs his things, so I run down here to see you." Big smile. "Didn't want to get here so late I had to haul you out of bed. That wouldn't be polite."

Tommy? It took me a moment to translate: Tomlinson.

I told her, "We don't want to keep Tommy waiting. I've got his stuff sacked, ready to go."

"You going to invite me in?"

I hesitated, then said, "Sure."

She closed the ice locker and followed me up the stairs to the house. Oohed and aahed at my fish tank. Asked me questions about the telescope—"That planet with the rings around it. Can you see those?"—then focused her attention on the bookshelves. Because I have the volumes arranged alphabetically, by author, she had to get down on hands and knees to search. I knew what she was looking for—one of Tomlinson's books. But instead of helping, I stood there and watched. It was hard not to watch: big woman in slick yellow pants, haunches poked up into the air, the pendulum swing of loose breasts against damp T-shirt. She seemed to fill the room; filled it with her size, and with a musky odor of girl-sweat, fish, strong soap, and salt water. Felt the urge to change the music on the tape player—get rid of that damn Gregorian chant stuff—and offer her some of that finely aged wine in my refrigerator.

"Here's one!" She had one of Tomlinson's books. Was opening it as she stood. "Even got his picture in the back. Isn't he a cutey?" Now she was leafing to the front. "Whew, this one's a little *heavy*, though, huh? I've only come across four or five words that I understand."

"Not what you would call easy reading," I agreed. "It has to do with the concept of infinity . . . I think. Something about all motion and change being an illusion. That reality is actually static and immutable."

Hannah had an index finger to her lip, trying to follow along. Said, "That's why I like you two guys. You're smart, both of you—not that I'm not. I'm probably just as smart, only sometimes I wished I'd gone to college."

"With Tomlinson, a college education is no help. I'm

just repeating what he told me. It's like . . . if you drop a rock, the rock has to fall half the distance to the ground before it can fall the remaining half. Right? But then the rock must fall half the distance of *that*. So on and so on. Logically, the rock should never reach the ground. What his book does is question the existence of distance and motion.''

She closed the book and looked at the dust jacket. The title was: *No End in Sight*.

''How many copies you think it sold?''

''I think Tomlinson probably gave away more copies than he sold.''

She thought that over. ''Well, my book is going to sell. I want people to know about the kind of people we are. And the mullet fishermen, what's being taken away from us. So I don't want any of that falling-rock bullshit in my book. I'll remind him when I get back. Oh yeah, I almost forgot—'' She reached down into her Farmer Johns and handed me a folded sheaf of papers. ''It's the first chapter. Tommy's already working on the sixth or maybe the seventh. He wants to know what you think. He said you'd be a good . . . what'd he call it? . . . a good barometer for the average reader.''

I took the sheaf of papers. Said, ''What a nice thing for Tommy to say.''

I OPENED THE PAPERS AND LOOKED AT THE COVER PAGE. It read: *People of the Same Fire*.

Hannah was watching over my shoulder. ''That's Tommy's title idea. He says the Indians up in the Carolinas and Georgia—the ones who moved down to Florida and net-fished?—that's what they called people from . . . not exactly the same tribe, but who were related.

Yeah, related. The Creeks, I think he said.''

I started to fold the page over, but she stopped me. ''I was thinking maybe just call it 'The Hannah Smith Story.' Real simple, you know?''

Turning the page, I said, ''You may want to trust Tomlinson's judgment on this one,'' and I began to read:

''I am the direct descendant of Sarah Smith, one of four incredible giant Smith sisters who did as much to settle this Florida wilderness as any eight men half their size. They may have not been net fishermen, but they had fishermen's blood in their veins.

''Sarah was my great-grandmother, and was known as the Ox Woman throughout the Everglades. My great-aunt, Hannah Smith, was my namesake. Hannah was called Big Six because of her height. She made her own way in the world until some bad men down on the Chatham River murdered her and, it is said, used a knife to cut the unborn baby from her stomach before they tossed her carcass into the river. But Hannah was stubborn. She still wouldn't sink.

''I am the spiritual sister of both women. But between the two, I probably favor Hannah. So I am well named. . . .''

I refolded the chapter, placed it on my writing desk. ''Tomlinson wrote this?''

''I wrote it, then he changed it, then I changed what he wrote. That's the way we're doing it,'' she said. ''It's my book. He's just helping.''

''Pretty gruesome story about your great-aunt—''

''Gruesome or not, it's the truth. That's what I mean to do, tell the truth. Sarah and Hannah woulda both wanted it that way. Believe me, I know because—''

"Because you were born with a veil over your face?"

She fixed me with a sly look of appraisal. "That's right. I know all kinds of things because of that. The gift of second sight—that's what my mama called it. What I'm askin' you is, do you think it'll sell? The book, I mean. From what you read."

"With your picture on the cover, I think it'll sell a lot better than *No End in Sight*."

"Is that like a compliment? Or just a tricky way of sayin' you don't like it?"

"It's a compliment. I'll read more later, but I liked the first page just fine."

She thought about that. Then: "So what you're sayin' is you think I'm pretty." Talking about the cover I had suggested.

"Pretty's not quite the word. Attractive. Very attractive."

"Dressed the way I am, soaked from fishin'?"

"That's part of your appeal."

Hannah had a wide, full mouth with sun-chapped lips that didn't seem to hurt her when she smiled. She was smiling now, a kind of sleepy, lazy, amused smile. She put the book down and walked toward me until her bare feet were nearly touching my toes. "I like you, Ford. You're big enough to look me right in the eyes, only"— she made her bell-tone chuckling sound—"only you don't spend a lot of time looking at my eyes."

Which, of course, caused me to stare directly into her eyes: dark, dark eyes; irises flecked with gold beneath the glittering windows of cornea.

Heard her say, "Is it true?"

"Is *what* true?"

"What the guys around the docks tell me? They say

my nipples show their shape even through a rain jacket.''

I was just starting to reply to that when Hannah touched her fingers to the back of my head, pulled my face to hers. Kissed me very softly . . . then used her tongue to wet my lips . . . kissed me again, harder—until I took her by the shoulders, swung her around, and held her fast against the wall. Smiled at her, and said, ''Hannah, I'm at your service. But before we go any farther, I want to know just what the hell it is you want from me.''

''See? No bullshit.'' She was laughing—enjoying it. ''That's just what I told you, Ford; just what I like about you. The way you go right for that little soft part of the throat.''

''With Tomlinson, it was the book. What do you want from me? That's all I'm asking.''

She levered her arms up over mine and freed herself. ''Oh-h-h . . . I see what you're gettin' at. You think I screw guys just to get something.'' She wagged her index finger at me: *Naughty, naughty, naughty.* ''That's where you're headed. Well, you're wrong. How many men you think I've taken to bed in my life?''

''That's none of my—''

''Come on, now admit it. Damn right you want to know. You're thinkin', Yeah, I'd *like* to, but you're not the type to just hop in the sack with any ol' slut.''

''Wait a minute, Hannah, I never—''

''Hell, I don't blame you. The way some women go around jumpin' on any pecker that can stand up and smile. Me? I've had five men, counting Jimmy, which I wish I didn't have to. That don't include the playin' around, touchy-feely make-somebody-happy business.

The just-for-fun stuff. Five.'' Now she clamped her hands on my shoulders. I was shaking my head—a *tough* woman to deal with—as I allowed her to pivot me around and press me against the same wall. She pursed her lips, like a teacher questioning a rowdy student. ''Now what about you? More than five?''

''Well, I'm older than you—''

''More than a dozen?''

''I used to travel a lot; never been married—''

''More than twenty?'' She saw my expression and hooted, ''So who's the slut, Ford? Men, they're the sluts, and boy oh boy, you don't like it when the tables get turned!'' She released me, found the back of my neck with her hand. ''You want to know what I want from you, Ford? Yeah, pick your brain about fish farming. That's what I want. I'll do that, 'cause fish farming's about the only thing left when they ban the nets, and that's the business I'm starting. I can see you up there at Gumbo Limbo, giving me advice on where to dig ponds, what kind'a pumps to use. That'd make me happy, sure. But from me? If banks accepted blow jobs, you'd never have a nickel to your name.''

''So why the strong come-on?''

''Goddamn, Ford! You got to have everything spelled out?''

''Let's just say I'm the shy type.''

''*Sure*. Like I'm the queen of Paris, France.''

''I want to know what the rules are, that's all—''

''No rules. Not for you, not for me. No rules ever—''

''Then I want to know *why*.''

She cupped my face in her hands, and leaned forward until our noses were nearly touching. ''I like you. Is that

so hard to believe? I like the way you look, the way you
move. I like the way your brain works. It's because I
saw you, and I *knew*, that's why. That evening I saw
you outside, taking your shower. Took one look and I
thought, yep, we'll get our chance one day. You think I
go 'round asking the name of every man I meet? Then
up to Tallahassee, I heard you at that meeting. Same
thing: It came right into my mind, the picture of you
and me. You didn't strike me as the crazy jealous type.
The type to yammer at my heels like most of 'em.'' She
moved her hands on my face; paused to straighten my
glasses. ''If you knew how many men I got tailing after
me, half sick with tryin' to get me in bed. . . . Well, you
wouldn't be standing there talking, 'cause I can change
my mind anytime I want.''

I stared into her eyes, and said, ''Nope. No you can't.
Time's up.'' Pulled her to me, kissed her . . . felt her
mouth open and kissed her harder. Found the suspender
straps, nudged them from off her shoulders . . . and the
rubber rain pants dropped to her ankles. She lifted her
knees and kicked them away.

Nothing on beneath but cheap white cotton panties.

I had my hands cupped over her skinny little rump,
still kissing her . . . let my hand drift up over the wash-
board convexity of ribs . . . felt her sharp intake of breath
as my fingers found the heavy underside of her breast,
then traced that soft curvature to the length and heat of
nipple.

Hannah pulled away abruptly, stripped the T-shirt up
over her head, and shook her hair free of its red ribbon.
Stood there naked but for the drooping panties, and I
released a long, slow breath, staring at her: *Whew* . . .

Which caused Hannah to smile—*See what you would*

have missed?—and then she said in a husky, sleepy voice, "You can jump out of 'em now, or I'll yank 'em off for you."

Meaning my pants.

Moments later she had her long fingers curled around me, leading me toward my single bed as if steering a cart. "Big Six," she was saying. "Big Six . . ."

Wondered: As in number six?—as I listened to her make her bell note sound; a woman living her vision, enjoying it.

THIRTEEN

HANNAH INSISTED ON FISHING. SAID, "I'VE GOT house payments to make, and no money comin' in as of July." Also insisted that I go with her. "When you're feeling up to it again, I want somethin' between us besides distance." Bawdy, hungry tone to her voice.

So I went mullet fishing with Hannah. The logistics were tricky. I didn't want to get on her boat and have to spend the night in Gumbo Limbo. I didn't know if Tomlinson could be counted among Hannah's six lovers or not—she was so damn touchy about her independence I was afraid to ask. Whether he was or whether he wasn't, it would have been too weird, all three of us in the same house together, because Hannah was not a subdued and noiseless bed partner. She had whooped and moaned and made my small bed crash like a tambourine. Later, on the floor, she had thumped the walls with her heels. Same thing, later still, out on the deck.

Those are not sounds to be shared through thin walls with a friend.

Also . . . I wasn't entirely sure that I had the energy to help her produce those sounds again. Hannah made love without a hint of self-consciousness. She had one of the most spectacular bodies I had ever seen. But we all have our limits. Hannah had pushed me to mine—then helped baby me along until I had exceeded them.

So, what we decided was, Hannah had access to a little fish house off the southern point of Sulphur Wells, not far from the village of Curlew. Arlis Futch owned the house, though he had all but given it to her. By boat, Curlew was about halfway to Gumbo Limbo, only thirty minutes. I would lash Tomlinson's Zodiac onto my Hewes, then follow her to the fish house and tie my boat there. When we were done fishing, she would take the Zodiac in tow, and I would return to Dinkin's Bay.

She kept saying, "I don't know why you don't just come up and stay with me for a few days. Tommy, he wouldn't mind a bit."

I said, "Tommy will understand," wondering if he would—hoping he wouldn't.

Now it was after ten p.m., and we were in Hannah's boat. She stood forward of the engine well, using the PVC pipe to steer. I stood just behind her, right leg braced against the well for balance. When Hannah was at the controls, balance was required because of the way she veered in and out of islands. When we were behind a lee shore, out of the wind, she would twist the throttle open, and the little skiff would seem to gather buoyancy as it flew us across the mud banks. No moon, no running lights, no spotlight. She ran everything from memory. Said she loved speed, the force of the wind on her face.

"You get scared, just grab my shoulder!"

She had to holler above the engine noise to make herself heard.

I put my chin next to her ear. "If I grab your shoulder, it won't be because I'm scared."

Every now and then, she'd lean against my chest so that I could support the weight of her. Let her hair flap in my face, then reach back and squeeze my thigh. Mostly, though, she concentrated on finding fish.

When we were off Pine Island, just southeast on Mondongo Island, she slowed the boat abruptly. We were in slightly more than two feet of water, and I could see the green bioluminescent tracer-streaks of mullet flushing ahead of us. I had already squatted to grab the gunwale when she yelled, "Hang on!" then gunned the engine while, at the same instant, tossing out an anchor that was connected to the gill net.

The net began to peel out behind us as Hannah made a high-speed circle around the fish. She circled them a second time, then a third, using the bailing can to bang on the deck. The noise would spook the fish into the mesh. Finally, she killed the engine, and switched on a bare twelve-volt light bulb that was suspended from a wooden arm above the icebox. Felt our own wake catch us, rolling the boat, as Hannah said, "That's the fun part. Now I'll put you to work."

HANNAH CALLED IT PICKING MULLET. IT WASN'T TOO bad with both of us aboard. But one person alone? No wonder the woman's body was stripped bare of fat, corded with muscle. The hardest part was wrestling the net over the transom. We stood on opposite sides of the stern, pulling the net hand over hand, piling it in the well. When a mullet came thrashing into the boat, she would twist the fish free of the net and lob it into the icebox. I did the same, trying to mimic her smooth motion. It took a while to get the hang of it.

"You still pooped out, Ford?"

"Me? Fresh as a daisy."

With Hannah, facial expressions were a second language. Clearly, she was dubious. "I'll tell you somethin' I've never told nobody. Running this boat by myself at night makes me horny as hell. The way the engine vibrates? It runs through the wood right up my legs. When we get going again, I wouldn't mind you bending me right over the engine well. While I'm still steering, I mean. Never done that in my life, and I would purely love to. In my mind—when I had the vision of you and me being lovers?—that's what I saw you doing to me."

"Jesus, Hannah, I thought you were talking about fishing. Was I too tired to fish—that's what I thought you meant."

Wild whoop of laughter. "I embarrass you? Well . . . get *used* to it. I'll never say nothing in front of anybody else, but you—*you*, I'll tell just how I feel." She was untangling a gaffsail catfish that had spun itself in the net. I watched her rotate the fish's lateral barb, remove the fish cleanly, and toss it overboard. "When I was a little girl," she said, "I used to love to ride on a train, only I almost never got the chance. Now that I'm grown, turns out it's the same with men. If a woman's fussy, if she waits till her body and her mind both tell her it's okay, then not very many trains come along. But when one *does* . . ." More bawdy laughter.

"A train, huh? I guess I'm flattered."

"Damn straight you should be flattered. Your problem is, you lose your sense of humor when you lose your energy. Not that it didn't take a while. Here—" She reached into the icebox and brought out a jar of her tea. "You drink some of this. It'll fix you right up."

I drank her tea—felt the caffeine jolt. I picked fish and nudged the conversation toward safer topics. A few minutes later, she was telling me, "The way it used to work was, we'd take our mullet in and sell them to Arlis. Sell them in what we call the round, meaning the whole fish. Anytime but December and January—the roe season—he'd pay us maybe forty cents a pound. Not much, and Arlis didn't make much either. But roe season, like now, he'd pay us maybe two bucks a pound, then sell them for maybe two-forty to the big wholesale fish plants in Tampa or Cortez. Freezer trucks would come around and pick them up.

"Up there," she said, "the fish go on a conveyor belt. They got women who cut the roe out of them—they use these ball-pointed knives so they won't nick the sacs— and they grade the roe by color and weight. The big plants, like Sigma and Bell, they'll sell the best roe for maybe twenty-two dollars a pound to exporters. The exporters ship it to the Philippines, or Hong Kong—places like that—where *they* sell it to wholesalers for maybe eighty or a hundred bucks a pound. You can imagine what it sells for on the street."

Hannah twisted a mullet from the net, held it out and squeezed the flesh around the anal fin. Tiny yellow globules began to ooze out: fish eggs. "We call it red roe, but it's really more like gold. Get it? Not just the color, but what it's worth."

I said, "But now you have a better deal because of Raymond Tullock. Didn't you tell me that?"

She was nodding; collected the mullet roe on her index finger before she tossed the fish into the box. Held

the gooey finger out to me. "It's not bad. In Asia, they
dry it into little cakes and give it as gifts. During the
Chinese New Year, it's like the best gift you can give,
'cause it's supposed to be an aphrodisiac. Puts lead in
their pencils. Couldn't hurt you to take a taste."

I thought it would surprise her when I licked some
off her finger—the tiny eggs burst between my teeth,
gelatinous and rich—but she only looked blankly at the
roe that remained before putting the finger in her own
mouth and slurping it clean.

She said, "Raymond went to Asia—this was a couple
of years ago—and hunted around until he made his own
contacts. I know he got some Japanese backers for
money. But the importer he made friends with is in Indonesia, only sometimes he calls it something else.
Where he goes, I mean."

"Jakarta?" I guessed.

"You mean, like a city? No, it wasn't Jakarta. A
funny name . . . it had a weird sound."

The Republic of Indonesia is comprised of many
thousands of islands, but I tried again. "Borneo? New
Guinea?"

"No. . . ."

"Sumatra?"

She snapped her fingers. "That's it! How'd you
know?"

I reminded her that I had once traveled a lot.

She accepted that, but her expression told me she
wanted to ask questions—How were the girls over
there?—but instead, she said, "I guess that's the main
thing in the international seafood business. Having contacts? Like the guy who runs the big Tampa export business, he's got important family connections in the

Philippines. Another guy has Hong Kong all locked up. I'm talking about mullet roe now. You ever go to one of those big fish export places?''

I had, but I wanted to hear Hannah tell it.

"It's like the way you would picture the New York stock market,'' she said. "Computers and fax machines all over. These huge rooms full of people, everyone yelling into telephones. Only you can't understand them because they're speakin' Japanese or French or some other language that I wouldn't recognize if I heard it. Right up there in Tampa. Somebody in Germany needs swordfish? They arrange it; maybe have one of their brokers ship it out from California that day. Tokyo needs stone crab claws? Same thing. They've got these blast freezers the size of a gymnasium. But even if they don't have the fish in stock, they know someone who does, and they take their cut. People don't realize that the international seafood market is like a multibillion-dollar business. We do the catchin', but everybody else makes the real money. We go down, the other countries will just fish that much harder. And of course, they got no regulations at all.''

I said, "That's the business Tullock started after he quit his job working as a marine extension agent?''

"Kind'a, but he just rents space from one of the big export companies. His contacts—where we sell to now?—it's all to Sumatra. He calls it a 'niche' market. They're not as rich as the Philippines, but it still works out pretty good. Raymond handles everything, so Arlis sells to him exclusively. Now, instead of selling fish whole, we butcher them ourselves and end up makin' five times the profit. See what I mean about contacts in Asia bein' important?''

"I bet Raymond does pretty well too."

"Yeah, but he works for his money. Raymond rents freezer space in Tampa till he gets a container full— that's like a semitrailer that fits on an oceangoing freighter. He's already shipped one container, and in a few days, he's gonna get on a plane so he can fly over and meet it." She locked onto me with her eyes before adding, "He wants me to go along . . . and I plan to."

What she was looking for was an expression of jealousy from me, any indication that I would limit her by trying to possess her. I tossed the last of the mullet into the box, and said, "You ought to go. It's a fascinating island, Sumatra."

"You been there?"

"Once."

"What I want to do is learn everything I can about the business so I . . . so I—"

"So you won't need Raymond anymore? Make your own contacts?"

She was taken aback for a moment . . . slowly recovered . . . then spoke in a tone that I had not heard her use. The tone was resolute, uncompromising—yet not severe. She wasn't defending herself, just telling me how it was. Said, "You know how to make it hurt, don't you? Only it doesn't bother me a bit, 'cause it's the same thing you'd do. Aren't you the independent type? Damn right I'll try to steal Raymond's contacts. It's business, and in business, that's part of the game—or so the menfolk tell me." Gave that a homey, ladylike twist before adding: "Raymond's tried plenty of times to use me— hell, *using* me is about all that poor bastard has on his mind."

"You mean as in—"

"I mean as in fuckin' me. Yeah." Looked hard at me to see how that was accepted. "That's part of it. I haven't given him the first taste, which just makes him crazier for it, but it also makes him easier to handle."

I said, "Maybe the other part is that you know Raymond was never against the net ban. A buddy of mine told me Raymond lobbied for the ban behind your back."

A thin, noncommittal smile. "Maybe."

"But if he makes his money selling mullet roe, why would he—"

"Don't you worry about my business, Ford. I know all about Raymond . . . but Raymond, he doesn't know all about me. That's just the way I want it." She was tromping the last of the net down, getting the boat ready to go. Stopped for a moment and stared toward the southwest. A pale, luminescent cloud marked the night strongholds of the barrier islands: Captiva Island, its lights twinkling; Sanibel, a gray bloom beyond. She put her hand on my shoulder and said, "See that?" She meant the lights. "When I was little, my daddy would fish so close to that island that I could smell the fresh-cut grass. All those big, rich houses, and the golf course—Yankee millionaires, that's what Daddy called everybody who lived there."

"A lot different than Sulphur Wells," I agreed.

"We lived on Cedar Key then, but yeah, about the same thing. Daddy always said if I was smart, I'd marry one of them. He'd pick out some good-looking man on the golf course, or some guy sweating on the tennis courts, and he'd say, 'There ya go, Hannah. Marry him, you'll never have to worry about another thing all your life.' Being a little girl, I'd always think, yeah, right, some rich man would marry *me*?

"About the time I turned seventeen, though, those rich men started staring back. Started giving me that little smile—like, *hello*, young lady. That's when I knew. I knew I could hunt around, play it right, and pick just about any one of them golfers or tennis players I wanted. Let them pay for me while I laid around in a bikini. I'd be one of their pretty ornaments and they'd let me pretend to be their partner." Hannah squeezed my shoulder; gave me a little shake. "You may not believe it, but if I put a dress and stockings on, I could walk into the fanciest restaurant on that island, and no man inside would think I was a mullet fisherman. Even if they thought it, they wouldn't much care." She kissed me on the cheek. "Maybe I'll do that for you sometime. Get all dressed up."

I said, "So why didn't you? Tell me the rest of it."

"Why I didn't snag a rich guy? I coulda. Hell, I *thought* about it. Have a real nice car, somebody to do the housework. Plan out dinner parties for my husband's clients—" She laughed. "Can't you just see me doin' that?"

"Yes, I can," I said softly. "I think you'd be good at whatever you chose to do."

"Well, what I've chosen is the life I'm meant to have. Tommy says it's my karma. Build my own business, live with my own kind of people. Net ban or not, that's exactly what I'm goin' to do. Whenever I get restless, whenever I'm on the water alone and the lights of those big houses start winking at me, I just remind myself what happened to Big Six when she messed with outsiders."

It took me a moment to cross-reference that—she was talking about her great-aunt.

Hannah waved off my reply—subject closed—and leaned over the engine well to start the Yamaha. As she jumped the boat onto plane, she yelled above the noise, "You feel it? *That's* the vibration I'm talking about."

CLOSE TO MIDNIGHT, BOTH OF US NAKED, TANGLED TO-gether on a bare mattress in a dilapidated stilt house near the village of Curlew, some portion of my subconscious kept nagging at me; would yank me back through the film of awareness each time I drifted downward, downward into the gauzy gray world of sleep.

Then, gradually, the subconscious found an unworn brain conduit, and the question that was nagging at me finally burst to the surface. I sat upright in the darkness . . . felt around for Hannah's shoulder and shook her. "Hannah, are you awake? Hey—wake up." She stirred. "What the hell's in your tea?"

Heard her soft murmur of laughter.

"Damn it, there's something strange about it. The way it affects me."

Enough light came through the window that I could see the charcoal shape of her: long panels of flesh tone . . . a segment of cheek . . . a wedge of matted pubic hair . . . one dark eye blinking up at me.

"Go to sleep. You worry too much."

Shook her again. "No, there's something strange about it. Makes me feel about half drunk. The same thing happened at Gumbo Limbo."

Her hand explored around until it found my chest, then patted its way downward along ribs, stomach . . . groin. When she found me, her fingers began to gently massage. "Um-m-m-m," she said lazily. "You don't feel drunk. More like warm wood."

"That's another thing. It's not normal. It's not . . . it's not even human. It won't go away. I could get *gangrene*."

She rolled over onto me, then used her teeth to pull at my chest hair; her tongue to trace the abdominal expanse. Said, "I'm no doctor, but I do know a little first aid," before ingesting me. I felt the siphoning draw of her lips, her tongue . . . lay back momentarily . . . then fought my way upright again. Took her hair in my hands and lifted her head. "No you don't. First tell me what's in the tea."

She hesitated, staring at me in the darkness, then scooched her way up and kissed me on the lips. "Is it real important?"

"Then I'm right?"

"I'll show you, but I want you to remember somethin'—you didn't have a drop before the first time. Tonight at your place, I mean. That's what I want you to remember. It was just you and me, both of us feelin' the way we felt. My tea didn't have a thing to do with it."

I was thinking: Jesus, the woman has *drugged* me. But said agreeably, "Nothing's going to change that. Just the two of us. Our own free will. Exactly."

"We're lovers?" She seemed worried; vulnerable for the first time, which I found touching.

Kissed her on the forehead, then on the lips. "Yep, lovers."

She got to her feet; moved around carefully in the darkness. "I'd like that. You and me; neither of us the marrying kind. I'll have my house at Gumbo Limbo, you'll be over on Sanibel, and when either one of us gets the urge to be together . . ." There was the flare of a kitchen match, a sulfur stink. I watched Hannah's face, bathed in gold, as she lit an oil lamp. ". . . you call me, or I'll call you. We can have our own lives, but we can have each other, too. We'll be like . . . secret partners."

I stood behind her, put my hands on her shoulders. "You don't need to get me drunk to have that."

"You sure? I'm gonna tell you, but I want to be sure."

Turned her to me and kissed her. "I'm sure. Now tell me what's in the tea."

She smiled, moved away—naked; comfortable with it—and began to lift away boards from what I thought was a solid wall. "This is Arlis's old hidey-hole. For a time there, he never trusted banks, so he built this himself way back in the thirties. When he was young." From the wall, she carefully removed a black duffel and held it open to me. Inside were a dozen or so small brown bottles, a nub of white candle, a leather-bound book, and an opaque sphere made of green glass. I remembered seeing similar glass balls on the mantel over her fireplace.

She took out one of the bottles and the glass ball. Held up the glass ball and said, "This one's a powder made from the bark of an African tree. It's called yohimbe. It's supposed to grow hair, but it's also supposed to be about the only aphrodisiac that really works." She looked down at me. "By golly, it seems to!" Was still laughing at that as she indicated the bottle. "In here, I've got a combination of what they call blue stone from Haiti and oil from a leaf they call iron tree. Mix the two, plus a drop of turpentine, and you've got a love potion. That's what I put in the tea."

I took the glass ball from her and held it up to the lamp. It appeared to be hand-blown glass, very old, with air bubbles frozen within. It had an ingenious fluted stopper.

Hannah said, "Pretty, isn't it? It used to be my great-aunt's. Hannah's? This one and a couple of more, that's all I've got of hers."

I handed the ball back. "You sure you didn't put something else in the tea?"

"If I wanted to lie to you, I wouldn't've shown you this much."

I was relieved. No amphetamines or amphetamine-tranquilizer mix. Even so, it made me angry. Why pull such a stunt? I said, "No more potions, okay? Ever. You really believe in that stuff? Voodoo?"

She seemed suddenly uneasy. "I can't tell you about it. Sorry, I can't."

I sat her down and made her tell me. It took a while. She had once taken an oath—back when she was in Louisiana—and I had to take an oath in turn. Hannah was very serious about it. I pretended I was, too. When she was convinced I would never share her secret—I was honest about that, at least—she told me that Jimmy Darroux's mother had indoctrinated her. The reason was, the mother so distrusted her own son that she didn't want to see Hannah get hurt. Jimmy's mother was certain that he had fed Hannah a "love potion." To prove it, the mother had demonstrated exactly what Jimmy used to make it. Hannah had such a natural fervor for folk medicines that the mother spent the next several days instructing her. "She wouldn't let me write anything down," Hannah told me. We were on the mattress again, lying naked, my arms around her. "There were some things she wouldn't tell me—some of the real important religious stuff. But it explained why I got so hot for Jimmy so quick.''

I said, ''Yeah, but why do it to me? You just happened to have the stuff there waiting, and I show up—''

''I recognized you at the door, that's why. I knew we'd be lovers''—she made a sound of self-deprecation—''but you, you took some convincing. You showed up at the door, and I just thought . . . looked in the 'frigerator and all the Cokes were gone, so I just *did* it. I didn't make the tea planning on you coming. But I knew we would meet someday.''

''Then why *did* you make it?''

''I . . . keep it in the house for Arlis.''

''For Arlis? For Arlis . . . and you?''

''That's right. Arlis and me.''

I fought off the twinge of jealousy I felt; said in a tone of manufactured indifference: ''I knew you were close.''

She rolled over so that we were face-to-face. ''That don't bother you?''

''Why should it?''

Hannah snuggled up close to me, very pleased. ''That's what *I* think! Arlis, he's an old man. He's sweet as he can be, and . . . he's one of us. One of the old Cracker people. Like, him and me are part of the same tribe.''

I guessed that she was parroting some past remark by Tomlinson, but did not comment.

''Arlis, his wife died more than two years ago. There's no other women on the island he gives a damn about, so . . . sometimes, when he's in a wanting mood,

I help him feel like a man again. At his age, he needs the tea to help him. I don't do it out of pity. I care about the old bastard, and he cares about me. It's . . . private . . . and it's real sweet.''

"That's why Arlis was glad when Jimmy died.''

"Arlis hated Jimmy; he'd tell you the same himself. Arlis was so mad at me when I married him that he wouldn't even talk to me for a week. But he came around when he realized it was just me bein' . . . bein' me. I'm . . . kind'a a different sort of woman. I told you that before.''

I kissed her cheek, then her lips; told her I was finally beginning to believe that. Then I asked, "Did Arlis hate Jimmy enough to kill him?''

She got up on one elbow, chin braced in hand. "The bomb, you mean?'' She shook her head. "Arlis was glad about it. Real glad. But no, Arlis didn't have nothing to do with it.'' She paused for a moment, looking into my eyes, then said, "I'm the one that fixed it. I'm the one that killed Jimmy.''

She said it so matter-of-factly that it took a moment for it to register. "You *what*?''

"About three weeks ago, he broke in the house and he hit me again. I told him what I was gonna do, and I did it.''

"But how? Jimmy was alone. He brought the bomb to my marina—''

"I'll show you how,'' she said. Reached over and dragged the black duffel within reach, and took out the leather-bound book. "Jimmy's mama sent this to me just before she died. She was a good woman, but sometimes . . .'' Hannah had the book open; was leafing through it. "Sometimes good women produce assholes for sons. I guess she knew that and thought maybe I needed protection. So she wanted me to have this.''

The book was very old; had the nutty, musty smell of autumn leaves. It was written in French, a language I cannot read.

''What this is, it's the lost books of the Bible,'' Hannah said. ''The eighth, ninth, and tenth books of Moses. You can't find it anywhere anymore—I checked around after I got it. Some people don't even believe that the books exist, but here they are.'' She had found what she was looking for and showed me. An entire page had been crossed out with black tape. ''I used this to put what they call an 'assault obeah' on Jimmy. This and a ceremony his mama had told me about. Wrote his name on Chipman paper, then burned it with a candle. The thing with Chipman paper is, it'll burn, but the writing on it won't. The writing shows right through the ashes. I called Jimmy up to the house three days before he died and showed him this Bible, showed him the ashes. He acted like it didn't scare him a bit, but it did. His face went sort of funny; kind of twitchin'.''

''That's all you did?'' I suspected she could hear the relief in my voice. ''You didn't have anything to do with the bomb?''

She said, ''Nope, you can relax about that,'' and closed the book. ''Whether you believe in this stuff or not—Jimmy, he believed. Maybe he was carryin' that bomb and got jumpy, knowing he didn't have long to live no matter what. Probably hit the wrong switch—drunk as usual. Or maybe nobody explained exactly how it worked. When he told Tommy to 'take care of Hannah'? The asshole meant take *care* of me. Like Jimmy was always gonna 'take care' of so-and-so; that's the way he always said it. You know—beat the hell out of them.''

I didn't want to press her, but I had to. ''Who didn't explain to Jimmy how the bomb worked? You need to tell me, Hannah. Who built the bomb?''

She stared at me a moment, then returned the book to the duffel bag and pushed it away. ''I don't know who did it and I don't want to know.''

''But you have some ideas.''

''That's right, I've got some ideas. If I told you, would it be the same as telling the cops?''

I thought about lying to her; looked into those eyes and realized that she would know the truth anyway. ''Yeah,'' I said, finally, ''I'd pass the information along.''

Which, for some reason, made her smile. ''Let me think about it. Give me some time. Why don't the two of us just . . . relax a little before we do any more talking?'' She had her hands on me, massaging my chest with strong fingers, her breasts hanging pendulously, brushing my face. Heard her say, ''Hoo! Looky there— the big guy's finally gone back to the barn!''

I was about to make some reply to that—tell her no, I wanted to talk *now*—when the door of the house crashed open. I heard a man's voice yell, ''Jesus Christ, what are you *doing*?'' Jumped to my feet to see Raymond Tullock filling the low doorway, his expression grotesque, a combination of outrage and shock. The beam of the flashlight in his hand was brighter than the oil lamp. He shone it on Hannah, then on me. Heard him say, ''This guy? You're fucking *this* guy?''

My voice was surprisingly calm considering how hard my heart was beating. I said, ''Get the light out of my eyes, Raymond, or this guy thinks you'll be eating that flashlight.'' The whole time, I was fishing around for pants, shirt—anything to use as a covering.

Tullock lowered the flashlight, but he still wore the grotesque expression. ''Do you realize what you're doing to me, Hannah? Do you have any *idea*?'' As he stared at her, I had the strong impression that he had never seen her naked before . . . that he was feeling both pain and wonder.

Hannah made no effort to cover herself. Said, ''Raymond, you've got a special talent for acting like a dumb ass.''

''Don't you dare lecture me! Don't you dare!'' As he stepped toward her, I moved between them, ready to shove him away. But he stepped back immediately. Seemed to gather himself, and said in a cold, controlled voice, ''I've been looking for you all night. Trying to call you on the radio, driving all over the island. There're men out in boats trying to find you.''

''You serious, Raymond? You damn well better not be joking—''

''No joke. Arlis is the one who finally told me to check here.'' Raymond bent down, picked up Hannah's T-shirt, seeming to take perverse delight in what he said next: ''That long-haired boyfriend of yours? A couple hours ago, some tourist found him out on the road, beaten nearly to death. Probably *is* dead by now.'' He tossed the T-shirt in her face. ''They took him to the hospital, in case you're interested.''

FOURTEEN

TO SEE TOMLINSON, I HAD TO LOOK THROUGH A wall of Plexiglas. He was lying on a stainless steel table, a sheet over his bare hips, his body a nexus of tubes and wires and monitoring equipment. The most troubling linkage was a fogged green hose—it was segmented like a worm—that arched away from the concrete wall, then snaked through his mouth, down his throat. The hose, the table were all part of the respirator that was now doing his breathing. When the table contracted, Tomlinson's body inflated, then deflated rhythmically, like a metronome. The ventilator machine made a cold, hydraulic *keesh-ah-h . . . keesh-ah-h . . . keesh-ah-h* whisper, steady as a mechanical heartbeat, and Tomlinson's limp body jolted with each breath like a skinny bellows.

It was after two a.m. Around me, in a tight little group, were all of the regulars from Dinkin's Bay: Mack, Jeth, Rhonda, JoAnn, Harry Burdock and wife Wendy, Big Nick Clements, Javier Castillo, and some others, plus Janet Mueller as well. Felix and Nels didn't live at the marina, but they had been contacted and were on their way.

Jeth moved up close to me, fighting hard to control his emotions. Said, "Why . . . why would some bastard hurt a sweet guy like . . . like . . . He was such a guh-good man. . . ." Then lost it; didn't try to go on anymore. Sniffed loudly . . . covered his mouth and made a coughing noise as he shoved his way toward the back of the little room that the hospital had set up for us in the intensive care unit. Which set off the others . . . a lot of throat clearing and sniffing and the soft siren sound of restrained sobbing.

Tomlinson had made a lot of friends, touched a lot of people, in his years at Dinkin's Bay.

"Goddamn it," Mack said fiercely, "the buggers went too far this time! I'm going down to the sheriff's department in the morning. Tell them if they can't protect my people, I'll find a way to bloody well do it myself."

Something Tomlinson had once told me—*Anger is the concession to fear*—floated to mind as I said to Mack, "Now, now—I'm sure the police are doing everything they can." Said it in a tone that seemed to originate from some other person; a tone so cheerfully indifferent that it surprised even me.

Mack gave me an odd, troubled look and moved away.

That Tomlinson was on a respirator was bad enough. But worse was the uneven, broken shape of his head and face. Even through the bandages, I could tell that all the delicate bonework of chin and cheeks had been pounded askew. Also, his face and head had been shaved for the emergency surgery the doctors had already done . . . and for the surgery they had yet to do.

Janet came up and slipped under my arm, hugging

herself to me. "He's got a chance," she sniffed. "When the doctor comes, I bet that's what he tells us. Have you talked to anybody?"

"The doctor, you mean? Not yet—she'll be up in a little bit." I patted Janet's shoulder. "It's not as bad as it looks. Tomlinson can't feel anything; doesn't have any pain at all." I pointed through the Plexiglas. "Notice his hands?"

Tomlinson's hands were folded across his stomach. Janet was confused. "What about his hands, Doc?"

"No broken fingers. No swelling. Do you understand the implications of that?" I smiled at her. "*No defensive wounds*. He made no attempt to defend himself. See? Tomlinson preached passive resistance all his life." The blank expression on Janet's face told me that she still didn't get it. "This is the way he *wanted* it." I pressed. "Don't you understand? He wanted to end up like a slab of meat on a table. It was his choice! That's why he wouldn't fight back."

Janet had me by both arms, looking up into my face. "Are you okay, Doc? Maybe you need to sit down."

I waved her away. "I'm fine, Janet. You worry too much."

"Doc . . . ?"

"Yes, Janet?"

"I think you need to go home and get some sleep. I'll be over in the morning to take care of the tarpon, okay? I'll feed them, then start the procedure. You just sleep in."

I smiled at Janet and nodded agreeably . . . which, for some reason, caused her to break down in tears.

More people were in the little room now . . . people I had never seen before. Mostly men and a few women.

The men wore T-shirts and ball caps; the women wore plain-looking blouses, inexpensive slacks. Couldn't figure out what all these strangers were doing in the room, until I finally recognized one of the men: Tootsie Cribbs, who ran a small fish house in Curlew on Sulphur Wells. Hadn't seen him since high school. Went over and shook hands. Listened to Tootsie tell me that he hoped we didn't mind, but he and his church group had driven over in a caravan to see if they could help. "I only met Tommy a couple days ago," he said, "but he struck me as being . . . well, a nice fella. Different, but nice. Honestly interested in what we are going through with this net ban business, and . . ." Tootsie shrugged. "Truth is, I feel sick about it, Doc. We all do. We've got good people on our island. We work hard, raise our kids the right way. But we also got a few bad ones. Scum, that's all they are . . . anybody who'd—" He glanced through the Plexiglas at Tomlinson. "Anybody who'd beat a person like Tommy so bad, that's what they are. Just scum."

Tootsie, I decided, could be an interesting source of information. I began to ask a few questions. The tourist who had found Tomlinson, Tootsie told me, was on his way back to a Sulphur Wells mobile home park when he saw, in his headlights, what he thought was a big animal crawling along beside the road. The animal turned out to be Tomlinson, who kept right on crawling despite the pleas of the tourist to stop. When an ambulance finally arrived, the EMT's first guess was that Tomlinson had been hit by a car—he was that badly hurt. But then after they cut Tomlinson's clothes off him, sponged off the wounds, they found the word *SPY* sliced into his forehead.

"Spy?" I said—at least they hadn't cut his nose off. "I didn't know that, Tootsie. No way to tell with all those bandages on his head." Then I added, in an off-hand, disinterested way, "Any idea who did it?"

Tootsie was silent for a time, looking at the floor, before he said, "Everything I know, anyone I suspect, I'll tell the cops. You can be sure of that. Hannah Smith's down talking to the detective now, and when she's done, I'll volunteer everything I've got. After that, my group is gonna hold a prayer meeting in the hospital chapel. You're welcome to come."

"Come on, Tootsie," I said easily, "just for my own information."

Tootsie was shaking his head. "I'm not like the others, Doc. I knew you . . . I knew you before you moved away; went off to do whatever it is you did. I'd like to tell you, but I won't." Then he added, "I've seen that look in your eyes before."

THE DOCTOR'S NAME WAS MARIA CORALES. I FOUND her name heartening because I know how smart and tough Hispanic-American professionals tend to be. She used phrases such as "bad head injury" and "lung problems" until I demonstrated enough familiarity with human physiology to force her into specifics.

She said, "Okay, Mr. Ford, it's like this. The ER people did a good job with him. They got enough Ringer's lactate into him, fed him enough antibiotics empirically, enough Ancef to get him stabilized. But he was still having respiratory problems, and the routine blood tests showed his electrolytes were way down. He was co-matose by that time—obviously had a severe concus-

sion—so they got him prepped for a CAT scan and had
him all ready by the time I arrived.''

Dr. Corales paused—she had the bedrock steadiness
but slightly distracted, haunted look I have come to associate with neurosurgeons. Said, ''Are you still with
me?''

''What did the CAT scan show?'' I asked.

''It wasn't good. Intraabdominal injuries, some signs
of hemopneumothorax—bleeding in the chest cavity because of a broken rib—and some obvious swelling of
the brain. I decided we had to go right in and have a
look. I found a severe subdural hematoma. Again, not
good. I did what I could, but I want my full team with
me before I go back in and try to do any more. Also,
we're still having trouble getting his electrolytes stabilized. For now, we're hyperventilating him, trying to
lower the CO_2; get the brain swelling down. A general
surgeon will be in to look after the internal injuries—
they're all manageable. Actually, they're rather minor in
comparison. The head injury is the real problem. I want
to keep him under close observation. But if things don't
improve very quickly, we'll have to go back in. Before
the weekend, probably.''

''The prognosis?'' I asked.

Dr. Corales hesitated before answering. ''Are you related to Mr. Tomlinson?''

''A close friend,'' I said. ''A very old, close friend.''

''Do you know if Mr. Tomlinson has family living in
the area?''

''No, he doesn't. He has a daughter in Boston, but
she's very young. The girl's mother is a friend of Tomlinson's—I can notify her. Tomlinson's mother passed

away many years ago, but he still stays in touch with
his father . . . and a brother, too.''

''Was he ever married to the mother of his daughter?''
''No.''

''Would you know how we can contact either the father or the brother?''

I didn't like the sound of that. I said, ''The father is
a paleontologist. I think he's doing fieldwork somewhere
in Bolivia. But he's way back in; been living in the bush
for years. He and Tomlinson stayed in touch through the
mail. But only occasionally. Like once or twice a year.''

''Do you have an address?''

''I can try to find one. The brother, he'll be difficult
to contact as well. He lives in Burma. In Rangoon, I
believe. I'm sure I can find an address, but it's my understanding that he's . . . a heroin addict.''

Dr. Corales's expression remained bland. Physicians
have to work hard at being nonjudgmental. I said, ''You
were about to tell me the prognosis, Doctor.''

The woman looked at the clipboard in her hand,
looked at me, then hunched her shoulders into a long,
weary sigh. ''I'm afraid I just did, Mr. Ford. But we'll
do what we can.''

I WAS LOOKING FOR HANNAH—HAD BEEN GIVEN DIREC-
tions to a downstairs conference room—and was striding
down the hallway, glancing at numbers on doors as I
hurried along, when Hannah and Detective Ron Jackson
stepped out into the hall. They were still talking; didn't
notice me until I was only a few yards away. Hannah
glanced up, focused, seemed to refocus, then held her
arms out so that I could take her into mine. Into my ear,
she whispered, ''I'm so sorry. Please believe me, if I'd

known anything about it, I'da stopped it."

I held her away from me. Said, "I'm sure of that, Hannah," as Jackson cleared his throat and said, "I take it you two know each other."

I manufactured a weary but congenial smile. "They got you up early for this one, Ron."

"Early? I never got to bed. As I was telling Mrs. Darroux, I've been assigned to this . . . particular community problem." He made an open-palmed so-here-I-am gesture.

"Any idea who did it?"

"Not a lot to go on, I'm afraid. Still trying to assemble what I can, and we'll take it from there." I could tell he didn't want to talk about it in front of Hannah. He asked, "How's your buddy?"

I told them both what the doctor told me, but I tried to make it sound better than it was. I'm not sure why. Tomlinson was the one who believed in the power of positive thought waves, not me. Tomlinson, I said, would remain in intensive care under observation, and if need be, he would go back into surgery in a day or so. The doctors had high hopes. Judging from the way Hannah was looking at me, she knew I was lying. Maybe Jackson knew it too, but he played along. When I had the chance, I said to Hannah, "Would you excuse us just for a minute?" She stood there, obviously confused, as I took Jackson by the arm and walked with him a little way down the hall. When we were far enough, I said in a hoarse whisper, "They tried to kill him, Ron. Did you talk to the doctor? They did everything but run over him with a truck."

Jackson had already considered that; was shaking his head. "No . . . if they wanted to kill him, they would have used the knife to cut his throat instead of cutting letters into his head. I don't think they *cared* if he died. I think what happened was, somehow they got the idea your buddy was spying on them, and they beat the living shit out of him because of it. Left him out along the roadside, like: *Don't come over here and screw with us.*"

I glanced back at Hannah. I hadn't seen her since I'd jumped into my boat and blasted full speed back to Dinkin's Bay to alert the locals and then drive to the hospital. She had her hair tied back in a blue and white kerchief. She had changed into jeans and a black turtleneck sweater. It was the first time I'd ever seen her in shoes. Brown leather deck shoes. She gave me a troubled, quizzical look—*Don't you trust me*?

To Jackson, I said, "Maybe that's what happened. Maybe some outlaw netters thought Tomlinson was spying on them, but it could also be just a ruse. Somebody smart enough to lay a false trail."

He said, "What? What are you talking about, Ford?"

"There's a guy I want you to check out. A guy named Raymond Tullock."

"Never heard of him. He's one of the commercial guys?"

I told Jackson what I knew about Tullock's background. I didn't know where the man lived, but his business number could be found in the yellow pages. I asked him not to mention Tullock's name to Hannah—why risk tipping him off? Jackson said, "You have some solid reason to believe that he's involved?"

"Nope. Nothing solid. But I think the guy's a flake. I saw him in action tonight. I think he's obsessive-compulsive when it comes to Mrs. Darroux. First Jimmy

Darroux gets blown up. Now the guy who's living with her—Tomlinson—ends up comatose in a hospital. Maybe there's a connection, maybe there isn't. I don't know if Tullock had the opportunity, and I don't know if he's twisted enough to do it. But the motive is there.''

Jackson thought that over. "Mrs. Darroux, the way she looks . . . she packs a wallop. Funny thing is, I didn't notice it at first. But just now, when we were alone in the room . . . *whew*. Yeah, I can see it.'' He glanced up at me. "That's all you've got? A hunch?''

Tomlinson would have found that amusing—me functioning on instinct rather than reason. "That's all,'' I said. "A hunch.''

"I don't know. That other name you gave me is looking pretty good. Kemper Waits? The guy's been in and out of prison. Cocaine trafficking, assault and battery. He was up on a manslaughter charge, but it was dropped. I went to work on it this afternoon after talking to you. But it's all computer stuff. I need more before I try to nail him.''

I said, "How about if I drive up to Sulphur Wells tomorrow, do some poking around? See if I can come up with some information on Waits and Raymond Tullock.''

"I don't know. . . .'' Jackson was studying me, a severe cop-expression on his face. "I think it might be getting too personal for you, Ford. I don't like the tone in your voice. It's a little too light and breezy. You know what they say: Don't try to bullshit a bullshitter.''

"I'm just trying to help, Ron—''

"You've already helped. You gave me a good lead.'' He was still staring at me. "Yeah, I think that's how we'll leave it. You get some rest; go home and have a beer. Let me and my partner work on things. We'll find whoever did it, and I'll let you know. If you want, maybe even let you tag along on the bust.''

I smiled amiably. "Geez, Ron. That would be nice.''

I WAS WALKING WITH HANNAH. HAD MY LEFT ARM OVER her shoulder. She had her fingers knotted into my left hand. Ahead of us, far down the hall, Detective Jackson stood impatiently at the elevator. I wanted to time it right so that he would have to take the elevator without us. When the doors opened, he looked at us, glanced at his watch. I called, "Go ahead, Ron. We'll catch the next one." He stepped aboard; the elevator doors closed.

Ahead of us, down the hall, was an open, darkened room. When Hannah and I were abreast of the doorway, I swung her into the room. Held her there, my face inches from hers, and said, "Who did it? You know, and you're going to tell me: Who jumped Tomlinson?''

"Hey . . . Ford! You're hurting me!''

"Tell me, goddamn it. No more games. No more secrets. Talk to me!''

She wrestled out of my grip and stepped back, rubbing her arms. "I already told him everything I know," she said stubbornly. Meaning Jackson.

"Yeah? So now you're going to tell me.''

"You don't believe me?''

"That's right. I don't believe you. The bad publicity might stall that precious money you're counting on from Tallahassee.''

Enough light came through the doorway that I could see the expression on her face: astonishment, a touch of disappointment, mostly anguish. She touched a hand to her forehead, stood poised for a moment . . . then stumbled forward and fell into my arms. I felt a convulsive tremor move through her body that exited as a sob. "He's going to die," she whispered. "You know that, don't you? I . . . should have seen it comin'. Maybe Tommy did see it—his powers were stronger than mine. But I didn't see it, and now he's going to die."

I stood there holding her, feeling her tears hot on my face . . . but felt no emotion of my own, nothing, except for a mild surprise that a woman so strong could shatter so completely . . . and that she trusted me enough to allow me to see it happen.

There was a leather couch against one wall—it was some kind of consulting room—and I steered her toward it, then sat, still holding her tightly. "If Tomlinson dies, he dies," I said. "Either way, I'm going to find out who did it—and you're going to help me."

"I don't *know* who did it. You wouldn't believe me anyway!"

"Maybe I will, maybe I won't. You're going to sit right here until you've told me everything. More than you told Jackson. With me, you're not going to leave out a single, self-interested detail."

She sat up on her own, stripped the kerchief from her hair and used it to dry her eyes. Took her time, seemed very tired. I expected anger. Instead, her face only registered pain. Watched her take a deep breath, hesitate, then breathe out through her mouth. "Okay. I'm not sayin' they did it, but there are . . . some guys camped north of Gumbo Limbo. A little stretch of beach—we call it Copper Rim, but you won't find it on the chart. They're netters, but mostly outsiders: Georgia, a few from Texas, North Florida . . . like that. Friends of Jimmy's. His drinkin' buddies."

"What makes you think it was them?"

"Give me a chance, I'll tell you. The last few years, they've come down for the roe season and camped there. Copper Rim's got enough water for their boats, plus there's a little footpath through the mangroves out to the main road. I know they got in thick with a local man, Kemper Waits, and I think it's them that's been stealin' boats and stuff. Maybe Kemper was behind the bombing, I don't know—he talks real mean and he's about half crazy. But the boat stealin', I'm pretty sure about. They strip the engines off, hide them somewhere—I don't know where—then somehow ship them north to sell for parts."

"Did you tell Jackson this?"

She sat silently for a time, then said in a small voice, "No. Not the part about the boat stealing."

"Where the tourist found Tomlinson—was it near the footpath that leads to Copper Rim?"

She had her face in her hands. "That's why I'm not sure. They found Tommy way, way south. A lot closer to Curlew than Gumbo Limbo or Rancho."

"But you suspect them."

She looked up, made a helpless gesture. "I don't *know*. Yesterday, Tommy, he said something about how it sure would help our cause if we could stop them boys from stealin' boats, stringing cables. That kind of business. He said maybe somebody ought to go up and talk with them. Try to reason with 'em."

I could hear Tomlinson on the telephone saying, *Should the scientific observer ever allow himself to intercede*?

"Is that all he said?"

"Yeah, that's all he said. He had my truck if he

wanted to use it. That's the way he spent his days—
writing away on my book, driving around and talkin' to
the fishermen. He was . . . happy. Everybody he met on
the island liked him. Nobody I ever talked to even hinted
about him maybe bein' there to spy on us.''

I said, "When you went home and changed clothes
tonight, was your truck still there?"

"Uh-huh, that's how I got into town, but . . ." She
paused for a moment, reflecting. "Now that I think
about it, the truck wasn't parked the way we usually
park it. We always back it in. I guess I didn't even notice, I was so upset about Tommy."

"Someone involved with the attack on Tomlinson
could have brought the truck back."

"I guess . . . yeah. The keys were in the ignition. I
looked all over the house, and that's where I finally
found them."

I said, "Do you think there's any chance that Raymond Tullock was behind it?"

That surprised her. "Raymond? Why would he . . . ?"

"Come on, Hannah. Tonight can't be the first time
Tullock's behaved like some jealous freak."

"Well, no . . . he's always jealous of me. Every man
he ever sees me talkin' to, he's jealous. He's in love
with me. He says he wants to marry me. But I don't
think he could do something like—"

"Was he jealous of Tomlinson?"

" 'Course he was. He hated the idea of Tommy sleeping there under the same roof. Tommy and me were
never lovers. Not that I would've told Raymond. What
business was it of his? But aside from some real sweet
. . . stuff, Tommy and I never—"

I didn't want to hear it. "What about Arlis Futch? Was Tullock jealous of Arlis?"

She was shaking her head. "Raymond never knew about Arlis. You're the only one I ever told about that. He knew Arlis and I were close. He didn't trust Arlis, but he had no reason to be jealous."

I thought: Arlis Futch is still alive. "So why do you keep Raymond around, Hannah? That's the part you're leaving out. Because he found a better market for your fish? Because it's a chance for you to meet some contacts in Asia? That's bullshit. Tell me *why*."

"Because I was using him, that's why!" Hannah yelled it, as she yanked her arm away, then stood. "I was using him just the way he planned to use me! Is that so hard to understand?" She crossed the room, felt around on the wall . . . and the shadows were suddenly flooded out by a sterile glare of neon light. She closed the door and turned before saying in a calmer, more controlled voice: "Raymond wants the land, Ford. Him and some of his Tallahassee buddies. They want Arlis's fish house and his pasture acreage so they can build a marina and a condominium village to go with it. They knew the net ban would put us out of business. That's the only reason Raymond ever came sniffin' around Gumbo Limbo. Yeah, he's been makin' money brokering our fish. But he'll make a hell of a lot more brokering our land."

"Does he know you realize that?"

She made a fluttering sound with her lips. "Raymond's too busy bein' tricky to worry about what anyone else knows. Now the poor bastard wants me as much as he wants the land. Hell, me and the land, we've come to be 'bout the same thing in his mind. So Raymond's been real careful about what he says. He kind'a hinted around to Arlis and me that yeah, since we had to give up mullet fishin' anyway, why not let him handle things? See if he could sweet-talk some investors into taking all that property off our hands. Or maybe the investors would let Arlis and me keep a little percentage. Like he's doing us a big favor.'' Hannah smiled—not a very nice smile. "So Arlis and me, we played along with it. Raymond says, 'I fought hard against that net ban,' we say, 'Sure you did, Raymond. You're a good ol' boy, just like one of us.' "

I said, "I don't see how that's using him."

"The men Raymond's got as backers? They're what he calls 'professional environmentalists.' What they really do is all the surveys and studies so developers can get their state permits. They're old buddies of his from the Fisheries Conservation Board. We told Raymond we might be willing to include them in some kind of corporation, but first we wanted them to go ahead and get the zoning changed on our land from agricultural to commercial. Like about seven or eight thousand dollars' worth of work—just to show their heart's in the right place.''

"But Arlis's fish house is already zoned commercial. It has to be—"

"The cattle pasture across the road isn't," she said. "Arlis's fifteen acres and my three acres. Where they want their condominium project to go."

"Did you sign any sort of contract?"

"You keep thinking I'm dumb, Ford. I'm a lot of things, but dumb is not one of them. Besides, the only contract Raymond's interested in is the one I keep between my legs. Nope, no contract. I want the zoning

changed so I can get my fish farm goin'. That and maybe
a little marina. Just Arlis and me. We couldn't afford to
get it changed on our own—even if we do get our
money from the state.'' She was shaking out the bandanna, retying it in her hair. ''So now I guess you think
I'm a sneaky little bitch, using Raymond the way I am.''
She was looking at me, expecting an answer.

''Would it matter to you if I did?''

She made a small noise of exasperation as she opened
the door, then stood in the doorway, studying me with
her dark eyes. ''Know what, Ford? It *would* matter to
me. It'd matter a lot.'' As she turned to leave, I heard
her say, ''But you probably wouldn't believe that, either.''

FIFTEEN

THAT MORNING—A WINTER-BRIGHT EARLY WEDNES-
day morning—I bolted the door after entering my
house, and I hunted around through the desk until I
found two small stainless steel keys. One key fit the
bottom drawer of my fireproof clothes locker. I used the
key to open the drawer, then removed the neat stacks of
clothing therein. Also unlocked and removed the
drawer's false bottom—which revealed equally neat
stacks of folders, two bogus passports, some clothing,
and other detritus from a life I thought I had abandoned
long ago.

I took out a manila envelope that had *OPERATION
PHOENIX* stamped on the cover. Took out another envelope that had the words "Dirección: Blanca Managua" written on a label in red felt-tip pen. Fought the
urge, once again, to burn the envelopes—and some similar files—in a private little fire. I lingered over the image of that, enjoying the freedom those imaginary flames
produced . . . before reminding myself how unwise it
would be to destroy my only wedge against potential
legal problems from which no statute of limitations
would ever protect me.

Set the envelopes aside. Squatted there staring, for a time, at the nine-millimeter Sig Sauer P-226 semi-automatic handgun that lay, in its shoulder holster, atop a black navy watch sweater that I had not worn in years. Removed the Sig Sauer from the holster, feeling the weight of it. Popped the clip, flipped the slide lock, and removed the barrel. The weapon had an industrial-black finish . . . the spring and metalwork still mirror-clean beneath a layer of oil.

I lifted up the sweater and found the leather case within which was a six-inch custom-built sound arrestor. Screwed the silencer onto the barrel, admiring the precise machining . . . swung the weapon in a fast arc, re-testing the once familiar balance of it . . . recalled the amplified blowgun noise it made when fired: *THOOP-ah*. Then paused, considering the wisdom of carrying it. I had no intention of using the Sig as an offensive weapon, but everyone in America was carrying firearms these days, from frightened housewives to feral children gone wild in ghettos . . . and probably itinerant mullet fishermen, too. What if they heard me and were idiotic enough to start plinking away at unidentified sounds?

Then I thought: But they'll never hear me. I sprayed another coat of oil onto the Sig and its sound arrestor before putting them away.

Ultimately, the only articles I removed from the drawer were the watch sweater, some well-worn Australian S.A.S. field pants in dark battle pattern, a black silk balaclava face hood, leather gloves, a thin-bladed knife in a plastic scabbard that had been given to me by an Israeli friend assigned to the Mossad, and finally, a small, weighty waterproof bag. I opened the bag and removed a set of Starlite goggles and placed them on my bed. With its twin monoculars and padded face frame, the Starlite unit resembled a gadget that might be used by a mad scientist more than the sophisticated—but outdated—second-generation night-vision system that it was.

I had to go into the lab to find the double-A batteries I needed. Unscrewed the power tube, mounted the batteries, then checked to make sure the rubber lens covers were tightly in place before switching the Starlite goggles on. I held the goggles to my face, then strapped them tight. Even with the lens caps on, the photo cathode within the Starlite's optical tube reassembled the light electrons efficiently. The room became a stage of green and eerie, sparkling elements—bed . . . stove . . . Crunch & Des, the black cat, peering at me . . . the bolted door.

I took the goggles off, relieved that they still worked.

When I was finished, I neatened the drawer—I am compulsive about such things—then placed the articles under my bed. Finally, I unlocked the door, went to my outside storage locker. My ancient jungle boots were there in a box. A spider had built her home in them. I shooed the spider away. Found my old Rocket swim fins, a good dive mask plus snorkel . . . and assembled a few other bits of hardware that I might need. Also got my hated contact lenses out of the medicine cabinet, and put them with the other things.

I wouldn't be able to wear my glasses tonight.

When I had everything ready, I stripped down to my underwear and lay down to sleep . . . and had just started to doze when I felt the vibration of someone walking up my dock. I glanced out the window—it was Janet. Checked the clock: 6:30 a.m. sharp.

The woman was punctual. She had stayed with Tomlinson at the hospital only a few hours less than I.

Lay back down and gauged Janet's movements by sounds that came through the screen door. Heard her stop at the fish tank. Heard her struggle momentarily as she opened the heavy lid. Then: "How we doin' this morning, Green Flag? Where's . . . where's . . . ? *There* you are. You're looking handsome this morning. Ready for breakfast?"

I guessed she was talking to the tarpon she called Red Threat.

Heard her coming up the steps to my house. Thought about getting up to greet her . . . but decided I didn't feel like talking to someone as nice as Janet Mueller. Didn't want to risk softening the cold, cold mood I was in—a mood I would need to keep and protect through the day and well into the night.

Heard her stop at the screen door. I kept my eyes closed. Knew that she could look in and see me lying there, a blanket pulled across my hips. Hoped she would see that I was asleep and return to her work with the tarpon. Instead, I heard the door creak open . . . felt her pad across the room . . . sensed her standing next to the bed, close to me.

"Sweet dreams." Words whispered so softly that I barely heard them. Felt warm lips touch my forehead . . . nothing else for several seconds . . . then felt her fingers on my chest, a touch so light, so hesitant that it seemed experimental . . . then felt her lips on mine . . . briefly, very briefly . . . and then she was gone, out the door.

I waited awhile before opening my eyes and to look through the window. Janet was out there in khaki slacks and the same brown sweatshirt, feeding my fish. She was making a cheerful little whistling noise, lips pursed, while she worked.

I AWOKE JUST AFTER ONE P.M., DREAMING OF HANNAH. It was a restless, troubled dream, rife with frustration. I sat up groggily. The details had already faded. Something that had to do with chasing a bus that roared away each time I drew near. Maybe Hannah was on the bus. Or maybe she was chugging right along behind me. I couldn't remember.

The phone rang. I got up, a little surprised to realize that I hoped it was Hannah calling. Give me a chance to make amends—I'd been way too rough on her. But surely she would understand. . . .

It wasn't Hannah. It was a Dr. Wesley Evans calling from the University of Minnesota, wondering if I could ship four dozen fresh cannonball jellyfish to the biology department. I told Dr. Evans that come August, I could ship him four thousand fresh cannonball jellyfish, but none at all in January.

Tried to sleep a little more, but kept thinking of Hannah. Her voice drifted in and out of my mind: *I like the way you look, the way you move. I like the way your brain works*.

Lay there and admitted to myself that the feelings were reciprocal. I did, indeed, like the way Hannah Smith looked, the way she moved . . . and was intrigued, at least, by the way her mind worked. Also admitted that the feelings were real. They had nothing to do with that herbal tea concoction she had fed me—a stunt that still made me mad when I thought about it. Hannah was . . . different. No doubt about that. But . . . damn if I didn't like her anyway. In fact, that was precisely *why* I liked her. A big, strong woman who was wild and hard-tethered with confidence; a woman who didn't hesitate to tell you exactly what she wanted and when she wanted it. The kind who would keep things . . . private. Heard her say: *I'll have my place, you'll have yours . . . like secret partners.*

Heard Tomlinson's voice say: *You and Hannah are both extreme people.*

Which is when I threw the covers back and dialed Hannah's number. On the push-button phone, her number sounded like an abbreviated stanza of "Twinkle Twinkle Little Star."

I let it ring and ring. No answer. There was another thing I liked about her: She was one of the two or three people remaining in America who did not use an answering machine.

I dressed and went outside. I used my mooring pulley-system to haul my flats skiff close enough, then mounted the White Shark trolling motor on the bow—just in case I needed to move quickly and silently through the night. Afterward, I idled over to the marina to top off the fuel tank; then I got in my truck and drove into town to visit Tomlinson.

Something new had been added to Tomlinson's retinue of tubes and wires: an electroencephalogram monitoring system. While I listened to the respirator do his breathing—*keesh-ah . . . keesh-ah*—and listened to the heart monitor echo the pulse of his heart—*bleep . . . bleep . . . bleep*—I could now watch Tomlinson's brain waves track across a green CRT screen. They had wheeled him over beneath an oblong window. Light from the window washed over him, and he looked very tiny, paper-thin, and frail.

I stood there for an hour or more watching the screen, eyes fixed to the monotonous flow of oscillations. For long stretches of time, the waves drifted along incrementally. Small, even bumps that were widely spaced. But every now and then the man would reward me with a fast series of snow-cone shaped peaks, letting me know that he was still in there, still alive beneath all the gauze and damaged skull bone.

Hang in there, Tomlinson. Fight your ass off and dream good dreams.

Dr. Corales wasn't around, but I ingratiated myself with a pretty little red-haired nurse who had runner's legs and killer green eyes. Her name was Debbie. Debbie checked the chart for me, and her reluctance to pass along information told me that the prognosis still wasn't good. She told me, "You never know with head injuries. People can recover in a few weeks, or . . ."

I finished her sentence without speaking it: Or a few years . . . or they never recover, ever.

She said, "Please don't tell anyone I told you, but I think Dr. Corales is planning another surgery for him tonight, or maybe early Thursday morning. She believes head injury patients do better if she operates at midnight or later. Some people say she's cold, not very emotional—not much of a spiritual side, I guess—but she's still about the best around, so you don't have to worry about that."

I told Nurse Debbie that I was certain Tomlinson was getting excellent care.

Rhonda Lister arrived. The Dinkin's Bay people were visiting Tomlinson in shifts now. I went off and tried to call Hannah again—still no answer—before returning to the intensive care unit, where Rhonda and I stood and watched the EEG screen, not saying much. Rhonda left and Nels showed up. He was doing his charters in an old Suncoast that he was renting. The deck was trampoline-soft with age, but it had good bait wells and he was making money again. We made no mention of the explosion that had ruined his new boat, but neither was there any awkwardness between us. Tomlinson—his condition—had leached away any lingering and private bitterness that remained.

Jeth showed up at five. Took one look at Tomlinson and got weepy again. We took the elevator down to the cafeteria. One of life's great ironies is that hospitals, despite their staffs of professional nutritionists, produce the world's worst food.

I didn't care. I didn't want to eat. I wanted to remain lean and light. I didn't want digestion to slow my thinking processes.

As Jeth wolfed down pasty mashed potatoes, he looked at me and said, "You're gettin' those black things under your eyes, Doc. Like circles? You don't need to stay here no more. Mack's gonna be in around suh-suh-suh-six."

I told Jeth I'd stay a little longer. What I didn't tell him was that I wanted to keep my mind occupied until well after dark.

HANNAH WAS RIGHT. THE NAUTICAL CHARTS DID NOT show Copper Rim. But I knew it was north of Gumbo Limbo, some vacant stretch of mangrove fringe, and that was all I needed to know.

At just after ten p.m., I left the wooden channel markers at the mouth of Dinkin's Bay and pointed my skiff into a thumping, blustery northwest wind that seemed to blow down out of the stars. Dark night with scudding clouds and rolling black seas. I banged along at half throttle, bow trimmed high, trying to sense a rhythm to the waves so that I could find the driest, most effective speed.

But there was no rhythm, no order. Just the ice-gray combing of breakers that I could not see until they were on me. Each time I miscalculated, my boat would slam belly-hard into the trough and the hull would vibrate like a wounded animal. I thought about using the Starlite goggles, but didn't want to risk getting them soaked. So I took it easy. Pounded along, taking the occasional wave over the bow-quarter. Considering the conditions, the skiff powered me comfortably enough. Sweet-riding boat on a nasty, nasty night. There was no rush. None at all. I wanted to give the squatters at Copper Rim plenty of time to finish the night's fishing—or the night's drinking—and get back to camp. The more men there, the better my chances of singling out the ones who had attacked Tomlinson.

When I was below Blind Pass, I angled in close to shore. With the exception of Sanibel, the barrier islands of Florida's west coast run north and south. Now those islands provided an effective windbreak. I got the engine trimmed high and fast. There was still some chop, but not enough to soak me. Reached beneath the console, removed the night-vision goggles and strapped them over my eyes. Darkness was transformed into pale green dusk. The charcoal smear of islands became hedges of mangrove trees, singular and distinct. South of Redfish Pass, there were unlit mooring buoys. Picked them up well in advance, no problem. Using the goggles was like viewing the world through a jade tunnel that was hazed with glitter. Off to my left, the house lights of Captiva ascended star-bright into view. To each incandescent bulb, the goggles added the illusion of a streaking meteor's tail; created a glowing arc of fire that shocked the eye and penetrated to the brain.

I looked away.

Thought about Hannah; the story she had told me. Prior to leaving my house, I'd tried to call her once more. Still no answer. She was probably out in her boat, maybe not far from where I was now. Maybe working in the lee of some nearby island, picking mullet, alone.

The thought of that created an odd surge of emotion within me, the sensation of the heart being squeezed. But it was not useful to linger over such thoughts or feelings, so I turned my mind to other things.

It took more than two hours to get to the northern tip of Sulphur Wells. I'd taken off the night-vision goggles by then—didn't need them in open water—and resealed them in their case. I did an experimental run along the perimeter of the island, standing a mile or so off shore. To the south was Gumbo Limbo. Inland and to the north was the village of Rancho: a glimmer of yellow windows. Between lay the unbroken darkness of mangrove swamp . . . and then I saw what I knew had to be Copper Rim: a golden swash of campfire light.

I took my time. Didn't want anyone there to suspect a boat was approaching. An ideal night water insertion requires that at least two people be aboard. One drives past the point of insertion at full speed while the other lies on the gunwale . . . does a quick push-up . . . then rolls into the water holding his mask in place. The method is silent and also strategically advantageous: A boat sped past in the night. Big deal.

But I didn't want anyone with me; couldn't risk it. And I had done this sort of thing, alone, before.

I ran a mile or more upwind, then shoreward before switching off my engine. Then I set about collecting my gear as I let the wind drift me down, down, ever closer to Copper Rim. Twice I had to use the trolling motor to maintain the driftline I wanted. Then, when I was slightly downwind but still at least a quarter-mile from the beach, I dropped anchor.

The campfire threw a halo of light over what appeared to be a tiny stretch of marl beach. There were half a dozen mullet skiffs pulled up onto the beach, and I could see the dark shapes of men moving around the fire. There were tents in the background; a radio was blaring. The wind swept the jarring heavy-metal racket past me. I checked behind me to make certain I wasn't silhouetted by a marker light—there were none—then I pulled on the balaclava face hood, the gloves, and gathered the A.L.I.C.E. pack in which I had stashed my emergency gear. Finally, I strapped fins over my jungle boots and slid, fully clothed, into the water.

The water was cold and as salty as the open sea. I stayed otter-deep in the water, fins working silently beneath the surface. Found myself counting each leg kick out of old habit. But there was no need for that. Swam nearly to the beach, then had to walk myself hand over hand, belly-down, through the shallows.

There were seven men lounging near the fire, passing a bottle around. The only one I recognized was Julie, the tall fisherman with the biceps who'd given Tomlinson and me a hard time at Arlis Futch's fish house. His buddy J. D. was nowhere to be seen. They didn't see me as I went from boat to boat, slithering over the gunwales to cut each and every fuel hose. I had to do it. One thing I wanted to avoid was a boat chase. My skiff was undoubtedly faster and it ran very shallow indeed. But no boat can run as shallow as a mullet boat. A mullet boat can jump sandbars and travel across flats where shorebirds can stand. It is because a mullet boat's engine is mounted forward near the bow in its own well. To catch me, all they had to do was spread out and run cross-country until they cut me off. Even if I did manage to dodge them, they might have weapons, and a bullet will win a boat race every time.

When I had their fuel systems disabled, I hugged myself down against one of the boats to listen. But because of the music and the wind, I could only decipher snatches of random conversation. Once I heard Julie shout, ''An' if you ever tell a living soul what I jes' said . . .'' but the rest of his words were indistinguishable. Tried to get a little closer, but couldn't get close enough to hear if there was any discussion of what had happened to Tomlinson.

It wasn't good. My original plan, conceived in rage, was to identify the guilty parties, wait until they were asleep, slice through the tent walls, and then punish them, one by one. Nothing bloody or brutal—using my Israeli knife to carve SPY into their foreheads was never a consideration. But there were ways, several subtle and perfectly quiet ways, to make the guilty men regret for the rest of their lives what they had done to my friend.

Yet I had abandoned that plan for a couple of reasons. One was that Ron Jackson was no fool. He would know who had done it and why it had been done. But the second reason was more compelling: After I had cooled down, I was reluctant to believe—didn't want to believe—that I was capable of such behavior. I was a legitimate biologist, for Christ's sake!

So I had settled upon a simpler plan: gather all the information I could surreptitiously, then take it back to Ron Jackson. By eavesdropping, I might be able to assemble data that was key to the assault on Tomlinson ... maybe on the bombing and the boat theft ring as well. I'd give Jackson names, dates, and places. Wouldn't be able to tell him how I'd gotten the information, of course, but I would hand him the solutions on a platter, and leave the rest up to him. Everything nice and legal ... relatively legal. The outlaw netters wouldn't even know that I had been there.

But there was too much wind, too much loud music.

I lay there in the water for more than an hour, hoping they'd shut that damn radio off. They never did. The only time they moved away from the fire—or the bottle—was to wander off into the mangroves. Because this was a two-month base camp, I guessed they'd had the good sense to designate a latrine area.

When I realized that, I realized my plan could still work—but with some tough modifications.

For some reason, that pleased me very much.

I reached into one of the boats and stole a coil of nylon rope. Then crawled out into water deep enough to float me, before swimming log-slow southward from their camp, toward the mangrove fringe. When I was shielded by the trees, I sat up, took off my fins, and wedged them tight into the A.L.I.C.E. pack. Then I put on the night-vision goggles and began to work my way carefully, quietly over the monkey-bar conduit of tree roots. January or not, mosquitoes found me. Cold or not, I was sweating by the time I finally found the little clearing. There was a wooden bench. A roll of toilet paper had been fitted onto a broken limb.

Through instinct and long conditioning, a human being knows that if there is enough light to see, then there is enough light to be seen. That instinct must be ignored while wearing Starlite goggles, particularly if you are hunched down in a swamp, lying stump-still . . . and on the hunt for other humans.

I decided to wait for Julie. I didn't like the bastard anyway, and he, at least, had a motive for attacking Tomlinson. I could picture the wolfish look he had given me while calmly lying to Arlis Futch. And I was still curious about the fragment of sentence I had heard: *If you ever tell another living soul what I just said . . .*

But Julie apparently had a plumbing system of iron. Or he was too lazy to leave the beach. Over the space of the next hour, four men stumbled through the bushes, did their business, and left. I was close enough to each man to reach out and grab him had I wanted. One of them carried a flashlight, which almost caused me to jump up into sprint position. But I remained frozen . . . closed my eyes as the light panned across the roots within which I lay . . . and he did not notice.

Tomlinson had once told me that too many people see only what they expect to see. It was true.

Finally, I heard the by now familiar rattle of bushes, and Julie came down the path. He was fiddling with his belt, already unzipping his pants. A cigarette hung from his lips. Through the Starlite goggles, the ash of the cigarette glowed like an infrared eye. I watched him drop his pants and take a seat on the bench.

I waited until he was done. Waited until he reached down for his underwear, and then I jumped him.

Clapped my hand over his mouth as he went down, jammed my elbow hard into the base of his skull. When he made a meek effort to struggle, I whispered into his ear, "Make a sound . . . try to fight me . . . I'll cut your throat." Then I sapped him with my elbow again.

I felt his body go limp beneath me. Maybe he was unconscious, maybe he wasn't. Fear is the most powerful tranquilizer there is. I used electrical tape on him: hands, ankles, eyes, and mouth.

Then I hoisted Julie onto my shoulder, carried him to the water, and swam him out to my boat.

SIXTEEN

IDIDN'T REMOVE THE TAPE FROM JULIE'S MOUTH UN-
til we were fifteen miles or so away, on a deserted
island named Patricio. Patricio had once been home
to a couple of hardscrabble, turn-of-the-century farming
families. All that remained of those long-gone lives were
a couple of shell-mortar water cisterns and contours of
high mounds the farmers had once plowed.

In South Florida, jungle is quick to reclaim the trans-
gressions of man.

I'd used the stolen rope to tie Julie by the ankles.
Tossed the rope over the thick limb of a ficus tree, then
hauled him high, suspending him like a trophy fish. Let
him swing helplessly for a few minutes, hands bound
behind his back, before I walked over and stripped the
tape away.

His voice had a shrill energy. "Goddamn, this is a
joke? This better be a joke! Untie me, take this damn
tape off my eyes!"

Listened to him rattle on for a while; recognized the
sound of fear in him—an overoxygenated breathless-
ness. Finally, in a low voice, I silenced him, saying,

"Nope. No joke." Gave it a Deep South inflection: Nawp. No-o-o joke.

"Then what? Why? Who the hell are you!"

On the ride to Patricio, I'd decided how I was going to work it. Now I let Julie hear the voice of my imaginary accomplice—cupped my hands around my mouth, turned my back to him, and spoke a few sentences of cold, nasal Spanish.

"You guys Cubans? Jesus, what *is* this?"

I said, "I ain't no Cuban. And it ain't none of your business what my boss is. He says he wants you to talk. I was you, I'd start talkin'."

"About what? Shit! Cut me down. Hell, whatever you want to know, I'll tell you. I can't think like this. Feels like my head's 'bout to explode."

"We listened to you boys on the beach. That's what he wants to know about."

"Huh?"

"My boss and me heard you tell that real interestin' story. The guy you beat."

"The hippie, you mean? That's why—because of what we did to the hippie?"

I thought: Got you, you bastard.

More Spanish. I pretended to translate: "The hippie don't mean nothin' to my boss, but he says maybe we should hear you tell it again anyway. See if you tell it twice the same way. My boss, I guess he thinks you might try an' lie to us. That wouldn't be good, you lied to us."

Through the night-vision goggles, Julie's face had begun to resemble an engorged green grape. His breathing had become so rapid that I wondered if he would pass out. Snatch a person out of familiar surroundings, tape him, soak him, then short-circuit his equilibrium, and an existential terror will erase all the familiar groundings of self. I took no joy in his reaction . . . and was relieved that I didn't—only the truly twisted find pleasure in wielding dominance over another human life. Yet neither did I feel much pity.

''He's not gonna . . . kill me, is he?''

He was asking about my boss.

''You talk, probably not. That's up to him.''

''I mean it, I'll tell you anything you boys want to know. Hell, you and me . . . the way you sound, we prob'ly got some of the same friends. You from around here? I know lots'a people from around here. You cut me down, I'll answer all the questions you got. Man, I'll *help* you.''

I said, ''Nope. The man pays me, so I do what he says. I hear what you're sayin', but these Colombians, they ain't like us, buddy-row.'' Listened to a sound of pure anguish escape from Julie—*Colombians*—before continuing. ''My advice is, you start talkin' straight. My boss, he listens to me sometimes. You help us, I'll try to help you. You give us the information he wants and I don't see no particular need to kill you. I'll tell him that. But if he does give me the order, partner, I promise you this: A coupl'a country boys like you and me, well . . . I'll make it so you won't feel a thing. That's not somethin' I do for ever'body.''

''Oh God . . .''

Julie began to talk. He talked nonstop. What had happened, he said, was Tomlinson had walked right into their camp. Julie, of course, recognized him—''He an' this big dude jumped me a while back''—and there was a rumor being spread around the island that Tomlinson was a spy. To them, it made sense. Some of the other men in the camp knew that Tomlinson had been talking to commercial fishermen on Sulphur Wells, asking lots of questions. What Tomlinson was, said Julie, was an informer sent to snoop around by some government agency. So they had slapped him around a little, trying to make him confess, but Tomlinson wouldn't talk.

"You should've *made* him talk," I said encouragingly.

"Man, we tried! But he just kept sayin' weird shit, not at all what we was askin' him. Like this stupid poetry crap and Bible verses. And was too scared to fight back a'tall. So what you gonna do? I made an example out of him. Hell, we had plans to track that hippie down and nail him anyway. So I thumped him pretty good. We dumped him off on the road, and we dropped his girlfriend's truck back where he was livin'. How else you gonna deal with somebody like that?"

I was feeling no pity at all for Julie now. But I said, "Sounds like the pure damn truth to me."

"Hell yes, it's the truth. I'll be straight with you guys. I'll *work* with you."

I told Julie that I appreciated that. Told him I was going to try and convince my boss that Julie was actually a pretty good guy. I moved off through the bushes and had a whispered conversation, South American Spanish, then slow Spanish with a Deep South accent. Returned to Julie's side—his body convulsed at my touch—and said, "Thing is, now my boss wants me to ask you some other questions. . . ."

"If I know the answer, you got it!"

Julie didn't realize how much he knew. It took a long, long while to scrape pieces of information out of him.

It wasn't that he wasn't willing to talk—"I'll tell you anything I know, man!"—but what he might think was some mundane, unimportant incident might, to me, be a key bit of data.

So I took my time with him. Showed a lot of patience. I became his buddy. Played good cop to my Colombian boss's bad cop. I didn't want Julie so desperate that he would begin inventing information just to please us. I comforted him, I complimented his memory when he reached down deep and brought out a name or some other forgotten fact. Gradually, very gradually, I pieced together the information I wanted.

Julie knew a lot about a lot of things. He told me how the boat-theft ring worked. They trucked the stolen engines to a little house Kemper Waits had back in the palmetto flats. There was a shallow freshwater pond behind the house. They dumped the engines in the pond— no one would ever think to look there—and then waited until it was safe to truck them north to Georgia where Waits had connections with a professional chop shop. The fresh water didn't hurt the engine components, and the chop shop paid off in cash, or in cocaine. Waits preferred cocaine. It was a lot more valuable to him— particularly now, since the local netters were going to have so much more time on their hands. Waits believed the net ban would help open up a whole new market. Give the younger ones enough free cocaine to get them interested, then get them involved in the stolen outboard motor business. Waits didn't like or trust the Sulphur Wells locals, and they didn't like or trust him. For Waits, it was just one more way to even the score.

Julie knew less about the bomb that had killed Jimmy Darroux, but he knew enough. Once again, Waits had played a central role. Julie didn't know for certain, but he thought Waits had built the bomb in a little concrete block shed near his house. Only he had heard that maybe, just maybe, Waits had botched the bomb intentionally as a favor to a friend. "Jimmy Darroux, hell, he was a pretty good buddy of mine," Julie said. "But I think he may'a stepped on the wrong toes, probably over that bitch of a wife he had."

I didn't want to press the issue too hard. I wanted Julie to leave the island with an entirely different impression about why he was being questioned. I nudged the conversation off the topic, then nudged it back again. Then I listened very carefully, as Julie said, "There's this guy used to work for the state. Him an' Kemper, they're pretty tight. Might go into business together. This guy used to come around an' inspect Kemper's boats an' stuff, give him advice about how he could fish better. He's the one says we can't take this net ban bullshit laying down. He told us he didn't recommend breaking any laws, but the only way to get Tallahassee's attention is to do like a white man's riot. You know, like burn baby burn. Hell, those people *always* get their way. The man's been up there in Tallahassee working; part of it all. So he'd know. I think it was him that give Kemper some book on how to make a bomb. I heard he told Kemper he prob'ly shouldn't do it, but Kemper, he went ahead and did it anyway."

I wondered if Raymond Tullock had also told them they probably shouldn't beat Tomlinson senseless—*after* confiding that his Tallahassee contacts had confirmed that Tomlinson had been sent to Sulphur Wells as an informant.

Didn't ask. Didn't need to ask. Instead, I got Julie

talking about the cocaine trade. I didn't care about it, but I wanted him to think that I did. He kept asking for water—his throat was so dry. I told him he could have all the water when we were done. He tried to ingratiate himself—"Only a coupl'a good ol' boys like you an' me'd understand that!"—and through his abject eagerness to cooperate, he begged for his life.

I grew sick of him. I was sickened by the whole situation. One of the locker room maxims of hydrology is that shit never flows uphill. The maxim applies to human social dynamics as well. When the good ones, the hardworking hill climbers, are displaced for any reason—bad legislation, ghetto diffusion, or political leveraging—social sewage will flood in to fill the void. It was too damn bad. I wondered if the paper Tomlinson had intended to write on Sulphur Wells would have touched on that dynamic. Decided that Tomlinson's paper would have addressed that, along with subtleties that were beyond my power to understand.

I looked at Julie hanging there. He looked lifeless and mummified, like a mounted fish. Allowed myself to picture, for a moment, this big, loose-limbed goon pounding Tomlinson's face . . . quickly forced the image out of my mind because I didn't know if I could tolerate the cold and calculating rage that filled me.

I said, "Tuck your chin up against your chest," and I cut him down. The shock of the landing knocked the wind out of him. I rolled him over onto his belly, and as I sliced through the tape on his wrists, I said, "My boss says I can let you live, but there're a couple of conditions—Get your damn hands away from that tape on your eyes!"

Julie dropped his hands immediately. "Anything,

man. Name it.'' He was sitting up, rubbing his wrists, massaging his cheeks.

''My boss's got what you might call an import-export business of his own. Only it's no piddly-shit operation like you're used to. He was thinkin' about usin' that guy Kemper Waits to expand into the area, only, after what you told us, Waits sounds like some dumb ass hick.''

''He is! Kemper . . . Kemper, he's about half crazy.''

''My boss is thinkin' maybe you might be a better choice. Set you up here, let you work into it slow. Rules are simple: We supply the product, you find your own distributors. Screw up and we kill you.''

I could see Julie shiver at the thought of that. ''I'd . . . I'd get paid, right?''

''Make more money'n you ever made in your life. Move down here full-time, Julius. Buy yourself a nice place—that's right, we know who ya are, where you're from. First thing we got to do, though, is knock Kemper Waits away from the trough.''

''You want me to kill—''

''I want you to keep your damn mouth shut till I'm done. The way we're gonna work it is, we got a man on our payroll in the area. A local cop by the name'a Jackson. Now, Julius, you ever so much as hint to Jackson or anybody else that you know he's on our payroll, you're gonna be one of those ones I told you about. The ones I'm not always so nice to?'' I waited for Julie to nod his head eagerly before continuing. ''We're gonna have Jackson come down hard on Waits. You're gonna cooperate. Tell him everything you know. Might even have him arrest you on some piddly-ass little thing just to make it look good. Don't worry about it. Jackson'll be told you're one of us when the time's right. When

Kemper Waits is out of the way, that's when you'll take over.''

I patted him on the head; felt him flinch. Said, ''It'll be light in another hour or so. You flag yourself down a ride. Wait for us to get in touch. You handled yourself pretty good tonight, Julius. Most times, they bawl like babies. That's how we know you'll fit right in. My boss, he's pretty impressed.''

Julie wasn't sure he was allowed to speak. ''You mean this was like a sort of . . . test?''

I was already walking away, making enough noise for two people. ''My boss runs a class operation. Can't just let any shit-stomper in.''

I was almost to the water when I heard Julie call through the trees, ''Hey—fellas? FELLAS? You boys . . . you boys made the *right* decision. Thanks!''

AS I TOOK MY TIME RUNNING BACK TO DINKIN'S BAY, the first smear of daylight hung foglike over Sulphur Wells . . . then expanded out of the Pine Island tree line: a stratum of gray membrane that, gradually, was streaked with conch pink and violet. Somewhere—over Bimini, maybe; someplace in the Bahamas chain—the sun was wheeling hard around the rim of earth, moving incrementally across the Gulf Stream toward Florida.

I was thinking about Raymond Tullock. I had seen him only twice, yet the image of him was picture-sharp in my brain: not as tall as Hannah, but still a big man. Six feet, six one maybe. Tight muscularity. Hundred and eighty pounds, maybe one-ninety. The kind who worked out, stayed fit. Probably had a NordicTrack at home or a weight machine. Maybe a membership to a good health and tennis club. Early to mid thirties, and very careful about his appearance. The night he had surprised Hannah and me, he had arrived wild-eyed but well groomed. Dusty blond hair styled neatly. Wearing the carefully pressed travel-adventure khakis of a kind favored by the affluent armchair traveler. The Banana Republic style of outfit that is worn to make a statement. Tullock had a bony, angular face of a type that I associated with country club tennis players: athletic but articulate. With his face and hair, he resembled one of the doctors on the television show M*A*S*H. Hawkeye's second sidekick? Yeah, that was the one.

I wondered what motivated the guy. It was not surprising that he had become obsessive about Hannah Smith. A case could be made that I was also guilty of that. Nor was it surprising that he and others were working behind the scenes, plotting ways to turn the net ban into a personal windfall. Tullock was an ex-state employee, so he knew the ins and outs of the bureaucracy. It was not unusual that he and his cohorts would use that knowledge to their own advantage. What *was* unusual was that Tullock didn't hesitate to cross dangerous lines. He had told desperate commercial fishermen that they had to riot to get Tallahassee's attention. He had provided Kemper Waits—an unstable man, by all accounts—with a book on how to build a bomb. And it was Tullock, I was certain, who had seeded the rumor that Tomlinson was an informant. But the man was shrewd. Each time, he had tacked on just the right addendum to absolve himself of responsibility. I could hear him giving a deposition, telling some assistant district attorney that the only advice he remembered ever giving anybody was not to riot, not to burn, and not to retaliate. Could also picture the commercial fishermen that he had manipulated sitting there, handcuffed, admitting, yeah, Tullock *had* told them they shouldn't.

I wondered how that would play with Ron Jackson. I didn't know enough about the law to guess. Suspected that Tullock was operating in the gray fringe areas, and it depended on just how hard the DA's office wanted to go after him—if they went after him. What hard evidence was there, after all? Some black market book on terrorism? If Tullock was shrewd enough to remain safely in the background, pulling all the little puppet strings, then he was shrewd enough to buy a book in a way that was difficult to trace.

I was certain of one thing: Raymond Tullock had some dangerous kinks in his brain. He was fixated on having Hannah. The expression on his face the night he found us together had been grotesque. I could hear Hannah saying that in Tullock's mind, she and the land had become one. Tullock was determined to have them both, and somehow, that determination had grown into an obsession; an irrational craving that had nudged him toward the edge. It would be difficult to prove—perhaps impossible to prove—but I was convinced that Jimmy Darroux had been killed because of that craving . . . and perhaps Tomlinson, too.

When I was off Captiva Pass, I had to begin angling eastward into unprotected water. There was not so much wind now, but it was still gusting briskly out of the northwest. The wind had a bite to it; an Arctic Sea edge. My clothes had the leaden feel of dried salt and dampness. But the sweater and the good S.A.S. field pants were both made of wool, and I had also gotten my foul-weather jacket out of the stern locker and zipped it on. So I was soggy but warm. Surfed along with a following sea, thinking about Tullock, trying to determine the best way to smoke him out. No way was I going to let the bastard remain aloof from all the damage he had done . . . and would continue to do through surrogates. He was one of the behind-the-scenes guys; one of the cool manipulators. Well . . . I had some experience in that arena myself.

I was his next logical target, of course. Quite literally, he had caught Hannah and me with our pants down. For Tomlinson, Tullock had only required suspicion to act. The question was, how would he come after me? Tullock wasn't the one-on-one type—he'd had his opportunity that night at the Curlew fish house. And after I told Ron Jackson what I knew, neither the Copper Rim netters nor Kemper Waits would be in a position to do Tullock's dirty work.

That left Tullock powerless against me . . . for a while anyway. At least until he found another stooge.

I took some pleasure in that. I'd already stuck Tullock pretty good—the man didn't even know it. Then Hannah would stick him again when she broke the news about her fish farm. But I wanted to nail him in a way that hurt, really hurt, and I needed some time to do that. Time was something I would have. Tullock might be obsessive, but his each and every act was, at least, logical. Again, that was to my advantage. Logic dictated that he wait a good safe period before risking an attack on me. Too many dead men in too short a period and the full mass of state law enforcement would come snooping around his little island.

I took pleasure in that, too; the pure reasonableness of it.

I was still musing over ways to trap Tullock as I ran

through the old Mail Boat Channel—a couple of markers made of broken limbs and Clorox bottles—and happened to notice a fast mullet skiff angling down on me. It was a green plywood boat slapping along, throwing high spray. One person aboard dressed in a full yellow rain suit. Watched the boat jump a sandbar, coming closer . . . saw the driver motion for me to stop . . . and realized it was Hannah.

What the hell was she doing out here?

I levered the throttle back; waited.

HANNAH WAS IDLING TOWARD ME, HER SKIFF ROLLING and bucking as waves slid beneath the hull. She had to holler to make herself heard. Couldn't understand her, at first. Then: "Ford! Have you been home yet? Don't go home!"

I began to reply, but did not. There was something strange about the look of her face. . . .

"I've been trying to find you all night! I called and kept calling!"

She had the rain hood up. I was squinting, trying to see her clearly. My damn contact lenses . . .

"They told me at the hospital you didn't come back last night. So then I decided . . . Ford? Ford! Are you hearing me okay?"

She was close enough now. What I was hoping would turn out to be only a shadow or a grease mark was not a shadow or a grease mark. Her left eye was swollen nearly shut, her cheek a blush of eggplant purple.

I whispered a groaning sound before I yelled, "What happened to your face?"

Her boat was alongside mine now; we had to jockey our engines to keep the boats from slamming into each other. She touched her fingers experimentally to her cheek. It was as if she had forgotten that she was injured . . . or as if she had not had time to look in the mirror. Said, "It don't even hurt. It's somethin' we don't need to worry about right now—"

"Did somebody hit you?"

"Would you listen for a second—"

"Who hit you?" I shouted. "Was it Raymond? Goddamn it, I warned you about that guy—"

"That's what I'm tryin' to tell you!" There was a frenetic quality to her tone that demanded I shut up and let her speak. I did. She called, "Yesterday I started thinking about Raymond. Went down and talked to Arlis. He agreed. What you said about Raymond started makin' sense once we fit all the little pieces together. Then last night, after I got back from the hospital, it was pretty late and Raymond, he just opened the door and walked right into my house. It made me so mad that I . . . I probably shouldn't have, but I asked him about it. About what happened to Tommy . . . and Jimmy. Then I told him about my fish farm, too."

I looked at her; could see in her expression—*her poor face*—that she knew how foolish that had been. I said, "I don't care what you said, he had no right to hit you—"

"That's not why he hit me. He hit me 'cause I refused to stop seeing you. Then he hit me again because I wouldn't take off to Asia with him. He had my ticket, all the papers, everything all set to go. The midnight flight to Los Angeles. It was like he'd gone crazy. Started rummaging around my house, taking photographs of me, stuff off the mantelpiece, jamming it all into a briefcase. Like he was stealin' little pieces of me to take along. But that's not what I'm talking about, Ford.''

"You called the police. Tell me you called the police.''

"Yeah, but I called them because I was worried. Listen to what I'm telling you! I think Raymond musta knocked me out or something. I woke up on the floor and I had this terrible . . . I don't know . . . *feeling*. It had to do with the last thing I remember him sayin' to me. What he said was something about 'after your boyfriend gets home . . . ' Or, 'Don't expect your boyfriend to call after he gets home.' Something like that.''

I nodded agreeably. Hannah didn't seem to be tracking well. Tullock had probably given her a slight concussion. Why was that happening lately to all the people I cared about? I wished the wind weren't rolling our boats around so badly. I wanted to take her into my arms and hold her . . . wanted to apologize to her for my suspicions, for my coldness. I wanted to make her believe that not all angry men used their fists.

"Don't you see what I'm saying? By then it was almost three in the morning. I called your house and kept callin'. Called the hospital, and then I finally called the Sanibel police. They didn't want to listen to some hicky-voiced girl like me, but I made one of them drive to your place and have a look. It took him about forever to call back. All he said was your house was fine, and your truck was there, but your boat was gone.''

"My place—that's where we're going right now. I'm going to put you in bed and have a doctor buddy of mine—''

"No!'' Her tone said: *Why are you being so slow?* "Listen to me! 'After your boyfriend gets home.' That's what Raymond said. Don't you get it? How did he know you *weren't* home, Ford?''

I thought about that. For a moment, it threw a chilly little shadow over the shiny-bright chain of logic that I had constructed to predict Raymond Tullock's next move. But it didn't make sense. Moving so quickly against me just wasn't reasonable.

I explained that to Hannah. Added, ''I think he was trying to scare you. Or maybe you misunderstood. We've both been up all night.'' I glanced at my watch: 6:30 a.m. ''I want a doctor to look at you, then we'll get some sleep.''

For a moment, our boats were close enough, and I reached out and grasped Hannah's extended hand. Felt her long, cool fingers . . . felt the private little squeeze. An apology offered; an apology accepted.

She pushed the rain hood off her head and ran those same fingers through her Navajo hair. ''You really do think it's okay?''

''Yes.'' I looked at my watch again: 6:30.

''I had this awful feeling, Ford. I can't describe it. This feeling that somethin' really . . . bad was going to happen. I had the same feeling the night my mama died, so I got in my boat, scared to death, lookin' for you. . . .''

She paused as she noticed me stare at my watch a third time: *6:30*.

''What's wrong, Ford?''

''It's . . . nothing.''

''There's something wrong. Don't lie to me. I can see it in your face.''

I kept my voice calm—told myself there was nothing to worry about. ''I just remembered that there's a woman due at my house right now. A friend of mine named Janet Mueller. She's been taking care of my fish.''

"Doc . . . we've got to warn her. Even if you're right about Raymond.''

I began to think out loud. ''The police officer you called, he's already been there. . . . He had to walk out on the dock, maybe even knocked on the door.'' I was picturing it in my head: the cop walking out, shining his flashlight around. Walking up the steps to the breezeway that separated the lab from my house entrance, then peering over the rail to check my boats. I knew most of the Sanibel cops. If my truck was parked out front but my Hewes was gone, the cop would assume I was on the water. Pictured the cop turning, maybe shining the flashlight into a window or two before returning to his car.

Finally had to admit to myself that a brief inspection by a policeman did not mean that my house was safe. Also admitted that I was already thinking in terms of a bomb. If Tullock wanted to target me, he would make it very personal; rig it in a way that wouldn't be prematurely triggered by some idle visitor. He'd select some element of the house that was used by me and me alone. That's where he would put it. With all the marina contacts he had through his government work it was possible—hell, likely—that he knew far more about my lifestyle than I knew about his.

I thought about the door to my house . . . I thought about the door to my lab . . . then I thought about the heavy lid that covered my fish tank. Thought about Janet Mueller, always so punctual.

Six-thirty . . .

Don't worry, I'll take care of your fish.

I looked into Hannah's face and felt a contagious panic sweep through me. Said, "Follow me in!" and gunned my boat. Heard Hannah yell something in reply—something, I realized later, that I should have already known: In Hannah's boat, the trip would have been quicker.

In Hannah's boat, there was a chance . . . a slim, slim chance . . . that I would arrive at my dock before Janet did.

SEVENTEEN

INKIN'S BAY IS A LOPSIDED LAKE OF BRACKISH water that is enclosed by mangroves. There are only two narrow holes through the mangroves into that lake. One opening is to the northeast—slightly more than two miles from the marina and my stilt house. Because the water there is deep, it is known as the mouth to Dinkin's Bay. Channel markers create a twisting, navigable road to and from the mouth.

The other opening is to the northwest. It is much closer to the marina—a quarter-mile away, maybe less. That cut is also deep, but there are sandbars on either side which seal it closed. Because of its configuration, the cut is known to the fishing guides as Auger Hole. The Auger Hole is not considered navigable, unless you are in a canoe, or unless you are in a thin-draft boat like mine and it is a very, very high tide.

That morning, the tide was not very, very high. In fact, it was closer to low tide because the dynamics of a northwest wind push water out of the sound, then hold it offshore. As I raced away from Hannah, I pointed my bow directly at the mouth of Dinkin's Bay. From the corner of my eye, I noticed Hannah also speeding away, but she was steering much farther toward the south; she appeared to be heading into another bay, which the guides call Horseshoe.

That made no sense . . . until I realized what she was doing. She was going to attempt to lop off a couple of miles; shorten the distance between herself and the marina. She was going to try and jump the bars and cross through Auger Hole into Dinkin's Bay.

I thought: not on this tide. Not even in a mullet boat.

I watched her for a while: she and her skiff getting smaller and smaller, our angles of passage expanding the distance. Then the outside wall of Dinkin's Bay interceded, and she disappeared.

At Woodring Point, I turned hard to the south into the mouth of the bay. I ignored the channel markers and trimmed the engine high. The mangroves provided a break from the wind, so the water was much calmer. I jammed the throttle forward and watched the tachometer needle jump to six thousand RPM—sixty miles an hour, maybe faster. The speed made my lips flutter and teared my eyes. I used the nose on my boat like a rifle sight: kept it pointed on my tiny gray house, two miles away.

As I drove, I fished beneath the console and pulled out my portable VHF radio. I tried to call the fishing guides on channel 8.

No reply. If they were at the docks this early, they hadn't yet turned their radios on.

Hit a button and tried to call the marina on channel 16.

No reply. The marina didn't open until seven. Mack usually didn't get around to turning the radio on until later.

Put the radio away and made a ridiculous attempt to

try one of Tomlinson's tricks, a telepathic message to Janet Mueller: *Sleep late . . . sleep late . . . sleep late. . . . Stay away from the aquarium. . . .*

Pictured Janet's face: the pudgy face with steady, steady eyes that had already seen way too much pain. Pictured her in her baggy pants and sweatshirt . . . saw her expression of astonishment as she marveled at the behavior of the tarpon . . . saw her in her gaudy peach ball gown before Perbcot: a shy, private girl in a grown-up's party clothes.

Felt the panic in me grow stronger; attempted to use logic like an antidote: Raymond Tullock wouldn't do it. Not now. Not this damn soon!

Heard a small voice say: *You're wrong*.

I was so fixated on my fish house, straining so hard to will Janet away from it, that I didn't notice Hannah until she came sweeping across the channel a mile or so ahead of me, her plywood boat throwing a funneling wake. Felt shock close to disbelief—She *made* it?—followed by pure admiration. There are people in this world who are so strong, who possess such power of character, that the very attributes that set them apart also make the validity of their character suspect.

Heard the small voice say: *You were wrong again*.

It was true. Wrong about many things. Very wrong about Hannah.

I was gaining on her small green boat. Now I was close enough to see the empty porch that encircles my house . . . and the empty platform below it on which sat my big wooden fish tank. Was close enough to see the rambling, rickety yards of empty boardwalk which lead from my house to the mangrove shore. Was close enough to see . . . to see Janet Mueller come through the mangroves and step up onto the boardwalk, walking swiftly. New outfit on this chilly morning: furry red miracle-fabric jacket and green shorts.

It seemed, then, that I could not make my boat go fast enough . . . seemed as if everything was being dragged down by a leaden gravity created by my own anxiety . . . seemed as if time and movement were being dilated into a terrible slow motion. I leaned over the windshield of my boat, my weight full on the throttle, as if, by urging my boat along, I might free the both of us from gravity's grip. It did not help.

I watched Hannah standing at the throttle of her boat, going fast, waving frantically, trying to get Janet's attention. . . .

Watched Janet, as if lost in her own thoughts, walk obliviously to the end of the boardwalk and step up onto the platform below my house. Realized that she was headed for the fish tank. . . .

Saw Hannah, now no more than a hundred yards away, raise both hands over her head and flag her arms back and forth. . . .

Watched Janet stop at the fish tank, look up at the windows of my house, then reach for the lid of the fish tank. Couldn't she hear the boat bearing down on her? . . .

Saw Hannah cup both hands to her mouth—she was shouting now—as her boat dolphined closer and closer to the house, still going full speed. . . .

Watched Janet lifting the lid . . . lifting it up on its hinges . . . pushing the weight of the lid higher. . . .

Then saw Janet suddenly look at the approaching boat and jump back as if in surprise. Saw the lid slap shut just as Hannah's boat slid to a fast stop below my house, the chines of her boat plowing up a curtain of bright spray that soaked the platform and Janet, too. . . .

Hannah was now talking to Janet, hands motioning animatedly. Janet hesitated. Said something back to Hannah . . . listened for another moment. Then Janet turned and hurried off the platform, jogging along the boardwalk toward shore. . . .

Thank God.

I was a little more than fifty yards away now, already backing off on the throttle, slowing down. Hannah turned to look at me and grinned—a tall, gawky, handsome woman in a cheap yellow rain suit. Her grin so bright that her swollen eye seemed insignificant; did not detract at all from her beauty. She made a clownish show of wiping the sweat off her brow and slinging it away. Mouthed the words: "I told her."

I raised a fist over my head and shook it—*Good job!*—and motioned her toward the pilings where she could tie up while I checked the place out. She idled around the corner of the house . . . caught the only available line of my mooring pulley system, and pulled it. But the counterweight didn't budge.

I thought: That's odd, as I watched Hannah give the rope another yank. And yet another.

My brain took its time; scanned dumbly for an explanation; neuron conduits began the electrochemical process of deduction . . . and suddenly, the message relays were seared by the acid shock of a single, numbing thought: *Trip wire!*

But I realized it much, much too late to stop Hannah from pulling the rope a final time. Much, much too late to scream a warning, though I tried. And much too late to stab my hand out to stop her—an absurd gesture because I was still forty or more yards away. Yet I attempted to do that, too.

Later, Ron Jackson would tell me the A.T.F. guys calculated that the radiant power of the bomb was no more than that of a quarter-stick of dynamite. It was a small and personalized little bomb, created for just one person; placed against a piling and triggered off the mooring rope so that a returning boater—me—could not possibly avoid it.

So Hannah could not have avoided what happened to her. When she pulled the rope free, I saw a bloom of thermal energy shoot skyward, and in the same instant, I was knocked to the deck by the shock of the noise and rifled debris. When I got to my feet again, I saw that the platform and the back wall of my lab were on fire . . . saw Hannah facedown in the water, blown far from her listing, burning boat.

Days afterward, Janet Mueller, who saw it all, would tell me that I gunned my boat toward Hannah, and when I was close enough, I jumped into the water beside her without pulling the throttle back or switching off the engine. Janet told me that, because I couldn't remember how I had gotten Hannah to shore, or how and why my boat had ended up high and dry, wrecked in the mangroves.

What I could remember was the look of Hannah's face as I held her head in my lap. A pretty face, and peaceful, but her dark eyes were . . . *wrong* . . . because of the force of the explosion. Could remember the hoarse and strangely amused quality in Hannah's voice trying to ask me something . . . or trying to tell me something . . . trying to make me understand.

Leaned to touch my lips to hers. "Don't try to talk, love."

But she was stubborn; wouldn't be silent. In a final effort to be heard, she lurched her face up toward mine and whispered words that, for a long time, made no sense: "Ford? Like before, I . . . didn't . . . *sink*."

Though her eyes remained open, Hannah Smith did not speak again.

I remembered that. And I remembered threatening to punch one of the paramedics if he did not allow me to sit at Hannah's side as they flew us to the hospital— "What's the big deal about a bruise on my forehead!"— and I remember the expression on the emergency room doctor when he turned to me . . . after pulling the sheet up over Hannah's face.

The only other thing I remember clearly about that morning was standing alone, in an empty hospital corridor—I don't know how I got there—and watching Dr. Maria Corales walking toward me. She was wearing soiled surgical scrubs. She looked very tired. The way she put her hand on my shoulder communicated genuine concern. She told me, "We'll keep the respirator going until we hear from the family, or until the hospital's Human Subjects Panel meets. But the surgery didn't go well. I'm afraid I lost him this morning."

It took me a long, dull moment to realize what she meant. She was talking about Tomlinson.

THEY BURIED HANNAH FOUR DAYS LATER, JANUARY 16, a Monday, one day after the official close of Florida's last mullet roe season. I couldn't decide whether it was good timing or cruel irony. Buried her in an incongruously modern cemetery on the mainland—one of those fairway-neat memorial parks that use standardized brass markers to make it easier on the mowing crews. The cemetery was close enough to the main highway so that all the tourist traffic made it difficult to hear the minister's words.

I don't know how many hundreds of people attended. Enough to render the island of Sulphur Wells nearly empty that afternoon. Enough to illustrate Tomlinson's theory about Hannah's position in the community. When a chieftain dies, the whole tribe turns out. I stood and talked with Tootsie Cribbs for a while. Met his nice wife and three children. His kids looked so uncomfortable in their Sunday clothes that I guessed they would have preferred to be in school.

I didn't blame them.

Also met Hannah's two brothers. There was Bob, who'd flown in from Atlanta, and Cletus, who now lived in Orlando. They weren't at all what I had expected them to be. Both were huge, hulking men, but their expressions were mild, faintly bovine; they didn't have Hannah's wild eyes. Nor were they fishermen. Bob was an attorney; Cletus worked in administration for Disney. It was Bob who told me, "Hannah was a romantic. With her grades and with her talent—all-state basketball; class president three years in a row—she could have gotten a scholarship, no problem. Florida State wanted her, one of those ritzy Ivy League women's schools, too. But she'd get her mind set on something and nobody could talk sense into her. Our dad fished day and night so his kids wouldn't have to fish. So what's Hannah do? She becomes one of those back-to-the-roots people. I loved her dearly; she was one of my favorite people in the world, but Hannah was . . . different.''

I could not argue.

Mostly, I looked after Arlis Futch. The man was miserable. He looked as if the last few days had aged him twenty years. He walked around in a fog, too tough to cry, in too much pain not to. Looked up at me more than once and said, "I sure 'nuff hope they catch the ones that kilt her."

More than once, I answered, "You can count on it, Arlis."

THE FIRE DEPARTMENT HAD DONE A SUPERB JOB OF SAVing my stilt house. Even so, much of the lower decking had been destroyed and most of my lab, too. My optical equipment had either cracked or fogged because of the heat. Many of my slides were ruined and whole rows of specimen jars had exploded. Because my one-room house is under the same tin roof, heat-saturated smoke had invaded the place, ruining my telescope, melting some of my record albums, and the stink of the smoke was on everything I owned.

The only bright spot was that Crunch & Des, the black cat, had been panhandling around the marina at the time of the explosion, so he was still his lazy, healthy, indifferent self.

For several days after Hannah's death, I was led to believe that the explosion and fire had also somehow killed all the specimens in my fish tank. But Janet Mueller finally told me the truth: The reason she had dropped the lid so abruptly that Thursday morning was not because she heard Hannah calling to her, but because she had been shocked to find all the fish, including our six tarpon, swirling around in a green chemical foam. She decided that my raw-water pump had somehow sucked in some kind of pollutant, but didn't want to tell me right away. Wanted to give me time to recover from the concussion she insisted that I had suffered. "A big chunk of wood hit you right in the head, Doc. I saw it. That's why I still think you need to see a doctor."

I didn't want to see a doctor. It was my own stupidity that had allowed the explosion to occur. A mild concussion didn't seem penalty enough for the harm I had caused. Nor did I tell Janet what I suspected was the truth: A couple of drunk sportfishermen in a pickup truck had poisoned my fish as punishment for my traitorous association with the netters. Didn't mention my suspicions to Nels Esterline, either. Why reopen old wounds?

Everyone from the marina community joined together in an attempt to help me. No one worked harder at that than Janet. A change had come over her since the explosion. She was no longer the weepy, nerve-shattered woman she had been when she arrived at Dinkin's Bay. Maybe it was because she had finally come to terms with what had happened in her life. Or maybe it was because the explosion required that she refocus her energies on the needs of others. Every day, I would find her picking through the wreckage of my lab, sorting and boxing and scrubbing.

Not that I was staying at my stilt house. No. I couldn't stand the smoky stink of the place; the images that flashed into my brain caused by just standing on the charred dock. I had spent the first night sleeping on Tomlinson's sailboat, but there were too many ghosts there, too. Finally, I rented a one-bedroom condo unit down on the beach. I moved in enough personal items to be comfortable—my shortwave radio; a few books—

and had my telephone forwarded. It was a pretty tourist place called Casa Ybel. Each morning, I'd sleep just as late as I possibly could, then do a very long beach run, a very long surf swim. Each night, I'd force myself to stay awake just as late as I possibly could, my brain whirring away with devious little ideas; nasty, nasty scenarios.

When you are planning a trip to the other side of the world, it's best to nudge the body clock ahead long before departure.

One afternoon, Janet confronted me and said, "Look, Doc, I can relate to what you're going through. I've *been* through it. So I want to give you some advice that I wish somebody had given me: You've got to stay busy. Find something to do. Not big stuff. I think the little no-brainer stuff is best . . . like maybe help me get this place cleaned up? Or we could start building a new fish tank. I'll help!"

I had patted her arm affectionately, smiled my bland smile, and said, "But I *am* staying busy, Janet."

I was.

The first thing I had done was box all my important personal items; then rented space at a high-security storage business. The kind of business that gladly accepts cash in advance and isn't too fussy about identification. The kind of business favored by people who realize that a safety deposit box can be sealed and searched by authorities if a judge can be found to sign the right papers.

Through a much traveled friend, I also drew out a sizable chunk of cash from my account at the Royal Trust Ltd., Seven Mile Beach, Grand Cayman Island. Then I took a tiny piece of that cash around to several local banks and converted it into hefty bags of quarters.

When you are traveling from pay phone to pay phone, over a large area and over a period of several days, you don't want to be caught short of change, particularly if you are making tough but untraceable trunk calls to places such as Nicaragua, Singapore, Burma, and Medan, Sumatra.

I also converted a tidy chunk of that cash into two large money orders. I Fed Exed both of the checks, but to different parts of the world. One went to an acquaintance of mine in Miami, along with a passport-size photograph. Pretty nice photograph; didn't wear my glasses.

The days prior to Hannah's funeral were very busy days indeed.

ON TUESDAY AFTERNOON, JANUARY 17, RON JACKSON called and invited me to accompany him on a midnight bust he and some A.T.F. agents had planned. Even though I declined, he didn't tell me who they were going to hit, or why. He didn't need to. I had already given him all the information I had collected. After thinking long and hard about it, I had even told him my suspicions about Raymond Tullock. I didn't press the issue too hard. But I told him. If fate—or Tullock's good planning—made him impossible for the law to touch, then fate *wanted* me to intercede.

Tomlinson might have called the gesture an attempt to seek karmic approval.

On Wednesday morning, Jackson showed up at my condo apartment. His clothes were wrinkled; he looked tired. Probably hadn't been to bed all night. When I opened the door, he held up his gym bag. "Run?"

We ran.

They had swept the beach at Copper Rim, he told me.

They had bagged every man there on probable cause, including one Julian Claypool.

"Julian?" I said. I had called him Julius—another mistake to add to my list.

"Claypool may be the strangest man I've ever arrested," Jackson said as we chugged along, the hard sand sponging our waffle tracks. "The whole time, he just beamed and grinned. Not the least bit upset. Hell, Claypool seemed *glad* to see me. Like he was going to reach out and shake my hand. Yep, he'd beaten Mr. Tomlinson. Yep, he'd dropped him off along the road. Sure, he could tell me who helped—it was this guy and this guy and this guy. Didn't care about the others hearing him. Man, if looks could kill! I'm telling you, Ford, he made me nervous. I tried to get him to shut up. Didn't want him to say another word until we got the court to appoint him a lawyer." Jackson jogged along silently for a time, before adding, "I'm sorry about your friend, by the way. Wiped the smile right off Claypool's face when he found out he was up for murder."

I said, "I imagine it did. Florida's an electric chair state."

"Naw-w-w. Second degree maybe, but more likely they'll work it down to manslaughter. Claypool won't get the chair." More silence. Something was on his mind. I thought he was going to confront me with it but, instead, he told me about Kemper Waits. How the bust had gone.

It had gone very well. They had cuffed Waits and read him his rights. Unlike Claypool, Waits had not been cooperative. He had slobbered at the mouth and screamed about government conspiracies. Waits, Jackson told me, was a certifiable freak. Because Waits refused to provide a key, they had battered down the door of his cement shed. Inside, the A.T.F. agents had found wiring and timers and caps and fuses, along with four vacuum-packed sticks of dynamite, plus a tattered counterculture pamphlet with the words "Cook Book" in the title. It was a well-equipped little bomb factory.

"He wasn't going to stop with two," Jackson told me. "Kemper had a taste for it. He'd declared his own private war. A diet of drugs and whiskey can create paranoia, and that guy has a big-league case of it."

In the pond behind Waits's house, agents had waded in and confirmed that there were heavy, metal objects in the shallows that were presumably boat engines, but they wouldn't know how many until they started winching them out.

"The information was all good, Ford. Everything you gave me was dead on." We had run halfway to the San-ibel lighthouse, and now were on our way back. "A clean bust like that, it didn't hurt my reputation with the sheriff . . . or the federal boys, either, for that matter. I appreciate it. I really do. But what I'm worried about is . . . this thing that's been on my mind . . ."

I sensed what was troubling Jackson and decided to help him out. "The bomb that killed Hannah Smith had nothing to do with me gathering information on Sulphur Wells, Ron."

"I wish I could be as certain of it as you are. I'm the one who asked you to do it. I'd feel terrible—"

"I've already told you why that bomb was there. I think Kemper Waits probably made it, but I think Ray-mond Tullock put it there. You seem reluctant to believe that."

"Oh bullshit, Ford." He made a noise of friendly exasperation. "It's not that I'm reluctant, we just don't have anything on him. Waits played dumb about him; even Claypool said Tullock wasn't involved—and Claypool was squealing on everybody but his mother. Everything you told me makes sense. Yeah, I believe the guy's a flake. Do we have our suspicions? Damn right. Tullock flies off to Asia the night before the bomb explodes. Did I tell you he cleaned out his bank account?"

"No, but I'm not surprised." It was true. I wasn't surprised; had, in fact, already anticipated it.

"He cleans out his bank account, yeah. *And* his corporate account. Closes up his apartment and gets on a plane to Singapore." Jackson looked at me to emphasize his point. "I'll tell you one thing: The guy screws up in Asia, he'll wish he'd never left home. Some of those places, they still beat you bloody with a cane. Or worse. Like that American brat who spraypainted those cars?"

"Asians are pretty tough," I agreed.

"When the right paperwork comes through, the A.T.F. boys and I are going to have a look at Tullock's apartment." Jackson reached over and gave me an amiable slap on the shoulder. "If we find something good, we'll go to work on extradition. A week in one of those rathole dungeons would put a new bounce in Tullock's step. Or we'll be at the airport waiting on him if he's got the balls to come back. The computers show he's got a return ticket out of Singapore for the twenty-fifth."

I said, "Singapore, huh?" But I was thinking: Raymond Tullock isn't coming back.

I SPREAD THE WORD AROUND DINKIN'S BAY THAT I WAS flying off to Nicaragua. Told them I was going to watch a few ball games at Mad Monk Stadium in Managua, then drive clear down to the San Juan River—old Contra country—to do some research on the bull sharks that live in Lake Nicaragua. Or at least *had* lived in Lake Nicaragua until the Japanese fin merchants exterminated them.

I told my friends I needed a change of scenery. Told them that a month or so in the jungle would help me adjust. I didn't mention that in a world of tele-linkage and information highways, the only way to travel anonymously anymore is through one of the few remaining outlaw countries.

Cuba would have been okay, but I couldn't get the direct flight to Mexico City I needed. If I was late to Mexico City, I'd miss my Thai Airline connection to Fiji. Which meant that the rest of my itinerary—Fiji to Manila, Manila to Singapore, Singapore to Medan, Sumatra—would all fall through.

But the afternoon Managua-to-Mexico City flight would work out just fine. So I spread the story about Nicaragua. Told it so many times that I was actually beginning to believe it myself. Wide-eyed and a little breathless, Janet had asked me, "Isn't it dangerous in the rain forest? All those animals? You, all by yourself?"

I wondered if it was her shy way of hinting that she would like to accompany me.

I shook my head, telling Janet, "The rain forest is the safest place I know."

MY LAST DAY IN FLORIDA—MY LAST FOR MANY YEARS, I suspected—was Friday, January 20. It was the kind of winter-gray day that one associates with snow peaks or midwestern industrial cities. There were heavy rain

clouds to the north. The weather added a sarcastic edge
to my mood. I looked at the sky and thought: Perfect.

In the morning, I made the long, long drive to Sulphur
Wells. Had to pick the lock at Hannah's house to get in.
She and Tomlinson had set up the typewriter on the
breakfast table. There was a sheet of paper still rolled
into it. The incomplete manuscript—Hannah's book—
lay neatly in a box on the table. Tomlinson had finished
nearly eight chapters. Not seven, as Hannah had said.

The last entry was in Hannah's handwriting: "The
Yeaters and the Treadwells had a yard sale yesterday,
selling out. Mr. Yeater said he might be able to get work
in Detroit. Him and my daddy fished together when I
was a little girl, so . . ."

The note was unfinished. Wondered if Tullock had
interrupted her at the writing desk.

I took the manuscript, and collected Tomlinson's personal effects in his old brown leather suitcase. I then
made a slow tour of the house. There were still signs of
Tullock's last confrontation with Hannah: the arrangement of dried flowers that had once been on the mantelpiece was now scattered across the floor in front of
the fireplace. One of the green glass spheres lay shattered on the floor, though one remained unbroken. One,
perhaps two were missing. I remembered Hannah telling
me that they were heirlooms; the only thing she had of
her Great-Aunt Hannah's. I took the sphere that remained, then searched her bedroom. What I wanted was
a photograph of her; something else to remember her
by. Could hear Hannah say, *He was stealing little pieces
of me.* I wanted a few pieces for myself.

I finally found the scrapbook. It was a cheap blue
imitation-leather binder. Leafed through it. Saw a tintype

of a very tall woman in a long print dress and a white sun hat. She was standing by a team of oxen, holding a coil of rope in her left hand. Written on the back of the photograph in fountain pen was: Hannah "Big Six" Smith, Homestead, Fla. 1907.

I removed the print, then selected two photographs of Hannah. One was of her in a basketball uniform: stork legs; black, glittering eyes. The other was of her sitting beneath a tree, holding a book. A more reflective pose. Her hair was longer, parted in the middle and combed straight to her shoulders. She looked young and at ease. Very pretty.

I took the things, locked the house, and drove to a print business that was on the way to the hospital. It was called Kopy Kat. One of the big chains. I gave the woman at the counter the partial manuscript and two of the photographs. I told her how I wanted it done: printed book form, good quality paper, nice cover. I told her to print enough copies to send to every library in Florida. I paid cash in advance.

My going-away present.

When the clerk asked what should go on the cover, I took the order form and wrote: *The Hannah Smith Story*.

SINCE THE EXPLOSION, I HAD VISITED TOMLINSON ONLY once. Seeing his shrunken body, hearing the flatline hum of the electroencephalogram was just too unsettling. The man was gone, so why leave the plugs in?

I had arranged to meet Dr. Corales and two representatives of the hospital's Human Subjects Panel at a private room off the intensive care unit at eleven a.m.— less than an hour before my flight to Miami. She arrived slightly late, her hair and clothes soaked from the rainstorm that had rumbled and threatened all morning. We shook hands as she told me, "I appreciate you tracking down Mr. Tomlinson's brother. We received his telegram yesterday afternoon. It's . . . a little strange, but it's sufficient."

I wasn't surprised in the least. On the phone, from halfway around the world, Norvin Tomlinson had sounded vague, distracted, cynical, and desperately mercenary. Even in Burma, a drug addict's life required some income.

She handed me the telegram. I read it, then smiled at Dr. Corales. She looked less businesslike, more attractive because of her wet hair. "Isn't it odd," I said, "how siblings can be so different?"

Norvin Tomlinson's telegram had read: "KILL HIM, KILL THEM ALL!"

Dr. Corales returned my smile, agreeing, then took the telegram from me before saying, "Are you ready?"

I was ready. I was holding Tomlinson's hand when they disengaged the respirator. His hand was already cool. His face was the color and texture of a very, very old mushroom. I waited there alone with him for a minute or so while the thunderstorm whoofed and rumbled outside. I sent telepathic messages. I received no messages in reply. Then I exited the room and I handed Dr. Corales a brown paper bag. Tomlinson's sarong was in the bag and I instructed that he be wearing it when he was cremated. I also reminded her that the ashes were to go to Mack at Dinkin's Bay, so that they could be spread by boat following the little Buddhist ceremony I had already arranged.

The last thing I did before taking a cab to the airport was hand the doctor my truck's registration and keys. I told her to make a present of the truck to Janet Mueller, who would arrive later.

As I walked away, Dr. Corales said, "Have a good trip. Too bad you have to fly on a day like today." One of those bland comments that professionals sometimes use to gauge the mood and the stability of a patient.

I told Dr. Corales that *any* trip that had a layover at the American Eagle terminal in Miami was a bad day to fly.

A little joke. Just to let her know I was okay.

EIGHTEEN

I WAS IN AN ANCIENT GARUDA AIRLINER; SOME RE-cycled transport jet whose fuselage had been polished beer can-thin by all the hours of wind friction, all the years of jungle puddle-jumping, all the days of harsh Indonesian sunlight.

We banked to starboard and descended through vol-canic clouds. Below and ahead was Sumatra. We dropped down over mangrove plains off the Straits of Malacca and I could see a plateau of orange smog that was as vivid as the hot haze of a chemical fire. The smog lay over jungle—a stratum of red gas shimmering over emerald green. Then the jungle began to thin. There was a veinwork of dirt roads and brown rivers that ran through rice paddies. The landscape reminded me of Vietnam. Then I could see the city's outskirts: a coag-ulated mass of slums; thousands of bamboo shanties, each with a television antenna suspended from a bamboo pole. The city's center was to the north: a hazy, geo-metric clutter packed onto a delta created by the branch-ing of two muddy rivers.

The old plane wobbled, creaked; tires yelped before the reverse thrust of engines, and then a throng of tiny, brown shirtless men were wheeling the stairs toward the open cabin door.

Welcome to Sumatra, the second largest island in the nation of Indonesia. Welcome to Medan, the island's largest city, home to a million or more anonymous souls. Had I attacked the tarmac with a nuclear auger, drilled straight down through the center of the planet, through the thousands of miles of molten core, I would have exited the tunnel somewhere close to Nicaragua, not far from where I had started.

So, welcome to the back side of the earth. . . .

I went through customs, no problem. Expected to be met by an old contact of mine, Havildar Singbah. Havildar had been a staff sergeant in the Duke of Edinburgh's Own Gurkha Rifles. In military communities, the Gurkhas are considered to be the most fearsome infantry fighters on earth. They are also considered to be among the most trustworthy men on earth. Havildar had seen action in Vietnam and the Falklands. He is about five feet six inches tall, and he is one of the few men I've met in my life who truly frightens me. Not because of the way he looks—the man always had a mellow little smile on his face—but because of the stories I had heard about him while he and his troop served with the Brits.

Waiting for me with a car, though, was a man named Rengat Ungar. Rengat was maybe thirty years old, maybe fifty. He wore a dirty turban and rubber sandals. He told me Havildar had suddenly been called back to Nepal because his father was very ill. Rengat assured me I could like and trust him one hundred percent. "Just like Havildar, you bet!"

But I didn't like or trust Rengat. He chattered constantly in his broken English and chain-smoked Indonesian cigarettes that stank of cloves. He drove much too fast and the brakes on his little car were bad. Because Medan has no stoplights or stop signs, it was a dangerous combination.

I settled back and stared out the window, hoping that my indifference would cause him to concentrate on his driving.

If there were a million people in Medan, there seemed to be at least that many beat-up minibuses and motorized *becak* rickshaws on the narrow streets. Few of the vehicles had mufflers, but they all had horns, so the streets were a chaos of noise and exhaust that linked the open markets, filthy restaurants, sleazy bars, teenage prostitutes, swaggering cops, sleeping drunks, women cooking over wood fires, pretty children flirting from doorways, roaming goats, and the few stray dogs that had not yet been eaten.

"You want nice girl?" Rengat asked me cheerfully. "Very young, very cheap."

"Not right now," I told him.

"A nice young boy, then? I can offer you a selection of very clean young boys."

It is one of the great ironies of Indonesia that its Islamic communities are brutally strict about some laws, yet totally indifferent to others. Were I found guilty of stealing in Medan, my left hand would be chopped off. Were I caught with narcotics in my possession, I would be condemned to some hellhole prison for a year or more, then shot. No appeals considered, no questions asked, no concessions offered even to a well-moneyed American. But for a few thousand rupiah—the equivalent of about two dollars—I could purchase the innocence of any wandering child, and the local cops would turn their backs.

The few tourists who came to Sumatra—there weren't many—came for the lively sex trade. The only other draw was the timber trade. The Japanese, I knew, were logging the rain forests day and night. The industry had attracted a sizable enclave of Japanese—which explained the niche market Raymond Tullock had found for his mullet roe. That Sumatra was sexually lawless also explained the Japanese's need for it.

I told Rengat, "No children today, thanks."

Before he dropped me at my hotel, I had Rengat drive me through town and out toward the port of Belawan. It took me more than an hour of roaming around the docks, using Rengat as an interpreter, to find the boat I was to meet. It was a small brown-sailed junk made of red teak. The junk had a dragon's head carved into the bow, and golden Chinese characters on the stern. Beneath the characters was a word in English: *Rangoon*.

The captain of the vessel was a dour little man whose teeth were black from chewing betel nuts. He made a show of being angry at me. I was days late! He was now off schedule! Which was all bullshit—they had only just arrived, according to the junk's customs sheet, and had to stay in Sumatra for at least several days, as we both well knew. But I palmed him several twenties, and three evenly ripped halves of hundred-dollar bills to make him happy.

At customs, I showed the inspector one of my three false passports. I also showed him my international collector's permit. All the embossed lettering and stamps seemed to impress him. So did the innocuous ten-dollar bill I slipped him. The customs inspector opened the small Styrofoam box I had taken from the junk. Inside were three frozen ox-eyed tarpon, a species that is found only in Asia and is very common around the river mouths of Burma. To an American biologist such as myself, they were rare creatures indeed.

I raised my eyebrows at the inspector to illustrate my question, then made a sawing motion with my hand. Did he want me to cut the fish open?

The man shook his head, already bored with me, and waved me through.

I carried my package back to the little car and got in beside Rengat. As we neared the city, I suggested he make a quick stop at his home so that I might meet his wife and children. Rengat was reluctant. I pressed the issue, telling him I wanted to make small gifts of money to his children.

Ultimately, greed got the best of him. His tiny block house was just off a side street named Madong Lubis. I bowed to Rengat's wife and dipped a cup of kava from the wooden bowl in the tiny living room. In Asia, loud slurping is the sound of polite approval. I patted Rengat's children and gave them crisp greenbacks. As I held the bills out, only I seemed to notice that my hands were shaking.

Once we were back in the car, Rengat was not so talkative, and he seemed less eager for me to approve of him. Familiarity diminishes authority while increasing dependency. My visit had accomplished both. As he drove me to my hotel, I was aware that Rengat was aware that the price of any sort of betrayal had increased exponentially.

I now knew where the man lived.

•   •   •

A SEALED NOTE FROM HAVILDAR APOLOGIZED FOR HIS absence and told me that Raymond Tullock was staying at the Hotel Tiara, third floor, room 217.

The strange numbering system, I knew, was a hold-over from the old Dutch colonial days when Sumatra was one of the thriving dark corners of the rubber trade.

The Hotel Tiara was the best hotel in Medan—which is to say that it was about as plush, but not as clean, as the average Motel 6. It was a tall, squarish salmon-colored building on busy, potholed Cut Mutiah Street. Small men with rickshaws and pedicabs stood in a line outside the hotel, waiting for fares.

The room Havildar had arranged for me was opposite the Hotel Tiara and down less than a block. It was a native place named Selamat Sian—"Good day!" in Indonesian. The little rooming house was as dark and nar-row-staired as a New York tenement building. It smelled of curry and rotting durian fruit and Indonesian ciga-rettes. My room overlooked the street, so I could watch Tullock coming and going.

Havildar's note also told me that I should not trust Rengat, but not to fear him either. The note included the names I needed of a few local men, and it concluded by reminding me that Havildar and I still had unfinished business on the nearby island of Timor. In 1975, the Indonesian government had staged a brutal military take-over of East Timor. Military rule there—enforced by Indonesian death squads—continues even today.

Years ago, I had used Sumatra as a staging area for a surveillance operation that had accomplished abso-lutely nothing but earn me the friendship of the little Gurkha sergeant. I was sorry about Havildar's father, but I wished to hell Havildar were still in Medan, and not

working his way up to his native village in the Hima-
layas. It did more than change my plan. I would now
have to completely abandon certain elements of it.

There was one thing I didn't want to do, couldn't do:
spend much time in Medan. It was possible that the Indonesian government had learned about my earlier work.
If I was caught—particularly with three false passports
in my possession—I would be summarily jailed. Maybe
the American Embassy in Jakarta would be notified, but
that was unlikely. A more probable scenario was that I
would be locked anonymously away until an appropriate
time when I might be used as a bargaining tool. If that
opportunity never materialized—I could think of no reason that it would—then I would be left to die in the
local prison.

I had once driven past that prison—the Simpang Alas
it was called, named for a local river. Alas Prison was
a monstrous old fortress of rotting cement and concertina
wire built north of town. It had reminded me of Hoa Lo
prison in Hanoi, because the outside walls were painted
the same damp, mustard-yellow color. Its few windows
were as black and narrow as gunports; the yellow walls
were high. Two elements dominated the prison grounds:
the silence . . . and the smell. Simpang Alas possessed
the eerie silence of an abandoned city; the kind of silence that fills the void after someone has abruptly
ceased screaming. The wind that blew over the prison
carried the defecant odors of humans who have been
reduced to cave animals. That smell was the stench of
nightmares.

Even local travelers who passed Simpang Alas
averted their eyes, as if a dark vacuum radiated out be-

yond the prison walls and to look upon it put them at risk of being sucked into that darkness.

What I needed to do was hit Raymond Tullock quickly, then get the hell out. I would have preferred anything to even a year in Simpang Alas—a firing squad, a knife . . . anything.

But with Havildar gone, it would not be so easy.

FOR THREE STRAIGHT DAYS, I WATCHED TULLOCK FROM my window, or tagged along after him in a car, with Rengat driving. I watched him and made cryptic notes.

He was never hard to find. In the alleyways of Sumatra, a tall, blond American stands out in any crowd.

Tullock had three Japanese business associates. The four of them spent two mornings at the huge fish market in Belawan, not far from the port where I had met the junk days earlier. They also spent a day traveling around the foothills of the western mountains. I got the impression that Tullock was thinking about expanding into the timber business. Also got the impression that he was looking for an estate to buy or rent.

In Indonesia, a man with a monthly income of a couple thousand U.S. dollars could live like a sultan. Maids, gardeners, a chauffeur, cooks, and all the wives and mistresses he wanted.

I wondered if Tullock was afraid of the murder charge that might await him back in the states. He had cleaned out his bank accounts. So maybe that had been his plan all along. Hannah had made it plain that he would never have her, so why go back?

I also wondered if Tullock, through phone calls back to the States, had discovered that he had killed Hannah, not me.

I found it oddly irritating that I did not know.

Tullock was a punctual man of habit. Each day he returned to his hotel just after five and drank bottled Pellegrino water on the patio that overlooked the hotel garden. He would sit there in his catalogue-new safari clothes and listen to the eerie wail of the muezzin calling the Muslim faithful to prayer. Would sit there as the whole city came to a stop around him; as passersby threw prayer carpets onto the dirt walkways and bowed toward Mecca. He would continue to sip water and write in his ledger book, indifferent to it all. Then Tullock would return to his room and reappear an hour later, right at dusk, and go for a jog. His route was always the same: down the crowded streets, then north along the Deli River. His route followed dirt footpaths that wound through several patches of park that were as dark and wooded as jungle.

My original plan was to have Havildar sneak into Tullock's room while he was out. It would have been so simple, so damn easy. I could have chosen any time I wanted to confront Tullock—I *wanted* to confront him— then left the rest to Havildar and the men he had named in his note.

That wouldn't work now. Rengat couldn't be trusted, and like Tullock, I stood out in a crowd. People would notice me in his hotel. People would notice me on his floor.

I couldn't risk that . . . yet it seemed mad to proceed without knowing what was in the man's room.

I could hear Tomlinson's voice saying, *I take it on faith, man. On faith.* Could hear Hannah's voice saying, *I knew . . . I just knew.*

But I took little on faith, and I knew nothing instinctively.

What I did know was that revenge included risk, and risk had a price.

One night, I stood in my room and looked at myself in the flaked mirror that was nailed to the wall. I was a little drunk—I'd had a couple of liters of Tiger beer. In the mirror was the face of a stranger. It was like standing behind a wall, looking through a two-way mirror. If I moved my mouth, the stranger moved his mouth. If I rubbed a hand over the beard stubble on my chin, the stranger did the same. But the stranger's eyes were not my eyes. His were predator-bright. Mine felt bleary. It was as if the stranger were mocking me: *So just snatch the guy, bag him, and kill him!*

It seemed so easy to the stranger; everything clear-cut and neatly defined. And it *would* have been easy: Follow Tullock out on one of his runs, then hide along the river, in the trees. Crouch there watching the great hornbill birds fly over, their wings creaking; watch the giant fruit bats drop down out of the trees and cup the darkness with their five-foot wing spans. Wait for Tullock to jog back . . . then take him.

It was so easy that, each day at dusk, as I watched Tullock trot off, I had to fight the temptation . . . a temptation so strong that I found myself procrastinating, getting the man's patterns down for no other reason than to underline the simplicity of that stranger's simple solution.

Yet I didn't want it to end that way. Not for Raymond Tullock. More important, not for me.

I decided to proceed with a variation of my original

plan. I had taken risks before—not many, but a few. Now, at least, it seemed that I had much less to lose. . . .

FRIDAY IS A MUSLIM HOLY DAY, SO I SPENT IT TRANS-ferring my belongings into two canvas duffel bags that I had purchased at the Central Market which was just off Sutomo Street.

Into my old bags—which included my favorite Loomis travel rod satchel—I placed rags and chunks of wood that I had pilfered from the back of my boarding house. When the bags looked and felt about right, I used duct tape to seal them tight.

Then I dressed myself in a favorite pair of baggy Egyptian cotton slacks; the kind with the big cargo pockets. Into the right pocket, I stuffed a big bandanna and the opaque green glass orb I had taken from Hannah's house.

The little ball had a nice weight to it. It was granite-smooth except for the ingenious flanged stopper.

I spent half an hour practicing, but just couldn't seem to get it right. My hands were too big, my fingers too long and blunt. Once upon a time I had spent a deadly boring week in a boat off the coast of Cambodia. One of my companions had three small baggies filled with sand, and he had tried to teach me to juggle. I never did get it. My hands are fine for focusing a microscope, or for using a scalpel, but they are not clever in a way that I now needed.

Once I almost dropped the glass ball, and I thought: You're insane to try this without Havildar's help.

But I ignored the small, destructive internal voice. Blotted out the images of me squatting in some cell in Simpang Alas Prison. I kept at it. Kept practicing. Tried to picture the way it would be: me in the room, Raymond Tullock in the room, plus two, maybe three others. I had to point at something—anything to shift their attention—then draw the bandanna out of my pocket smoothly, very, very smoothly. . . .

When I thought I had it pretty good, I played around with my portable shortwave radio, then took up the bandanna again and practiced for another half an hour. I wanted to embed the move into the muscle memory; wanted to be able to do it mechanically, like it was second nature, without having to think.

In the early evening, while the city's bullhorns told the faithful that it was time to bow to Mecca, I decided that I had had enough. I put everything away, changed into different clothes. Then I took my three ox-eyed tarpon into the bathroom to dissect.

Later that night, I ate satay beef and rice, sitting across a restaurant table from Rengat. I told him that I would be leaving Medan the next evening. I told him to come by my boarding house promptly at sunset, so that he could take my luggage to Polonia Airport. I told him that because of a business engagement, I would arrive separately by private cab and might be a little late.

I watched the little man's eyes shift around as he projected great sadness that I had to leave Sumatra so soon. "Has something happened to displease you?" he asked.

I handed Rengat my Garuda Airline ticket so that he could check my luggage. "I'm afraid something very bad *has* happened," I told him. "I've been robbed."

WHEN RAYMOND TULLOCK RETURNED FROM HIS RUN the next evening, two Indonesian policemen and I were standing in the hallway, outside his room, waiting on him. For days, I had been looking forward to this moment; had anticipated, with great pleasure, the shock that seeing me would cause the man . . . had anticipated, with greater pleasure, the terror that would drain his face pale.

So I stood there, arms folded, a uniformed cop on either side of me. I could hear the squeak-squeaking of Tullock's rubber-soled shoes as he came up the linoleum steps, two at a time. Could see his head and shoulders come into view, and I fixed my eyes on his face. As Tullock got to the top of the stairs, he hesitated when he saw us. I watched closely as his eyes registered consternation and minor surprise; but nothing that communicated shock, nothing close to terror.

Not a good reaction . . .

He paused at the top of the stairs, collecting himself. He was wearing black spandex beneath burgundy running shorts. The rubber skin of his sweat pullover was shiny but dry—a vaguely reptilian touch. Tullock stared at me for a moment . . . then at the two cops . . . then back to me. Favored me with a thin, nervous smile before he said, "Well, well—long time no see. The name's Ford, isn't it? How's our girl Hannah doing, Ford?"

At least he doesn't know.

I said, "My girl Hannah is just fine. Me, too. We're all just fine."

Which seemed to cause him momentary discomfort. But he recovered quickly, showing me he didn't much care. Said, "Always good to see another American in these Third World countries," as he continued down the hall toward us. Then: "Is it true? I hear you've been robbed."

I thought: Rengat, you son of a bitch!

Tullock brushed past me just close enough so that his

shoulder collided with mine—a gesture designed to stake out territory—and he produced a key, then swung his door wide. "You're welcome to have a seat while I change, gentlemen. But I'm afraid I can't give you much time. I have a dinner appointment in less than an hour." Turned his head to give me a private, searing look. "So let's make it quick."

In Indonesia, law enforcement has an informal aspect. Visitors or individual citizens can seek out the help of specific cops. Havildar had given me the names of two who spoke English. One was Lieutenant Suradi, the other was Officer Prajurit. Both were small, dark men who wore navy-blue slacks and shirts that were brightened with red trim. Because I had used Havildar's name, they had come with me to the Hotel Tiara willingly enough—not that I could expect any favors from them. Already I could sense that Tullock's self-assurance had made Lieutenant Suradi, for one, dubious.

"This a very serious charge, sahr," he said to me as we entered the room. "You must be certain. You not very certain, sahr, maybe this man ask we arrest you!" Said it loud enough for Tullock to hear, letting him know that he was not taking sides in this squabble between two Americans.

Tullock was stripping off the rubber pullover, handling himself pretty well. Showing just the right mix of tolerance and indignation. "It's a damn serious charge, Ford. If you've never been to Indonesia before, maybe you don't know, but—over here?—they cut a man's hand off for stealing."

I gave a soft whistle, trying to play it just as cool. "Maybe you can get the doctors to fix you up with a hook, Ray. A man with your hobbies wouldn't want to get caught shorthanded.''

''Oh? What hobbies are those?''

''Wires and things. Timers? Things that can blow up in your face.''

Tullock was toweling himself down. Gave me a pained expression—*Fuck you*—before saying to Suradi, ''I suppose you're here to search my room.''

''Yes. If this man want.''

''You mind showing me the search warrant?''

Suradi was puzzled for a moment. ''Oh! No need warrant. This man want, we search.''

I got the impression that Tullock didn't care if we searched his room or not; was just playing a role. I wondered what kind of deal Rengat had worked with him. The little bastard had picked up my luggage right on time. Had probably reasoned that since I was flying out tonight, he no longer had a cause to fear me. So why not make some extra money? Could picture him telling Tullock, ''All week, this big man follow you! You pay, I tell you more!''

Obviously, Tullock had paid. The question was: When had Rengat told him, and how much could he know?

To Lieutenant Suradi, Tullock said, ''Tell me something. How are people who make false accusations treated in Sumatra? I'll cooperate, but I'll be damned if I'm going to let this guy get away with calling me a thief. I've got *business* interests in this country.'' Letting the cops know that he was an important man; a man with connections.

Suradi said, ''It very serious, sahr. Yes, very serious. Mr. Ford wrong, maybe we take him to jail. You charge him, we do it, yes sahr.'' The little man was glaring at me, giving me one last chance to back down.

Tullock made a sweeping motion with his hand. "In that case," he said, "search all you want."

Suradi was still looking at me. I thought it over. Thought: What the hell. I nodded at the lieutenant. Said, "The man's a thief. Search his room."

TULLOCK HAD PULLED ON A DRY T-SHIRT. HE TOOK A chair across from me, dabbing at his face with a towel as Suradi and Prajurit began to politely lift and poke their way through drawers and luggage. It was a large, sparsely furnished room. Hard brown linoleum floor, an open window that looked out over the city, off-white walls decorated only with two small paintings done in the gaudy colors of a cheap valentine card. Both paintings were weirdly abstract—one of a dark-faced girl, her hands extended in an Egyptian-like pose; the other was of a cart pulled by water buffalo. Cart and oxen—it caused the image of Hannah's face to flash into my mind.

"You tell me what you're looking for, maybe I can help." Tullock was sitting there, projecting indifference. His chair was against the open window. There was a floor lamp and a closet door to his left.

I told him, "You'll know when they find it," but I was thinking: If it starts to unravel, I'll shove him through the window.

"Ah-h-h," he said. "So it's going to be like that. I don't suppose you'd tell me when this supposed theft occurred?"

Suradi and Prajurit were leaving the conversation to us, just doing their jobs, not very happy about it.

"Yesterday," I said. "Late afternoon—just after the muezzin called the prayer."

"You mean that noise they blast over the streets?" Tullock had his legs crossed. He was a foot tapper—the only symptom of nervousness in the otherwise shielded demeanor of a bureaucrat who was probably seasoned by years of long meetings and public hearings. His foot continued to tap as he said, "In that case, I couldn't have done it, because that's when I take my daily run."

"Your running partner can confirm that?"

His foot slowed momentarily . . . then resumed its normal pace. "I had thousands of partners. Out there on the streets. They remember men who look like you and me, Ford. We all probably look *alike* to them."

Little did he know.

I said, "You were never alone, Ray? I seldom see anyone in the parks along the Deli River."

Tullock's foot began to lose speed . . . then stopped. He leaned toward me slightly and for a moment, just a moment, I could see the craziness that was in him. "You've made a terrible mistake, buddy. You have no idea just how deep the hole is you're digging—you should have done some reading before you came. I *know* about this country."

I said, "Ray, I've made mistakes that were a hell of a lot bigger than this. Mistakes I'm going to regret for the rest of my life. Like that bomb you left for me? I made a mistake and it ended up killing Hannah."

Slowly, very slowly, the color of his face changed from brown to red, and then to gray: Hawkeye's sidekick after hearing some shocking news. "You're . . . you're lying," he whispered.

"I wish I were. The mistake I made was not realizing just how scrambled your brain really is."

He had both feet on the linoleum now, both hands on the armrest. "She's not dead, she can't be dead. I put that thing—" He caught himself in time; realized that the two Indonesian cops had stopped their search and were listening. He sat back. "I don't know what the hell you're talking about."

"What I'm talking about, Ray, is what you stole from me." I used my head to gesture toward Lieutenant Suradi. In his hand he was holding the small opaque green ball that I had already described to him . . . and which I had just watched him remove from the open drawer of a dresser. To the lieutenant, I said, "That's it. He must have taken it from my room when I was out. It's extremely valuable."

"That's not his, it's *mine*! Don't you see what he's doing?" Tullock was on his feet now, beginning to lose it. Also getting some very hard looks from the cops. He forced himself to pause . . . took a very deep breath, fighting hard to recover. Actually managed to give Suradi a little smile as he said, "What if I prove that glass ball belongs to me? Will that make you happy?"

Lieutenant Suradi said in a chilly, formal voice, "He tell us it's here. We find it."

"But it was in my room all along! He's trying to make fools of you. I'll show you—" Tullock hustled over to his briefcase and pulled out a sheet of long pinkish paper, the color of a legal document in Sumatra. "I was expecting him to pull something like this. At the suggestion of my Japanese associates, I had their secretary list everything that I brought into the country. Everything I have in this room. See?" Tullock was showing them the paper. "It's listed right here. See this? 'Green glass ornament.' I carry it as a good luck charm." Gave the tone just the right inflection—an innocent admission of silliness made by an innocent man.

Now Suradi and Prajurit had turned their cold stares on me. My expression said, *Oh, shit . . .*

Tullock pressed the advantage. "The man's trying to frame me. Look at his face! He's trying to set me up—"

"What's the date on that list?" I asked Suradi.

He checked it. "Dated . . . two . . . no, three days ago." I watched his eyes shift from the paper to me. "You robbed yesterday, sahr. That's what you say."

I thought about how nice it would be to shake Rengat by the neck.

"They could have postdated it. The date on that paper means nothing."

Tullock had made a full recovery now. "I'm afraid it's your word against mine, sport. My word and the word of my business associates. All very respectable Japanese businessmen." He slapped the paper. "Listed right here in black and white."

I stood, took the bandanna from my pocket and wiped the sweat from my forehead. "May I see the glass ball?"

Suradi hesitated, then handed it to me.

"I guess I could have made a mistake, but it's very similar." I motioned to the floor lamp. "Can you pull that over so I can see a little better?" I stuffed the bandanna back in my pocket as I held the sphere up to the light. The glass was so old and fogged that the light succeeded only in changing its color from black green to jade green. I pushed my glasses up on my head, inspecting more closely. Cleared my throat—couldn't hide my nervousness—then, after a long pause, I said, "I'm afraid I owe Mr. Tullock an apology. This definitely isn't the object that was stolen from me."

"You can stick that apology right up your ass." Tullock had taken his seat, legs crossed, foot tapping. "Of course it's mine. You knew all along it was mine. Don't try to play coy now."

To Lieutenant Suradi, I said, "I'm very sorry. I heard a rumor that he had a similar object—an innocent mistake."

I crossed to the window, held the glass ball out to Tullock—a deferential gesture. "I admit it. You said it was yours and it *is* yours. You've proven it. Hope there are no hard feelings."

Tullock was reaching for the ball, saying, "Lieutenant? I want to press charges. This was a vicious attempt on Mr. Ford's part to create legal problems for me in my new home," as I allowed the ball to roll off my fingers much too soon . . . saw Tullock bat at it, trying to stop the sphere's fall . . . watched the sphere hit the floor and explode into shards of glass and plume of heavy gray dust.

"You clumsy bastard!" Tullock was on his feet, hands balled into fists. For a moment, I thought he was going to take a swing at me. I would have liked that. He shouted, "You can pay me for this right now. Pay me in cash!" But then he seemed to have a better idea. "Wait—" He turned to the two Indonesian policemen. "I want you to charge him with this, too. The intentional destruction of my private . . ." He allowed the sentence to trail off as he noticed that neither Suradi nor Prajurit was listening to him. Both were too intent on the mess at Tullock's feet to hear.

Among the shards of glass was a substantial mound of grayish powder, fine as talcum.

"What's that?" Tullock asked—the voice of a confused adolescent.

I had backed against the open chest of drawers when the ball shattered, the bandanna once again in my hands. Now I stepped away from the chest of drawers, shrugged, and said, "I wouldn't know. Like you said, Ray: It's not mine."

Lieutenant Suradi was on one knee, studying the powder. Sumatra, apparently, was one of the few remaining places in the world where police officers actually touched and tasted unidentified chemicals. I wondered if it tasted of fish.

Maybe it did. Suradi tasted his finger once more, then spat. He looked from Officer Prajurit to Raymond Tullock, then back to Officer Prajurit. Then he spoke in very fast Bahasa Indonesian; long, involved directive sentences that had the ring of discovery.

Tullock's confusion began to overwhelm him. "What are they saying? What the hell's going on here!"

Prajurit had a portable radio out and was talking into it. He banged the radio a few times, trying to get it to work. It wouldn't work, so he used the telephone. Suradi stood, felt around for the handcuffs on his belt as he tried to take Tullock by the left wrist. Tullock yanked his wrist away. "Goddamn it, what *is* that stuff?"

I watched his face very closely as I said, "I think I heard them say the word 'heroin.'"

"Heroin?" The expression on his face reminded me of the night he had caught Hannah and me together: bug-eyed crazy . . . wild with rage . . . grotesque. He said,

"Do you know how they *deal* with that? What . . . what the *punishment* is for that?"

I wanted to ask, *Have you ever seen Simpang Alas Prison?* Instead, I gave him a private little wink. Said, "You crossed the borders, Ray. That's always risky."

What happened next was not pretty. Tullock lunged at me, screaming, "He did this! Search him!" as Suradi tried to get a wrist handcuffed. Suradi interpreted the movement as an attempt to escape. He went to work on Tullock with a wooden baton. Suradi was a tough and determined little man, but Raymond Tullock had a wild tenacity that one associates with the truly insane . . . or with those who have absolutely nothing left to lose. When Tullock went down for the fourth time, he lay on the linoleum, alternately cursing me and pleading for my help. *We're both Americans, for God's sake.*

I watched his face closely, enjoying it, as I said, "Ray, you're only half right."

When the backup cops arrived, Suradi *did* search me. He was no fool and, by now, he was also in a fighting mood. I cooperated fully in what was a very thorough search. In my pockets, he found a clip full of American money. In my zippered leather belt, he found more money. He also found a single passport and tourist card, on which the money had been accurately declared. Aside from a few shiny-bright tarpon scales—he puzzled over those—he found nothing more.

Later, when Suradi and the others did an equally thorough search of Tullock's room, they would certainly find a second ball of opaque green glass in the chest of drawers . . . where, minutes earlier, I had placed it . . . and what remained of a bag of Burmese heroin—heroin for which a Rangoon bank draft, wired to Norvin Tomlinson, still awaited my final approval.

But that was Raymond Tullock's problem, not mine.

Still . . . Lieutenant Suradi didn't like it. Like all cops, he was cynical and suspicious. Coincidence and drug smugglers were two things he did not suffer gladly. Before releasing me, he took my passport—my real passport—along with my tourist card. "When you leave Medan?" he asked.

I told him truthfully that my plane was due to leave in less than an hour. Pictured Rengat waiting at the airport with my ticket and luggage—luggage full of wood scraps, taped tight—although it was more likely that Rengat had dropped both ticket and luggage at the Garuda counter before taking his family into the mountains for a convenient vacation.

Suradi shook my passport meaningfully. "You no go to airport tonight. You no go to airport till I say."

I promised him that I would not go to the airport.

Outside, on the busy night streets of Medan, the cab I had hired was waiting, my new duffel bags locked in the trunk. I opened the trunk and took out one of my false passports . . . not the passport I had recently had made; not the one that listed my name as Raymond Alan Walley; not the one I had used to clean out Tullock's bank account earlier that afternoon. Could hear Tullock saying, *We all look* alike *to them.* Could hear the teller at the Dutch East Indian Bank tell me, "Have nice day, sahr!" as I walked away with a briefcase full of 50,000-denomination rupiah notes—about $110,000 worth.

I put the false passport in my pocket, swung into the back seat with the briefcase. Told the driver, "Port of

Belawan,'' as I checked to make sure that I still had the torn halves of the hundred-dollar bills so that I could pay my passage to the captain of the red teak junk out of Rangoon.

EPILOGUE

HERE IS WHY I DECIDED, AND HOW I DECIDED, TO return to my home at Dinkin's Bay, on Sanibel Island:

Because I did not trust the betel nut-chewing captain of the Burmese junk, and because I became convinced that he and his crew of Bougie pirates planned to rob me, I jumped ship at the island of Phuket on the Isthmus of Thailand, and spent the next few weeks traveling around Indochina. I needed the time; felt I had rooted myself too deeply in the community that was South Florida, and now was an opportunity to sever those roots. Why had I stayed on Sanibel so long? The accoutrements of a modern life—and the obligations they imply—grow as slowly but as surely as a strangler fig. They also suffocate just as completely.

One night, at Raffles Hotel in Singapore, I sat outside in the tropical garden and realized, with some surprise, just how completely I had allowed myself to become entwined by the bonds of my island home. I was on committees, I was on boards, I paid electric, water, phone, and insurance. I had become a convenient source of advice and comfort and conversation for the dozens of friends who had come to depend on me almost as much as I had come to depend on them. I had a schedule; I had a routine. I had become one of the *regulars*, for God's sake. But all human interrelationships exact a price, and for me, that price was the lost look in Hannah's eyes just before she died, and the chill limpness of Tomlinson's hand.

I wanted to cut free. Revolted at the idea of ever risking it again. Tomlinson believed, he truly believed, in the symmetry of life and in a Creator's universe that was warmed by what he called sentient consciousness. Hannah had possessed the same mystic instincts. She *knew*. . . .

But the only thing I knew or believed was that all life—my life included—was a definable, weighable process. That process was brief indeed. For a while at least, I wanted to be free of the tethers. I wanted to be wild and alone and on the loose. So what I did was buy a big-frame backpack and a jungle tent from another one of my Gurkha friends—this was in Kuala Lumpur—and I set off on foot, and by public bus, on my tour of Indochina. What I found was what I expected to find: Asia was on the move. It was chopping, building, and bulldozing its way out of the oxcart world, directly into the world of computer chips. It was financing the transition with the bounty paid—usually by the Japanese—on rain forest timber and increasingly rare sea products. Denotations on maps such as "national park" were euphemisms meaningful only in that they marked regions that bulldozers had not yet reached. The term "net ban" was meaningful only in that it symbolized the increased value of Asia's own unregulated and desperately overused fishery.

I roamed around, observing, taking notes. Americans who call themselves environmentalists would have found the wholesale destruction I saw shocking. I did not. It was tragic, yes. But not shocking. When stray dogs become a part of the citizenry's menu, professorial speeches about the long-term benefits of virgin forests and sea conservation won't turn a single head—particularly when those speeches come from people who have never had to stalk their neighborhood's pets.

I loved the people, but ultimately, I grew tired of Indochina. The people I met were as smart as they were kind; they were as generous as they were tough. The reason I left was trivial: I yearned to hear English spoken. It happens sometimes, when you have been away too long in a foreign land. I had my portable shortwave radio, true. And in places such as Thailand and Cambodia, the V.O.A.—Voice of America—came in fairly strong. But it wasn't enough, so I caught a Qantas flight in Phnom Penh and flew to Darwin.

Australia and its Northern Territory are the English-speaking world's future . . . just as Asia is currently designing the rest of the world's future. After Cambodia, I was unprepared for the horizon of wild space and pure sea light that rims Darwin. The land has a hot, primeval aspect. Tendrils of steam seep upward, as if the process of chemical genesis still continues. Darwin is an outback town; a frontier town, despite its parks and modern architecture. In too many cities around the world, sidewalk travelers wear expressions of introspective rage. Not in Darwin. In Darwin, people had a blue-collar glow, as if they were just damn glad to live in a world that had electricity and indoor plumbing. Strangers grinned at me on the street, tipped their Akubra cowboy hats and said, "Ga'day!" or, "How ya goin', mate?"

It was from Darwin that I mailed—via a buddy of mine in Managua—the second of my only two letters to Mack at Dinkin's Bay. The first had included a brief note explaining that I had decided to do some traveling and would be back in about a month. The second letter, sent seven weeks later, explained that I might be gone for six months, maybe more. It included private notes to Janet Mueller, Jeth, and Rhonda and JoAnn aboard the *Tiger Lilly*. I offered no return address. Still felt the need to be on the loose, untethered.

East of Darwin, I had a friend who owned six hundred square kilometers of land. It was grazing land and eucalyptus forest that fronted the Timor Sea. My friend was reluctant—didn't think it was hospitable—but he finally agreed to chopper me out to the most desolate stretch of beach on his property, and leave me there. I told him I wanted to spend a few weeks living off the land, collecting specimens from the mud flats. My friend told me that I was bloody nuts, unloaded my gear, and flew off.

That is where I decided to return to Dinkin's Bay. But here is how and why: I had built a sapling hut that was close enough to the sea so that I could feel the rumbling surf, but far enough away from the beach so that the giant estuarine crocodiles wouldn't crawl up and eat me in the night. I had covered the hut with a tight palm-frond thatching to keep out the monsoon rains, and I had constructed what I thought was a very ingenious all-weather fire pit. Made myself a nice little jungle camp, complete with everything but a sign outside that read: *Beware the Big Dumb Shit.*

For food, there were plenty of mud crabs, plus the occasional snaredumb feral hog. I also caught barra-mundi—a fish which looks and behaves remarkably like a snook. For water, I had the monsoons, as well as a Pur hand-pump water filter. It was a good life. I loved the solitude of it . . . all the potential that the sea and that wild country offered. Some days, just for the hell of it, I'd pull out the little mirror in my toilet kit and take a look at myself: long tangle of salt-bleached hair . . . red beard . . . sea-gray eyes that gradually, very gradually and over several weeks, lost the predator's gleam.

I told myself I was a hermit. I told myself that I had become the captive of my own wild instincts. But we are all creatures of habit, and soon I had carved out a new routine that was very similar to my old routine. I ran along the beach each morning, collected specimens and took notes during the day; then I'd lie in my palm shack at night, listening to my shortwave radio.

It was something I heard on the shortwave that caused me to finally return to Florida. I was lying by the fire, using what remained of my clothes as a pillow. I had the radio's antenna extended as far as it would go, and I was tinkering with the slide tuner. I was trying to pick up something—anything—in Spanish, when I happened to come across a medical talk program on Voice of America. There was a lot of static, a lot of whiny elec-tronic garble, but I listened because there seemed to be something very familiar about the voice of the woman being interviewed.

Heard her say: ". . . always considered myself to be a logical woman who is well grounded in the sciences, but I have no explanation for . . ."

Static.

I stood naked beside the fire and held the radio up in the air, turning slowly, trying to vector in on the signal.

Heard the woman's voice say, "... lightning strike, perhaps ... filled the room with a brilliant white light. ... *May* explain it, although ... yes, there were a number of wires still attached ..."

Static.

"... still talks about an alien presence in space, which he insists ... never dead, only traveling ... The man still describes his body as a spaceship. ..."

Static.

Pulled the radio down to my ear because I was certain that I recognized the woman's voice. Heard Dr. Maria Corales say, "... only one other known case of such a recovery. Even so, for my own peace of mind as a surgeon ... for my own spiritual peace of mind ... doing more tests ... Odd thing is? He believes, and I'm beginning to believe too. ... Yes ... God ... I'm talking about God. ..."

It took me all the next day to hike out to a dirt road, where I caught a lift into Darwin. The following morning—it was March 24, a Friday—I caught a Qantas flight home to see my friend Tomlinson.

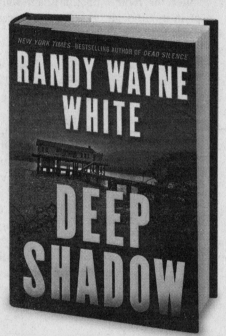

BLACK WIDOW

FROM *NEW YORK TIMES* BESTSELLING AUTHOR

Randy Wayne White

Doc Ford is drawn into a deadly battle when his god-daughter Shay is blackmailed. Someone filmed her at an out-of-control bachelorette party—and they want big money to keep it quiet. When Ford investigates, he finds that the woman responsible is an agent of corruption unlike any Ford has ever encountered before. And she may be the last encounter he ever has.

penguin.com